Silver Rose

Elizabeth Jane Morgan

Cover Design by Vila Design

Book Design by Ebook Launch

Published by Elizabeth Jane Morgan

Printed by IngramSpark

ISBN: 978-0-692-04614-2

Silver Rose, #1

First American Edition: August 2017

10 9 8 7 6 5 4 3 2 1

To my mom, Jackie and dad, Jeff.

Also my brothers Daniel and Bill, my fellow writers at heart.

Chapter One

Strange Encounters

I

T ALL STARTED WHEN A BRIGHT RED FLASH darted past the castle's mullioned windows. I gasped, my hands flying to my mouth, which caused the water pitcher I was carrying to clatter to the floor, shattering to pieces and spilling water on myself. What was that? I thought, rushing to the window. I had glimpsed a triangular head, scales, and a long, tapered tail. It couldn't be. I scanned the courtyard below. Something red by the ground caught my attention. I squinted, but I couldn't see anything. Don't be ridiculous, I told myself. They weren't real. They were just a myth. They inhabited the mists of old tales. They were on the fringes of stories, stealing, killing, and wreaking havoc.

"Penelope! What is the meaning of this?"

Quaking, I turned and looked up into the face of the matron in charge of housekeeping, Mrs. Sophia Thompson. Her hands were on her perfectly starched waist and her mouth was a thin line of displeasure. I became fascinated with my black shoes, trying to ignore my hammering heart and the sodden hem of my handmaiden dress.

"Miss Bogg, kindly explain yourself."

"I dropped the pitcher on the floor. My apologies," I mumbled.

"Are you injured?" Mrs. Thompson asked, inspecting me from head to foot.

I shook my head. My cheeks were burning.

"Well, if you are positive, report to the Queen's private chambers. She is expecting you."

I waited until Mrs. Thompson had rounded the corner before gathering the pieces of broken pottery and placing them in a nearby rubbish bin. Satisfied with my work, though cringing at the damp spot that remained, I headed toward the queen's apartments on the third floor.

A noise attracted my attention on the stairs. There was a lit torch burning off to my left, but it was too dim to make out any details. Just my imagination, I thought, when suddenly a dark red shadow detached and started toward me. I backed up hastily, my foot slipping on the step. I waved my arms wildly, trying to keep my balance, when something tackled me from behind, sending me sprawling to the ground.

"Lydia!" I grunted, as I righted myself and turned to see my younger sister. She helped me to my feet and the figure disappeared into the shadows again. "What are you doing here? You know you're supposed to wait in your room while I'm working."

My twelve-year-old sister pouted. "I was bored," she said. "I was walking down the hall when I heard something break. I ran past Hazel going in the opposite direction. Are you all right?"

I stared intently at her, touched. She was tall for her age at almost five feet, no matter my four years and three inches on her. "Yes, I'm fine. Why don't you visit Constance in the village?"

Lydia perked up immediately at the mention of her best friend. She took off running down the stairs, taking them two at a time.

"Don't forget!" I called after her. "Malcolm will be home later today. Be back in half-an-hour." Malcolm was our older brother and the captain of the castle's guards. He had been gone for the last few days on a special mission for the queen. Something to do with werewolves.

As I started away from the staircase, I could hear footsteps heading in my direction. Thinking it was Lydia again, I turned, but it wasn't her. Instead, the figure on the stairs stood watching me. It was difficult to tell whether it was a she or a he, but whoever it was wore a dark, almost blood red hooded cloak. The figure was at least half a foot taller than me.

We stared at each other for a full minute. The figure was completely still, except for the fingers of its left hand, which were drumming against its leg. Is this person going to speak or not? I thought.

I had just turned away, when the figure spoke. It had a raspy, yet feminine, voice. "Penelope Bogg, I must talk to you."

"Who are you?" I asked.

"A friend," she said, stepping forward, past another torch bracket on the wall. The torch inside was spluttering fretfully. "Please, Miss Bogg, you must help me."

But, I heard no more. The girl had stopped near the sputtering torch, which had suddenly flared to life. My eyes widened with shock. "Magic!" I whispered. How did she get magic? I knew only two people with that kind of power: my late mother and the court wizard, Casimir. I took one last frightened look at the girl before I took off running down the hall toward the queen's rooms. Stopping before the third door on the left, I knocked smartly on the wooden surface.

"Enter," the queen's voice said.

I yanked the door open and slipped inside, closing it with a soft click.

"Penelope, there you are," Queen Alana said. She was a beautiful woman with long, black hair, piercing blue eyes, and a kind smile. She was wearing a green velvet dress with a white bow encircling her waist. She was standing in front of a full-length mirror decorated with carved roses.

The room itself was a pale turquoise. Several chairs and a couch decorated the center of the room. There was an old desk in the corner. I loved that desk. I saw it at least once a day. It reminded me of the desk my mother used to own. A portrait of a blonde-haired woman with Queen Alana's blue eyes hung above the couch, staring out across the room. She was wearing a necklace shaped like a crescent moon. I smiled. This was Queen Rebecca, Queen Alana's grandmother and founder of Kelton Castle.

Queen Alana had inherited her grandmother's good sense. She was never rash or impulsive, but ruled the entire kingdom of Alsmora fairly. On her desk, I could see Malcolm's latest report about the current state of the werewolf population.

"I don't know, Malcolm," the queen had once said to him, while I cleaned the room around them. "The werewolves are getting out of control. There are more attacks daily."

"We could attack back, Your Highness," my captain of the guards brother had suggested.

"No, they are normal most of the time, except when the moon is full. We must come up with another solution."

Queen Alana had been agonizing over this for weeks, trying to decide whether to give werewolves more or less rights. She had finally sent Malcolm to investigate a werewolf attack in the west of Alsmora. While there, he was to arrange a meeting between an ambassador werewolf and Queen Alana.

I turned my attention to the rest of the room. Another handmaiden was there, buttoning Queen Alana's forest green dress.

"Milady," I said, with a curtsey.

The other handmaiden, Hazel, smiled at me, but it didn't quite reach her cold, gray eyes. She had never liked me, ever since she had discovered that my mother, Alice Bogg, had been an old friend of Queen Alana's. Hazel thought it was wrong for a handmaiden and the captain of the guards to have known Queen Alana since childhood.

"Precious Penelope," she had once muttered loudly as I passed. "Thinks she can get away with anything, just because her mother was friends with the Queen."

I averted my eyes, mumbling a greeting to Hazel.

"Penelope, hand me that shawl," Queen Alana said, extending her hand.

I spotted the shawl in question, a dark red that complimented the green beautifully, but reminded me forcefully of the figure outside the room.

Handing it to the queen, I stood beside her, waiting for further instructions. I could see myself in the mirror. I stared at myself thoughtfully. Lydia and I looked the same. We both had brown hair, round brown eyes, and fair skin. Lydia's hair was longer, though. It reached as far as her waist. Mine, on the other hand, fell to slightly below my shoulders. My handmaiden uniform was a dark blue dress and a white mobcap.

Hazel stepped back, her task complete. "I am finished, Your Highness."

Queen Alana withdrew from the mirror and sat in one of the chairs. "Hazel, go find Viola and see how my dress for the gala tonight is coming along."

"Yes, milady." She exited through the open door.

I was left alone in the room with the queen.

"Penelope, find me the pale blue dress in the wardrobe."

While I was searching, pushing aside at least three green dresses, the queen said, "Hazel has reported that Lydia was running in the halls. She shouldn't do that."

I turned around and saw that Queen Alana's eyes were twinkling with humor.

"How old is she?" Queen Alana continued.

"Lydia?" I said, returning to my task, my hand slipping on some yellow fabric. "Twelve."

"Has she shown any signs of magic yet?"

"No," I said, looking through a dozen pale blue dresses. Which one did she want? "But, her birthday will be soon."

I lapsed into thoughtful silence as I selected a pale blue with short sleeves. My mother had told me that thirteen was the age in which magic was said to appear in young children. She never knew why this was. It had never surfaced in me. At sixteen, I was much too old for it. Lydia, however, was the right age.

"If she shows, I would like to introduce her to my magical advisor, Casimir."

"That is a great honor, milady. I thank you."

Casimir was a mystery to most of the servants in the palace. He had appeared one stormy night two years ago, offering the king his magical services. King Marcus was Queen Alana's husband. He had scoffed at Casimir, telling the wizard to take his bag of tricks and depart at once. Unperturbed, Casimir had used a spell to calm the skies of their wrath. Impressed, the king accepted him as his magical advisor.

A little over a year ago, the king had gone off to stop an invading army. He drove them back into the sea from whence they came, but died from a stray arrow in the process.

Queen Alana had been in mourning for a year afterward. She took over the kingdom and had been a fair and just ruler ever since.

She kept Casimir around for his magic and because he had been on the field with King Marcus at the time. He had tried everything to save the king, but to no avail.

I tried to imagine Lydia learning magic from Casimir. At once, I could see Lydia becoming a witch. She would have the power to do whatever she pleased and wouldn't have to work as a handmaiden.

"Thank you," I said again, handing the pale blue dress over. "I will mention this to Lydia when she returns from the village." Speaking of which, nearly half-an-hour had passed. Where was she?

The queen smiled and patted my hand as Hazel stepped back into the room, accompanied by the third handmaiden, Viola.

Viola curtseyed; her eyelids drooped over her tired green eyes and her brown hair had come undone from its bun.

"My Queen," she said in a strained voice. "I am afraid your dress is not complete as such."

"Explain."

"The fabric is sewn and hemmed, but lacks lace."

"How much is missing?"

"We are almost complete. All that is left is the neck, but all the lace has disappeared."

"It is most peculiar," Hazel said. "Your ladyship sent me to buy lace only last week."

I frowned. I had been with Hazel during that outing and I remembered what at the time had seemed like a mountain of lace.

"Could we have used it up on something else?" Queen Alana asked.

"It is indeed possible, Your Highness," Viola said. "The seamstresses have been hard at work on your dresses for weeks."

"Penelope," the queen said. "Go down to the village and buy more lace from Mrs. Wilkins's shop."

I curtseyed and departed, shutting the door quietly on the sounds of the queen's continued conversation with Viola and Hazel.

I paused, staring down the hallway where I had seen the strange figure, but she had gone. The only evidence of her presence was the brightly burning torch. I skirted around it, making my way to the staircase and descending to the first floor. The pendant my mom had given me before she died two years ago thudded against my chest. The pendant was shaped like a star and in the center, like a large egg, sat a ruby.

I kept it on a chain around my neck, under my dress. The ruby must have cost a fortune and would have easily allowed me to quit my position as handmaiden, but I couldn't do it. My mother's voice echoed inside my head whenever I thought of selling it.

"This pendant is very powerful, Penny," she had said. She had still been quite young, only in her mid-forties, but an unknown sickness had claimed her. "It cannot fall into the wrong hands. Keep it safe for me."

I had for these last two years. Whenever I was sad or lonely, I would feel for the chain and smile at the pendant's familiar weight.

The cook greeted me as I entered the kitchen and headed for the servant's exit. "Morning, Miss Penelope." A pleasant, plump woman, she smiled good-naturedly at me, handing me a bit of bread.

"Good morning, Mrs. Appleton." I grabbed a basket from the table.

The air was crisp and full of the songs of birds as I made my way from the castle grounds. A black and fluffy cat watched me from a low bench. A paw was dangling over the edge. A pattern like an "M" could be seen on its furry forehead. The cat was rather small, unlike the old cat Constance Wilkins owned, who also had an "M" on her forehead, but Petals the Maine coon was at least twice the size of this cat.

I had always liked cats and this one appeared to be a stray, though a well-fed stray. I left the piece of bread beside it on the bench, noticing as I did so that the cat's front half was raised slightly higher than its back, like it was lying on something. I shrugged and continued on my way.

I followed the cobbled street into the village of Kelton. Near the edge of the village was the tanner's, where the smell from the cured hides assaulted my nose, making me cough. Beside the tanner, was the cobbler, his shoes visible through the window.

Rounding the corner, I stumbled to a halt. There, across from where I stood, was the figure in dark red that I had seen in the castle. A strange silver glow was coming from her right hand. My stomach plummeted. Not again.

A tense moment passed as we stared at each other. I took a deep breath and walked forward. The figure started across the street toward me as well.

"Who are you?" I demanded, stopping several feet from her. "Why are you following me?"

"I can see it now. You are definitely the right descendent, Penelope Bogg." She turned her right hand slightly and I saw a mass of silver and black. Before I could ask what she was talking about, a voice hailed me.

"Greetings, Penelope."

I turned to see the widowed owner of the general store, Mrs. Georgina Wilkins. She was a short woman, who was hardly taller than myself. She was watering her flowers in the window box in the front of her store. Mrs. Wilkins once told me that she thought the window box made her store feel more homey.

"Good morning, Mrs. Wilkins," I said, turning back toward the girl. She had disappeared again.

"Are you here for anything, dear?"

"...Yes, the Queen sent me to buy lace."

"Lace? I believe I have some in the back," Mrs. Wilkins said, leading me into the store. Within seconds, she had brought out the same white lace that was supposed to adorn Queen Alana's unfinished dress.

After I had paid for the lace and placed it in my basket, I left the store, thanking Mrs. Wilkins.

"Don't forget, dear," she called before the door slammed shut. "Constance and I will be in Dewdrop Village next week. Old Mr. Pewter will be looking after the store."

As I crossed the square back toward the castle, I heard laughter from behind Mrs. Wilkins's shop. It sounded like Lydia, so I decided to investigate.

Lydia and Constance Wilkins were standing, talking to a tall man with black hair and mismatched eyes. The left eye was brown, while the right was green.

"... and that, girls, is why you should never taunt a wild mushroom," the black-haired man said. "Ah, the elder Miss Bogg. Welcome."

"Greetings, Master Casimir," I said with a curtsey.

Casimir smiled and gave a long, sweeping bow. "Your sister and her friend have been a most enjoyable audience."

Lydia giggled. "I liked your story of the evil wild mushroom."

"Did you really slay it with nothing more than an onion stalk and the dye from a flower?" Constance asked in awe.

Casimir winked at me. "Don't forget the magic."

"Lydia, its time to return to the castle," I said. "Malcolm will be back soon and I have to get this lace back to the Queen."

"Allow me," Casimir said, pulling out his staff. He muttered something under his breath and the lace disappeared from my basket. "Queen Alana should be receiving it momentarily, along with a message claiming credit for you."

"Thank you," I said, frowning that he hadn't asked me first.

"My pleasure. I must be going now. I told the Queen I would be joining her for the gala this evening. I will be seeing you shortly, Miss Bogg, girls."

As he twisted and vanished in a gust of gray smoke, Lydia turned to me. "That was amazing. I wish I had magic."

I glanced at the empty basket. Queen Alana would be expecting me soon. "You might," I said. "You still have a few weeks. If you do show, the Queen would like you trained by Casimir himself."

Lydia looked excited, but I couldn't help shivering, even though it was a warm, clear, day.

Chapter Two

Rising Denial

AFTER ESCORTING CONSTANCE WILKINS TO her mother, I led Lydia back to the castle. Lydia was jumping up and down in excitement. "I can't believe I get to learn magic!"

"Slow down, Lydia. We won't know until you show and you still have a few more weeks before your birthday." If she didn't perform some act of magic by then, Lydia would simply be a mundane, like me and almost everyone else. Based on the two powerful magicals I knew, my mom and Casimir, magic gifted maybe one person per year, if you were lucky.

"But, I can feel it, Penny. The magic's bubbling inside of me."

I said nothing as we left the village, crossed a small dirt path, and entered the queen's garden. I had felt much the same way when I was twelve, almost thirteen, but nothing had ever happened.

Queen Alana's offer to train Lydia was kind, but we would have to wait and see. I didn't want to crush Lydia's hopes, however, so I changed the subject by pointing to the black cat that was still on the bench.

"Look at that, Lydia. I wouldn't want to get on the bad side of that cat. Would you? Those claws look sharp."

As Lydia turned toward the cat, she clapped a hand over her eyes. The bench began to rise into the air. It was rocking back and forth, threatening to throw the cat off, who sat up hurriedly. At the same time, my vision flickered so everything took on a silvery quality. I could see the cat's tiny, silver-tinged face peering down at me. Its mouth opened in an indignant squeak.

"Lydia, let the poor cat down."

She didn't answer. The bench continued to pitch dangerously.

"Lydia!" What was wrong with my baby sister?

I looked at her, panic-stricken. She had removed her hands from her eyes and seemed to be in some sort of trance. I took her by the shoulders and stared at her. "Lydia!" I shouted over the cat's ever-increasing complaints. It was starting to sound more like a lion's growls.

Lydia blinked. Her eyes were wide with shock as she turned to me, the cat meowing louder for attention. "I have magic!" she cried, sprinting for the castle, leaving the bench floating behind her.

"Lydia, wait!" I called starting forward, we had to figure this out, calmly, but she didn't look back.

"Get me down!" a voice called.

I jumped, looking for the source of the noise, but couldn't find anyone.

"Up here!" the voice yelled.

Craning my neck up, I saw the cat still sitting on the floating bench. Its mouth was moving, "You're the one controlling this thing! Put. Me. Down!"

If I hadn't seen it with my own eyes, I wouldn't have believed that the cat had spoken. The cat's words registered in my head and as my eyesight cleared, the bench wobbled and plummeted to the ground.

The cat's legs splayed as the bench struck the dirt. It scrambled upright and leapt off the bench to glare at me. Some kind of material slipped to the ground behind it. Its look was so icy it could have frozen me solid.

Now that I had a closer look at the cat, I could see it wasn't pure black. It had a tan mane and a white muzzle. Black triangles framed both its yellow eyes. Its legs were gray with thick black lines crisscrossing to its paws. Its body and tail were black with tan and gray mixed in. From what I could see of its stomach, it was white.

"Why did you drop me?" it demanded.

"I'm sorry," I said, sitting down gingerly on the bench. "I didn't know I was doing it. I thought my sister…"

"Oh, she lifted me," the cat said, grumpily, "but *you* were the one who kept me in the air after she bolted. Impressive that your magic overrode hers."

My head was spinning as I remembered the silver quality everything had taken. "But, I don't have magic," I insisted, pushing the thought from my mind. "I've never even attempted to use it before."

"Ah, well, you could be a late bloomer," the cat said, yawning in obvious boredom now. "I'm Cadmus. What's your name?"

"Penelope. Look," I said, my temper rising. "I don't know where you get the idea that I have magic, but I'm simply a handmaiden. I have too much to do to deal with magic. Whatever happened with the bench was a fluke, if it was even me. How are you talking anyway? You're just a cat."

Cadmus narrowed his eyes and flicked his tail. "Magic," he said.

"Magic?"

"Magic," he confirmed. "How often does your vision change color?"

I gaped at him. "How-"

"I have a friend who keeps me informed about magic. You might be meeting her quite soon. Incidentally, what color did you see?"

"Silver," I said, before I could stop myself. Unreasonable hope bloomed within my chest. Maybe it had finally surfaced, after all this time.... No, I chided myself, no. It couldn't be, not after everything.... I was deluding myself.

Cadmus's eyes grew wide and I heard him mutter, "... Must get word to Mag."

"Who's Mag?" I asked, bewildered.

Cadmus ignored me, threw back his head, and yowled at the top of his lungs. I clapped my hands to my ears, but I couldn't block out the plaintive wail. He stopped after a minute.

"What was that?" I demanded.

"I was calling Mag," he said calmly. "She should be here any moment."

"That's right. Hello, Miss Bogg, we meet again," a familiar, raspy voice said from right next to my shoulder.

Startled, I leapt off of the bench and spun around. Mid-spin, however, I got tangled in my skirts and fell in a heap. "Ow," I groaned from the ground.

A shadow loomed above me and I saw the figure again. Her hood was still up, obscuring most of her features, except for her eyes, which were like amber. I shuddered. Were those vertical pupils?

The girl must have sensed my gaze because her hood twitched, hiding her eyes.

Don't be ridiculous. Nobody has vertical pupils.

"Mag?" I asked.

"Indeed. Mag Everett, at your service." She held out her hand. I again noticed the slight silvery glow about it. I took her hand and Mag pulled me to my feet. She was strong.

As Mag released me, I stumbled forward and spotted the material that had fallen behind Cadmus. I stooped and snatched it from the ground. "What's this?" I shook the queen's lost lace in front of them. "Did you steal this?"

"Yes," Cadmus said, blinking lazily up at me. "I climbed through an open window, brought the lace outside, and took a nap on it."

"But... why?"

"We needed your attention," Mag said. "We've been trying to talk to you all day."

"Why?"

"You're Alice Bogg's oldest daughter. We have information about your magic."

"But I don't have magic," I protested, squashing down the glimmer of hope growing within me again.

"Penelope, you have magic whether you like it or not. We can train you not to waste it," Cadmus said.

"Waste it?" I wanted to scream, but kept my voice steady. "Where was this magic two years ago when my mother died? I was fourteen, a whole year after I was supposed to receive it. I might have been able to save her! But no, apparently I wasn't ready for it yet!"

Mag was leaning against the bench, while Cadmus gazed up at me. "I'm sorry that your mother died," he said. "But Alice had her own magic. Strange she didn't heal her own injuries."

Both Mag and Cadmus were staring at me curiously.

"She went to a neighboring town and never returned. They told us she had died and was buried there. We never saw the body," I explained, turning away from them. Magic hadn't appeared in me three years ago. There was no way I was going to get my hopes up. Not again.

"Perhaps a demonstration is in order," Mag said. She lifted the bench over her head and threw it as hard as she could at me. "Catch."

I was so startled, I almost couldn't move. I was quaking as I seized the chain of my pendant. I closed my eyes. A word formed in my mouth, a word I hadn't heard since my mother was alive: "Enchanta."

Wind rushed into my face from the sailing bench. Quickly, I dove out of the way. Something crashed behind me. Shakily, I opened my eyes and saw the bench lying on its side, exactly where I had been standing moments before.

"See," I said, getting to my feet. "I told you I didn't have magic."

"This can't be," Mag said stubbornly. "Penelope, you're the daughter of Alice Bogg. That spell should have worked. You must have magic. All the signs point to you."

"I'm sorry, but I simply can't help you."

Mag curled her lip and said, "Cadmus, grow."

Grow? Cadmus was already the size of a full-grown male housecat. How much more could he grow?

Cadmus sighed and threw me an apologetic look. He stood up, stretched, and crossed the space between us in four steps. On the first step he looked normal; on the second step he was the size of a bobcat; he resembled a cheetah on the third; and the fourth left me staring down a lion.

"N-nice k-kitty," I said, transfixed by the fangs now sprouting from his mouth.

Come on, move, I thought, but my legs refused to budge. He's a cat, I reminded myself. Just a plain, simple housecat.

Cadmus began to circle me, padding slowly and surely. As our eyes met, Cadmus winked.

Winked? Was he trying to distract me? He was stalking... Of course! This was a test! I quickly looked at Mag, in case she was sneaking up behind me. She hadn't moved.

"Penelope! To your left!" she called.

I ducked to my right without thinking and whipped around in time to see a huge paw breeze harmlessly over my head. Cadmus pulled his paw back and readied himself for another swipe.

"Penelope, try 'Beredan,'" Mag said, as panic prompted my legs to move. I scrambled out of the way, before he pounced. A shiver ran down my spine as Cadmus's claws scraped against the bench.

Some test, I thought. Out loud, I said, "Beredan," my tongue slipping over the unfamiliar sound.

Nothing happened. Cadmus continued to pad forward. With no more warning than a flick of his tail, he lunged at me. Wait for it, I told myself. *Now!* At the last moment, I rolled out of the way and the lion went sailing over my head. But before I could do more than stand up, Cadmus lunged again, his paws striking my chest, sending me sprawling to the ground.

It was over as quickly as it had begun. Winded, I stared up at the lion above me. One of his whiskers tickled my cheek.

Surely someone must have heard that. But nobody came and Cadmus simply peered down at me.

I blinked and the lion disappeared as did the weight on my chest. I looked around, confused. Then, I realized that a housecat was sitting on me, licking his paw.

"Nice try," he said.

I looked upside down at Mag. "No magic."

She glared at me as I scrambled to my feet. "I will prove it to you, Penelope. You have to have magic! The rose wouldn't have identified you otherwise."

"Wait, what?"

Mag opened her mouth to respond, but before she could say anything, there was the sound of racing footsteps as Lydia appeared.

"Penelope! Oh, hello." Lydia had spotted Mag.

"Greetings," Mag said without turning around.

"Penelope, the Queen wants to see me!" Lydia squealed.

"She probably wants to know about your magic," I said with a half-glance toward Mag and Cadmus.

"Penelope, Mag and I will see you here later," Cadmus whispered.

I nodded, as Lydia grabbed my hand and dragged me back to the castle.

I glanced back at Mag and Cadmus who were talking rapidly with much arm and paw waving.

As we entered the kitchens, Lydia began to talk, her words bubbling with excitement. "I can't wait to find out what spells I'm going to learn first. Did you say that Casimir is going to teach me? I hope I get to fight an evil wild mushroom, like him."

She continued in this vein all the way up the first and second floors. If only Mag had tested Lydia instead of me, I thought. I was sure she would have passed with flying colors on her first try. My heart swelled with pride for my baby sister.

As we mounted the stairs to the third floor, Lydia said, "That was a cute cat outside. I loved all his little meows and squeaks."

My blood ran cold. Clearing my throat, I said, "Y-you didn't hear him speak?"

Lydia wrinkled her brow. "Yes, his meows and squeaks were adorable."

"But, you didn't hear him say any human sentences?"

Lydia stopped dead and stared at me, her eyes wide with concern. "He's a cat, Penelope. He can't talk. Are you feeling all right?"

My head was spinning. How could Lydia receive her magic and not hear Cadmus? On the other hand, my magical status was questionable at best and I could hear him. I resolved to ask Mag and Cadmus later, preferably away from Lydia, since she didn't believe me anyway.

She was still staring at me.

I forced a laugh. "I was only kidding. You're right, that cat definitely did not talk." My insides squirmed at the lie. I tried to ignore it.

Lydia seemed to relax and we continued to the queen's room. I knocked on the door. Within moments, it was answered by Casimir, who ushered us inside. The only other person there was the queen.

"Your Highness," we said, curtseying.

"Penelope," Queen Alana said, in way of greeting, before addressing Lydia. "Lydia Bogg. Casimir has informed me that you have received your magic."

"Yes, ma'am, I have," Lydia said, trembling.

"Kindly demonstrate."

I watched as Lydia stepped forward. Her hands were visibly shaking.

"Lydia, repeat after me," Casimir said, banging his staff on the ground. "Sten henaus."

"Sten henaus."

A glittering stick appeared in Lydia's hand. I knew what it was immediately: a wand.

I stared at it, wondering if I was a fool for believing Cadmus and Mag when they said that I had magic and that they could instruct me in it. I shook my head. Mag's test with the bench and Cadmus chasing me as a lion had both come up blank, after all.

"Impressive," Queen Alana said. "Summoning a wand is not enough, though. You must prove yourself further."

Casimir whispered something into Lydia's ear. She nodded and said in barely more than a whisper, "Henatin." A pleasant feeling of warmth spread throughout my body, as if I were in the midst of a warm bath.

Queen Alana was talking to Lydia, but I didn't hear a word as I clapped a hand to my forehead. The warmth had suddenly turned into a dizzy sensation that passed through my head, leaving me seeing silver.

"Penelope?" Lydia said from a long way off.

I remained silent, my eyes growing wide with shock. A water pitcher on a small table in the corner of the room was rising slowly into the air. I trembled with exertion. The water pitcher seemed to react to my movement, for it began to wobble.

Recovering from my surprise, I focused on the pitcher. It steadied itself at once.

Realizing that I was holding my breath, I released it and the water pitcher set down on the table with a loud bump. I was half-aware that everyone was staring at me now.

My vision had returned to normal, but I had broken out in a cold sweat and couldn't seem to stop shaking.

Lydia touched me lightly on the shoulder and I saw silver again.

A framed painting of a man sitting astride a horse, with a hound at its heels was peeling itself from the wall behind the queen. I stared in horror as it rose above her head and started to drop upon her.

I gasped and looked around. Everyone was too busy watching me rather than the painting.

I concentrated with all my might on pushing the painting back. The portrait shuddered to a halt, then began to spin like a top.

Stop, I thought desperately, sinking to one knee.

Two sets of voices spoke over me and silver blasts came out of Lydia's wand and Casimir's staff. The two spells faded before they reached the portrait.

Please, whatever force is controlling the painting, stop.

Lydia entered my field of vision as she approached the painting. She shot another silver blast at it, but the portrait continued to spin. She had to jump away to avoid being clipped by the frame.

No, she'll be hurt. That cleared my head. There was no way I'd ever let anything harm Lydia.

The door opened and two pairs of feet crossed the threshold. The footsteps ceased as their owners must have taken in the scene, but I didn't care. I now knew what I had to do. I stood and grabbed my pendant to give me strength, and yelled, "Enchanta!"

Instantly, everything stopped. The portrait teetered dangerously for a moment, before it slowly resumed its former position on the wall with a thump.

Once it was secured in place, I wrenched myself from my concentration with difficulty and took a step back, my vision cleared, sweat beading my forehead.

Lydia was staring at me in awe. Queen Alana was addressing one of the new arrivals, a man dressed in white with snow-white hair. They were saying something about my "condition." Mag was standing next to me.

"Glad you could make it," I muttered, before I collapsed.

Chapter Three

Silver Reflections

"MISS BOGG, WAKE UP," MAG SAID, from above me.

I was lying on the floor of Queen Alana's chambers, staring up at the ceiling. I groaned and sat up, looking around. Papers were strewn everywhere. A werewolf report rested on my right foot. The now-still portrait was currently upside down on the wall. Casimir was watching me steadily, without blinking.

Mag held out her hand. I accepted it and she pulled me to my feet. The man with the white hair and the white cloak stood beside her.

"Magic," Mag said from behind her hood.

Stumbling away from her, I jumped when Lydia appeared at my shoulder.

"Penelope?" my sister said, worry etched in her voice.

"I'm fine," I mumbled.

"Thank you for seeing to my handmaiden, Master Aldrich," Queen Alana said, to the new arrival.

"Queen Alana," the man said. He had a deeper, but equally as raspy voice as Mag. "Thank you for receiving us. I am sorry that we just barged in, but we heard the commotion and came to see if we could help." He paid me a sidelong glance.

I looked at the floor. It wasn't my fault that my vision kept changing to silver and then strange things happened.

"Queen Alana, if I may be so bold, my grandfather and I have experience in this sort of thing. We may be able to help," Mag said.

I felt my face go warm at her words.

Queen Alana looked over my flushed and sweaty face and said, "Penelope, you may return to your room."

Blushing furiously, I turned on my heel, marching out of the chamber with as much dignity as I could muster.

I went back to my room, where I spent a sleepless hour tossing and turning. I couldn't quiet my mind or my nerves after the day I had had.

Mag was convinced it was magic. I wasn't. Couldn't it all be one giant mistake? Maybe Lydia's magic was somehow affecting me? Yes, that had to be it. And yet, I almost wanted to believe Mag. I had never given up my desire for magic.

Don't be stupid, I scolded myself. I'm simply too old for it. But Mag's persistence was starting to influence me.

"I have to know," I said out loud. "I have to know if Mag is right, or if I'm just deluding myself."

I tried to focus on lifting my blankets without touching them. The white fabric remained motionless. I concentrated harder, willing it to rise with my whole being. It moved a fraction of an inch at the bottom of the bed. I felt a thrill of excitement, before I realized that my foot had twitched.

Turning over, I fingered my pendant absently and faced the beige wall, a color chosen by the queen. I blinked and sat up straight, my arms falling to my sides. My eyes must have been playing tricks on me. The walls had suddenly changed to a silver-tinged, shocking pink. I swayed and fell back on the bed, dizzy.

Had I done that? I couldn't even lift the sheets on my bed, but I could change the color of my walls whenever I wanted?

I thought of the color red and waited for it to shift. Nothing happened. Red! I shouted mentally. Come on, change! Nothing. Blue. Green. The walls remained stubbornly pink. It crossed my mind that the queen would not be pleased if she saw her choice of beige had been covered by pink.

I shivered, as if I had the flu. I gripped the pendant and felt warmth spreading into my very being, as if my mom had just enveloped me in a hug. I wiped away a tear and watched as it fell sparkling onto the ruby. When I looked up, one of the walls had changed from pink to red.

Startled, I almost dropped the pendant. Now it changed to red, I thought, rolling my eyes. Blue, I thought, looking down at it. Sure enough, another wall shifted to blue.

I set the pendant on the nightstand. Green. The walls refused to change.

Yellow, I thought, grabbing the pendant again and focusing on the ceiling. The ceiling became yellow. Red, blue, green, pink, I thought, directing my attention at each wall in turn.

I stood, looking at my colorful room. I took a deep, shuddering breath, closing my fist around the pendant. It seemed to help clear the dizziness. What was that rhyme Mom always used to say when we were visiting the castle?

I started to mutter it, feeling calm for the first time all day.

> "When the situation is dire,
> Turn to the path, led by fire,
> Remember what was once said,
> And change to red."

I felt more exhausted than ever, but I forced myself to open my eyes. My jaw dropped as I looked at my room.

I was like I had stepped into a fireplace. Everything in my room, from the four walls to the ceiling to the floor was a deep red.

Even the torch in the bracket, which I never lit, had ignited, making everything brighter.

I jumped as someone knocked on the door.

I answered it and found Mag standing in front of me.

"Yes?" I said taking a deep breath to calm myself.

I felt as if I had discovered something important. I turned instinctively toward the torch. That wall seemed to be pulsing slightly with a ruby light.

"Penelope, please follow me," Mag said from behind me.

I tore my gaze away and looked up at Mag. She had already retreated down the hall and was rounding the corner. Hurrying after her as fast as my skirts would allow without running, I turned the corner and stumbled to a halt. The hallway was deserted.

"Mag?" I said uncertainly. A tapestry twitched. I crept toward it, but before I could peer around it, Mag stuck her head out.

"Are you coming or not?"

Following her behind it, I found that we were on a hidden staircase.

"What are we doing here?" I asked. "Where's Cadmus?"

"He's still in the garden, calling together members of his pride. Come with me." Mag turned and started off down the stairs.

Curious, I followed.

The staircase was made of gray, roughly hewn stone. It had definitely gone unused for quite some time. It was damp and smelled strongly of mildew. I kept stepping in small puddles that had accumulated on the stairs. Torch brackets lined the walls, but all the torches had burned out, so I had to squint to see what was ahead. There were no windows.

We walked in silence for several minutes, until Mag said, "How are you feeling?"

"Fine."

"You're shaking."

I ignored her, staring determinedly at the floor. But, I wasn't really seeing it. Mag was right: I was shaking. I crossed my arms in an effort to stop myself trembling. "Mag, what-"

"It's the shock."

"What?" I looked up sharply.

"The shock of using magic is draining you."

"Mag," I rasped. "What's happening to me?"

Mag shifted from foot to foot. "I'm sorry, Penelope, but I can't tell you anything until we meet with Aldrich."

I wracked my brain, trying to place the name. Mag must have noticed how perplexed I was, for she said, "My grandfather, Aldrich. The man dressed all in white. We have something we must tell you. I hope its not too late." I heard her last sentence as a whisper.

Before I could ask what she meant, we reached the foot of the staircase. Across a small landing was a door. The strange thing was, it didn't have a doorknob. Instead, there was a slight impression of a handprint.

Mag stepped forward and placed her hand on the impression. The wood around it started to glow red.

"The highest hill on the westernmost side of the castle, please," she said.

I gasped as a silver doorknob appeared. It had just grown out of the wood. "Magic," I whispered in awe.

Mag seized the doorknob with her other hand and turned it. She kept her right hand on the handprint.

"You have to do both simultaneously," she explained, pushing the door open. "Otherwise it won't work."

The doorknob disappeared again as I followed Mag outside. We were standing on a flat, green hill the size of a large house. Its entire eastern flank was covered in trees, so the only part of the castle I could see were the spires. Wildflowers dotted the hill.

I looked around and saw the doorway to the hidden staircase. It seemed to be suspended in mid-air. As I watched, the door closed on its own with a snap and disappeared completely, like it was never there.

"Its one-way," Mag said. "We can access it only from the inside of the castle, not the outside. Come, I want you to meet Aldrich. He just finished speaking with Queen Alana."

I turned and saw the man with the white hair and white cloak from the queen's room. He was standing in the center of the hill.

His eyes flicked to me, before he focused on Mag.

"Is it her, Mag?"

She glanced in my direction. "I believe so."

"What are you talking about?" I asked, exasperated. Why were they talking like I wasn't even there?

"Miss Bogg," the old man said. "It is a pleasure to meet you. I am Aldrich."

I bent my knees slightly in a curtsey, looking down at the ground. "The pleasure is all mine."

Then, addressing Mag, he said, "How can you be so sure she is the one?"

"The rose reacted when I saw her in the village," Mag said, facing me. "And her hair has started to change."

I automatically reached for my hair to examine it, but it seemed the same to me. Still brown.

"It's a slow process," Mag said. "But believe me, Penelope, it will happen. I'm sorry the task has fallen into your hands, but do not worry. It is my job to help you."

"What?"

"You were chosen, Penelope Bogg, for a great purpose. Chosen by this rose."

Mag raised her hand, the one with the silver glow. In her hand was a rose.

But the rose didn't look... normal. It was silver, instead of red, with a black stem and thorns. It was in full bloom and radiated the silver glow a full inch above its surface. I stared in open-mouthed wonder at Mag and Aldrich. Finding my voice, I said, "W-what does this have to do with me? What great purpose are you talking about?"

Mag took a deep breath, it seemed like she was steeling herself. "Penelope, have you ever heard of the dragons?"

Yes, I wanted to say, but I hesitated. After everything that had happened that day, was I prepared to believe that dragons were real? The more rational part of my brain said that nobody had ever seen a dragon. But, still, what else had scales, tails, and triangular heads? Choosing my words with care, I said, "Yes, but they were just a myth, they didn't really exist."

Aldrich snorted. "I can assure you, Miss Bogg, dragons are in fact real. They are living amongst you right now."

"Where are they, then?" I asked.

"We will get to that in a moment," Aldrich said. "First, you need a lesson in dragon lore."

He paused, staring off toward the castle. When he returned his attention to me, I could see that the eyes piercing me were golden.

"A long time ago, dragons inhabited the land. They were mighty in number, all cowered before them. But there were other powerful races as well. The elves kept to themselves and rarely left their leafy domain of the Konold Forest. The dwarves were tough and sturdy; living in their mountains, content to keep the evil trolls holed away, where they couldn't get to the rest of Alsmora. Giants were metalworkers in their own mountains, while the elusive fairies haven't been seen for years. That leaves the humans, the most numerous of all the races and the ones linked most closely with the dragons."

I couldn't take it anymore. "Where are the dragons, then?" I blurted. "If humans and dragons are linked, shouldn't there be dragons flying around? Was that really a dragon I saw this morning?" I paused to take a breath and Aldrich held out a hand to stop me.

"Slow down, Miss Bogg," Aldrich smiled. "Let me see. A hundred years ago, there was a war between humans and dragons. Or, I suppose I should say, a few misguided humans and a rogue dragon against the other dragons and their human allies. Long story short, a dragon named Cessala and an unknown witch defeated the rogue dragon. The enemy fled, leaving Alsmora in a period of peace.

"Cessala and the witch disappeared soon after, leaving behind the silver rose, with instructions for the dragons to prepare themselves. For when the rose blooms, it means the rogue dragon will rise again, and a new witch and dragon must work together to save Alsmora once more.

"That witch is you."

I burst out laughing. They were joking, surely. How could I save all of Alsmora? Mag and Aldrich looked affronted, causing me to laugh even harder.

"You must have made a mistake," I chortled. "I can't possibly help you. I don't even have magic, I think. Maybe you could try Casimir. He's the Queen's magical advisor, surely he could assist you."

"You don't understand," Aldrich said. "It has to be you."

"Why?"

"The rose bloomed in your presence. Cessala and the witch told us that it would bloom for a human and a dragon. Those two would have the greatest chance of saving Alsmora. Plus, we assumed the silver in your hair was a sign."

"What are you talking about?" I said. "I have brown hair, not silver."

"Miss Bogg, maybe you should look in this puddle," Aldrich said, gesturing toward a bit of water at the base of a tree.

I did as he said and gaped at my reflection. That couldn't be me. It looked like me, but not exactly. My hair was its usual brown, except for several strands. They were bright, glowing silver.

"T-this can't be," I whispered.

"It won't happen immediately. It will take some time for the magic to wear off and reveal your natural hair color. I'm impressed that the spell changing your hair to brown lasted so long. The fact that you've been in contact with the rose has weakened the magic. You should be back to normal, eventually," Mag said.

"This is not normal," I said in a strangled voice.

Mag and Aldrich exchanged looks.

"You were born with silver hair," Aldrich said, slowly. "I met your mother once. A clever woman. She recognized how distinctive your hair was. Something spooked her. She wanted to hide you in plain sight, so not even we could find you."

"My mother didn't want to save Alsmora?"

"No, she didn't want *you* to save Alsmora," Aldrich corrected me. "She knew the dangers you would face. Alice hoped that you could lead a normal life. But, that will sadly never happen. We need your help to defeat the rogue dragon again, or all is lost."

I sat down with my head in my hands. No, no, no, I thought. This could not be happening. I could accept magic, since my mother had it, but talking cats and two people telling me I had to save everyone from a ferocious rogue dragon was too much.

"Penelope," Mag said. I could sense her kneeling beside me. "Look at me."

I did so, but grudgingly. When she had my attention, Mag continued, "We need your help, Penelope, otherwise the dragons' hard work would have been in vain."

"You keep talking about the dragons as if they exist. Where are they?" I asked, latching onto the first question that popped into my head.

Mag and Aldrich exchanged another glance.

"First, Miss Bogg," Aldrich said, "we must know: will you assist us?"

I hesitated. Aldrich was asking a lot, especially considering the fact that I had no control over what had happened in the queen's room, or mine, for that matter. But I could learn. Maybe I didn't know what I was doing, but Mag and Aldrich seemed so nice.

I want to help them, I realized. I want to see a real dragon. The only problem was...

"Why are you so insistent that I have magic? I'm sixteen. I lost out on the possibility three years ago."

It was Mag's turn to hesitate. "I think," she said, "its time to show her."

She removed her cloak and I finally got a look at her face. It was angular, her eyes amber slits. Her hair was flaming red. She was young. She didn't look much older than myself.

Mag picked up a fallen branch. Her hair began to twist and writhe, as if it had a life of its own. As I watched, fascinated, tendrils of flame drifted toward the branch. The flames whipped their way across the top and when she stepped away, her hair lying flat once more, the makeshift torch was lit.

"How-" I began, but Mag took the burning branch in her hand and blew the flames in my direction. I would have been burnt to a crisp if I hadn't leapt up and grabbed my pendant in fright. I need a shield, I thought. A shield erupted from the center of the ruby, protecting me.

Mag ceased with the flames and blew out the branch, tossing it onto the ground.

"Is your hair made of *fire?*" I spluttered.

"Yes," Aldrich said. "Young Mag's method was crude, but I think we got our point across."

"I have magic?" How else could a shield materialize from my pendant when I asked for one? "This is not possible," I said, kneading the palms of my hands into my forehead, while at the same time elation flooded me. "Why now? Why not three years ago?"

"I believe," Aldrich said, "it is because the rose has bloomed. That was the signal that you were strong enough for this burden."

Then, Mag and Aldrich's shapes began to bubble like hot wax. Their features elongated. Their faces grew into snouts. Spikes were erupting all over their bodies. Tails were sprouting behind them, wings on their backs. Their hands and feet were turning into claws. Mag stopped growing long before Aldrich was through. She was twice as tall as a horse and four times as long. He was twice the size of Mag. All together, we just fit on the hill.

I gaped at the two dragons.

"I ask you again, Penelope Bogg," the larger, white dragon said in Aldrich's deep voice. "Will you help us?"

Chapter Four

Grandfathering

I CLOSED MY MOUTH HURRIEDLY, LEAST THEY notice my astonishment. But the only thought that ran through my head was, so this is the dragon from this morning. I sighed with relief. I wasn't crazy.

"How?" I asked.

"The magic it took to defeat the rogue dragon had strange effects on some of the races," the smaller, red dragon said. She sounded like Mag. "A pride of cats got the ability to grow into the size of lions. A nest of scorpions became the vicious predators known as yikties. Cessala worked so closely with a human that we dragons gained a human form. As far as I know, nothing happened to humans."

"That's not entirely true," Aldrich said. "After that day, there have been fewer magicals born. Magic isn't as prevalent now as it was a hundred years ago. All those old spells are beginning to fade."

"Why? I thought magic lasted for a long time," I said, remembering my mom's spell to promote her garden's growth. That one had lasted for years on end.

Mag shook her head. "A spell will fail if the caster is dead. Magic dies with its originator."

Mag and Aldrich were quiet for a long moment. Then, it dawned on me.

"My hair," I said, reaching toward it. "Its still brown. If my mother cast the spell on me and it hasn't changed since her death, then she's... she must be..." The word caught in my throat. Tears brimmed in my eyes. Could it be true? Could she really still be alive? If so, where was she?

"Miss Bogg," Aldrich said, gently. "Please, don't torture yourself with this. The fact that your hair is only now changing is evidence to that possibility, yes, but we can't know for sure. Please, don't get your hopes up. We must focus on the task at hand."

"But my mother could still be alive! I have to go find her! I haven't seen her for two years..." I trailed off.

Why hadn't she contacted me? Lydia? Malcolm? Two years was a long time to be absent. Where, oh where, was she?

"Please, Miss Bogg, I promise the dragons will do everything in our power to find your mother, but back to the matter at hand," Aldrich said.

They returned to their human forms and sat down next to me.

I turned away and glanced at myself in the puddle again. I looked tired. "I want to help," I said slowly. "But what about Lydia, Malcolm, my job? I can't just leave them."

"That won't be an issue. We will train you here, in the castle. We're staying as the Queen's guests for the time being."

"Can I have time to think?" I said, my head buzzing. "I need to rest." It was early afternoon. The gala wouldn't be until late that evening.

"No, I'm sorry, Miss Bogg, but we need to start your magical training," Aldrich said.

"It's busy at the castle at the moment. I'll have precious little time to train."

"We'll make time. You have to begin immediately."

"Why? What kind of training?"

"We will be starting you off on the basics," Aldrich said. "Oh, yes, and you'll also be learning sword fighting."

I kept from groaning out loud, but only barely.

"The longer we wait, the less time we'll have before the rogue dragon attacks," Mag said. "At least we have the rose."

I stared at her questioningly.

"The rose chose me, too. According to the unknown witch, now that the rose has bloomed, we can both tap into its power to heal and strengthen ourselves. With it, your vision will never turn silver. But, we must be careful. If we use it too much, it will fade to white, turning it into a normal rose. Its power would be lost, forever."

I fingered the pendant's chain as I considered Mag's words.

"What is that?" Mag said sharply.

I looked down and realized what I was doing. "A pendant my mother gave me," I said, pulling it into view and holding it up for Mag and Aldrich to see. The ruby glinted in the afternoon sun. "Why?"

"May I see it?" Mag asked, holding out her hand.

"What? No! I'm not letting this pendant out of my sight!"

"Please? I promise to give it back."

I frowned and shook my head.

Mag gave a short growl or annoyance. "What if I look at it without you taking it off?"

I hesitated. I had promised to look after it, but if it was going to be around my neck the whole time, I couldn't see the harm of allowing Mag to just look at it. I nodded my consent.

Mag began to examine it, squinting through it so her eye appeared more red than amber. She ran a finger over the ruby. "I know this amulet," she whispered.

"Don't you mean pendant?"

Aldrich spoke up, "No, it has magical properties making it an amulet. Like the rose, you can channel your magic through it, but unlike the rose, it still has the possibility of changing your vision to silver. I've seen this particular amulet before. I was present when it was given to your mother, Alice Bogg."

"Really?"

"Yes, she helped the dragons many years before you were born and earned that ruby," Aldrich said. "I have no idea where the star-shaped setting came from, though. But, I digress. Miss Bogg, it is past the time for your training to begin."

"I can't, Master Aldrich," I said. "I'm sorry, but I need to return to the castle soon. My brother will be back later today and I want to talk to him about... all this."

Mag bared her fangs, slightly. "Penelope, I'm not sure if you understand, but we don't know whom we can trust. Only the essential people may know."

I frowned. "I don't think *you* understand, Mag. I need to talk with Malcolm. He's the captain of the Queen's guards. He's trustworthy. He can advise me on what to do."

"Enough, both of you," Aldrich said, stepping between us. "Miss Bogg, I'm afraid you shouldn't tell your siblings. The fewer people who know, the better."

I stared at Aldrich before slowly saying, "Why?"

"Because the rogue dragon has survived for the last hundred years. He's grown more powerful and more deadly. We can't afford for him to learn our plans and the more who know, the greater the probability that that will happen."

I paused, mulling over his words. "I does make sense, I guess," I agreed reluctantly. Another pause. "All right, I'll help."

"Wait here," Aldrich said, transforming back into a dragon. He leaped into the sky and disappeared in the direction of the castle.

"I'm sorry," I said to Mag.

"No, I'm sorry," she said. "I shouldn't have pushed you to start your training. It's just... I long to soar through the skies once again, but these arms are useless."

"Weren't you flying earlier?" I asked. "I saw a red flash earlier."

"Yeah, well, that was necessary to get me here. For the most part, we don't fly unless we have to. Dragons operate on secrecy, Penelope. We always have, seeing as how the rest of the races see us as monsters."

"But..."

"Don't worry, I'm used to it," Mag said with a sad smile. "All the stories about how we steal and pillage for our hoards of treasure. It's not true, by the way. I've never stolen anything in my life."

She sighed and stretched. "Aldrich's coming. We'd better get your training started."

"What are we doing first?" I asked, glad for a change in topic.

When Aldrich landed, I saw that he had brought a white marble statue. "Miss Bogg, I want you to take the amulet and change the color of this statue."

I took one look at the statue and bristled. It depicted a man on a horse, one of King Marcus's ancestors. It usually stood in the center of the garden.

"Where did you get this?" I demanded. "This is supposed to be in the castle courtyard."

"I borrowed it. Don't worry, I'll return it, but we needed something white. Now, Miss Bogg, we're going to be teaching you focus and control. Take the amulet and think of a color. If you're concentrating hard enough, it should change," Aldrich said.

Like in my room, I thought, holding the amulet and focusing on the stone. A bird chirped in an orange tree, dropping an orange on the ground. Orange, I thought. Instantly, my vision turned silver. Not again. I closed my eyes and fell to my knees, clutching my head.

"Penelope," Mag said, from somewhere to my right. "Are you seeing silver again?"

With an effort, I nodded.

"Your body is trying to adjust to the magic," Mag explained. "Open your eyes and take three deep breaths. It'll clear."

There was a blast of silver as I did as she said. I took a deep breath and the dazzling silver became muted. I breathed a second time and everything looked black and white. A third breath and suddenly color flooded my eyesight. I blinked several times and my vision returned to normal. I continued to kneel there, shaking.

"Mag, would you mind taking Penelope back to her room? She needs time to acclimate to the magic."

"But, Aldrich, we have to keep training," Mag protested. "You can't grandfather everyone. Kindness and caring are all well and good, but we need action."

"There's no point in training if Penelope is tired. It would be counterproductive. What do you think, Penelope?"

My eyes were stinging from tiredness, but this was what I wanted, wasn't it? To be a witch. "I can keep going," I declared, swaying on my feet.

"Very well," Aldrich said, though he was frowning. "But let's leave magic for the moment and try you out on swords."

Mag produced a sword from a scabbard I didn't even know she had. It glinted in the sunlight and looked wickedly sharp.

I stood there, weaponless.

"Here," Aldrich said, handing me a sword from his own scabbard.

I examined it, marveling at how it felt like an extension of my arm. My sword looked as sharp as Mag's. We'll cut each other to ribbons, I thought nervously.

Aldrich smiled, and as if he could read my thoughts, said, "You can't."

"Can't what?"

"Hurt each other with these swords. The giants made them from tempered steel and enchanted them to never harm your opponent, unless you want them to. Perfect for training.

"Now Penelope, you and Mag will spar until one of you disarms the other."

Mag and I faced each other, swords directed at the other's chest.

I had never even held a sword before, but I knew the basic concept. I took a step forward and swung clumsily. Even with a balanced sword, I still felt awkward and unsure of my next move.

Mag easily sidestepped and then quickly rapped me on the arms several times with the flat of her blade. She didn't draw any blood, but it still stung.

I swung again, but with a clang of steel, Mag's sword met mine in mid-air. My arms trembled with exertion, but Mag calmly pressed me back until I was standing on one knee. She carelessly flicked her wrist and my sword clattered to the ground.

Sweat beaded my forehead and dripped into my eye, while Mag stood with her sword to my neck. I just knelt there, panting, not bothering to wipe the sweat away.

The next thing I knew, I was lying on my back in the cool grass. I blinked as the sun dazzled me. Mag and Aldrich were talking nearby. I sat up and looked around.

"How do you feel, Penelope?" Mag asked.

"Like I was beaten to a pulp. What happened?"

Mag rubbed the back on her neck sheepishly. "After I disarmed you, you fainted. Sorry if I overdid it for your first time." She held out a hand and pulled me to my feet, "Come on, I'll fly you back. We can't use the hidden staircase from here," Mag said. "Aldrich was right. We can train later."

"Mag, I don't think you should fly," Aldrich said sharply. "Someone might see you."

I gave a shaky laugh. "There was me, for one."

Aldrich nodded in my direction. "Exactly. If one person saw you, others might as well."

Mag gave a short growl. "It would take five minutes flying. Its over half-an-hour if we walk."

"No, Mag," Aldrich said firmly.

"Fine, come on, Penelope."

Mag led me to the trees on the east side of the hill. The trees weren't really thick and the castle loomed into view in a minute.

I breathed a sigh of relief. Mag took several steps away. "Stand back," she warned.

Curious, I watched as Mag transformed back into a dragon.

"Get on," she said.

I hesitated. "Mag, are you sure? You know what Aldrich said."

She rolled her eyes. "Just come on. I won't go as far as the castle, but I'm not walking when I can fly, especially with the trolls roaming around."

"Trolls?" I groaned. "They're back?" As if worrying about werewolves wasn't enough. Once a year, usually on the day of Queen Alana's annual gala, trolls would appear to steal from the guests while they were still on the road.

"I saw them from the air," Mag said.

I did not want to deal with trolls. I climbed awkwardly onto Mag's back and looked for a place to hold on. She leapt into the air and started toward the castle. I threw my arms around her snake-like neck to keep myself from falling.

The wind whipped past, causing my eyes to water and my hair to stream behind me. I wiped the tears away and laughed. My stomach felt as if I had left it behind on the ground. Flying among the fluffy clouds and looking down on the trees below, I felt giddy and it had nothing to do with seeing silver. I laughed even harder. This was where I belonged, up in the boundless sky, on top of a fierce, fire-breathing dragon.

I fingered my amulet again. Mom. I will find you and discover what happened two years ago. I had to know and helping the dragons seemed like the fastest way to find out.

Chapter Five

Invisibility Among Friends

MAG CIRCLED THE OUTSKIRTS OF THE castle by a little stand of secluded trees. The people below didn't even react to the bright red dragon flying overhead.

"Why can't they see you?" I asked.

"They can see me, but I'm so high up, I look like a hawk to the people on the ground," Mag said. "At least I assume so."

"Wait, what? How could you not know how people see you?"

"I've never seen myself from the ground," Mag said matter-of-factly, twisting around to look at me. "The unknown witch cast a spell, so nobody should recognize us as dragons. The silver rose is the only reason you aren't affected."

"I feel so honored," I said dryly. "But seriously, how do we know the people on the ground aren't seeing a dragon right now?"

"We don't, unless they start pointing and screaming."

"This just keeps getting better and better," I muttered darkly as Mag touched down on the ground next to the isolated trees, and I slid down. But I had to admit that nobody was pointing and screaming, so it looked like we were safe. As Mag returned to human, adjusting her cloak to cover her face, I leaned against a tree, watching as a bunny hopped past.

"Penelope, come on, we need to get back to the castle."

I stumbled after Mag, feeling the beginnings of a headache. As we crossed the garden, I spotted several cats lounging on benches, patrolling the area, and meowing to each other. It was bizarre to realize that I could understand them.

"Where are Cadmus and Grrwrath?" one gray tabby said, licking her paw.

"I think Grrwrath's patrolling the western flank," a black and tan striped cat yawned.

"Is it true that we're looking out for the Kaninens?" the gray continued.

The cats' voices faded. I turned to Mag. "How many cats are there?"

"Hmm? I would say around twenty cats make up Cadmus's pride."

"Can they all turn..."

"Turn into lions? A fair few. Maybe, half. The rest are ordinary cats."

We crossed from the cobbled garden path to the back door. An orange cat was sitting like a statue by the door.

There was nobody in the kitchen, so Mag and I slipped through unseen and went to my room on the first floor.

I opened the door and got a glimpse of my red room, before a voice hailed me from the floor.

"Mag. Penelope. It's about time you showed you." It was Cadmus.

"Cadmus? What are you doing here? How did you get in my room?"

"Through the open window. You should really lock it. Mag, we can smell the intruders."

She removed her hood and inclined her head. "I noticed them as well."

"What are you talking about?"

"Grab that torch and come with us," Mag said, grimly. "We'll show you. There's a Kaninen around."

"What's a Kaninen?" I asked, taking the burning torch from its bracket. Queen Alana insisted that every room have a torch, for nighttime emergencies.

There was a grating sound and I turned to see that a section of the wall beneath the torch had swung out, revealing an opening for a fairly small person into a dark passage beyond. I looked back at Mag and Cadmus. They were both staring in shock at the opening.

"Where did that come from?" Mag breathed.

"I don't know," I said, creeping toward it and poking my head inside. It was like the staircase behind the tapestry. It was damp, made of roughly hewn gray stone. I cautiously stepped into the passage and immediately there was another grating noise. I spun around in time to see Mag and Cadmus rushing to the increasingly smaller opening, before it closed without another sound. I was all alone in the dark and damp. Even worse, my torch spluttered out.

I pounded on the wall, but it was solid once again. No seam indicated where the exit used to be. "Mag! Cadmus!" I cried.

There was no response.

"Mag! Cadmus!"

"Who are you?"

I almost jumped out of my skin, for the voice had come from behind me. I squinted into the dark and saw a silhouette bearing down on me.

I screamed in alarm as whoever it was took hold of the torch and gently tugged it out of my hands. There was a pause, in which I heard a rock scraping against some kind of metal. A moment later, after a burst of sparks, the torch was lit once again and a boy's face swam into view.

He looked to be about my age, a couple inches taller than me, with blue eyes and blonde hair plastered to his face, like it was wet. A faded and torn green cloak covered his homespun shirt and trousers. He was holding a rock against an intricate-looking knife. He must have struck the two together, creating the spark that had ignited the torch. As he handed me back the torch, I saw him sheathing the knife into his belt.

"Who are you?" the boy said again.

"Penelope Bogg," I answered automatically. "Handmaiden to Queen Alana. Listen, my room's on the other side of this wall, do you know how I can get back in?"

The boy brushed past me and ran his hand over the wall. He passed by so close, that I took a step back.

After a moment, the boy touched a point about halfway up the wall. I saw him turn back toward me, before I slid down the wall in exhaustion.

"What's wrong?" he asked. I could hear him breathing beside me.

I looked up at him and gave a weak smile. "Let's just say, I've had a rough day."

The boy nodded knowingly. "Magic?"

I stared at him in surprise. "Yes, how did you know?"

It was the boy's turn to smile weakly. "My sister has magic. I know the signs. You're still reacting badly to seeing a color." He stood and held out his hand. "Arthur, but my friends call my Artie."

I took Artie's hand and he pulled me up. I swayed and had to catch myself on the wall. It was damp there too.

"I can help with that," Artie offered. "My sister told me about a plant that can temporarily cure this sort of thing."

"Really?" I couldn't keep the hopefulness out of my voice.

"Yes, its outside the castle. The thing is, I can't lead you."

My heart sank. "You said you could help."

"I can, but I don't know my way around in here. You're going to have to lead us."

Who is he? I wondered. How could he tell me that he could help me, when he didn't even know how to find his way outside?

"Why are you in here?" I asked.

Artie had gone pale. "I was... avoiding someone. I ducked into the other end of the passage and got lost. I'm a mundane and this tunnel, along with several others in Alsmora, is enchanted so only a magical can find their way through. The tunnel will bend to your will. It will open up passageways for you, to help you find your way, where it wouldn't do that for me."

It seemed so extraordinary. How could a tunnel know who was traveling its depths? Why were magic users so special? On the other hand, I could tell from Artie's voice that he was sincere. He seemed so confident that only I could do it.

I squared my shoulders. "What do I have to do?"

"Hold the torch up, say where you want to go, in this case the forest outside of Kelton Castle, and start walking. Eventually, we're going to reach a dead end. I can let us out then."

I stared hard at Artie. How could we get out at a dead end? He stared back, calmly, and motioned for me to raise the torch.

This can't possibly work, I thought. Then, I remembered how Mag how used nothing but her hand to open the last secret passageway. Why not? I raised the torch high in the air with one hand and gripped my amulet with the other. "The forest outside Kelton Castle, please."

Nothing happened at first. I stood there, waiting for what seemed like ages when suddenly a pulsing arrow of light appeared in the center of the path, pointing to an arch to the left. I gasped.

"What is it?" Artie said urgently.

"You don't see it? There's a light leading to that arch," I said, pointing.

"This is great, Penelope. Follow it. It's your magic leading us out."

I took a deep breath and stepped forward. The light quickened, flashing with each step. I paused at the arch and looked into the next room.

I could see the faint impression of the rocks and what looked like a giant, sleeping scorpion.

"Scorp-" I cried in alarm, but Artie covered my mouth and tugged me back into the other room.

I was almost hyperventilating as Artie removed his hand. "I'm sorry, but I couldn't let you wake up the yikty."

"Yikties," I managed to gasp. Giant scorpions the size of humans with a paralyzing sting.

"Don't like scorpions?" Artie guessed.

"Hate them," I shuddered. "Ever since-" I paused. That was strange. I couldn't remember.

Artie didn't press me.

I peeked around the corner and saw the yikty sleeping right in front of another lighted arch. That's where we had to go. The question was, how to get past the yikty?

"I have an idea," Artie said slowly, "but you're not going to like it."

"Why? What is it?"

"We're going to turn invisible."

Invisible? Why wouldn't I like that? I'd always wanted to turn invisible, especially the night-

I frowned, unable to remember.

"Will it hurt?"

"In a way. It might bring on your colored vision again."

No, not that! I couldn't take another instant of silver. I started shivering just thinking about it.

"Artie, no," I said, balling my hands into fists. "I can't."

"Penelope, you can't be afraid of your colored vision. I know its hard, but believe me, it will pass. It just takes time, practice, and the courage to try in the first place."

"What if it wakes up?" I rubbed my arms to rid myself of goose bumps.

"It might, but that's a chance we're going to have to take."

"What about alternate routes?"

Artie frowned. "Maybe. Turn around and say, 'The forest outside Kelton Castle, alternate route.'"

I did so and waited for another pulsing arrow. I scanned the room carefully, but everything remained in shadow. Artie raised his eyebrows. I shook my head and turned back to the room with the yikty. The arch behind it was flashing with a steady, white light.

"Is this the only way forward?" he asked.

"Past the scorpion," I confirmed, barely repressing a shudder. There was nothing else I could do, but—"How do we turn ourselves invisible?"

"Just say, 'Aun evas comren.' It will bend the existing light around whatever you're touching." As he took my hand again, he stared pointedly at the torch and I put it in the nearest bracket.

I took a deep breath and repeated, "Aun evas comren." The silver immediately returned and I sank to my knees. Artie squeezed my hand and I could see the surprised look on his face as his blue eyes turned to muted silver.

Is that what I look like when I see silver, I dimly wondered. As I watched, I realized that my vision was clearing and everything looked normal again.

"Silver, huh?" Artie said.

I started. "How did you know?"

"My sister taught me a simple technique for mundanes. If you take a magical's hand when their colored vision comes on, the color can be disbursed more quickly, through the mundane's body. It only works, though, if you're holding something of the same color." He tilted his silver knife toward me.

"How did you know it was silver?" I asked, curiously.

"Honestly, I just guessed. My knife has several colors on it, so it seemed like my best bet."

There were three jewels on the knife's black hilt: a ruby, sapphire, and emerald.

"Five different options," I said. "Smart."

I looked around the room and realized that Artie and I were in black and white. Everything else was in perfect color.

"What's going on?" I asked, turning my hand over, studying it in fascination.

"We're invisible," Artie said, simply.

"I can still see us."

"That's what happens when you're invisible. Everyone and everything in perfect color can't see us. Only those in black and white can see others in black and white."

"The yikty won't see us?"

"That's right. But, be careful, he can still hear us." Artie crept forward into the next chamber. I was right on his heels. "Which door?" he whispered.

"That one," I whispered back, pointing to the one directly behind the yikty.

We stole silently toward the yikty. Its tail was curled over its back. All we had to do was somehow climb over it.

"I'll go first," I said, letting go of Artie's hand.

The yikty's leg was as thick as a tree trunk. I backed up and ran forward; ready to leap over the yikty, when it shifted and brought its tail right in my path. I was already in the air; I was going to crash right into the sting. I had no time to change course.

Artie tackled me from behind and we sailed right under the sting, landing on the other side with twin thumps.

"Ouch!" I said and looked around. Artie was lying on the ground beside me.

"Are you all right?" he said, helping me to my feet.

"Yes. Thank you," I said quietly.

Artie didn't answer, but as he turned away, I saw that he was blushing. "Where to now?" he said.

I grabbed a new torch and Artie lit it. I held it up and saw that we were twenty feet from a dead end.

"We're here," Artie said, approaching the blank wall. He took out his knife and began to carve something into the rock. I caught a glimpse of what looked like a circle with a line coming out of the side.

As I watched, a crack appeared at the top of the ceiling, went down the center of the circle, and ended at the floor. The two sides parted and opened outward to the outside.

"This was the hill I was on when I had to hide," Artie said, stepping through the doorway. "And there's the castle behind us."

I followed Artie, my mouth hanging open. As the late afternoon sun warmed me, I noticed that his hair was turning back to blonde and his cloak to green. My skirts were currently a dark blue. The castle loomed tall in the north.

"Here we are," Artie said, pointing to a small, red flower that grew on the top of the hill.

I walked up to the flower and leaned down, pressing my ear gently against it. I closed my eyes and breathed deeply. Instantly, a dozen sounds filled my head: water dripping, roots growing, and petals uncurling toward the sun.

"Thank you," I said, standing and turning to the flower, before picking it. Artie was looking at me curiously. "What?" I asked.

"What were you doing?"

"Listening to the flower," I said, simply.

When he continued to look confused, I tried to explain, "You see, there's a multitude of life living in the plants-"

But Artie cut me off, pulling me to the ground. He was crouching, staring intently at something in the valley below us.

I looked down and saw two people riding astride horses: a man with shoulder-length dark brown hair and a woman with long, flowing blonde hair. I squinted at the man. "Malcolm," I said. I didn't recognize the woman, though. They were heading for the castle. "Who is she?"

Artie didn't answer. I turned to look at him, but he was striding away, back toward the rock tunnel.

"Artie?"

"You have to get back through the tunnel, Penelope," he said, without looking at me. "You have to make it back before them. Its not safe for you out here."

"What about you?"

"I can't go. Not now."

My blood started to run cold. "But, I can't open the door to get back into my room. And if it's not safe out here, you should come with me." Please, I added silently.

Artie finally turned to face me. "I can handle anything thrown at me. As for getting back into your room, there's nothing special about me, Penelope, it's all in the knife. My... sister infused it with powerful magic, so it can open the many secret passageways and tunnels in Alsmora. All you have to do is carve the symbol I drew earlier into the rock wall."

"You mean the circle with the line coming out the side?"

"You could say that." Artie smiled faintly and pressed the hilt of the knife into my hand, wrapping my fingers around it. After a moment, he added the sheath.

I tried to hand the knife back. "Artie, I can't-"

"Keep it, at least for now," he said firmly. "You're going to need it."

I stared into his determined blue eyes and nodded reluctantly. "All right, for now. But, how will I get the knife back to you?"

"Come to this hill tomorrow morning at dawn, I'll be waiting."

"Artie, please, come back with me. I don't want to face that yikty by myself."

"I'll tell you what," he said. "I'll come with you inside the tunnel and all the way to the dead end where I can come in if I have to, but if the torch leads you down an alternate route, away from the yikty, I'm coming back out immediately. I'll hold the door open on this end, until I know which way the magic will lead you. I can't go into the castle right now, Penelope. I'm sorry. Remember to eat that flower as soon as possible."

I struggled to find a counterargument. Any counterargument. Finally, I was forced to say, "Deal."

As I chewed the plant, we walked back to the tunnel entrance. New strength flowed through me. I looked back one more time and saw Malcolm and the girl riding away from us. But just for a second, the girl seemed to turn and stare straight at us, with a knowing grin on her face.

Chapter Six

A Thief for a Guest

ARTIE HELD OPEN THE TUNNEL ENTRANCE, then disappeared after the torch pointed me toward a completely new arch. I was a little disappointed. He had been good company. It was an uneventful trip. I went through two empty rooms before I found the dead end again. The only thing out of the ordinary was a blue-tinged rabbit darting past me as I left the first room.

In front of the dead end, I took out Artie's knife and started to carve the circle with a line through the side. The crack appeared through the middle of the circle, opening outward. I hurried into the room beyond and heard several gasps.

"There you are, Penelope!" Mag said, as she and Cadmus turned toward me. There was a persistent knocking on the door. "Where were you?"

"Later," I muttered, as the knocking grew louder. I dropped the knife and sheath on the nightstand and opened the door to find Mrs. Thompson glaring down at me.

"I've been knocking for five minutes," she said grumpily. "You didn't answer."

I hung my head. "I'm deeply sorry. It won't happen again."

"See that it doesn't. The Queen wants you in her chambers. There's a very important guest at the gate." And she marched off down the hall.

"She's pleasant," Mag snorted.

"I'd better go," I said, glancing at Artie's knife. Should I leave it or take it with me? It would probably be a bad idea if Queen Alana saw me with it, but at the same time, I didn't want to let it out of my sight.

I wrapped a cord around my middle and stuck the sheathed knife in it.

"What is that?" Mag asked.

I ignored her and said without hesitation, "Aun evas comren." The sheath turned invisible at once. And there was no silver!

"Nice spell," Cadmus said. "Where did you learn that?"

"A boy I met in the passageway taught it to me. He helped me to get out again," I said, checking to make sure the sheath was really hidden. It had completely disappeared from my view. But I hadn't.

Maybe because I had been focusing on the knife instead of me? Possible.

"There was a boy in the secret passageway?" Mag asked. "That's odd. Do you know who he is?"

"His name's Artie."

There was an awkward pause as Mag and Cadmus stared at me. When I didn't elaborate, Mag gestured with her hand. "And?"

"That's it," I said, blushing. I didn't even know Artie's last name. "I met him, we helped each other get outside, ran into a yikty, and collected a flower before coming back in. What?" I asked, noticing their shocked expressions.

"A yikty?!" Mag demanded.

"Yes, but don't worry, it was asleep."

Mag closed her eyes and breathed deeply, like she was trying to calm herself. Cadmus, meanwhile, said, "Penelope, if there's a yikty in the passageway, we need to get in there and destroy it."

"I'm going in," Mag said, taking a step forward.

"Hold on a second," I said, stepping between Mag and the secret entrance. "You can't."

"Sure, I can," Mag said, brushing past me.

"No, you can't," I said, stepping in front of her again. "The only way to get back out of the tunnel is to use Artie's knife to carve a symbol into the wall. I'm not letting this knife out of my sight until I give it back to Artie tomorrow morning."

Mag opened her mouth to protest.

"Plus," I said, holding up my hand to silence her. "I have to go to Queen Alana's chambers and I'm running late."

I didn't add that I would sooner let Hazel boss me around for a week than see the yikty again. I wanted to stay as far away from that monster as I could.

Mag gave a low growl. "You're a bad as Aldrich. Neither of you ever left me have any fun. Fine, I'll go with you, at least to the door, then I'll have to find Aldrich." And she headed out of the room without further complaint.

I paused at the door and looked back to see Cadmus standing on the window frame.

"Cadmus?"

"You go ahead," he said. "I need to check on the other cats. See how they're doing patrolling the perimeter."

"Patrolling against what?" I asked. They still hadn't told me exactly why I needed the torch that opened the secret passageway in the first place.

"Rabbits," he said simply.

"Rabbits?" I repeated. What was so dangerous about cute, little bunnies? I saw them all the time in the garden. There was nothing threatening about them.

Mag appeared at my shoulder. "Are we going or not?" she asked.

Without another word, I turned on my heel and made my way up to the two flights to Queen Alana's chambers. Mag was right behind me.

After several minutes of walking in silence, I turned toward Mag and said, "Why did you two want to use a torch against a rabbit?"

Mag's shoulders slumped. "It's a long story," she warned.

"We have a little time before we reach Queen Alana's rooms," I pointed out.

Mag didn't say anything until we were in front of Queen Alana's door. "Ice," she muttered.

"What?"

"Ice," she repeated and knocked on the door.

The door was pulled open by Viola, who curtseyed when she saw Mag, who promptly went back down the stairs to search for Aldrich. Viola blocked my way in, though.

"You're really pushing it, Penelope," Viola hissed. The taller, brunette handmaiden seized my arm and dragged me a few feet away. "Where were you?"

"Downstairs," I whispered. "Is Queen Alana angry?"

"She hasn't noticed. She's been too busy discussing security measures with Casimir. He left through the other door. He's creepy, isn't he?"

I nodded. Those mismatched eyes unnerved me as well.

"Girls, could you button my dress, please?" Queen Alana said, cutting across our conversation.

Viola and I lurched forward to assist the queen. She had changed from the green dress with the bow encircling her waist to an elegant blue dress with buttons in the back. The white lace I had picked up from town was around the neck and sleeves. It seemed as if Casimir's magic had reached Queen Alana after all. Hazel was holding up jewelry for Alana to inspect.

After Viola had buttoned the dress, there was a knock on the door, which I answered. A page of about twelve in velvet livery was standing before me.

"The ambassador to see Queen Alana," he said, before saluting and departing.

Alana smoothed down her dress and motioned for us to follow.

We went in through a side door to the throne room, where Queen Alana sat primly on her seat. Viola, Hazel, and I stood on either side of the door. As the queen's handmaidens, we were privileged to be allowed access to court proceedings. If she needed anything, we would be there.

Within moments, Casimir arrived and stood behind Queen Alana and slightly to the left.

The same page walked into the room and announced, "Now presenting, from the west of Alsmora, the ambassador Sylvia Quick."

My stomach dropped as the boy turned on his heel and walked smartly off. Not the Quicks! They were a group of villainous thieves that preyed on the westernmost cities. They were elusive. Only they knew the location of their secret headquarters. It was outlandish to think one could be here now.

The gilded double doors opened to reveal a girl of about eighteen. She was blonde, with ice-cold blue eyes, a pointed nose, and a smirk on her face. She was wearing a white dress that made her look like a fairy princess, if rather a cold one.

Her eyes swept once over the room, traveling over the handmaidens and Casimir. They flicked between Queen Alana and myself. She seemed to glare at me, before settling on the queen and relaxing her expression.

"Your Majesty," she said with a deep curtsey.

"Miss Quick," Queen Alana said politely. "It is a pleasure to see you. How was your journey?"

"Exhausting. Traveling halfway across the country is no mean feat."

"I will have a room prepared for you," Queen Alana said.

They continued with this vein of pleasantries for several minutes.

While they talked, I watched Sylvia's hands, distrustful of the thief, but she didn't move.

Finally, Queen Alana broached the reason for Sylvia's visit. "I must admit to some surprise to seeing you in the center of Alsmora. I thought your family stuck to the west. What does your father want, to send you so far from home?"

"My father sends his regards and would like to ask your assistance in finding someone. A boy of sixteen."

My heart skipped a beat. No, it couldn't be him, I thought, there are plenty of boys my age, but the invisible knife around my waist started to feel heavy.

"Whatever Leopold Quick holds against one of my subjects," Queen Alana said, "we can surely work it out here."

"That would be true under normal circumstances, Queen Alana," Sylvia said. "But, no, that will not suffice. The person I seek is a thief himself and must be brought before my father immediately."

Queen Alana cleared her throat and said, "What is the boy's name?"

Sylvia's eyes rested on Hazel, Viola, and me in turn. "Not in front of them," she said, barely opening her mouth. "The less people that know, the fewer that can tip him off."

It was the same rationale Mag and Aldrich had used to keep me from telling Malcolm and Lydia about my magic. It seemed, like Mag and Aldrich, Sylvia didn't know whom she could trust.

"I understand," the queen said. "Viola, Hazel, Penelope, could you wait for me outside, please?"

The three of us filed out. I was the last one at the door. My eyes lingered on Queen Alana, Casimir, and Sylvia still in the room, before I closed it with a click.

Once we were out of earshot, Viola and Hazel started a furious argument about who the girl was searching for.

"He must be a thief that stole from their ruler," Hazel said. "Why else would the king of thieves himself be so eager to find him?"

"He sent his own daughter," Viola mused. "This has to be personal. Maybe it was her boyfriend and her father disapproves of him. He could be waiting to punish this boy."

I remained quiet. Artie had saved me from the yikty, got me the flower I needed, and even left me his knife so I could return through the tunnel. It couldn't be him. Ah, a little voice in my head reminded me, but what do you really know about him?

I was gazing out the nearest window, when a movement outside caught my attention. Checking to make sure Viola and Hazel were still deep in discussion, I hurried to the window and looked out. Artie was slinking rapidly through the secluded standing of trees a little past the garden. Even from this distance, I recognized his green cloak and blonde hair.

As I watched, he stopped and looked back every few feet, as if checking for pursuers. Finally, he crept further into the shade of the trees and was lost to sight.

"Penelope." Someone tapped me on the shoulder. It was Viola.

"Yes?"

"Queen Alana has summoned us back into the throne room."

"Be right there," I said, sneaking one last glance out the window. I couldn't shake the feeling that Artie was indeed being followed. But I had no other proof than Artie's strange behavior in the tunnel or just now outside.

I sighed and followed Viola back into the throne room.

Sylvia Quick was leaning against the wall, watching us with unblinking eyes as we filed back in. Queen Alana and Casimir were discussing something in whispers.

"Girls, there you are," Queen Alana said, breaking off her conversation with Casimir. Her eyes looked glazed. "Miss Quick will remain in the castle for the next few days. She'll be attending the gala. We'll be putting her into the... blue room. Yes, that's it. Now, we must prepare for the festivities."

* * *

"Wait!" someone called as I was leaving the room. I turned around and saw Sylvia Quick approaching rapidly, with a frown on her face. "Follow me," she said.

Puzzled, I trailed after her, down the stairs to the second floor, and into an empty sitting room. She planted herself on a chair. "Sit," she commanded.

I never took my eyes off her hands as I sat gingerly on the edge of the chair opposite her.

"That's an interesting knife you have around your waist. Where did you get it?" Sylvia asked casually. Her hands never wavered from her lap.

I blinked in surprise. "What knife?"

Sylvia glared at me. "I can see the knife, you know. Its right there on your waist."

I looked down. Sure enough, it was visible.

"I don't understand. It's supposed to be invisible," I murmured softly.

"Ah, I see," Sylvia said. "You're just starting out with magic, aren't you? Well, let me give you a helpful tip. Spells can wear off. I can teach you a spell that will extend how long a spell lasts."

"Really? What's that?" I asked, wary of anything this thief could teach me.

"Its called 'Lanasan.' It's a spell to slow down timed spells. For instance, if a spell is only supposed to last a minute, saying 'Lanasan' will increase your time to two minutes."

"Aun evas comren," I said and the knife and sheath disappeared again. I sagged against the wall. "Lanasan," I gasped out, as silver flooded my vision. The flower must have worn off already. Too much magic in one day, I thought, sliding down the wall completely.

"Well, that should hold for a while," Sylvia said.

"Thank you," I said. "...Why did you help me?"

Sylvia smiled faintly. "Maybe because I know what you're going through. Now, could you show me to my room? Queen Alana said it would be the one on the second floor. The one with the blue door."

"I know the one," I said, standing up. "Strange, though."

"What is?"

"That particular door is usually locked. Since King Marcus died, Queen Alana has forbidden anyone from ever going inside. Why would she put you in there?"

"Why, indeed?" Sylvia mused as I lead her out the room and a couple of doors down.

"Here we are," I said, taking the key from Sylvia and reaching for the doorknob. It was freezing cold and wouldn't turn. I shivered as the doorknob slipped out of my hand.

"Allow me," Sylvia said, shaking her wrist free of her sleeve. I could see a shiny blue bracelet glittering there. She muttered something and the doorknob began to drip water.

Then it hit me: the doorknob hadn't just been cold. It had been covered with completely smooth ice!

Sylvia fitted in the key and the door creaked open. The room was a solid mass of black, with a thin sliver of light from a small window.

"Hello?" I called into the gloom.

The only answer was a short growl and a frightened squeak.

"Who's there?" I said, louder.

Sylvia seized my arm and pulled me back. "There's something in here," she said, eyes narrowed. "Something big."

She said another unintelligible spell and a ball of light appeared over her hand.

I blinked at the sudden brightness and saw the something big Sylvia had been talking about. A huge orange shape was crouched at the foot of the bed, trying to get at something underneath.

Sylvia raised her hand, probably to cast another spell, when something small and blue-white rushed out from under the bed, closely followed by something small and black. Orange jumped forward in front of Blue-White, when I recognized Black and gasped, "Cadmus!"

Orange, startled, took a swipe at Blue-White and missed. Blue-White turned, breathed something blue and sparkly at Orange, and escaped, running past Sylvia and me in the doorway and down the hall. I shivered. Whatever Blue-White had done was cold. The room felt like ice.

Black, who was indeed Cadmus, stepped forward. "We were so close," he said. "Ah, Penelope, there you are. You're just in time to help us." And he walked back into the room.

"Cats?" Sylvia said.

"The black's name is Cadmus," I said, stepping into the room. Sylvia and her light followed.

"Is he your cat?" she asked.

"No, I just met him today."

"Then, how do you know his name?"

I hesitated, remembering that Lydia hadn't understood Cadmus either. "What did Cadmus do when he came out?" I asked.

Sylvia frowned. "He meowed and walked back into the room."

Before I could stop myself, I said, "Were his meows... in English?"

"...No."

Sylvia and I were in the center of the room. I gasped for the second time in so many minutes. Orange was next to the bed, a housecat the size of a lion, and it was frozen in a block of ice. Everything except its head and tail, that is. The tail was twitching in agitation.

"Get me out of here," the cat meowed.

"Penelope," Cadmus said from on top of the bed. "Meet Charlotte. My second in command."

"Hello, Charlotte," I said slowly approaching.

"You!" she cried. "You're the cause of all this! We had that Kaninen cornered, then you distracted me!"

"Kaninen?"

"An ice rabbit," Sylvia said. "As far as I can tell, they can appear and disappear like magic in a flash of blue light and can freeze anything with a single breath." She indicated Charlotte. "Its so dark, how did you know that was a Kaninen?"

"Cadmus and Charlotte..." I said, before breaking off.

Sylvia's eyes seemed to bore right into me, but she didn't say anything.

"Get me out of here," Charlotte repeated.

"Of course, I... Sylvia, do you know how to free Charlotte?"

Sylvia shook her head. "My magical focus is water. We need fire. A light is all right, but any true flame cannot pass through my bracelet."

"Wait, I have it," I said. "Mag."

"The ambassador from Draval?"

Draval? Where's that? I wondered, but what I actually said was, "Yes?"

"Mm-hmm," Sylvia said. "If it's the same red-cloaked girl I saw when I first arrived, she's outside right now. I can see her through the window."

I spun around to the window and saw that Mag was indeed striding toward the nearby tree line, but going in the opposite direction of Artie.

"I'll go and get her," I said. "Miss Quick, would you mind waiting in here with Cadmus and Charlotte? Mag knows me."

"And I might have a harder time convincing her to come," Sylvia said. "Very well, but hurry, please. There is a matter of great urgency that I must address with you. Despite what you may think of me, I do like animals."

I nodded, hiked up my skirts, and sped out of the room, accompanied by the shrill sound of Charlotte yowling to be released. Who would have thought, the daughter of a fearsome thief lord, an animal lover? Maybe she wasn't as heartless as I originally thought. I raced through the kitchen and out into the garden. Mag was only a little way ahead of me.

"Mag! Wait up!"

She paused and waited for me to catch up. I stood there, my hands on my knees, panting.

"Mag... we need... your... help," I gasped out. "Cat has been... frozen."

"I'd be happy to help, Penelope, but I'm looking for the infestation of Kaninens. They're coming in from somewhere." Mag was interrupted by a curious noise. It sounded like a scream.

I could tell Mag had heard it too. She had gone stiff with surprise.

"Mag, we have to go check it out," I said, going cold with dread.

"It could be a trick, to lure us away from the castle," Mag said.

I wasn't listening. That scream had come from the west. The same direction Artie had been traveling in when he disappeared amongst the trees. I rushed forward, seizing my amulet as I went. "There's no time! We have to help him!"

Mag had no choice. She followed me from the grounds and into a deserted field beyond the castle. We hid behind a hill and looked down on the scene below.

Two trolls—eight feet tall, humanoid, a slight greenish hue to their skin—with clubs stood over a boy, roughly my age. I inhaled sharply when I again recognized the blonde hair and green cloak.

"Artie," I breathed. I had hoped to be wrong. His head lolled listlessly to the side, like he was on the verge of unconsciousness. One troll held his arms behind his back as the bigger and stockier of the two addressed their captive. It was then that I noticed the smaller bundle in the bigger troll's hands. I squinted. It looked bluish-white, like the creature that had run from Sylvia's room. A Kaninen.

"Mag, is that...?" I whispered, pointing.

"Yes," she whispered back bitterly. "That's an ice rabbit. Strange that they caught it. They're small and usually impossible to trap."

"I am tired of these games, boy," the bigger troll snapped, shaking the rabbit. There was a white cloth tied over its mouth. Its ears drooped miserably. "Now, tell me where the hideout is!"

Artie raised his head shakily. "Don't know. Never been there."

The smaller troll grunted, "Lying won't save you, boy."

Artie kicked out at the larger troll, missing the ice rabbit by inches. "I told you, I don't know! And I wouldn't tell you if I did!"

I narrowed my eyes, furious at the cruel treatment toward them.

Mag pulled me down quickly. "What are you doing? This could still be a trap. Kaninens working together with trolls to capture or kill you."

"Trap or no trap, I'm not going to let either of them die, Mag! That's Artie! And that poor rabbit must be scared stiff," I gestured wildly in their direction. "Now, are you with me or not?"

Mag stared into my eyes, amber into brown, and grinned. "Ice rabbits are not my friends, but I'm with you, Penelope. Let's go, but don't expect my full dragon form. Aldrich would be furious if he knew I broke my cover. One of these days, I may even have to go before the dragon council, as Aldrich would say."

Mag and I stood upon a steep, grassy hill, dotted with trees. We would have to tread carefully, least we faltered and fell, sprawling at the trolls' feet. We started out descent.

When we were halfway to the bottom, and I was picking my way between two large oak trees, Artie looked up and saw us. His eyes went wide. He stared for too long, however.

"What are you looking at?" the head troll snarled.

"Nothing," Artie said quickly.

I flung myself behind the largest of the two oaks, pulling Mag with me. We held our breath for several tense moments. If the trolls came to investigate, the only upside would be that we had the advantage of higher ground.

"Go check it out," the bigger troll snapped at the smaller one.

Grunting, the troll released Artie into its fellow's clutches and lumbered in our direction.

"Now what?" I mouthed at Mag.

She studied the scene below us and motioned for me to prepare myself.

As the troll ambled closer, she transformed halfway and readied her claws and tail. I took a starting position, waiting for her signal.

The troll was feet away from Mag. She pounced, sending him sprawling across the ground.

"Go!" she yelled, whipping her tail back and forth.

I dashed from my hiding space and recklessly pelted toward the head troll. Artie and the rabbit were slung over its back.

I cut the distance separating us at an angle, slowing to a stop in front of the troll.

"Fool," it growled, dropping Artie and the ice rabbit on the ground. They looked dazed, but at least the white cloth had slipped free from the rabbit's mouth. "You will never defeat me! Me, Laborc the Mighty!"

"You think a lot of yourself," I said. Holding forth the amulet, I shot a blast of red energy at the troll.

Laborc swung his club and destroyed the spell as easily as I might swat a fly.

The rabbit hopped to its feet, jerking its head from side-to-side, taking in the scene. I reached down to try and calm it and get it out of the way, but it leapt at my throat and latched on to my amulet, tearing it free from my neck. Before I could do more than stare at it in disbelief, with the ends of the chain flapping around the rabbit like writhing snakes, it disappeared in a flash of blue.

I stood in shocked silence, too stunned to move.

"Penelope!" Mag yelled, jolting me to my senses. I dived out of the way as Laborc's club came crashing down where I had been standing seconds before.

Rolling upright, I found myself beside Artie. He tugged weakly on my arm. "Knife," he said, his hands shaking as he pointed to the sheath on my waist. I fumbled with the hilt, finally managing to grasp it awkwardly in my hand. It was much smaller than a sword. I would have to get within club range if I wanted to attack.

Laborc ran at me, swinging his club as he went, yelling, "Feel honored, human. You will fall to Laborc, prince of the trolls!" I braced myself for the impact of the huge troll, when I realized I wasn't the target; Artie was! I leapt in front of him, holding the knifepoint up as the troll bore down on us. The troll couldn't stop his headlong charge as the knifepoint struck him in the arm. He shuddered for a moment, the club slipping from his grip. He seized his arm.

I dropped the knife in alarm and backed away from the troll. It hardly seemed like a scratch against his massive bulk.

Laborc glared at me and growled, "You'll pay for that." He charged again, stretching out his arms to grab me. I grasped whatever was closest, which was Artie's hand and closed my eyes, but nothing happened.

After several seconds, I peeked out. Laborc stood five feet in front of me, banging with his good arm on the blue shield I had somehow conjured to protect us.

"Curse you!" Laborc screamed.

I slumped forward in exhaustion, trying to stay conscious. Silver was threatening to engulf my vision. Mag was on the other side of the shield, tripping the second troll with her tail and breathing fire in his face.

"Beware, human," Laborc growled. "You have brought the full wrath of the house of Kelraz upon your head." He pounded against the shield with renewed force, but it stayed glittering intact. He pounded again, but the shield didn't like that. It shot a beam of silver-white energy at both trolls, sending them flying through the air. I couldn't see where they landed, but I heard two loud thumps.

"Nice spell," Mag said, crossing the barrier when Laborc couldn't and stopping by my side. "Your shield should protect us from the trolls."

"Mag," I blinked blearily and saw the blue glow was over the whole castle. "The ice rabbit has my amulet." It hurt to think. "What did I do?" I asked blankly.

"You extended your shield," Mag said, with a pained, pinched expression. "Impressive bit of spell work, especially without your amulet. I'll have to inform Aldrich when I see him, omitting of course, that I transformed halfway. Penelope, I don't know why the silver rose chose us, but Aldrich made one point perfectly clear: we need that amulet. The Kaninens cannot get away with this."

I frowned. I didn't feel as if I deserved any praise. I had panicked when Laborc ran at me. And what was this about my amulet? What did Aldrich know that he wasn't telling me?

Saving those thoughts for later, I said, "So, Laborc can't get in?"

"No, not until the spell wears off, which should take a couple of hours," Mag said, scooping up the fallen knife and feeling its point, before handing it back to me. "Excellent blade. This is strongly made. If I had to guess, I'd say it was tempered silver. We'd better treat the boy who owns it. He looks on the verge of collapse."

"His name's Artie," I said, protectively. We placed his arms over our shoulders and walked him back to the castle. I stumbled slightly under his weight.

"Huh? Who?" Artie blinked dazedly.

"Shh," I whispered. "Its me. Penelope. This is my friend, Mag."

"My head feels like its split open," Artie said, rubbing his temple.

I resisted the urge to do the same. "We're taking you back to the castle. The nurse, Mrs. Hexley, will treat you there. We'll have to be quiet, though. They're having the gala tonight."

Artie began to cough uncontrollably. We had to stop, because he was shaking so much. "Ugh," he said. "Will Sylvia be there?"

"Yes," I said slowly. How did Artie know who she was? Was he...? No, he couldn't be.

Artie nodded. "Can I have my knife back?"

I placed it in Artie's hands and he seemed to sag against me.

I gave a sigh of relief. "Just relax, Artie. That's it. We'll be at the castle before you know it."

I almost dropped his arm when he took my hand in his own. It felt as if I had received an electric shock, which jolted me back to full awareness.

"Thank you," he whispered, before his eyes rolled into unconsciousness, leaving me staring at the burnished silver of his knife. Who are you, Artie? I thought.

A faint smile touched his lips, as though he could hear my question.

Chapter Seven

Fire to Water

MAG AND I STAGGERED INTO THE CASTLE with Artie. We gently deposited him on the floor of the entrance hall.

"Whew," I said, massaging my arms. "We made it."

"We're not there yet," Mag said. "We still need to treat him."

"There's an infirmary on the first floor," I said.

Sliding our hands under Artie's armpits, Mag and I lifted him again, but before we could go two feet, Artie opened his eyes and blinked blearily. "Who? What? Where?"

"You're safe," I said, gently. "We're at Kelton Castle. We're taking you to the infirmary."

Artie shook his head, vehemently. "Penelope, you have to get Sylvia. Promise me you'll find her."

"Of course, Artie. We'll drop you off at the infirmary and then I'll fetch Sylvia." Then, in barely more than a whisper, I said, "You should come, too, Mag. Charlotte, Cadmus's friend, is trapped in ice. Only your fire can save her."

"Where is she?"

"On the second floor, with Cadmus and Sylvia," I said.

"And the infirmary?"

"On the first floor, down the right hallway."

"Get Sylvia and bring her down here," Mag said. "Then, I'll go and free Charlotte. Don't worry, I can carry Artie by myself."

"I'm fine," he mumbled. "You can put me down."

"I don't think so. The way you're shaking, you'll simply fall over in a heap," Mag said. "Go on, Penelope."

I gently let go of Artie and Mag picked him up, slowly heading toward the right hall. I turned and hurried up the stairs, taking them two at a time. I hurtled headfirst into the room with Sylvia and the two cats, but Sylvia wasn't there. Instead, I found the two cats, one black and one orange staring up at me.

"Where's Sylvia?" I gasped.

"She had to go to the gala. She couldn't say no, the Queen invited her herself," Cadmus said. "If she refused, the messenger would have reported to Queen Alana and she would have sent somebody to check it out."

"But, you're back," Charlotte said happily. Her fur beneath the ice was starting to look blue-orange, but she looked a lot calmer than when we first met. "Where's Mag? You said she could free me."

"She's in the castle," I said. "But, first we need Sylvia's help with something."

Both Cadmus's and Charlotte's faces fell.

"Would you mind hurrying?" Charlotte said, an edge creeping back into her voice. "I can't stay like this much longer."

"Can't you shrink and then grow again?" I asked. "Wouldn't that expand the ice, breaking it?"

"Already tried it," Cadmus said gloomily. "Charlotte can't change size until she's free."

Charlotte grimaced in concentration. A moment later, she gasped as if in pain. "No good. The ice is blocking my powers."

I winced in sympathy as she turned a silver blue-orange. I rubbed my head in confusion. How had that happened? I hadn't even been trying to use a spell. My throat tightened as fear took hold. Would the silver never leave until I held my amulet once more? Even Artie's plant hadn't truly helped. I felt emotionally and physically weakened. That amulet had been my mother's last gift to me and without it, I felt empty.

"I'll be-" I coughed to clear my stinging throat and started over again. "I'll be as fast as I can."

I took off running down the stairs and immediately turned right. I was heading in the same direction as the infirmary, but before I reached it, I took a sharp left. I was panting with my hands on my knees when I skidded to a stop outside the ballroom's double doors. They each had a handle in the shape of a griffin.

I opened the right door cautiously. I had to grab onto the handle with both hands. I peeked inside and saw the ballroom completely filled with people. Some were whirling in dances, others were standing around talking, and still others were greeting Queen Alana.

I scanned the room, looking for Sylvia. I saw Viola and Hazel moving around, serving drinks. Casimir was passing a great stone fireplace at the other end of the room. Finally, I spotted Sylvia. She was standing by a table laden with food, from chicken to salads to puddings. She took a bite from a sandwich filled with cucumbers.

"Sylvia!" I said, rushing up.

"Hello," she said brightly. "Find Mag?"

"Yes," I panted, "but we need your help."

Sylvia frowned and put her sandwich back on her plate. "Why? What's wrong?"

"A new friend of mine was injured. Mag took him to the infirmary. His name's Artie."

Sylvia had taken another bite, but at my words she started to choke. As her fit subsided, she looked at me with streaming eyes, and said, "Artie? He's here?"

"Yes, when we brought him inside, he said that he wanted to talk to you." I quickly gave her directions to the infirmary.

Sylvia shoved the plate with the half-eaten sandwich into my hands, before rushing out the double doors.

I put the plate down on the nearest table and moved to follow, but somebody hailed me. I spun around and found myself face-to-face with a tall, muscular boy with shoulder-length dark brown hair, piercing green eyes, and a crooked smile. He was wearing a dark blue uniform dress shirt and black pants. I could see his sword at his belt.

"Malcolm," I said, smiling widely. "When did you get here?"

"A few hours ago. Sorry I didn't come see you and Lydia sooner, but I was reporting to Queen Alana," he said, gesturing back to the queen, who was still greeting guests. "I saw you talking with Sylvia Quick. Where did she go? I need to talk to her."

I sighed. "Long story. She went off to see my new friend. She should be back soon. In fact, I should go check on him, as well," I said reluctantly. Even if I couldn't tell him about the dragons, I at least wanted to chat with my brother for a few minutes, but Mag and Charlotte were waiting. And Artie.

"I'll come with you," Malcolm offered.

I frowned and looked around the ballroom, which was crowded with people. "But, doesn't the Queen need you here?"

"She ordered me to find Sylvia Quick. Besides, my men are here."

I glanced around again and saw a dozen guards, all dressed like Malcolm, standing to the sides of the room.

"The Queen and her guests will be well protected," Malcolm assured me.

"All right," I relented, heading for the doors.

"Where are we going?" he asked, looking around expectantly.

"The infirmary."

"Come on, then," Malcolm said, setting off at once. We fell into step and headed down the hall.

"I hate infirmaries," he said, holding open the door when we arrived. "I'll wait out here."

I stepped inside and found Artie propped up in a bed with Sylvia standing above him. Mag and Aldrich, both with their hoods up, were talking rapidly in a corner. Mag nodded as I entered the room. Aldrich flipped open a gold pocket watch and studied it. A blue star on the inside cover caught my attention. After consulting his watch, Aldrich left through the open door, patting me on the shoulder on his way out.

"Okay, Artie, I promise," Sylvia said. "I hope you know what you're doing."

"I do, Sylvia, don't worry. Penelope, there you are," Artie said, turning to face me.

"Hi, Artie. How are you?" I said, approaching with my brightest smile.

He rolled his eyes. "I've been better. Thanks for finding Sylvia."

"You're welcome," I said. My smile wavered slightly.

Mrs. Hexley, a gray-haired woman with large, square glasses perched on the tip of her nose came bustling over. She was a widowed witch that specialized in healing magic and potions. She smiled. "Penelope, what brings you here?"

"Artie was attacked by trolls."

Mrs. Hexley clicked her tongue. "Its always trolls this time of year. Let's see what we can do about that." She busied herself with examining Artie.

"Do not worry yourself, Mrs. Hexley. I've already seen to him," Sylvia said.

I sighed with relief, my smile returning. "Thank you, Sylvia. Mag, we should go and take care of that other problem upstairs."

"Cadmus is waiting for us, right? This shouldn't take long," Mag said, stretching and moving forward.

"Where are you going, now?" Artie asked anxiously.

"Problem in Sylvia's room. Mag knows how to solve it."

"I'll wait here," Sylvia said, sitting in one of the two chairs by Artie's bed.

"Come back quickly," Artie called pleadingly as I gently shut the door. Malcolm was still outside.

"Hi, Penelope. Is Sylvia in there?" he asked. "And you are...?"

"Malcolm, meet Mag, ambassador of Draval. Mag, Malcolm Bogg, Queen Alana's captain of the guards and my brother."

"It is a pleasure to meet you," Malcolm said, with a bow.

"The pleasure's all mine." Even with her long, floor-length red-cloak, Mag curtseyed all the same. "The second floor, right, Penelope?"

"Yes, you can't miss it. It's the blue door."

"Wait a second," Malcolm said, holding out his hands. "The blue door? You've got to be kidding me. Queen Alana actually opened up the blue room?"

"I'm as surprised as you are," I said. "But, there's a problem in there, one that only Mag can solve."

"Well, don't let me stop you," Malcolm said, stepping aside to let us pass. "I'll just speak to Sylvia and meet you there." His eyes were wide with concern.

Mag and I glanced at each other, before I nodded to Malcolm.

"Is he always like this?" Mag whispered, as soon as we were out of earshot.

"Yes, ever since Mom died, he's become more protective of Lydia and me, if that's even possible."

In front of the blue door, Malcolm caught up with us. He stood with his hand on the doorknob. "Ready?" he asked.

"Yes," Mag said, "but maybe you should wait out here."

Malcolm didn't appear to have heard Mag, because he turned the doorknob and pushed his way in. A second later, he gasped.

Inside the room, I found Malcolm standing five feet from Charlotte, still in the block of ice, but her whiskers had begun to turn blue. Cadmus was busy tugging a blanket off the bed toward Charlotte.

"Pefelapee, mat pfast," he grunted, his mouth full of blanket.

"What?" I said, blinking in confusion.

Cadmus spit out the blanket. "I said, 'Penelope, at last.' Help me pull this blanket over Charlotte. With any luck, it will keep her from freezing even faster."

"No need," Mag said, stepping forward and removing the hood of her cloak.

"Oh, Mag, thank goodness," Cadmus said, leaping onto the bed. "You might want to move out of the way, Penelope."

I climbed on top of the bed bedside Cadmus. Malcolm just stood by the door, confused.

"Penelope, what-"

But Malcolm got no further. Mag's hair had suddenly burst into flames and began to writhe, rippling between red, orange, and yellow. Malcolm gave a small cry of surprise and joined Cadmus and me out of the way.

Mag cupped her hand and blew into it. A fist-sized fireball materialized in it. She threw it at the ice covering Charlotte. Instantly, the ice around her right front leg shattered, leaving her soaking wet, with tiny crystal ice shards around her foot. Mag did the same thing again, and again, and again, until Charlotte stood before us, dripping wet, but unfrozen.

She shook herself, sending water droplets everywhere. "Thanks," she said.

Malcolm turned to me, his eyebrows raised in shock. "Penelope, what just happened?"

"Magic," Aldrich said. He was standing in the doorway with Queen Alana. Mag quickly put her hair out and covered her eyes with her hood once more.

"Queen Alana," I said. "Master Aldrich."

"Penelope," he said. "As you can see Queen Alana, I was telling the truth."

"Aldrich..." Mag said cautiously. "What truth might that be?"

"Why, that we're dragons, of course," Aldrich said calmly. There was stunned silence, broken only by the two cats hissing and racing out of the room.

"Aldrich!" Mag finally spluttered. "Nobody was supposed to know except Penelope!"

"Indeed?" Queen Alana said. "And why was it so important for my handmaiden to know?" When nobody answered, she sighed, "Its because of Alice isn't it? Penelope has inherited her magic, hasn't she?"

I glanced up sharply. "How did you know?"

Queen Alana smiled wryly. "When your best friend is a witch and her daughter starts acting strangely, it doesn't take a genius to figure it out."

Malcolm smiled, but it didn't quite reach his yellow eyes. "Good for you, Penelope!"

I frowned. Malcolm's eyes weren't yellow. But I blinked and they were suddenly green once more. It must have been a trick of the light, I decided.

"The rose chose Penelope," Aldrich explained, quietly. "You know what that means, Alana."

Queen Alana stood there, fingering her necklace as she considered. I assumed she would be angry, but she just stood there, looking thoughtful. Finally, she looked at me and said solemnly, "Penelope, you are no longer bound to me. Go and help the dragons. If and when you return, you will not be a handmaiden. I will make you a magical advisor, like Casimir."

Stunned, I curtseyed and said in a choked voice, "Thank you, Queen Alana."

She patted me on the shoulder as I rose. "Its what Alice would have wanted. She would be so proud if she could see you now."

I ducked my head in embarrassment, but I was secretly pleased. Then, I remembered my lost amulet.

"Oh! But, Queen Alana, my amulet has been stolen!"

Queen Alana put a hand to her mouth. "An amulet? But, wasn't that Alice's?"

I nodded miserably. "An ice rabbit took it."

"Penelope and I saved the Kaninen and a boy named Artie from a troll," Mag said. "The Kaninen stole the amulet. We have to get it back before we can do anything else."

"Of course," Queen Alana said. "You will have the castle's full support. When you are in true danger and are in need of help, find the healer of Cherry Grove."

"What do you mean? What kind of danger?" Malcolm asked.

"I don't know," Queen Alana said. "Alice wouldn't tell me."

Everyone turned to me.

I shook my head. "Don't look at me."

Malcolm bowed to Queen Alana and said abruptly, "With your permission, Your Majesty, I'll go check on the gala again. Excuse me."

He had only been gone for a few minutes when a voice by the door said, "Penelope?"

I looked over and saw Artie leaning against the doorframe. "Artie! What are you doing here? I thought you were resting."

"I did rest. Sylvia told me there was no damage. Apparently, my thick skull protected me from the fall."

I giggled, but I couldn't help feeling a stab of annoyance that Artie was spending so much time with Sylvia.

"Did I hear you say that you're going to find that ice rabbit?" Artie asked.

"Yes," Mag huffed. "Those rabbits are vicious and must be stopped."

"I'm not entirely sure about that," Artie said, slowly. "When we were both captured by the trolls, the Kaninen attempted to save both of us with its ice. It couldn't summon the ice until *after* its mouth was free of the cloth, but still, it tried to help."

"Oh, come off it, you can't possibly tell me you fell for that!" Mag cried. "Don't you see, Artie, it was trying to trick you into thinking its harmless!"

"Enough, Mag," Aldrich said quietly.

"I want to come with you," Artie plunged on. "When we find the Kaninen, it might recognize me and simply return the amulet. Its worth a try."

Artie had already helped me so much, getting me out of the tunnel, reminding me of the knife when facing off against the troll, and somehow removing my weariness through a touch. There was really no question. "Artie, we would be happy for you to travel with us."

Mag looked doubtful, but after a moment, "I agree with Penelope. You seem to know your way around that knife and you know how to handle Sylvia Quick."

Artie blushed and refused to meet my eyes.

"It is decided," Aldrich said. "You must seek out the Kaninens and question them about the amulet. I will go on ahead and alert the dragon council. Penelope, Mag, and Artie, you will start tomorrow and meet me in Dragon Valley. Do you understand, Mag? You are not to engage the Kaninens in any kind of communication, positive or negative, until you hear from the council."

Mag grumbled, but she didn't argue. "Fine, but only because ice is brutal against dragons."

"It is?" Artie asked.

"Trust me," Mag said. "It takes forever to pick ice crystals out of your scales and hair, even with fire."

I turned toward Queen Alana. She seemed oddly quiet and was staring blankly ahead, like when she placed Sylvia in the blue room. I opened my mouth, to ask if she was feeling all right, when-

Boom! The floor shook. We all grabbed onto something to stay on our feet, everyone but Mag and Aldrich. They had spread their hands and their claws had popped out, ready for action.

A page ran into the room. He had a pair of askew glasses on his nose. "Queen Alana!" he gasped. "Fire in the ballroom!"

Chapter Eight

Advice from a Cat

I STOOD STOCK-STILL. I COULDN'T BELIEVE IT. Queen Alana and Aldrich went rushing for the door.

"Penelope!" Mag cried as she and Artie hurried me along. "We have to go, *now!*"

I stumbled after Mag, Artie trailing behind as a sort of guard.

The ballroom doors were crammed with people surging away from the distant fireplace. Mag led us through a side door. I could see black smoke and flames lapping at the tapestries on the walls. Malcolm and his guards were standing in the center of the room, trying to direct people out. He looked at me briefly, before a rush of people obscured him from view.

"Malcolm!" I cried.

"Penelope!" Queen Alana said, appearing at my shoulder. Her eyes were no longer blank and empty, but alert and focused. "Go, now! We'll take care of this! Casimir! Malcolm! To me!" She turned and was swallowed by the crowd.

"In here," Mag said, turning us around and pushing us into a thankfully empty room.

Panting, I collapsed onto a chair. I was shaking from terror at the fire and sheer exhaustion. I kept running the image over and over again in my mind. There was Malcolm, trying to help people escape. I had done nothing but stand and gape as the smoke consumed the ballroom. I shuddered. It reminded me of that terrible night when—that was strange. What did it remind me of?

I glanced up to find my reflection gazing sadly at me from a cracked and dirty mirror. Nobody had been in to clean for a while. I looked older, with constant streaks of silver crisscrossing my hair. I stroked a patch of brown and my fingers came away, looking as if they were dyed with brown. The hair I had touched was now gleaming silver. The enchantment was fading away. Mag and Artie were by the door, peering into the hall.

Artie dropped into the chair beside me. "Penelope, I'm sorry. Malcolm will be all right. He wasn't too close to the blaze." He bestowed upon me an awkward hug. "I like the silver in your hair," he offered. "It makes you look more dignified."

I returned the hug, just as awkwardly, grateful for his words.

"Ahem," Mag said, causing us to jump apart. "If you're through, we have to get away from the fire and make our way to Dragon Valley. We should discuss this with the dragon elders. Aldrich's already gone ahead. After that, it should be relatively easy to gather the other dragons and force the Kaninens to return your amulet."

* * *

It was eerily quiet when we left the castle. All the corridors were deserted. I hoped everyone had made it out safely, but no one passed that I could ask.

"Penelope, its time for another lesson," Mag said as we came across a burning corridor. A loose ember from the ballroom fire had escaped and now it stood in our path. "*Bevasnor* is a useful spell that summons water from the nearest source," Mag explained.

"Bevasnor," I said. I held my head as silver water bubbled up from beneath the fires and extinguished them.

"Its good to drink," Mag said. "Wherever its source, magic purifies it."

"Why am I so tired?" I asked. "More so than usual."

"Your magic is dragging the water," Mag replied. "Distance matters. Also, magic is more difficult without a focus. Sorry, I forgot to warn you."

Artie took my hand and the silver dissipated somewhat. As my vision cleared fully, he released my hand and took several steps back. Like me, he was breathing rapidly and I remembered that he could see the silver, too.

After checking to make sure all the fires were out, we slipped outside through the darkness, making our way across the garden.

"So, you're leaving?" a familiar voice said from above.

"Hello, Cadmus," I said, allowing Mag and Artie to draw ahead. "You and Charlotte made it out all right?"

Cadmus leapt lightly from a nearby tree and stretched at my feet. "Yes, its amazing how people will just ignore us cats, even when we're standing right in front of them. We are the center of the universe, after all." He yawned. "Where are you three off to?"

After I had explained the trouble in the castle and how the Kaninen had stolen my amulet, he pierced me with his yellow-eyed stare and said, "I cannot go with you, but I can give you some advice: when you're done talking with the dragon elders, go to the village of Cherry Grove, in the west. There lives an interesting woman by the name of Mad Maude. She can train you in magic."

"Penelope!" Artie called.

"I have to go," I said. "Thank you, Cadmus! Look after Lydia!"

"Wait!" Cadmus called. "There is more. A dog has been howling tonight."

"So?"

"Penelope?" Artie said again, his voice nearer and full of concern.

"So, what is tonight?" Cadmus said, ignoring Artie's summons.

I frowned and looked away at a patch of moonlight. My eyes widened as it clicked. The howling of dogs and the full moon could only mean one thing...

"Cadmus," I gasped. "You don't mean *werewolves*, do you?"

Cadmus extended his claws. "I do, indeed. Now listen, Penelope," he said hurriedly as Artie stepped onto the path to join us, "just because cats and dogs don't typically like each other doesn't mean they can't learn to get along."

"What do you mean?" I said, but Artie slipped his hand into mine and squeezed it gently.

"Come on, Penelope, we have to go," he said.

I nodded and followed him a few paces, but paused to look back at Cadmus.

"I can tell you no more," he said. "You are an intelligent cat, Penelope. You can figure out who the dogs are for yourself."

And with that, Cadmus leapt back into the tree and vanished into the night.

Chapter Nine

Healing Rose

E STUMBLED AWAY FROM THE castle toward the forest, guided by the full moon. It was after midnight and all was silent.

An hour later, we halted in a clearing surrounded by trees and without speaking, we all settled against the fallen leaves and drifted to sleep. It didn't occur to me until later that we should have set a watch.

I awoke to a terrified squeak. As everything focused around me, I saw that Mag was up, her tail twitching threateningly, as she crouched behind a nearby stump, watching a figure at the tree line. I wanted to laugh at the bizarre image of a human with a dragon tail, when my eyes fell on the intruders.

"Lydia? Cadmus?" I said, brushing past Mag to stand beside my sister. "What are you doing here?"

"I followed you." She seemed transfixed by Mag's tail. "I heard you say you were going to find Mom's necklace. I want to help, too."

"Sorry, Penelope, she slipped right past me," Cadmus said.

I glanced back. Mag was busy inspecting her claws. Artie grimaced and shrugged.

Gesturing for Mag and Artie to follow, I retreated across the clearing away from Lydia and Cadmus. The other two joined me in a tight huddle.

"What do you think?" I whispered.

"She'll only get in the way," Mag said immediately. "I say we send her back."

"I agree," Artie said. He held up his hands at my squawk of annoyance and continued, "I agree, but I think we should give her a job to do. She'll feel as if she's helping and who knows, it might prove useful."

I opened my mouth to argue, when I remembered Aldrich's words. To involve Lydia might put her in danger.

"All right," I agreed reluctantly.

Artie gave me a sad, little smile.

"I'm sorry, Lydia," I said, returning to her side. "But, I can't allow you to come with us."

"Why not?" she protested.

"Because we have an important mission for you back at the castle. One only you can do."

Lydia's chest swelled with pride. All thoughts of joining us gone. "You can count on me."

"We need you to find whoever started the fire. It'll be tricky. We don't know who they are or what they look like. They could also be dangerous, so use caution. See if Malcolm will help. Once you find them, go to Queen Alana and Casimir. They can apprehend them."

Lydia saluted and dashed off into the night, back toward the castle, Cadmus close behind.

"Cute kid," Mag said.

"Thanks," I said. "Let's just hope she doesn't get hurt."

Artie stifled a yawn. "Come on. It's not yet dawn. We can still get a couple more hours of sleep. Then, we should head off."

"Where?" I said, my thoughts now slow and dim-witted, my eyes prickling with tiredness.

"To Dragon Valley, of course," Mag said. "The dragon council will be meeting tomorrow at noon and we have to be there to see it start."

* * *

I was still yawning when we set out the next morning. Artie didn't seem much better rested. He kept squinting in the bright sun.

Mag was the only one who acted as if she were truly awake, encouraging us to go faster.

We exited the trees and walked across a hill with a flat plain below, when a voice spoke, causing me to jump. "I wouldn't step there, if I were you."

I looked everywhere, but couldn't find anyone. "Where are you?"

"You need better eyesight. Up here."

There was a single, stunted tree beside us. In its branches sat an ordinary brown squirrel, but that's where ordinary stopped. This particular squirrel was wearing a green jerkin and held a miniature bow, a quiver full of arrows rested on its back.

"I'm Willow, leader of the Woodland Warriors," the squirrel said. It had a squeaky little voice that made it impossible to determine gender.

"Are you a *girl?*" Artie asked incredulously.

Willow rolled her eyes. "Well, of course I'm a girl! What did you think I was, a turnip?"

"I–"

"Mag, it's been a long time," Willow said, turning away from Artie.

"Yes, it has," Mag agreed.

"How's Aldrich?"

"Still fiery."

I took that as a compliment for dragons.

"Maybe you can help us, Willow," Mag went on. "There's trouble at Kelton castle. We need to reach Dragon Valley before the council meets at noon."

"Hmm? Walking, it could take days. Flying, however, you might make it," Willow mused. "But you'd better leave quickly. You don't have much time."

"Why?" I said. "And why did you tell me not to step there?"

"It's a hidden pit. One false move and you would've fallen into a yikty's lair."

We immediately surged away from the hole.

"This whole area is full of entrances to their foul nests," Willow said, shaking her head. "You'll have to be extremely careful where you step, least you fall and come face-to-face with one."

I took another step back, shuddering slightly.

"You'd better get going, before it's too late," Willow said, turning to leave. "The yikty leader Wansetop is coming this way. He looked hungry." She turned and vanished with a flick of her bushy tail.

* * *

Mag paced back and forth, curling her lip in disgust as she gazed out at the scarred land from the safety of our hill.

"Yikties," she muttered. "I despise them."

"What are they exactly?" Artie asked, sitting beside me. I was leaning against Willow's tree. "All I truly know about them is that they're scorpions."

"Monsters," I said grimly. "Giant scorpions the size of humans. They have black shells to protect themselves and they hunt at night so they blend in with their surroundings."

Artie went pale. "What happens if they sting you?"

"You're paralyzed. It will wear off, but not for twenty-four hours. They eat their prey, so there's no chance of escape."

"And we're supposed to cross a land filled with them?" Artie said, staring horrified at the ground below.

"I would love to stay and eradicate those things," Mag said, halting in her pacing. "But if we're going to make it to the meeting on time, we really must leave now."

Mag's features elongated. Her nose was lengthening into a snout. Spikes were sprouting on her back and her tail whipped behind her. Her wings unfurled. Claws were where her fingers used to be.

The transformation finished, the dragon stood before Artie and me on her hind legs.

Mag revealed her fanged smile. Her red scales glittered in the early morning sunlight. Artie looked thunderstruck and I reminded myself that this was his first time seeing Mag as a dragon.

"Ah, that's better," she said. "Its good to be myself again."

"We'd better get going," I said, hoisting myself onto Mag's back. Artie hesitated for a split second before he slowly climbed up and sat behind me, gripping me firming by the waist so he wouldn't fall off. I looked determinedly in front of me, trying to ignore my quickening heart.

"Hold on," Mag said and pushed off hard against the ground. I closed my eyes, flung my arms around her neck, and held on for dear life. Her wings beat furiously until we were airborne.

"Penelope, you have to see this," Artie said.

I opened my eyes and looked down. At first, I had a feeling of vertigo. The earth swam beneath me. The trees became dots as we rose. Mag leveled out and suddenly I could see what Artie meant.

Below us was a valley of green with black holes blinking up at us. Beings were moving on the ground, but they seemed... wrong. Their gait, the way they swung their bodies as they moved, was off. If I didn't know any better, I would have said they were crawling.

"Yikties," Mag said in disgust.

I squinted and saw that she was right. What I took to be people standing upright were actually long, barbed tails curved to wickedly sharp points. I shivered, glad they were down there and we were up here.

Then everything went wrong. Mag began to vibrate beneath us, her tail jerking back and forth in agitation.

"Mag-" I started, but I was cut off as Mag flew through what felt like honey and resumed her human form. Her arms were spread as if she still had wings.

We were falling. Artie was to my right, Mag to my left. I grabbed for Artie's hand as a scream ripped from my throat and we plummeted to the ground. The figures below were making guttural noises that I could hear from fifty feet in the air. I closed my eyes, too dizzy to keep them open.

A word tore from my throat. I couldn't hear it over the rushing wind. Then, as quickly as the fall had begun, it stopped. I opened my eyes. My face was an inch from the grassy earth. My magic had saved us. I ended the spell and we collapsed to the ground.

Spitting grass from my mouth, I sat up dazedly, blinking silver. "Artie, Mag, are you all right?" I said with a groan.

"Never better," Artie moaned.

"How touching," a bored voice said behind us. "But ultimately pointless. There was little chance you would get through the wizard's barrier. No dragons can enter."

I spun around, my hands digging into the dirt to keep myself balanced. I caught my breath. I was face-to-face with an arachnid the size of a large man. It had pincers, shiny black armor covering its body, and a long, barbed tail curled over its back.

Artie and Mag had jumped to their feet. Mag unsheathed her sword with a flourish and Artie drew his knife from his belt. I stayed where I was on the ground, too frightened to move.

My mouth had gone dry. I wet my lips and said, "You're a yikty, aren't you?"

"Yes, I am," it said in a bored voice, examining its pincer. "You are on our territory. I'm going to have to kill you now."

"We're not going anywhere," Mag growled.

"You cannot stop us, young dragon," it said. It began to chitter. Before I could even move, a dozen giant scorpions had surrounded us, blocking our escape.

"Lord Wansetop," a dozen grating voices whispered in unison. They looked smaller and more compact than the first, who seemed to be the leader.

"Now," Wansetop said, "any last words?"

"Yes," Artie said, reaching out and grasping my hand, pulling me to my feet. "Which of you wants to die first?"

Wansetop hissed and spread his pincers. The other yikities followed his example. The nearest one lunged at Artie and they rolled away, struggling.

"Take this," Mag said, pressing her sword and sheath into my hands.

"But-"

Mag growled, drowning out my words, as she plunged into the center of our attackers, her claws outstretched.

I dropped the sheath on the ground, I wouldn't need it, and fumbled for the hilt. I held the blade awkwardly from my body.

Wansetop hadn't moved. He laughed at the sight of me. "Do you really think you have what it takes to defeat me? *Me!* Leader of the yikties? But, if you wish for a quick death, I will be happy to oblige."

Trembling, I leaned forward and slashed clumsily at Wansetop's head, but he simply deflected it with his tail. While I was exposed, he whipped his tail back and easily slipped past my guard. I managed to leap aside before he struck, but I could feel the wind rushing over me.

"Yield," Wansetop hissed.

"Never," I said, more bravely than I felt, swinging the sword again.

Wansetop was quicker this time. He caught my sword in his pincers, lashing his tail toward my unprotected right. I groaned in agony as the needle sharp point buried itself into my arm before it was yanked out again.

I fell to the ground with a crash, releasing Mag's sword as I convulsed. I could feel the paralyzing venom coursing through my veins.

"You've lost, little hero," Wansetop said quietly. He reached out a pincer and took the sheath from where I left it on the ground. He shook it in my face, "Not even a dragon's sword could best me!"

Something fell out of the sheath and landed on top of me.

Wansetop hissed and drew his pincer back sharply. "What treachery is this?"

I used the last of my strength to look down at my chest. The silver rose was lying across my heart. It was glowing white-hot. The warmth spread throughout my entire body. I could feel the venom draining from me completely. I grabbed the rose and got unsteadily to my feet.

"Bah," Wansetop spat, flinging the sheath aside. "It does not matter, you still cannot defeat me."

He was right. No matter how magical the rose was I still couldn't hope to vanquish him.

I took a step back, stumbling as I did so on a rock jutting from the ground by my foot. I waved my arms wildly to stop myself from falling, flailing the still warm rose as I did so.

Wansetop hissed, "Heat," and backed away. It sounded like he was cursing.

Heat. Hadn't Casimir shown Lydia a spell that produced heat? What was it, Hentalin? No, *Henatin!*

"Henatin!" I yelled and fire erupted from the center of the rose, scorching Wansetop's glistening black armor. There was no silver this time, in fact, I felt great, and stronger than ever! I looked around and saw that Artie and Mag were still knee-deep in the yikty army.

"Mag!" I cried. "They respond to heat!"

Mag glanced in my direction, allowing the yikties to leap on top of her in her distraction.

Wansetop had retreated from the radius of my spell and was glaring down at me. Red blisters were popping up all over his black armor.

"You will pay-" he began, but stopped. It became clear what had distracted him when fire erupted from the mass of yikties over Mag and a fully-grown red dragon appeared.

Mag shot fire at the yikties, sending them streaming back to their underground dens. She whipped her tail back, knocking the ones menacing Artie askew. They too hurried out of sight.

The only yikty left was Wansetop. Mag faced him; smoke spewing from her mouth. I scrambled away from Wansetop, least I was charred by Mag's flames.

"You have not won," Wansetop hissed, holding his ground. "Go ahead, take this battle, but you have only awoken the wrath of the yikties. When our dark master rises, none will stand in his way."

Fire shot from Mag's mouth. Wansetop promptly disappeared down one of the holes.

"Good riddance," Artie muttered.

"Come on," I said, seizing the sheath and returning Mag's sword to it. I grabbed Artie's hand, and pulled him toward Mag. I didn't like the sound of that dark master. "Can you fly?"

"For the moment," Mag said, her eyes darting back and forth, clearly looking for more giant scorpions. "That yikty said I couldn't enter as a dragon. He never said I couldn't leave as one."

Once we were in the air, heading to Dragon Valley, I examined the place where Wansetop had stung me. There was no mark or blemish to indicate that I had ever been hurt. I stared at the silver rose, still clutched in my hand. It caught the light and twinkled innocently back.

Chapter Ten

Rivalry with a Rabbit

"WATCH IT!" ARTIE YELLED AS MAG almost collided into the side of a lone mountain. I clutched the nearest spike as Mag veered to the right.

"Sorry," she said, yawning, exposing her wickedly sharp fangs.

I studied Mag's wings. They were beating slowly, confirming that she was exhausted. We had left the yikty's lair three hours ago and Mag had been flying nonstop.

"Maybe we should stop," I suggested tentatively.

"No," Mag said, stubbornly. "I can do this." She dipped lower in the sky.

"When was the last time you flew for long stretches of time?" Artie asked, steadying himself.

Mag seemed to think about it. "Two years ago," she decided.

"What?" I said. "Why so long? What about yesterday morning?"

"I've been attending the Dragon Guardian Institute in Dragon Valley," Mag explained. "They take the most promising dragons and teach us how to interact with humans. I've spent most of the last two years as a human, proving that I can control my transformations. We can't suddenly return to dragon form in the middle of a crowded area. After passing a series of tests, proving that humans won't recognize us for what we are, we have the privilege of approaching the silver rose.

"It bloomed for me, meaning that I had the best chance of staying hidden during our mission."

I hurriedly coughed into my hand. Best chance of staying hidden? Since meeting her, Mag took every opportunity of transforming into a dragon, even if it was just her tail.

"Aldrich and I walked most of the way, to better conceal ourselves, but I transformed to avoid the trolls."

As the last of the lush, green hillsides passed away, a line of gray peaks rose up out of the ground. I was sure it hadn't been there moments before.

"What is that?" I said.

"The peaks of Dragon Valley. We've arrived," Mag said tiredly.

"Wow," Artie said.

"Wow," I agreed.

Mag swooped in between two peaks, the tip of her left wing barely missing the jutting rocks. A sandy-colored cliff was revealed high atop a mountain. It was protected on all sides by the gray peaks, but I could just see what appeared to be a narrow trail winding its way up the side of the mountain toward the cliff.

Mag began to shudder beneath me. Her outline began to blur; I could see her human form, wrapped in a layer of magic, surrounded by the hollow frame of a dragon. She gave a defiant roar and her human form disappeared, she felt solid again.

"Hold on!" Mag shouted over the rush of wind as she pelted toward the cliff.

Nervously, I reached out and seized Artie's hand to steady myself. My heart pounded in my chest, but I wasn't sure if it was from the rapid descent, or... something more.

Artie opened his mouth, probably to tell me not to worry, that everything would be all right, but before he could utter a single word, a tremor shook through Mag's body, jolting us. I slipped from her side, dragging Artie with me.

I closed my eyes, expecting a crash, but it never came. Instead it was more of a thump. I peeked out and saw that Artie and I were on the cliff, safe and sound.

Mag was panting beside us, her tongue lolling to the side. Then, before my eyes, she shrank back into a human.

"What happened?" Artie said, helping me to my feet.

"I'd already landed on the cliff," Mag explained, taking back the sword and sheath when I offered them, "so you only fell about three feet."

She fingered the top of the sheath before continuing, "Penelope, I'm also going to need the rose."

I blinked in surprise. I hadn't even realized I was still holding it. "But, why?"

"There are some dragons who don't take kindly to humans," Mag explained gently. "Mostly the older generation, who remembers fighting the golden dragon's human allies. Yes," she said, forestalling my objection, "there were humans against the golden dragon, but there weren't as many as you might think.

"If you, a human, walk into Dragon Valley with our most precious magical artifact, there will be chaos. Some will denounce you as a thief, while others will try to protect you."

"But, don't they know I'm coming?"

Mag exhaled deeply. "Only six dragons knew about the mission to Kelton Castle: myself, Aldrich, and the rest of the council. You need to be as non-threatening as possible if we're going to persuade everyone to trust you. Dragons are slow to change, Penelope, remember that."

I turned to Artie, who had been deathly quiet during the whole exchange. "What do you think?"

Artie's voice was a dull croak, "I agree with Mag. The dragons are our allies. You don't want to alienate them, simply because of a misunderstanding."

I looked between one serious face to the next, before I relinquished the rose to Mag.

She put it into her sheath. "Thank-" she began, when a roar, deeper and so unlike Mag's, echoed throughout the clearing.

"Follow me," Mag said, sweeping past us. "That sounded like a dragon in pain."

She took off running toward the sound. We ran after her as fast as we could.

"Penelope!" Artie said, as I stumbled over a foot long polished stone, almost taking him down with me. He kept me from falling, but I realized we were still holding hands. I quickly let go.

"Um, thanks," I said.

"No problem," he said, his voice strangely husky.

I glanced back at the object that I had almost tripped over. It was oval, perfectly smooth, and green. No, it was red. Now blue. The stone changed colors every thirty seconds or so.

"What are they?" I said, in wonder.

"No idea," Artie said. "Come on, we should go."

I allowed him to steer me from the clearing, still marveling at the stones. There must have been hundreds of them, all guarded by strict-looking men and women with various shades of hair and eyes, ranging from purple to pink to green to red to blue to yellow to black to white to orange to gray.

They glared at us as we rounded a corner and started toward a group of assorted dragons in both their human and true forms clustered in a tight circle. Mag was at the edge of the crowd.

She was talking quietly and urgently with Aldrich. Something gold glittered in her hand. He got here quickly, I thought. He frowned and shook his head, his arms crossed.

"Mag, what are those stones?" Artie whispered, jerking his thumb back the way we came.

"Eggs," Mag said, distractedly.

Eggs? I had never seen an egg that changed color before, but I let it go when I saw whom the group was gathered around: a boy with green hair, beaded with sweat, clutching his leg.

"Who is that?" I asked in a low voice.

Several of the people turned to face me. Their eyes grew bright when they spotted me. I blushed when I realized these people, these dragons, were staring at my hair. The silver must be growing in. I may have been currently without the rose, but my presence was still recognized.

"His name is Venn." Aldrich said, jarring me from my thoughts. "Hello, Penelope, Artie. I'm glad to see you made it pass the dragon knights. They protect Dragon Valley from outsiders," he added, his eyes twinkling.

"Those people guarding the eggs?"

"Dragon knights and mothers," Aldrich confirmed. "The dragon knights are the protectors of Dragon Valley. They take their jobs seriously."

"I, uh, didn't hurt that egg when I tripped over it, did I?"

Aldrich shook his head. "I wouldn't worry about it. Dragon eggs are tough. Venn, however, was injured by a yikty."

I shuddered, remembering when Wansetop had pierced my arm. "Is there anything we can do to help?"

"Maybe there is," Aldrich said slowly. "Venn needs the Lenahen Plum Flower."

Mag sucked in her breath. "But, Grandfather, that's impossible. You know dragons can't go into Kaninen territory."

"We have no choice," Aldrich said grimly. "Yikty venom is more lethal in dragons than the other races. We must retrieve this flower, otherwise Venn will die."

"Why can't you go get it?" I asked. "It can't be too far away."

Mag laughed bitterly. "Distance is no object, it's just on the other side of the valley. What lives there is the problem: the Kaninens."

"Oh, come on," Artie said, throwing his hands into the air. "The one I met was pretty cute."

He quailed under Mag's amber-eyed stare. With forced calm, she said, "The Kaninens and the dragons are mortal enemies. They are beings of ice; we are of fire. We used to get along, until one day a Kaninen attacked a dragon.

"It was a brutal deception. A young dragon named Marsa was innocently flying over Kaninen territory, even though there were no boundaries then, when the Kaninen Koal leapt up and froze her solid with no provocation.

"Marsa survived, but we dragons have never forgot this injustice."

"That's horrible!" I said. "Sylvia said that Kaninens only have to breathe to freeze you."

"That is correct. They're small, but extremely fierce," Aldrich acknowledged. "Their hatred towards us runs deep. If we're seen anywhere on their land, they will attack unmercifully."

"Yes, if *we* go," Mag said thoughtfully. "But, not Penelope and Artie."

"No," a dragon with pink hair said forcefully. "The girl is too valuable. We can't afford to lose her. At least the rose chose *her*."

"But, if she doesn't, we'll lose Venn," Mag growled. "This has nothing to do with the rose, Amarina. I've told you before, it's *not* my fault."

"Enough," Aldrich said, before the argument could escalate further. "It is Penelope and Artie's decision. They may go if they wish. We do not control them."

The pink-haired dragon, Amarina, glared resentfully at us, but remained silent.

I didn't understand this dragon's hostility. I looked down at Venn. He was so still that it took me a moment to realize he was asleep.

"I'm going," I said, with a long, steady look at Artie.

He stared into the distance, without answering. I thought he would refuse and stay, when, "I'm going with you."

"Thank you," Aldrich said solemnly. "We are in your debt."

"When should we leave?" I asked.

"Immediately," Mag said, her eyes alight with gratitude and relief. "I'll take you as far as the boundary line, but after that, you're on your own."

Chapter Eleven

Ice of Despair

WE WERE ABOUT TO LEAVE WHEN Venn stirred. Aldrich had been giving us our final instructions, "And remember, the Lenahen Plum is purple with red thorns."

"Bright," Artie commented.

"That makes it all the more easier to spot," Aldrich said, inclining his head. "Now is the time you must depart. It's getting dark. The Kaninens will be burrowing in their dens before long."

"I'd like to see them try and get past the Kaninens unscathed," the pink-haired dragon muttered. She seemed to be in a perpetually bad mood.

Artie and I exchanged skeptical looks. How could the dragons be afraid of something as puny as a rabbit, even if they did have ice powers?

Behind us, Mag gasped. I turned in time to see her rush to Venn's side. One bleary eye was opened and he mumbled, "What-"

"Shh," Mag whispered, gently. "All will be well, Venn, but you need sleep."

"My leg," Venn muttered, lifting his head. An emerald eye shined in my direction. "It feels like a thousand sharp fiery knives all aimed for my leg at once."

"You should go to sleep, Venn. Mag, could you sing him a lullaby? A more natural sleep is what he needs now," Aldrich said.

Mag took a deep breath and began to sing a slow lilting tune about a dragon who went off to the mountains, only to return to his beloved at the base. It seemed to seize the very air in the clearing.

> "The mountains, the mountains,
> Suffused with purple light
> Is dull compared
> To your sweetness bright."

I watched as Venn's eyelids drooped and resisted the urge to comply myself. All around me, the other dragons began to nod their heads in drowsy stupors.

"Penelope." Artie was suddenly shaking my arm.

"Huh?" I slurred dazedly.

"You were almost asleep."

"But you weren't," I pointed out with a yawn.

"No," Artie agreed, confused.

"It's because you're not a dragon," Aldrich said. "Or connected to the dragons. The song's magic only affects us."

"Why?" I said.

"The lullaby is ancient magic, the dragons have perfected it over the years to affect only our kind."

"Come on," Mag said, swiping a few errant tears from her eyes. "We have to go. Venn doesn't have much time."

"Good luck," Aldrich said.

I waved at him as Artie and I followed Mag down the cliff. Several of the dragons cheered as we passed. Others glared. The pink-haired dragon huffed and turned away.

"I don't want to get on the bad side of those dragons," Artie whispered.

I glanced back at them. Steam was streaming from the pink dragon's nostrils behind Aldrich's back.

"Me neither."

* * *

"Penelope!" Artie cried, reaching out and catching my wrist, pulling me to safety.

"Thanks," I gasped, staring down the incline in which I had almost fallen. The path was treacherous, with loose rocks shifting under our feet. Artie and I continued downhill with our arms outstretched to keep our balance on the winding path.

Mag plodded on fearlessly, like it was solid ground. "Here is the edge of Dragon Valley," she said gravely.

We were standing on solid rock at the bottom of the cliff, panting. Mag led us to a stretch of grass next to a clump of trees.

"I must stop," she said. "I cannot go any further into the woods."

I stared at the boundary line between Dragon Valley and the Kaninens' territory. Was it my imagination, or did some of those trees look slightly... frozen?

"I told Aldrich about the amulet," Mag said. "Make sure you get it back. The hopes of the dragons rest with you." Then she hurried back up the path and out of sight.

"No pressure. Ready, Artie?"

He squeezed my hand. "As ready as I'll ever be."

* * *

We ran the first time we saw the rabbit. Artie and I had been wandering the woods, searching for the Lenahen Plum Flower, but no purple or red was visible.

"Where are they?" I said, exasperated.

Artie pushed aside some bushes with a rustle. "Look."

I joined him and saw a light blue bunny against a bright red backdrop, cleaning its whiskers.

"A Kaninen," I breathed. "Its so cute. How is it the mortal enemy of the dragons?"

"Penelope," Artie said. "The flowers. The rabbit is protecting the Lenahens."

The rabbit looked at us inquisitively before motioning with a paw to two other light blue rabbits who had just arrived.

The three stared up at us with beady eyes, twitching their noses.

Artie reached for the flowers, when a sound of breaking twigs caught my attention. Artie froze, his hand suspended in midair. The rabbits were alert, watching as a deer entered the clearing. It appeared to be grazing.

The bunnies began to growl, low in their throats. The deer raised its head and nervously took a step back. The three rabbits were a blur of blue and white as they converged on the intruder, forming a rough triangular shape. Their teeth flashed, sharp claws extended from their paws, their eyes were a cold, ice blue.

They opened their mouths and shot beams of ice at the deer. I could feel the frigidness from where I stood ten feet away. Alarmed, I seized Artie's left hand for reassurance.

The rabbits retreated and I could see the deer properly. It was frozen solid in a block of ice. I shuddered, glad for Artie's support.

At the sight of Artie's right hand, still reaching for the flowers, the bunnies growled and began to converge on us.

"Run!" I shouted, yanking Artie away. He abandoned the flowers and joined me in running for our lives.

A rabbit leapt onto my shoulder, snapping at my neck. I stumbled, which probably saved my life. The rabbit overbalanced and dropped to the ground.

"There!" Artie yelled, pointing at an outcropping of rocks. It looked very solid.

"Are you crazy?" I demanded.

"Trust me! Anoffen!" he shouted back and dived for the rocks.

I followed, closing my eyes, expecting to crash, but nothing happened. I opened my eyes slowly, but all I could see was darkness.

"Artie!" I said in a terrified whisper.

There was a moment's pause in which I thought I was alone, when Artie responded from beside my shoulder, "I'm here."

I raised my hand to wipe my sweaty brow, when I realized my right hand was still clamped to Artie's left. I dropped his hand quickly, blushing. Hoping he couldn't see me, I cast about for something to say. "Where are we?"

"In a safe house. Well, it's more along the lines of a cave, but its close enough."

"How did you know it was here?"

"Some friends of mine left it," he mumbled. "We'll be safe as long as we stay in here."

I blinked rapidly, trying to adjust my eyes to the dark. "I can't see anything." I reached for my amulet before I remembered that I didn't have it anymore.

There was the sound of two sticks scraping across each other and then a small pinpoint of light appeared.

Artie handed me the torch and reached across me. I stiffened but he was focusing on a patch of stone beside my head. "It has to be here somewhere," he muttered, more to himself than to me.

"What?"

"The hidden lever that opens the door."

"You didn't need one to get us in," I protested.

"No," he agreed absently, still running his hand along the rock's surface. "It's kept open for any th... for any of my friends, in case they need a quick getaway. It closes automatically when someone is using it."

"But you can open it, right?" The thought of spending the rest of my life in the cave was not appealing.

"Of course I can open it," Artie said, dismissively. "As soon as I can find the lever. Ah, here it is."

His hand rested upon a projection of rock. It was so slight I hadn't realized it was there. Artie had only found it through touch.

"When I pull this lever, we'll be able to see what's going on, but all they'll see is a blank rock. Either way, they can still hear us. Don't go running out until I say so, because once you leave this hideout, the magic that protects it will cease to work on you," he cautioned.

I nodded my understanding and Artie pulled down on the outcropping of rock. A section of the wall shimmered and dissolved until I had a perfect view of the outside.

The three Kaninens were patrolling the area. A fourth, smaller Kaninen came running up with a gold chain clamped in its mouth. The amulet glittered on the other end.

I tensed when I saw it, but Artie gave me a warning look.

Off in the distance, I could see the sparkle of the frozen deer. If only I could unfreeze it, I thought, that would prove a fine distraction.

I glanced back at Artie. He had said something while seeking safety in the cave. Anoffen. It sounded like a spell. I placed my hands to my temple. I had a splitting headache that refused to pass. Was Artie a wizard? Could he use spells, and if he could, why was he hiding it from me?

He hadn't used a wand or an amulet or any other magical items that I could see. I no longer had my amulet or the silver rose. Maybe if he could do it without the aid of a magical focus, I could do it too.

"Henatin," I murmured, thinking of the deer again.

"No! Stop!" Artie cried.

But it was too late. I could feel the heat spreading out with me as its center. It gave me courage, but it also alerted the Kaninens to our presence.

They sniffed the air, their noses twitching. They must have caught our scent, because they turned toward us and stalked ever so closer to the cave.

"Penelope, end the magic!" Artie said, not even bothering to keep his voice down.

I didn't wait to be told twice. A split second before I severed my connection to the magic, I could hear something shattering in the distance. I smiled. I was light-headed, but somehow I knew the deer was free.

I slumped to the ground beside Artie, who was holding a glinting object in his hand. Silver vision, his knife, I thought sluggishly. And then everything turned black.

* * *

"... Penelope! Penelope, wake up!" My eyes snapped open. I tried to sit up, groaning.

"Easy," Artie said, helping me into a sitting position.

"What happened?" I asked. My tongue felt swollen, as if I hadn't had any water for days. Then, with a start, I realized the sky was over bright. Noon.

"How long was I out?" I asked slowly.

"A few hours. The Kaninens are gone. They were scared off by some help our deer friend called in."

I braced my hands and pushed off the ground. Once I was up, however, I swayed slightly and had to lean against the wall for support.

"You should rest," Artie said, gripping my arm to steady me. His words were tinged with worry.

"No," I said thickly. "We have to get the Lenahens back to Venn. It could already be too late."

"All right," he said reluctantly. "But, there's something you should know. The Kaninens disappeared with the amulet."

I stared at him in despair.

"We can get it back," Artie assured me. "Our reinforcements have promised to help."

"Who are our reinforcements?" I asked.

"You'll see." Artie allowed me to lean my weight against him as he led me from the rock hideout.

As we passed under the trees, I said, "How did we get into the cave?"

"My witch sister enchanted all of our hideouts to open with the word 'Anoffen,' which is the spell for 'open.' Its just a password, so even mundanes like me can use it."

"You're more than just a mundane, Artie," I murmured.

I thought I caught a smile on Artie's face out of the corner of my eye, but by the time I looked again, it had disappeared.

Chapter Twelve

Dragon Pride

"**C**ADMUS!" I SAID, STOPPING DEAD IN my tracks.

"You were expecting someone else?" the cat purred.

"No, its just... what are you doing here?" I gestured around the clearing. "Aren't you afraid of the Kaninens? Why aren't you watching Lydia?"

Artie had led me back to the site of the Kaninens' attack, before we ran to the safety of the cave. There, waiting for us, was Cadmus along with several other cats, all larger and fiercer-looking.

Cadmus sniffed in disgust. "Those rabbits are as much the enemies of the lions as they are of the dragons. As for your sister, I left her in Charlotte's care."

"Well, that's a relief. At least she isn't on her own. Why are these other lions so much bigger than you?" I had never before seen such a small lion or indeed one with black fur.

"I'm a young lion," Cadmus explained. "I won't reach full maturity for another year. Besides, I happen to like being the size of a housecat. Makes it easier to hide in plain sight. But, I digress. You're here for the flowers to save the dragon Venn, correct?"

"Yes, but how did you know?"

"I'm a cat. I know these things. Come on, I'll introduce you to Grrwrath, the leader of the pride."

"Penelope, how can I understand him?" Artie asked, his face a mask of panic.

"I don't know," I said truthfully.

"Were you in contact with anything magical lately?" Cadmus asked.

"I don't think so," Artie said, frowning.

"We'll figure this out," I promised. I had no idea whether this was a promise I could keep.

Cadmus led us further into the clearing to the biggest lion. He was tan in color, with a dark brown mane.

"Remember, speak only when he addresses you," Cadmus said in a whisper. "Don't lie, Grrwrath hates that. And none of your tricks, Artie."

"Why would Artie lie?" I said, confused.

"You haven't told her?" Cadmus asked, incredulously.

"No," Artie muttered.

"Told me what?" I demanded.

"Its not my place to say," Cadmus said, then in a louder voice, "Grrwrath, I have brought you the witch Penelope and the... mundane Artie."

Cadmus slipped away as Grrwrath stared at us with liquid-looking black eyes and said in a deep rumble, "Welcome, young travellers. I trust you journey well."

"I'm afraid not," Artie said. He gave me a look that said: *Let me handle this.*

Grrwrath shifted on his mighty paws. "What seems to be the problem?"

"Its my amulet," I blurted out. "The Kaninens have stolen it."

"Hmm?" Grrwrath said, flicking his tail. "That is indeed unfortunate. You will have to learn magic without its aid."

"But, sir," Artie said. "That's just not possible. Penelope already used magic without the aid of a focus and passed out from the strain."

I blushed. Artie hadn't meant to be unkind.

"She'll just have to become a lioness without the experience of a cub," Grrwrath said. "I know of someone who could be of assistance."

"Who?"

"Her name is Mad Maude. She lives in a town called Cherry Grove on the west side of Alsmora. You'll know her because she keeps a tiny, purple lizard as a pet. She is difficult to find, but she possesses a great deal of magic."

That was two lions who wanted me to find Mad Maude so far. "She must be a good friend of the dragons," I said cautiously. Something was nagging me about the lizard, but I couldn't place it. "Why a lizard?"

Grrwrath growled. "I don't know, do I? You're going to have to find Maude and ask her yourself."

"We meant no disrespect," Artie said, raising his hands to placate the lion.

"You're just like your sister," Grrwrath grunted. "Polite, but impossibly, stubbornly persistent."

Artie blanched. "S-she was here?"

"Indeed, three weeks ago. She used a spell to temporarily talk to us. She was looking for information on you."

I studied Artie carefully. Who was this boy who's sister would seek him out through lions?

"What did you tell her?" Artie asked in a choked voice.

"Nothing, I didn't know who you were."

"Sir," Artie said loudly. "We need your help to steal Penelope's amulet back."

"Interesting choice of words," Grrwrath said, allowing the change of subject. "Cadmus!"

Cadmus appeared at my ankles. "Here," he said, his voice muffled with the flowers in his mouth.

I took them and realized they were purple with red thorns: the Lenahen Plum flowers.

"Thank you," I said, looking between Cadmus and Grrwrath.

Without a word, Cadmus disappeared with a flick of his tail.

Grrwrath gazed approvingly after him. "My son has done well."

"Your son?"

"Yes, he will eventually become the leader of the pride."

Artie kicked the dirt with his shoe. This caught Grrwrath's attention. "Its not too late for you to mend matters with your own father, Arthur."

I was dying to ask what they meant, but before I could, the sound of crashing branches reached my ears. I turned just in time to see Mag rush into the clearing, Cadmus at her heels.

"What happened?" she demanded. "Cadmus told me something was wrong? Did the Kaninens harm you?"

I smiled ruefully. "Not us, but I'm glad you're here. I saw the Kaninen with my amulet."

"What?!" Mag cried.

"They attacked us," I said, ignoring the heat rushing to my cheeks.

"We have to get it back!" Mag said, her hair whipping into flames again.

"I can lead you," Cadmus offered. "I make it a point to know the lairs of my enemies."

"Thank you," I said. I turned to follow him, when I caught sight of Grrwrath. I stopped abruptly and curtsied. "Our sincerest gratitude, oh mighty Grrwrath."

He inclined his head. "May you have success in your hunt."

"Come," Cadmus said. Then, in a whisper, "We'll get your amulet back, Penelope, I swear it."

* * *

After checking on Venn, Mag had been waiting for us at the boundary line, when Cadmus had arrived and convinced her to follow him. He hadn't said much, but apparently it had been enough for Mag. She had taken off running immediately.

"The other dragons won't be pleased that I came onto the Kaninens' territory," Mag said as we walked. "As long as the

Kaninens don't recognize me, this probably won't get back to Aldrich."

"The lions could tell them," I pointed out, though I didn't believe it. Grrwrath had been kind enough to send another young lion to Dragon Valley with the Lenahen Plum Flowers.

Cadmus snorted in front of us.

"Dragons have a better chance at becoming vegetarians than the lions betraying us," Mag said.

"Penelope, dragons and lions have historically been on friendly terms," Artie said. "There have been numerous stories about the two species working together."

"We both despise the Kaninens," Mag said, curling her lip. "The dragons' and Kaninens' powers over fire and ice are so different that we couldn't possibly get along."

"And the lions?"

Cadmus shrugged. "Lions are predators. Rabbits are prey. What else do you need?"

We continued in silence for a while, then Cadmus stopped. We were in front of a cave, which was emitting a soft blue glow.

"Shh!" Cadmus said, though nobody had spoken.

Voices could be heard inside.

"What is it?"

"I don't know."

"It sure is pretty, though."

"Artie, could you get a closer look?" Cadmus hissed.

I was about to protest, when Artie overrode me, "Don't worry, I'll be right back." He crept forward.

"We could hang it up on the wall," a thoughtful voice continued from inside the cave.

"Ouch! It burned me!"

Artie knelt by the entrance. He was concealed by a bush, but he was still bathed in the eerie blue light.

"I bet the dragons allowed Flurry to find it, knowing it would burn us," the first voice said.

There were murmurs of agreement.

Artie inched forward. I wanted to scream at him to come back, but I was forced to watch silently. He stuck his head a foot into the cave and remained there for a breathless moment. Then, he retracted his head and mouthed "amulet" in my direction. He rose to return to us, but before he could take more than a step, three Kaninens burst from the cave. Their presence lent an icy chill to the air, freezing Artie solid.

"What do we have here?" one bunny snarled.

"Intruders," the one on the left said, looking straight at me.

"And a dragon," the right one said.

"What are you doing here, dragon," the middle rabbit said.

"You stole my friend's amulet. We're just here to retrieve it," Mag snapped.

"What? You mean this thing? Here, take it. It burned us."

"No," a deeper voice said and a Kaninen twice the size of housecat Cadmus stalked out of the cave. There was a smaller ice rabbit bobbing about its feet. I recognized the smaller Kaninen as the one I had saved from the trolls. "The amulet belongs to the dragons. You want it back so you can destroy us," the bigger Kaninen continued. "We cannot allow this."

"Yes, Blizzard," the three Kaninens murmured.

"Come, Flurry," the leader said to the smallest rabbit and he turned to go.

"Wait!" I said. "That amulet is mine! My mother gave it to me! Give it back!"

The leader half turned back to me. "I'm sorry, but if the amulet will help the dragons, I can't return it. You're just going to have to go without it."

I darted around, forcing the leader to look at me.

"That Kaninen," I said, pointing at a motionless Flurry, "stole my amulet. Give it back, now!"

"Dad," Flurry said, "they saved me from the trolls! I grabbed their amulet by mistake! Please, we have to return it!"

Blizzard shook his head at his daughter. "No, we can't. Have you forgotten? The dragons are our mortal enemies."

Mag took a threatening step forward, but I waved her down. We did not need to escalate this.

"I wish I had Frost, Snow, and Ice back," Flurry sighed. "They're much better than some old amulet."

Blizzard's head jerked up. "You have just given me an idea, Flurry. Human, follow me. You may unfreeze him," he indicated Artie, "but your friends must remain outside. You will not be harmed."

"You have a lot of nerve," Mag cried, but I cut her off.

"Will this get me my amulet back?"

"Perhaps," Blizzard said, before he, Flurry, and the other three Kaninens went back into the cave.

"You don't have to do this, Penelope," Cadmus said quietly.

"Yes, I do. I need my amulet back," I said stubbornly.

Artie shivered as Mag unfroze him. "A-at least we got the a-amulet back. R-right Penelope? Penelope?"

I explained everything as quickly as I could and Artie groaned.

"I'm going in," I said, determinedly, facing the cave.

Artie nodded and set his shoulders.

I marched to the mouth of the cave when Cadmus called, "Wait!"

"You're not going to change my mind, Cadmus."

"I won't," Cadmus promised. "I'm coming with you, no matter what the Kaninens say."

"Me too," Artie said.

"Thank you," I said, touched.

We all looked at Mag. She grunted. "I can't go in, remember? The Kaninens would attack me on sight. Cadmus might be able to get away with the housecat excuse, but I'll stay out here and guard against others in the area. They won't get past me."

I turned to Artie and Cadmus. They looked determined and ready. I took a deep breath and we plunged into the icy darkness of the cave. I gasped at the change of temperature. I was still wearing my dark blue handmaiden dress. It was made for summer, but in here, it felt like a blizzard.

Artie's teeth were chattering and Cadmus's fur was standing on end.

"They're close," Cadmus whispered.

We crept further into the cave, huddled close together for warmth. I stepped on a patch of ice and threw out my arms, catching myself on the wall. While I steadied myself, I noticed a slight red smudge underneath my hand. I tried to stifle my panic, but it wasn't blood as I suspected. It was berry juice.

"It's a drawing!" Artie said in wonder.

I squinted at the stains. He was right. There were three pictures on the wall. I had smeared the middle drawing.

"What are they?" Cadmus asked, placing his front paws on the wall to get a better look.

"The story of Koal."

We spun around. Blizzard was watching us with beady eyes. But, he wasn't threatening. In fact, he looked weary.

"This would be a much more pleasant conversation with names," he said in an attempt at politeness.

"Penelope, Artie, and Cadmus," I said. "What do you mean, the story of Koal? Mag said Koal attacked an innocent dragon."

"I take it Mag's the dragon outside," Blizzard said bitterly. "You should have left the cat outside as well."

"It was Koal's fault," Cadmus said, heatedly, ignoring Blizzard's comment. "He started it."

"Lies," Blizzard said. "Look at the first picture." It showed a Kaninen farming a row of carrots. "That was Koal, a peaceful Kaninen.

"The second drawing depicts the dragon Marsa attacking him for no cause. She was far from innocent." The part I had smudged was a stream of fire from a dragon's mouth. Koal's image scattered and carrots flew everywhere. I felt sick to look at it.

"The last one is of Koal swearing vengeance against the dragons." Koal was now standing on a mound of flaming carrots; his paw raised into a fist in the air.

"As you can see," Blizzard said, "the dragons brought this upon themselves."

Cadmus snorted and turned away. Artie and I exchanged uneasy looks. That was not the story Mag told.

"What about my amulet?"

"Ah, I was getting to that," Blizzard sighed, still gazing at the drawings. His head snapped forward. "Besides Flurry, three other Kaninens were kidnapped: Frost, Snow, and Ice. We don't know who kidnapped them, where they were taken, or even why. All Flurry told me was that her captor said to take one to Everburn Swamp, where Aneurin the sea serpent was waiting.

"You'll have to search out the other two on your own. Do this and I'll return your amulet. Fail, and the dragons will never rise again."

Before any of us could react, Blizzard disappeared in an icy blast, pushing us out of the cave, in the process.

"Guess it's decided," Artie muttered.

* * *

"Aldrich is going to kill me," Mag said. We had just left Cadmus with the other lions and were hurrying back to Dragon Valley.

"He won't really," I said.

"No," Mag said, "but he won't be happy. The amulet is with the enemy *and* I went into Kaninen territory. And worse, *you made a deal with them!*

"It will be difficult, but you can be taught magic without a focus," she continued. "But, just to make absolutely sure, we'll have to resume your practical training with swords."

I suppressed a groan. Not more swords.

The ground changed from springy grass to hard dirt and then rock. I stumbled at the shift, but Artie caught my arm to steady me.

I looked up as a flash of pink caught my eye.

"Was that the pink-haired dragon?" I asked, squinting at a pink, hawk-like shape flying above us.

"Amarina?" Mag said, keeping her eyes on the path. "You'll want to watch out for her. She hates me with a deep-seated passion... and she'll want to use you, Penelope."

"Use me?"

"Yes," she sighed. "You see, Amarina thinks I go out of my way to mess with her."

"Do you?" I blurted. I regretted the words as soon as I said them, but Mag just chuckled.

"No, but that's what she thinks. Aldrich is the oldest member of the dragon council and that earns him a lot of respect.

"As his granddaughter, everyone naturally knows who I am. It doesn't translate into respect, but Amarina thinks I use Aldrich's image to my advantage."

"Like a spoiled child," Artie breathed, his eyes wide.

"Exactly. Anything I have and Amarina wants, I must have flaunted Aldrich's name to get.

"The last straw came with the rose. We both graduated from the Dragon Academy the same year, though my grades were higher. When the rose chose me over her, clearly I must have cheated."

"That's ridiculous," I scoffed.

"Penelope," Mag said, carefully. "Think about it. You lost the amulet while we were saving Artie. Since it was under my watch, she'll claim it's *my* fault. She might incite some of the council to her side and attempt to remove me as a dragon guardian. If that happens, my position moves to the next best in line, which would be Amarina."

"But, the rose-"

"Chose me," Mag finished. "Yes, but if I'm right, and Amarina suspects it too, she could scare the dragon council into agreeing with her."

"What are you talking about?" Artie asked. "What do you suspect?"

Mag opened her mouth to respond, when-

"There you are!" an angry voice called.

I looked up and had to shield my eyes against the sun. A girl came into focus and I spotted the pink hair. It was Amarina as a human. She must have spotted us from the air, and raced to intercept us.

"Mag, where were you? I knew we shouldn't have sent the Rose to retrieve the Lenahen flower! Some cat just delivered a bouquet of them to Aldrich!"

"The Rose?" I asked Mag quietly.

"Its what some dragons know you as," she whispered back. "We didn't know the identity of the human chosen one, so we referred to your existence as 'the Rose.'"

"You don't care about stopping the golden dragon, do you, Mag?" Amarina spat. "You selfishly sent the Rose into danger."

Mag looked as if Amarina had slapped her. "Selfish?" she said, her voice quivering. "Venn is in pain, Amarina! He could *die!* And all you care about is yourself! In case you haven't noticed, Penelope is the Rose, but I didn't force her to search for the Lenahen, she and Artie decided to do that on their own."

"I'm also right here," I said, annoyed that they were talking about me as if I wasn't.

They ignored me.

"Well, I'm sorry if I don't cheat," Amarina snapped. "Not everyone is willing to use their grandfather's name to bribe the judges. I, at least, have some dignity."

"Watch it, Amarina," Mag said quietly.

"Or you'll do what, exactly?" Amarina taunted.

Mag growled, dropping her sword and sheath to the ground. Her form changed until she was her true dragon self again.

Amarina transformed too. Artie and I stood small beside the two massive giants.

"Mag!" I called to her, but she didn't look at me. She was too busy watching her pink-haired rival.

"Penelope, we have to go," Artie said. "There's nothing we can do to stop them. They'll crush us if we get too close."

I knew Artie was right, but I couldn't bring myself to leave Mag and Amarina to tear each other's throat out.

"Go," I said, surprising Artie as I shoved him toward the path. "Tell Aldrich what's happening. I'll stay and try to calm them down."

"Penelope-"

"Go! Before its too late!" I scooped up the fallen sword and sheath, and attached them to my waist. I ran forward, stepping in between the red and pink dragons. "Stop!" I yelled.

Mag flicked her eyes downward to rest upon me for a brief moment. That was all Amarina needed to gain the upper hand and pounce. I scrambled out of the way as the two dragons came crashing to the ground. Dust flew everywhere, almost choking me.

Mag roared in frustration and shot fire at Amarina's head, but she shielded herself just in time with her wings.

I rushed to Mag's side and boosted myself onto her back. It was dangerous, especially if Amarina decided to spring upon us, but it was the only way I could think of to force Mag to listen.

"Enough, Mag!" I yelled.

She glanced at me, extending her snake-like neck, and growled, "This does not concern you. Get off before you are injured."

Before I could answer, Amarina lowered her wings, apparently realizing that Mag had ended her attack. She dove at Mag again, who readied herself for the blow.

The rose! It was still in the sheath. I fumbled for it hastily. As soon as my thumb brushed the stem, I yelled, "Enchauta!"

Amarina froze in mid-pounce, her teeth an inch from Mag's throat.

I leaned against one of Mag's spikes, but thanks to the rose, my vision remained normal.

"That wasn't necessary," she said. She sounded slightly disappointed. "I could have taken her."

I simply nodded and slid off her back.

"Whoa!" I stumbled as the silver rose jerked in my grip. I grabbed it in both hands, but it continued to shudder violently. As I wrestled with it, I spotted something gold and glittery on the ground.

"Mag, what's that?"

She returned to her human form and picked it up. "This," she said, "is a dragon scale."

It was oval, with flat, horizontal ridges going down its length.

"Its... pretty," I said hesitantly, leaning in for a closer look, but the rose jumped in my hand.

Mag glared at me. "Penelope, what I'm going to tell you, you can't share with anyone else. Not even Artie."

I stared blankly at her. Surely, she must be joking... right?

"Mag," I managed as soon as I had found my voice, "why?"

"Look, Penelope," she said, hurriedly. "Artie is nice and skilled with a knife, but what do we know about him? Do you even know his last name?"

I opened my mouth, but shut it again when I realized she was right, at least partially. What *was* Artie's last name?

"Exactly. This scale has to do with our mission. I know it does. Until we know more about Artie, I think it best not to tell him anything."

No, I wanted to protest. Artie's our friend. We can trust him. Ah, a traitorous thought whispered, but what do you truly know about him? You barely met him yesterday. I was almost relieved when the rose shuddered again. It distracted me from my uneasy musings. I'm sorry, Artie, I thought. Out loud, I said, "Fine, I won't tell Artie" *unless necessary.*

"Gold is not a normal coloring for dragons," Mag said, so fast her words almost blended together. I noticed Amarina twitching slightly. The spell was weakening. Mag talked even faster.

"Onlyonedragonhaseverbeengold."

I blinked, startled. "What?"

At that moment, the spell broke and Amarina pounced where dragon Mag used to be. She spun around quickly, almost stepping on us, when someone called out my name.

I looked up, shading my eyes as a blindingly white dragon appeared, hovering over us. It landed and Artie jumped from his perch on its back and ran to me.

Mag stuffed the golden dragon scale out of sight. The rose stopped fighting me at once.

"Are you all right?" Artie panted.

"Yes."

"Mag! Amarina! What have you done?" the white dragon said, transforming back into Aldrich.

"Mag attacked me," Amarina whined, returning to her human form.

"Magma, is this true?"

Mag fell silent at once. It took me a moment to realize that Aldrich was referring to her. It was a strange name, but it fit.

When she spoke again, it was in a growl, "I will not deny that I had a part in this battle, but Amarina is just as responsible as I am."

"Penelope, explain, please," Aldrich said, turning to me.

"Amarina waylaid us as we exited the woods," I said, explaining the battle as best I could, not mentioning my stopping Amarina with magic or my conversation with Mag afterward. I carefully avoided Artie's eye.

"I am very disappointed in you both," Aldrich said to Mag and Amarina. "You allowed your emotions to get the better of you. As punishment, you will both be on sentry duty, watching after Venn all night."

I could have sworn that Mag smiled.

"You are not the Rose," Amarina stated flatly and stalked off.

I stared after her, stung by her words.

Aldrich sighed and rubbed his temple. "You must forgive Amarina. Her heart is in the right place, but she has a long way to go before she learns control."

"How's Venn?" I asked.

"Better," Artie said. "The fever's gone. We left him sleeping gently. He should be better in a few days."

We started slowly up the path, when Mag and Aldrich stiffened.

"What is it?" I said, stopping with them.

"Kaninen," Aldrich growled.

I followed his gaze to the edge of the tree line. There, clearly in Kaninen territory, was a small, blue-white rabbit.

"Flurry," I said, taking a step back in her direction. "I wonder what she wants."

Someone seized my arm, stopping me in my tracks.

"No, Penelope," Mag said in my ear. "It could be a trap."

"No, Mag," I said, shaking her off. "What purpose would it serve? I've already agreed to help them."

"But..."

"But, nothing," I said firmly. "I'll stay on dragon territory, while Flurry stays on her side. You'll be watching the entire time, won't you?"

"Yes."

"Then, what's the problem?"

Mag glared in Flurry's direction, but said nothing.

"I'll go with you," Artie volunteered. "If this is a trap, you won't be alone."

"Thanks," I said. I didn't truly believe Flurry would attack, but I was secretly glad Artie was coming along.

I looked back at Mag and Aldrich only once on the way down. Aldrich frowned and crossed his arms, but made no move to stop us. Meanwhile, Mag's wings were out and a tendril of smoke was coming out of her very human nostrils.

"Let's hope we can solve this quickly," I muttered to Artie. "Otherwise, Mag's going to swoop down on poor Flurry."

"What do you think is wrong with her?" Artie asked, nodding at the young ice rabbit. She was pacing, but each step left behind another frozen paw print.

Flurry didn't look up until we were kneeling beside her. "Penelope, Artie, I'm sorry and thank you!" she cried as she put her front paws on my knee and looked up at me.

Luckily, my knee didn't start freezing, as well.

"Slow down, Flurry," Artie said. "I want you to take a deep breath, let it out slowly, and then tell us what's going on."

Flurry took a moment to do just that, for which I was grateful. My leg, while not frozen, was beginning to get a little cold. It started to warm up again after she had calmed down.

"I'm sorry for what my father did to you. After you left, I tried to convince him to simply give you your amulet back, but he wouldn't budge."

Still, I felt my gratitude swelling for the tiny rabbit. "Thanks, Flurry."

She smiled sadly. "Well, it's my fault you lost it in the first place." There was a pause, then, "Thank you, both of you."

"For what?"

Flurry looked me straight in the eye and said, "For saving my friends, of course. You'll find Snow, Ice, and Frost. I know it."

Between Blizzard's threats and Flurry's confidence in me, I was more scared of Flurry. There was no way I wanted to disappoint such an expectant, hopeful face, but if I didn't find all three of her friends, that's exactly what would happen.

Chapter Thirteen

Rainbow Hollow

"WHERE ARE WE GOING?" ARTIE ASKED as we followed Mag.

"Come on. We're nearly there," was all Mag offered in reply.

The moment we had reached the cliff, Aldrich had taken the rose and left to check on Venn, while at the same time instructing Mag to take us to some kind of hollow. Now, she led us to a cave set against the side of the cliff, where every other dragon seemed to be heading.

"Remember, don't speak unless addressed," Mag warned. "Too many echoes. If everyone tried talking at once, nobody would be able to hear themselves think."

We arrived at an arena-like depression at the back of the cave. A table with five chairs sat in the center. The silver rose stood of its own accord on the table's polished surface. All around us, dragons in both their true and human forms were filing into stadium seats that rose above us.

"How do you fit everyone?" I asked in amazement.

"Magic," Mag said, like it was obvious.

Artie nudged me. "Penelope, look."

I followed his gaze and saw that the walls glittered different colors. At first, I thought it was the many dragons in the room, but that couldn't be. None of the dragons glowed in their human forms. The lights were bouncing around, illuminating various objects and only occasionally dragons.

"What is it?" I asked.

"Shells," Mag said. "The cave walls are imbued with the remnants of our eggs."

"Come again?"

"After we hatch, our shells are pressed against the walls. The strength that we used to break free lends its power to the cave."

"What is this place? Why are we here?" Artie asked, a nervous edge to his voice.

"Rainbow Hollow. This is where we hold all of our meetings."

Mag led us to three seats in the front row.

"No, can we sit by the door?" Artie asked. He looked frightened as Mag ushered us along.

"No, we have to sit here, behind Aldrich," she said.

I gently pushed Artie into a seat and sat beside him.

"Calm down, Artie. Nothing's going to happen," I reassured him.

He nodded, but his eyes kept darting to the exit.

I was gazing at the silver rose when it dawned on me. "Artie!" I whispered excitedly.

"What?" he asked, alarmed.

"The silver rose!"

"What about it?"

I rolled my eyes. "Artie, I came into contact with the rose and I could suddenly understand Cadmus. We've had the rose ever since we left the castle. The same must have happened to you!"

Artie's eyes grew wide. He breathed, "I can talk to animals! That is so cool!" He broke off as the door opened.

Five dragons in their human forms were taking their places around the table. The council included Aldrich, a yellow, a red, a purple, and a black.

"The yellow is Irena, the red is Alkira, the purple is Blaz, and the black is Obelix," Mag whispered, as Aldrich pounded his fist on the table for silence. The noise died down immediately.

"Welcome one and all to Rainbow Hallow," Aldrich said. "This is a special meeting concerning the request of the Kaninens upon Penelope."

"I protest that anything has to be done," Blaz said at once. "The Kaninens are our enemies. Why should we help them?"

"I disagree," Obelix said. "Aldrich has already informed me that three young and innocent Kaninens were kidnapped. They may be our enemies, but isn't it our duty as dragons to assist them?"

"Why, Obelix?" Alkira said. "Dragons are loyal, but to our own kind. How do we know this isn't a trap? Remember, you can't trust an ice rabbit."

I gaped at Alkira and Blaz incredulously. Their remarks were so... so callous. It was unthinkable to label Flurry as 'the enemy.' I had looked into her eyes when she had apologized and thanked me in advance for saving her friends. There was no trap. Artie and I were right on the edge of Kaninen territory. If it had been a trap, Flurry could have lured us to her side. We would have followed the poor, frightened bunny to calm her down. The perfect opportunity to freeze us when the dragons couldn't help us.

No, Flurry could be trusted. I felt certain of that.

Irena was speaking. I pulled my attention back to the present in time to hear her say, "Alkira! How can you say such a thing? All life is precious. I believe young Magma and her friends. We can't allow three young Kaninens to suffer. They are still innocent children, after all."

"So you say," Alkira muttered.

"Watch it, Alkira," Obelix growled.

"She can say whatever she wants," Blaz snapped.

"Peace," Irena said.

"Oh, be quiet, Irena," Alkira waved her hand dismissively. "Nobody cares about you and your softheartedness."

Irena blushed furiously.

"They're acting like little kids," I murmured to Artie. "I've met five-year-olds with better sense."

"Tell me about it," he whispered back. "Where I'm from, even we don't dissolve into argument this quickly, usually."

"Where-" I began, but Mag nudged me and I fell silent.

"I'm ashamed of you," Aldrich was saying. "We are the council of dragon elders, and yet you are behaving like hatchlings. We should put this to a vote. All those in favor of allowing Mag and her friends every resource we can provide to search for the Kaninens, raise your hand."

Irena and Obelix did so, along with Aldrich.

"All those opposed?"

Alkira and Blaz, glaring, raised their hands.

"It is decided," Aldrich said. "Mag, Penelope, Artie, our thoughts and hearts go with you on your search for the Kaninens. Do not fail us." And with those encouraging words, the meeting abruptly ended. I smiled wryly. No pressure.

Chapter Fourteen

Memories

"THANK YOU AGAIN FOR YOUR hospitality," I said as Artie loaded the bags on dragon Mag's back the following morning. I readjusted the new sword and sheath the dragons had given me.

"It was the least we could do after you saved Venn," Aldrich said, checking his gold pocket watch with the blue star on the inside cover. "I'm sorry about Amarina."

"You don't have to apologize," I said.

"No, I should have recognized Amarina's ambitions. Even as a hatchling, she wanted to be the dragon guardian. When Mag became the guardian instead, Amarina became a dragon knight. Still a prestigious job, but-"

"She's bitter," I finished.

"Indeed. Amarina's always been fascinated by the rose, but she can only get near it if she's the guardian."

I glanced down at the rose, tucked into a side pocket of the sheath. It sparkled in the morning light. "Aldrich, yesterday the rose did something odd-" As I described the rose healing me from Wansetop's sting, Aldrich's eyes grew wide.

"The unknown witch," he whispered when I was done.

"The one who helped Cessala defeat the rogue dragon?"

"The very same. She put a spell on the rose: Bechulen."

"Protect," I translated. I blinked in confusion. How had I known that?

"Yes. The witch placed a one-time protection spell on it. It wouldn't drain the rose and would heal you of anything instantly. It won't happen again."

I looked across the clearing at Mag and Artie in the gray, predawn light. Artie was just climbing onto her back.

"Aldrich, I'm not sure if I can do this," I said in a rush, turning back to him. My new sword felt heavy around my waist. Who was I, a handmaiden to Queen Alana, to be the Rose?

"Penelope," Aldrich said gently. "You have a lot of power. I know you're scared, but Mag has been training for this her entire life and Artie will be there to help."

I blushed and turned away, so Aldrich wouldn't see.

"Hurry up, Penelope," Mag called. "We have to get moving."

"Thank you, Aldrich," I said, before hurrying over and boosting myself up beside Artie as Mag reared to her feet. Aldrich went to stand beside Venn, who was looking better. At least he was sitting up.

"We will see you soon, Grandfather," Mag said. And without another word, she soared into the sky, leaving Dragon Valley to fade like a winking star behind us.

"Good luck, Mag," Venn called in a raspy voice, as he and Aldrich shrunk to nothing more than dots.

I tried to keep them in sight as long as I could, but the wind was merciless and made my eyes water.

To distract myself, I watched the pinks and purples of the sunrise.

"Beautiful, isn't it?" Artie said, stretching out on Mag's back.

"Yes," I agreed. "Beautiful."

We continued in silence for a while, until Mag angled downward. "We're stopping here for now," she said, her voice strained.

"Why?"

But, my question was answered for me when, without warning, Mag suddenly turned back to human, leaving the three of us to plummet to earth.

A scream tore from my mouth on the way down. All the rations Aldrich had given us tumbled from the bags to the ground. I barely had time to wonder what people on the ground would think of raining food, when there was a flash of red in the corner of my eye and I landed with a thump on something hard and scaly.

"Hold on," Mag said and I realized she had transformed back into a dragon.

I reached out my hand and gripped Artie's, reassuring myself that he was still there.

He squeezed back as Mag touched down on the grass. I slid off her immediately, as she became human once more.

"Was that...?" I began.

"Yes, another barrier," Mag groaned. She sounded exhausted. "But there shouldn't be anyone here now. The magic I flew through felt deep, powerful, and old, like it was cast nearly a decade ago."

"There's a village nearby," Artie said, venturing further into the underbrush. "As long as it's safe, I'm going into town to search for our missing supplies."

"I don't like this. Its too quiet," Mag muttered as he disappeared.

I had to agree. It was as if the whole village was deserted.

"There's a sign! The village is called Tealeaf!" Artie said, skidding back into the clearing.

I stared in horror at Artie.

"The whole town is destroyed," he said, "not a villager or store to speak of, but at least now we know where we—what's wrong?"

I swallowed and said, "Tealeaf. I grew up in this village, before it was destroyed. There should be nothing left, apart from a few ramshackle houses and buildings."

"That's all I found," Artie confirmed, with a sideways look at me. "Maybe we should leave."

"Good idea," Mag said, quickly. "The barrier won't keep us from leaving. We can fly somewhere else."

I ignored them as I proceeded into the destroyed Tealeaf.

Mag and Artie hurried in my wake, as I finally relived that fateful night in my mind.

* * *

I ran eagerly from building to building. My small, eight-year-old body knew no bounds as I darted through the streets. There was the village blacksmith, Marcus Pewter, pounding away on his anvil, crafting what looked like a sword. I waved at him, Mr. Pewter waved back.

I plodded silently through the sad, dusty streets of Tealeaf. Glancing up, I saw the old blacksmith hut, where good old Mr. Pewter had honed his craft. A crow was now sitting on the roof, watching me with beady eyes.

I skipped happily toward the local healer, known simply as M. She was a crazy old witch who had been struck by one too many spells and her brain had gone slightly fuzzy. I loved the sights and smells of M's cottage, packed to the brim with dried potion ingredients.

My eyes misted over with tears as M's hut hove into view. M had been odd, but she had always been willing to entertain my wild imagination, like when I told her several fairies had caused all the flowers in Mom's garden to bloom in constantly changing colors.

I ran into the small hut and exclaimed in my childish voice, "M! Eagle outside! Swooping down and grabbing things! Bam!" I imitated an eagle dive-bombing.

M gave a cackling screech. "Excellent, my pet. Now, I have a secret for thee."

"What?" I hopped up and down eagerly. M's purple lizard went scuttling past.

M held up an amulet attached to a golden chain. It was empty in the center, like it was waiting for something to go there. "I crafted it myself. Took me night and day for a week, but 'tis done."

"What does it do?" I asked in awe.

"Do? Well, nothing, at least not until you're ready."

"I'm ready!" I said, my eyes shining.

"It is written that the owner of this amulet will find the silver lagoon one day."

I giggled. "How's it written, if you just made it?"

"You'd be surprised," M said. "I wouldn't be giving it to you, if you weren't special, my dear."

I gave M a glowing smile.

I wiped the tears from my eyes. The amulet had been special, all right, but not because of any silver lagoon, but because of M herself. I never saw her again after that night.

I took the amulet and held it in my hand. "Thank-" but I was cut off by a chorus of screams.

"Dragon!"

I dashed outside, skidding to a stop on the cobbled street. I stared openmouthed as a huge golden dragon landed on the local tavern. Its talons raked the thatch roof, tearing off large chunks. I gasped as the dragon turned his green eyes toward me and roared.

A barrage of black flames streamed over the houses.

The dragon turned and I whimpered as he spoke in a dark and sinister voice. It felt as if my insides were freezing with fear.

"I have been expecting you, Penelope Bogg," the dragon hissed. "So, the rumors are true. Sadly, you will never get the chance to face me again."

I stood transfixed as the dragon opened his mouth wide. I braced myself for the onslaught of fire, when-

"NO!" a voice shouted and Mom appeared in front of me.

"You will not hurt one hair of my daughter's head," Mom whispered softly and dangerously, drawing her wand against the dragon. There was a steely glint in her eyes.

"Ah, Alice, how many times have you fallen to my might?"

"Not today," Mom said, still facing him. "Penelope, run home. Find your father, Malcolm, and Lydia and leave town. I'll catch up with you. And remember," she suddenly whispered. "Bechulen."

She began to duel the dragon; shooting fiery sparks at him. I staggered toward the center of town, coughing on a haze of thick smoke. I couldn't see, M was gone; people were jostling their neighbors, screaming, trying to escape. I was bumped into a wall, and as I slid down, the amulet slipped from my nerveless grip and everything went black.

I stooped and rubbed some dirt into my hand. There were still miniscule traces of ash after eight years. Somehow, my mom had found the amulet in this mess and placed the ruby in its center. I had almost forgotten it, until Mom gave it to me for a fourteenth birthday present.

I awoke hours later, with my head throbbing and the town deserted. I staggered upright and leaned against the wall to recover my bearings. The village had never been this quiet.

"Hello," I called, my voice echoing.

"What happened?"

I spun around, but didn't see anyone. "Where... where are you?"

"Above you."

I craned my neck up and saw the shape I had mistaken for an eagle gliding jerkily toward me. It wasn't an eagle; it was a dragon.

This wasn't the golden dragon, however. This dragon was ruby red, with amber eyes.

"Hello," the red dragon said politely, extending her claw.

I hesitantly shook it. "Hello, I'm Penelope."

"Nice to meet you, Penelope."

We sat across from one another in silence. Finally, I worked up the courage to say, "Who are you? You're not with that evil golden dragon, are you?"

The red dragon shook her head. "No. I don't know who he was."

"Where do you live?"

"In a place called Dragon Valley. Its that way," she indicted east with her tail, "but my grandfather wanted to visit someone named Alice Bogg."

"That's my mom! How come we've never met?"

"My grandfather just heard of your mom. He thinks she possesses something that could help us."

"Can I come visit you sometime?" I said eagerly.

"Sure, it'll be nice to hang out with an actual human for a change. My friends can be so serious. How old are you, by the way?"

"Eight and a half."

"I'm twelve. It'd be nice to have a younger sister."

While we talked, I glimpsed the silver orb of the moon rising in the distance.

"Do you know where my parents are?" I said suddenly.

The dragon's smile faltered. "No. I was hoping you knew where my grandfather was."

We looked into one another's eyes and I gave a small whimper. We were lost, with no idea how to find our families.

I sat on the burned stoop of a long deserted house. My head was pounding. Memories I had long forgotten were returning with startlingly clarity. I had a fuzzy recollection of sitting on this step with the red dragon all those years ago.

"Come on. Not far now," I said, leading my new friend by the claw.

"You said that ages ago."

"Well, this time I'm right."

We turned the corner and I gasped. There was my house all right, but it was burned to the ground.

"W-what happened?" I sobbed.

The dragon nudged the broken timber with her snout and sniffed. "Fire, and recent too."

I fell to my knees in horror. "Where's my family?" I wondered aloud.

"Hopefully with my grandfather," the dragon said, spreading her wings. "I'll fly up and check."

She flapped her wings and jumped, gliding into the sky.

I watched as she began to shrink to the size of an eagle again.

"Bogg!"

My blood froze as I slowly turned around. The ground shook slightly as the golden dragon landed in front of me. His brown eyes were blazing.

"Penelope Bogg," he growled. "You cannot escape me."

I backed away, tripping over the step. I shielded my eyes. "Bechulen!"

A flash of red light illuminated my hands. I felt my strength ebb. When I removed them, the golden dragon was gone.

I stood shakily, swaying unsteadily.

"Penelope!"

My mom appeared before me as my head swam.

"Mag! Aldrich! Help me!"

Two dragons, one red and one white were leaning over me.

"She'll be fine, Alice," the white dragon said. "But, I'm not sure about her memories."

* * *

I watched as Mag and Artie approached me cautiously. I wasn't crying, I felt too exhausted for tears.

"Mag, that was you the night Tealeaf was destroyed, right?" I asked.

"Yes, we had heard that Alice Bogg held the secret to the silver rose. Aldrich wanted to question her."

"Wouldn't you have discovered that Penelope was the Rose that night?" Artie asked, as the crow from Mr. Pewter's house landed in a nearby tree.

"No, we didn't have the rose on us," Mag replied. "The dragon council wouldn't risk sending it out on a possible dead-end mission."

I put my head in my hands. "I don't understand."

I could have sworn the crow was laughing.

"What?" Artie asked.

"Why couldn't I remember anything until we entered Tealeaf?"

"I can answer that," Mag said. "Aldrich explained that night that the trauma of what had happened might cause you to lose your memory."

"And you couldn't have told me this before?" I asked incredulously.

"Aldrich and I saw the golden dragon that night," Mag said, taking the golden dragon scale out of her cloak pocket. She glanced sideways at Artie before plunging on. "We reported it to the dragon council, but nobody has seen or heard from the rogue dragon since. We had no proof that he had returned. I didn't want to worry you two. But now..." her voice trailed off.

"Now we know the rogue dragon is out there," I said quietly. Then, "There was a flash of red light that night eight years ago. Do you know what that was?"

Artie wet his lips nervously. "It sounds... sounds like magic."

"It couldn't have been," I croaked. "According to Cadmus, I was a late bloomer."

Mag seemed to be turning white before my very eyes.

"Bechulen," she breathed.

"What?" Artie asked, perplexed.

"The protection spell," I said, recalling my conversation with Aldrich. "The same as the rose."

"Yes, but this," Mag said, gesturing at the various buildings of Tealeaf, "was on a much larger scale."

"But... how? It's the same spell, isn't it?"

"The intent is sometimes more important than the spell," Artie said.

"Exactly," Mag said. "Penelope, the intent the witch placed on the rose was to protect us from whatever danger we might come across. As a terrified eight-year-old, *you* were up against the rogue dragon. I wouldn't have been surprised if you panicked and your magic just assumed you wanted to be protected from *all* dragons."

"The barrier," I realized. "That was... me?"

"If I had to guess, yes," Mag said.

"Why?" I asked and judging from their mystified expressions, Mag and Artie had strayed to the same conundrum I had. And they couldn't answer it any better than I could.

Who was I to have performed magic so early in life, but lost it for eight years afterward?

Chapter Fifteen

Silence

WE RESTED BEHIND THE RUINED WALL OF M's old hut. The air was oddly chilly for midsummer, so Artie and I huddled close to dragon Mag for warmth.

"S-so, this is where the local healer used to live?" Artie asked, shivering slightly.

"Yes," I said, rubbing my arms to generate heat. "I spent many an afternoon here."

Mag cocked her head and studied us for a moment, before she started a small smokeless fire. "Much better," she said with a self-satisfied smirk. "Shall we have lunch?"

I reached into my bag. Nothing.

I blanched. "All the food, lost in the fall! Artie?"

He checked his own bag, but like me, found nothing. "Sorry, but we are currently out of food. Not a crumb to speak of."

Mag stretched. "You two stay here, I'll go and catch us some dinner. How do you feel about some wild hog, or deer and birds?"

I was sickened by the thought, but managed to say, "You go ahead, Mag, but I'm going to search for some fruits and vegetables. Artie?"

"Fruits and vegetables sound good," he sounded equally as queasy.

Mag shook her head sadly. "I'll never understand humans. You never enjoy any of the truly delicious food." She soared off, calling, "I'll be back soon!"

"I'll go see about those plants," I said, turning to go.

"Maybe I should come with you," Artie said, hurriedly. "As protection."

I smiled. "Thanks, but no thanks. You stay and tend the fire. I'll go and gather the plants. It won't take long."

"But, it could be dangerous. I should come along."

"No," I said, firmly. "Even I can perform the simplest of spells, if truly needed. You're not scared, are you, Artie?"

He puffed out his chest and said, "Me, scared? Never!" But, his eyes betrayed him; they were darting back and forth.

"There's no need for both of us to go. You stay and protect camp. I grew up here, I know the village like the back of my hand."

I walked toward the edge of the village, pausing for a second outside my former house. Was everything the same as how I left it? Would the eight intervening years have altered anything or would it be like stepping back in time to that night? Curiosity won out and I poked my head into the darkened interior. As my eyes adjusted to the dim light, I placed a hand on the doorframe. It rocked slightly beneath my grip and... what was that odd creaking noise? I looked up to see an old, rickety beam collapsing inward upon itself.

It would have flattened me, except for Artie's quick intervention. He tackled me a split second before I would have been crushed. We sat up, coughing on the billowing dust encasing us.

"Thanks," I managed.

"Any time. Will you change your mind now?"

I bit my lip. It was certainly true that I would have been a pancake, if Artie hadn't saved me from the beam, but all the same, this was more of a one-girl job, and a lookout could wait for Mag's return.

In the end, I relented. "All right, Artie." I dusted myself off and took one last look at the house's exterior. "You can come, but remember you must remain silent. The plants don't like disturbances."

If Artie found anything odd with that statement, he didn't show it, as he accompanied me in my search for the elusive wild plants.

We crept forward into the silence, picking our way over the uneven ground. "Ouch!" Artie cried out, tripping over a rock and laying sprawled at my feet.

"Shh!" I said, as I helped him up. I couldn't hear the plants over his cries of pain.

We reached the tree line of Tealeaf. I stepped past the village's boundary, crouching low to the ground.

"Here," I said, stopping. I could feel Artie watching me as I placed my ear close to the ground.

"Not this one," I said, frowning in concentration, turning to another plant. I listened intently. This time, I smiled as I plucked the plant, leaving its roots. "Thank you," I said to the ground as I straightened up.

"What was that about?"

"I'm listening to the plants to determine if they're safe to eat," I answered, as if this was the most natural thing in the world. "If I didn't listen, they wouldn't reveal their secrets to me. M taught me this trick."

When Artie continued to look confused, I sighed, grabbed his arm and tugged him down until his left ear was a foot from the leafy earth. "Now, place your ear against the ground, level out your breathing, and *listen*."

Artie did as he was told, but he didn't appear to hear anything. His expression remained confused. I sighed, shook my head in amusement, and closed my eyes. I concentrated on a flower. A buzzing filled my head. A bee was pollinating a plant off to my right. A sucking noise was coming from beneath me. A root was drinking a drop of water. The world of the plants was opened to me. I rose and said, "Thank you," to the plant, but didn't pick it. "Hear anything?"

"No," he said, trying to rise, but my voice held him in place.

"Listen," I whispered. "Listen to the sound of water trickling through a plant's roots. Listen to the roots growing. Listen to the bees droning, pollinating the flowers. Listen to the story the plants want to tell us."

Artie slowed his breathing and listened. I watched carefully as his expression went from skeptical to surprise.

"Hear it?"

Artie's eyes snapped opened and he rose to face me. "I—I did. What was that?"

I smiled. "What you heard was the plants' world. Not many people bother to listen. They miss a whole domain of life they would otherwise hear."

"Why doesn't anyone notice?"

"Because people are unfortunately short-sighted. If it doesn't affect their own lives, they don't care."

"Humans will ignore life?"

"To an extent. Don't get me wrong, humans are also loving, compassionate individuals, but a bee's life can be just as interesting as our own."

After listening to the plants for another ten minutes, I deemed we had enough and we set off back to the campsite.

Halfway through the eerie, deserted village, Artie paused and stood completely still.

"What's wrong?"

Artie didn't answer. Instead, I saw his eyes narrow and stare menacingly out toward the rickety beam that had almost crushed me. I thought I glimpsed a shadow detach itself from the beam and fly away. It was just the crow.

Beside me, Artie relaxed and took my hand. I smiled slightly as we set off again.

We reached the fire and I set to work preparing two small salads, from the various plants we had gathered.

"It won't be much, but at least its something." I borrowed Artie's knife and chopped the plants into pieces.

"Penelope, have you ever thought of wielding a knife, or even a sword?"

"Mag's mentioned it."

"I think you should seriously consider it. You handled my knife expertly against Laborc."

"Maybe," I said non-committedly, though I was secretly pleased. I handed him back his knife.

Artie wiped it off and stared at it thoughtfully. Then, without warning, he stood and pointed his knife at me.

I froze. What was he doing? Could he be—but it was impossible—the enemy?

"Come on, Penelope. The sooner we practice, the sooner we can eat."

I breathed a sigh of relief. Just practice.

I stood and drew my sword.

"You're going to drop your sword if you hold it like that," he said calmly.

I glanced down. The veins in my hand were bulging. I was holding the sword so fiercely.

"Too tight," Artie said, rapping my knuckles lightly with his hilt. I dropped my weapon in surprise. "Relax."

I took a deep breath and retrieved my sword. Artie corrected my grip, so I was holding it firmly and steadily.

"Ready, Penelope?"

"Artie, we can't fight with real swords, we'll cut each other to ribbons."

He thumped his forehead with his knife-free hand. "Thanks for reminding me. You're going to have to use Bechulen."

"Artie..."

He held up his hands defensively. "Hear me out. Concentrate on us and then on the magic of your surroundings, that way you won't drain your own reserves."

My jaw dropped. "I can do that?"

"Only in magically rich areas like this one. And because you cast the original protection spell."

Glad I didn't have to use the rose, I imagined a plant's protective thorns around the two of us. "Bechulen."

I held my breath, waiting for the silver.

Nothing.

It was then that I noticed both my sword and Artie's knife were glowing a faint green.

Artie studied his knife for a moment, before he raised it and slashed his own hand.

With a cry of alarm, I leapt forward and seized his hand, checking for injuries.

"Penelope, calm down."

"Calm down?" I shrieked. "I'm not the one who just sliced open my own palm!"

"Penelope, look!" Artie gently turned over his hand. There was no gaping wound, no sign of any damage at all.

"How?" I spluttered.

"By focusing on us, the protections surrounding Tealeaf extended to us. We can't be hurt until you release the magic. Perfect for training."

I could feel the magic tugging at the edge of my consciousness. I could sever the connection with one thought, but Artie was right. The energy fueling the spell was coming from around me, not from me.

Artie showed me several thrusts and parries in slow motion, which I attempted to copy.

"Right," he said, after he had disarmed me for the fifth time in a row, "let's try that in real time. First to disarm the other wins."

Maybe it was because I was tired of losing my sword, or perhaps I was simply fed up with practice, but my senses awoke. Artie was stabbing at my unprotected left, when with a flick of the wrist I brought my sword clanging against his knife. Artie looked momentarily shocked at the block, but then his face broke into a wide grin.

"Good job!" he said as he jumped back nimbly and feinted to my right. I blocked him again and when he retreated several steps, I went on the offensive, slashing at his ribcage. Artie stumbled back and I followed, pressing him until his back was against a tree. I smiled smugly. Artie had nowhere left to run. I had won.

I raised my sword to point at Artie, when he darted forward and elbowed me in the stomach.

Completely winded, I allowed my sword to clatter to the ground, while I held my stomach. I had lost.

I released the protection spell around us and just knelt, hunched over on the ground. When I was finally able to speak, I wheezed, "That's cheating!"

Artie laughed and held out his hand. I took it and he hauled me to my feet.

"I suppose it could be called cheating," he said, his eyes twinkling, "since I didn't defeat you with my knife. But, you did learn an important lesson."

"Always watch your elbows?"

Artie laughed again and this time I joined in.

"In a fight, always use what's available. It could be the difference between victory and, in extreme cases, death."

The back of my neck prickled at the last word.

"Always be aware of everything, Penelope. Your longer weapon gives you an advantage. You don't have to get as close to me as I have to do with you, but you never know when your opponent will elbow you into submission."

We cracked up again and, still chortling, collapsed on the ground to finish working on the plants.

We ate a pleasant lunch of vegetables. As we finished, Mag returned, licking her lips from her hunt.

"How was it?" I asked.

"Excellent," Mag said, as she returned to human. "I caught a young buck about thirty miles from the village."

That afternoon, as the sun rose higher above the mountains, a gentle mist spread. The crickets chirped their summer songs softly, the crow was sitting in a nearby tree, and the world itself was in a light doze. I awoke from a much-needed nap to find Artie ten feet away, with his ear pressed against the dirt.

"Artie?" I said, sleepily. "What are you doing?"

He gave an embarrassed laugh and straightened hurriedly. "Nothing. I just thought..."

"That you would listen to the plants again?" I asked, shrewdly.

Artie dropped his head. "Yes."

"There's nothing to be ashamed of," I said. "Did you hear anything?"

"No," he said, puzzled. "And after your tips today, I thought I must."

I crouched next to Artie and listened for myself. I shook my head. "Nobody can hear these plants."

"What?"

"There's nothing wrong with your hearing. They're simply silent."

"Plants can do that?"

"Beware of those," Mag said, starting awake. "Poisonous plants can wreak havoc on anyone."

"Poison!" Artie exclaimed, stepping away from the vegetation.

"They won't hurt you," I said as the crow chuckled in its tree. "As long as you don't eat them. There is a reason for their silence. It's a warning to stay away."

"If it was a warning, wouldn't they screech and throw a tantrum?" Artie said.

"Screech and throw a tantrum?" Mag said. "What good would that do?"

"Silence can speak louder than words. If I were upset with Mag and wouldn't talk to her, we would be able to settle things far sooner than if I were to yell insults at her. Not that I would do that in the first place."

Mag winked at me and said, "Predators are the most dangerous when they are hunting. Take earlier today. I circled that buck for ages, but I flew as silently as I could to prevent him from hearing me. I caught him, so my silence fooled him."

"So, the plants are warning us through their silence," Artie said slowly. "Because if we were to hear them, no matter what the message was, we would assume that they are safe?"

"Exactly," I said. "Silence is powerful, if only people would stop and listen."

* * *

"We'll need supplies when we reach the next village," I said, as Artie and I packed our bags with the remaining plants and secured them to Mag's back. "And also directions. Where is this Everburn Swamp, anyway?"

"Not sure," Artie said.

"What's the closest town to our location?"

Mag thought for a moment and said, "Silent Stream Village. It rests on the banks of the Duckweed River."

"Hmm. That village is a major trading post," I said. "Someone must have seen or heard something about the swamp."

We flew west over green, rolling hills, away from the ruins of my old home.

A few hours later, Mag stopped to rest. I didn't mind. This gave me the opportunity to consider M's cryptic words. *The owner of this amulet will find the silver lagoon one day.*

I thought and pondered until I was blue in the face, but no brilliant strokes of logic or understanding came to me. I even enlisted the help of Mag and Artie, but to no avail. Neither of them had the slightest idea of the amulet's secret.

"M's words have to mean *something*," I said. "I just know it."

"My parents never spoke of a silver lagoon," Artie said slowly, "and my sister would have told me if she knew. I doubt they've even heard of it."

"Who are your parents?" I asked, remembering with a jolt that I didn't even know Artie's last name.

Artie turned rather deaf and refused to look at me, until the subject was changed.

"Mag, do you know where the silver lagoon is?"

Artie visibility relaxed.

Mag frowned. "It does ring a bell. Grandfather must have told me something, but what that was, I have no idea."

We started again, following the twists and turns of the Duck-weed River. Artie was the first to see our destination.

"There!" he said.

I looked up from my musings, and saw a walled town sprawled along the edge of the river. Boats sailed lazily across the smooth, crystal clear water. A bridge was lowered across the water as we watched.

"Its huge," I gasped.

"Its Silent Stream," Mag said. "We have to tread carefully. Who knows what's waiting for us here."

* * *

Artie came to a halt halfway across the drawbridge.

"Come on, Artie. We're nearly there," Mag urged.

He gazed past us, staring fixedly at the top spire of a tower that peeked over the wall. "Silent Stream," Artie murmured. "I knew that name sounded familiar."

"What's familiar?" I asked.

"I've been here before," he whispered. "Years ago with my best friend Ben." He turned to me and said urgently, "We were framed for a crime we didn't commit. Ben got the worst of it, though, because they saw his face. We escaped, but barely."

"Could we finish this absorbing conversation later?" Mag said. "I think people are beginning to stare."

It was true. People passing by to enter the city were indeed staring at the three teenagers whispering, one of whom had her face completely covered with a blood red hooded cloak. We were also blocking traffic in and out of the city. Some people were elbowing past us. One man, leading a carrot-laden donkey, bumped into me, almost sending me headfirst into the river.

We pushed our way off the bridge, away from Silent Stream, and into a nearby clump of trees.

"Should we go in, Artie?" I asked.

"... Yes. We need the supplies. We can't risk waiting for another town. I don't think they'll recognize me after three years. Besides, someone may have information about the swamp."

Mag and I couldn't think of a better plan, so we agreed. Artie donned a forest green cloak similar to the kind dragons preferred.

We stepped back onto the bridge, trying to act casual, but I glanced around self-consciously. People were still staring at us. Not surprising, really, considering that both my companions' faces were hidden by hoods. If we had wanted to remain hidden, we had failed miserably.

Once inside, we began to question the guards, shop owners, everyone we could find. "Have you seen a swamp anywhere in Alsmora, with a constantly burning fire?"

We always omitted the Kaninen. The answer was always no.

After these exchanges, we would thank the person for their time and hurry on. Artie's treatment in this city weighed heavily on my mind, so I didn't want to hang around any longer than necessary.

We discovered nothing concrete concerning the swamp, and our inquiries had led us to the center of the city, which contained a small park. A flash of movement by a secluded birch tree caught my attention. I squinted and spotted what looked like a dark shape leaning against the bark.

"I'm going to get supplies," Artie said. He was facing the other direction and hadn't seen anything. "My stomach is rumbling and we have nothing but plants to eat."

I could hear his stomach grumble from feet away. I smiled distractedly and said, "Mag and I will be fine on our own for a few minutes. We'll meet you there."

Artie hesitated, suddenly reluctant to leave. Slowly, he turned and headed out of the park. He kept looking back every few feet. Once he was out of sight, Mag pushed aside her hood and said, "What was all that about?"

I pointed toward the tree. "Look."

With her better eyesight, Mag spotted the shadow immediately. Together, we watched as it suddenly split into two. One of the shadows beckoned to us.

We tensed, Mag tasting the air.

We approached cautiously. There was a pause as neither side moved nor spoke, and then a voice rang from above. "Shell, look, new customers. I'm thinking the one about the lion, porcupine, and gazelle."

"Shh, be quiet, Mel. We can't draw attention to ourselves. Our job is to discover their intentions, and then ask, not just select any random riddle."

Two chipmunks dropped from the tree onto the ground.

"Greetings," one chipmunk said. This one had a feminine voice. "My name is Shell. This is my brother Mel. We are the Riddle Chipmunks."

"Penelope and Mag," I said, politely. "We're searching for a swamp. Have you seen it?"

"Maybe and maybe not," the male chipmunk, Mel, said impressively. "We know everything."

"There's a kidnapped Kaninen in its depths," Mag said.

Shell, the female, and Mel shared a mysterious look.

"We've seen it," Shell admitted, "but we can only tell you in a riddle."

"Why?"

"Those are the rules," a familiar voice said.

"Willow!" I said, as the squirrel leader of the Woodland Warriors dropped from a branch of the birch tree. Several squirrels and birds, who I assumed to be the Woodland Warriors, were watching silently.

"Shell. Mel," Willow said, nodding to the Riddle Chipmunks.

"Lady Willow," they said in unison.

Willow frowned. "Was I interrupting something?"

"Oh, no," Shell began, but Mel cut in.

"Yes, you were, Lady Willow. We were just about to test them with a riddle when you barged in."

Shell covered her mouth with her paws, but Willow didn't look at all upset.

"Maybe you want to tell *me* the riddle. Go on, I'll whisper my answer to Shell, so these two," she gestured toward Mag and me, "don't hear."

Mel puffed himself up and said,

> "I do not earn,
> I only take.
> What's yours is mine,
> But I give naught.
> Watch out,
> Or the mouse will visit your house.

What am I?"

"That's not exactly a riddle," Mag said in my ear.

Willow must have heard Mag, for she murmured, "Shell and Mel think they're riddles."

"Nobody's ever corrected them?" I asked in a whisper.

Willow shook her head.

We settled down to ponder the "riddle." Willow muttered it to herself for a minute, and then whispered in Shell's ear. Shell nodded and Willow beamed.

Mag and I started to talk out the riddle, in the hope that two heads were better than one.

"Well, obviously, this person isn't particularly honest."

"No," Mag agreed. "It sounds like a criminal to me."

"A smuggler, maybe," I mused. "They take, but don't earn."

"But they give their stolen treasure to clients for money," Mag said. "A robber, perhaps?"

"No, not a robber," I said, slowly, "but a..."

"Thief!" we finished together.

Willow nodded, obviously pleased. "Well done, Penelope and Mag!" She turned to Mel. "They have passed your test. You know the rules."

Mel grimaced and recited, "'If a challenger solves the riddle of a Riddle Chipmunk, said chipmunk must answer any one question from said challenger.'"

"Correct," Willow said. "Shell, would you be so kind as to answer their questions, while I have a word with Mel."

Shell bowed. "My pleasure, Lady Willow."

Willow led Mel aside and began what appeared to be a lecture on how to treat challengers respectfully.

Shell winced slightly as she turned to face us and Willow's voice rose an octave to drown out Mel's complaining. "You each receive one question, since you worked together to solve the puzzle."

I considered Shell's offer. Two free questions, from a chipmunk who apparently knew everything, or at least according to Mel.

"How do we save the Kaninens?"

Shell thought for a moment and then said,

> "Three to become one
> Time hard won.
> A rock, watery flames, and the shade,
> Defeat and see one fade.
> To find I must seek the woman letter
> And the red returned in spirits better."

I gaped at the chipmunk. "What kind of answer is that?"

"A riddle," Shell said, simply. "Your answer is hidden within. She turned to Mag. "And your question?"

Mag's eyes were strangely downcast as she said, "I know what must be done on this quest: we must rescue the ice rabbits. But, my question is of a more personal level."

"Ask and I'll attempt to help."

Mag fixed me with a piercing, amber-eyed stare, before she turned to Shell and said, "I've only ever known my grandfather. My mother died when I was young and I never knew my father. Tell me, is he still alive?"

I felt a lump form in my throat. So, both Mag and I had lost parents at a young age.

Shell closed her eyes and exhaled a long, slow breath, before answering,

> "Daughter of wind and daughter of Storm
> Your father asleep in the valley of thorn.
> Seek him out.
> Erase his doubt.
> Only you can set the record straight, bring relief,
> And end his grief."

Mag cocked her head to the side. "That's my answer? A confused jumble of words?"

"It will all make sense when the time is right," Shell said cryptically. "I'd better see how Mel is doing. Farewell!"

I watched as Shell scampered up the trunk and within the blink of an eye, the birds, chipmunks, and squirrels, except for Willow, had vanished.

"I'm sorry about Mel," Willow said. "He's always been irritating."

"Hellooo, Willow!" a singsong voice called.

"Speaking of irritating," Willow muttered. Then, louder, "Hello, Milo."

A crow had landed on the branch beside Willow.

"Aren't you the crow from Tealeaf?" I asked, frowning.

"She has hope after all," Milo, the crow, said with a mock bow.

"Don't mind Milo," Willow said. "He's channeling Mel."

"Ha! That chipmunk wishes he were as magnificent as me!" Milo's eyes narrowed as he turned to Mag. "Ah, Magma, still human, I see."

"Hi, Milo," Mag said through gritted teeth.

"You know each other?" I said.

"Unfortunately," Mag and Willow said together.

Milo touched a wing to his chest. "You wound me."

"What are you doing here, Milo?" Willow asked wearily.

"M sent me to inspect *her*," Milo said, nodding in my direction.

"Wait! M?" I said excitedly. "You know her? How do we find her?"

"Ah, now you're interested. I would *love* to tell you, but I don't want to give *everything* away." He spread his wings, preparing to go. "Coming, Willow?"

"Yes," Willow said, tossing down a single willow leaf beside the birch tree as a calling card of her return.

"We'll see each other again," she promised, disappearing into the foliage.

"Me as well," Milo cackled. "Oh, we'll have so much fun!" He departed, looking like a great dark shadow.

I stowed the leaf in my bag. "We should go back for Artie and warn him about Milo. Maybe he'll know what the riddles mean."

* * *

We found Artie bartering for food.

"You can't be serious? Ten kubits for an apple? I could get the same produce at a fraction of the cost next door," Artie was saying, gesturing to the stand on his left. Like Mag, he had abandoned his hood.

"Eight kubits and not one more," the greasy looking man selling the apples said.

"Five," Artie said, crossing his arms.

"Seven."

"Six."

"Deal!"

Artie grinned crookedly and handed the money to the man. "Pleasure doing business with you."

He turned to leave and I hurried forward.

"That was impressive," I said. "But what happened to remaining hidden?"

"Oh, that. I don't think anyone with recognize me here." His eyes darted around rapidly. "Besides, people were beginning to stare." He cleared his throat. "What about you?"

"Talking to chipmunks and an annoying crow," I said, telling him about Willow, Milo, and the Riddle Chipmunks. "Do you have the supplies?"

"Yes, just finished," Artie said, handing us each an apple. "These people don't know how to barter. Lucky for us, that man didn't know the price of his own goods. Those were my last kubits." He shook his head at the loss of the silver coins.

"I'll never understand your money," Mag said. "Trading your items for little bits of metal. What good is that in real life? You can't eat metal."

I had no response, so I remained quiet. So did Artie. Mag grunted, but didn't pursue the subject.

We strolled down the street of the outdoor market. I admired the wares in the merchants' carts. One had a beautiful set of pottery on display. A striking blue vase caught my eye. It had a slender neck, with a pattern like the sea splashed across its middle.

Another cart offered small earthenware pots and pans for carrying water. One was particularly elegant. It showed a bright orange dragon with its wings outstretched.

And yet another cart had flying carpets, the most popular method of travel for those who weren't privileged to ride a dragon. We walked past several kids admiring them.

We passed another stand, one where a mustached man smelling of fish was bartering with a woman with two tiny children by her side. The family was covered in torn and dirty rags. The older child, a girl of about five with wide, scared eyes, held her younger brother's shoulders, while her mother spoke with the man. I caught a few words and almost ran into Artie, who had stopped dead in his tracks.

"Please, kind sir, we do not have much, and we need that bread to survive. I'll pay you three kubits for it."

The man stroked his mustache. He had a variety of items for sale, including food, gourds of water, and even a handful of rusted weapons.

"Three kubits are hardly worth my wares. Take this fine melon, for example." My eyes blazed when I saw the children's eyes alight with hunger. "Easily worth twenty. Now, be gone, before your filthy faces taint my cart and I lose my business."

"Wait!" the woman cried, removing a thin purse. "This is all the money I possess. My late husband was not a wealthy man, but we lived comfortably, until his untimely death last year." She held up five gold coins, more valuable than the silver kubits.

The mustached man laughed. "Five crestas? That will not buy you bread for a day! Be gone, wench, and take these urchins with you."

I was as close to breathing fire as Mag at that moment. How could this horrible man just... dismiss them like that? I could see Artie felt the same way. He looked ready to spit poison. Mag's hair was sparking with flames.

"Wait here," Artie muttered out of the side of his mouth, as he replaced his hood over his head.

Before I could respond, he had removed a length of twine from his bag. He crept behind the man, who was still arguing with the woman, and carefully tied one end to the cart's wheel and the other to the man's ankle. The man didn't even flinch as Artie secured the twine.

Mag and I stared at each other inquisitively, but neither of us seemed to know what to make of his strange behavior.

Artie retreated behind a building, onto the next street. He nodded once in our direction and after the space of a heartbeat, sprinted from around the corner, yelling, "Thief! A thief has been sighted at the gate! Hurry!"

The man started and made as if to dart forward, but the twine tightened and he stumbled, crashing the cart into the street. I leapt back to avoid a battered dagger that flew from the cart and impaled itself into the ground, where my left foot had been moments before.

Quick as a flash, Artie changed directions and snatched various bits of food, several gourds of water, and even a ragged piece of paper from the cart, before taking hold of the woman's wrist and dragging her and her children out of sight, the man's angry shouts still audible.

"Run!" Artie yelled.

Mag and I sprinted after him. Artie led us and the family through a crisscross of streets and carts, dodging horses, shoppers, and even the occasional soldier, who bore Alana's crest on the front of their uniforms.

Artie stopped, holding his hand up for silence. Heavy footfalls could be heard approaching us... in *both* directions! Wild-eyed, Artie motioned us down a deserted alleyway. He held his hand up for silence. We halted, panting, in the shadows, watching the alley's mouth with bated breath.

"They ran this way, sir!" a soldier saluted to his captain.

"Pursue them," the captain said. "You say the young man stole from Martin? He won't get far."

The two departed without once glancing at our hiding spot. I released the breath I was holding with a whoosh. I turned to the family, who looked utterly bewildered. Before I could figure out what to say, Artie stepped in, "I'm sorry we had to drag you into this, but we couldn't stand by and watch that man cheat you."

With a glance in my direction, he divided the food and water he had taken. "Here," he said, handing half to the woman. "You take this, that man won't be able to cheat you again for quite a while."

He handed each of the children a piece of candy and moved to turn away, but the woman reached out a hand and gripped the back of his cloak.

"Thank you," she said, gesturing toward the rations he had sectioned off for them. "How can I ever repay you for your kindness?"

"Leave Silent Stream. Go somewhere safe," Mag said. "Many strange forces are loose in the land and you would do well to protect yourselves from them."

"Wait! What are your names?"

"My name is-" I began, but Artie cut me off.

"I am known simply as A. My companions are P and M. I'm sorry, but we have to go."

"Good-bye!" the two children called out in unison.

"We'll never forget you," their mother said.

Artie nodded and swept away, forcing Mag and me to follow.

"Good luck!" I called to the family before we rounded the corner and I lost sight of them. Artie was heading deeper into the depths of Silent Stream. He instructed us to keep to the shadows, before creeping past bustling streets full of townspeople, out for a day of shopping.

At one point, my heart almost stopped when a soldier turned in our direction and yelled, "Hey, you! Stop!" There was a crash and the sound of racing footsteps behind us. The soldier took off in pursuit. Hidden in the shadows, we held perfectly still, until the sounds of the soldier and his quarry disappeared around a corner.

Artie led us to the opposite side of town and stopped beside a two-story, dusky pink building. It had obviously once been red, but time and the sun had faded away its color. There was a rickety ladder attached to it.

"After you," Artie said, gesturing to me. I started to climb, while he held the ladder steady for me, for which I was grateful. Soon, I stood perched on the roof, gazing down at the city, like a glorious bird of prey.

Artie joined me a few minutes later. "Mag will be up in a minute," he said.

When she did rejoin us, it was by soaring over the top of the building and landing gracefully beside us. She had sprouted her wings, but for the most part, she had remained human.

Artie led us to a small shack, built on top of the roof. "We're about to meet one of my oldest friends," he said. "Don't worry, as long as you're with me, you'll be fine."

That did not exactly reassure me.

He turned and knocked three times on the shack's door.

A slot slid open. A pair of eyes peered suspiciously at us. "Password?"

"Q sent me."

The slot closed and the door banged open. A boy a little older than Artie stood framed in the threshold. "Q sent you, indeed! I heard you haven't spoken to him in months!"

Artie threw back his hood, stepped forward, and gave the boy a brotherly hug. "Darren, good to see you."

"Aye, you too, Artie."

They broke apart and Darren turned brightly toward us. "Hello, there. I'm Darren. Are you friends of Artie? I could tell you some stories."

"That's quite all right, Darren," Artie said loudly. "We're just here to ask a favor."

Darren waved us inside a lavishly furnished room. There were several plump armchairs and a fire danced merrily in a hearth. I sank gratefully into one of the chairs. Mag, meanwhile, stuck her whole hand into the hearth.

"Shouldn't we stop her?" Darren asked in alarm.

"No," I said. "She's good." And Mag was. She had a look of joy on her face and I knew that the fire must have felt good to a dragon. So much for remaining inconspicuous, though.

"Right," Darren said, nervously. "What brings you here, Artie?"

"Well, it's a long story..." He spent the next quarter of an hour relating the tale of the crooked merchant and of the family's plight. Darren's eyes grew wide during the narrative.

"...and the riot will extend to the family if we don't stop it, Darren," he finished. "Can I trust you to look after this family until they leave the city?"

"Of course, Art, you can rely on me," Darren said.

"Thanks, Darren," Artie said, rising to leave, but Darren held him back.

"I thought you were out of the game, Artie?"

Artie's eyes flicked to mine and I could see the vulnerable look. "... No, just a disagreement with my old man. Besides, I still have my standards."

"Right, right. 'Never the innocent,' I remember."

"What are you talking about?" I asked. Mag had removed her hand from the flames and was listening intently.

"You haven't told them yet?" Darren asked. He sounded shocked.

"No," Artie said with a shake of his head.

"You'd better tell them soon, before one of our... friends catch up with you."

"Why would we meet those *friends* on our journey?" Artie croaked.

"You haven't heard?"

Artie shook his head.

"You need to keep up. Word on the street is that your father is looking for you. Some powerful agents are ordered to find you, even... her. If they do, no matter what you're doing, they're ordered to drag you back, if necessary, to headquarters."

Artie groaned. "I got her assurance that she would leave me alone. But, I guess I should have known that dear, old dad wouldn't give up so easily."

"If it makes you feel any better, she told me she won't personally drag you back."

Artie sighed and nodded.

"Couldn't we explain to them that we're busy?" I asked.

"Penelope, I doubt Artie's friend would leave us alone because we asked them nicely," Mag snorted.

"Exactly," Darren agreed.

"What can we do?" I asked.

"The only thing you can do," Darren said. "Go into hiding until this blows over. You're all welcome to stay here with me."

As tempting as that sounded, I knew we had to continue. I needed to save the Kaninens if I ever wanted my amulet back. Artie and I locked eyes and we came to a silent agreement.

"Thanks, but no thanks, Darren. We have to keep going," he said firmly.

"Well, if we're going, we'd better leave quickly." Mag stretched. "It won't be long now until they discover our hiding place."

"I doubt it," Darren said. "They've never found me yet."

Then how did they catch Artie and Ben?

Pushing that thought aside for the moment, I reached into my bag to ensure that we still had the necessary supplies, when an idea struck me.

"Darren, do you know where Everburn Swamp is?"

He gazed into the fire before responding. "I have heard of a swamp further north, where the Duckweed River comes to an end, but it wasn't called Everburn Swamp."

"What was it called?"

To my surprise, Mag answered. "The Blue Rose Swamp," she breathed. "Of course."

"Wait, you know where it is?" Artie asked incredulously. "Why didn't you tell us this before?"

"Because I knew it under a different name. Legend has it that a sapphire in the shape of a rose is hidden somewhere in its depths. Find it, and you gain power over the west wind. At least, that's what they say."

With a destination in mind, we departed Darren's secret hideout and slid down the ladder, careful to avoid detection from the soldiers on patrol.

We darted from shadow to shadow, ducking out of sight whenever one of us spotted a guard. Artie was in the lead as we approached the front entrance, but he stopped so suddenly, I almost walked straight into him. I tried to look past him, but I couldn't see anything. Something didn't feel right. I listened to the rush of water from the stream that gave the village its name, and realized with a jolt that Silent Stream was too quiet. For the first time since we had arrived, Silent Stream was completely silent.

We couldn't stand there all day, however. We had to get outside. But, how? The drawbridge was already up for the night.

"I could turn into my dragon form and fly us out," Mag whispered.

I thought that sounded like a fine idea. The place was eerily quiet and I was eager to leave.

"No, that won't work," Artie murmured. "The buildings are too close together for your full wingspan, Mag. You could try flying us out one at a time in your half-dragon form, but it's too much of a risk going past the guards not once, but *three* times."

"So what do we do?" I asked.

Artie looked at me sadly. "Invisibility," he said quietly.

"Really, you know an invisibility spell?" Mag said, obviously impressed.

I nodded, but when I spoke, my voice sounded hoarse, "I've only used it once, when trying to get past that yikty."

"The one in the castle?" Mag asked, flexing her claws. "I never did get to fight it."

"Penelope, this should be like dodging the yikty. We avoid the soldiers, open the gate, and get out of here."

"Last time, I had my amulet," I pointed out, frowning. "I do have the silver rose, but... I can't. Aldrich told me to use it only in extreme emergencies, like healing. To get to the gate, I'll have to use magic without the aid of a focus."

"I can help with my mundane powers, like last time," Artie said, taking his knife in his left hand and offering me his right. "Trust me."

Artie did help disperse the magic last time. But, without a focus, would it work?

"All right," I said reluctantly, taking Artie's hand, while Mag gripped my shoulder. I can do this, I thought, brushing aside my doubts. I can do this. I had to.

"Aun evas comren," I said. Instantly, I began to shake as all the color was drained from me. I could see Mag and Artie losing color as well. There was a brief flash of silver and then I blinked. Everything was back to normal, except for the fact that the three of us were in black and white.

"So, this is what it feels like to be invisible," Mag said, letting go of my shoulder and looking down at herself. "Weird!"

Artie released my hand. "How are you feeling?"

"Relieved." I smiled. I had done it. "There was only one brief glimpse of silver."

Artie smiled back. "Come on, we have to work fast before the spell wears off."

He dashed to the big iron lever that controlled the bridge. Mag and I had a second where we looked at each other, before we hurried after him.

What we found was a rusty old metal bar parallel to the ground.

"We have to push up to lower the drawbridge," Artie explained.

That sounded a little backwards to me, but I joined in with the other two, pushing and heaving against it. Slowly, the lever began to creak upward.

"Just a little further," Mag grunted.

"Who's there?" a voice rang out through the quiet. Torchlight bobbed in our direction.

"Guards," Artie mouthed.

I froze, releasing the lever. Luckily, Mag and Artie were keeping it steady, though barely.

"What was that?" the voice continued, as the torchlight drew nearer.

"It was probably just your imagination," another voice answered.

"No, it definitely came from over there," the first voice insisted.

Don't worry, I told myself, trying hard not to panic. I'm invisible. They can't see me.

"Penelope, move!" Artie hissed urgently.

"What? Why?"

It was then that I clearly saw why. My dress was slowly turning blue once more. Artie and Mag were regaining their color as well.

"This spell requires concentration," Artie muttered.

My panic, I thought with horror. I was so terrified of being discovered, I hadn't maintained the spell. I tried to concentrate, to return us to black and white. It was no use. As the seconds ticked by, we became more and more colorful. The guards were almost on top of us.

"We have to go," Artie said.

"The drawbridge will seal us in if nobody guards the lever," Mag pointed out.

I took a deep breath, intending to tell the others to run; that I would sacrifice myself so they could reach safety. But, I was too slow. Mag pushed me out of the way, braced herself against the lever, and said, "Go! I'll hold it!"

"No, Mag, you can't!"

"Go, while there's still time!"

I opened my mouth to argue further, when Artie seized my wrist and pulled me toward the bridge at a run.

There were yells of surprise as the guards discovered Mag. I wanted to scream and fling myself at them to give her time to escape, but I simply gritted my teeth as Artie and I sprinted over the bridge and tumbled safely onto the grass on the opposite bank.

The drawbridge thudded shut behind us, leaving Mag trapped inside.

Chapter Sixteen

The Ruby Ship

"**N**O!" I SHOUTED, LEAPING TO MY FEET. I rushed forward, only to find myself teetering on the edge of the bank.

"Penelope!" Artie cried, hauling me back to safety. "There's nothing we can do now. Mag's going to have to look after herself."

"We could storm the walls," I said, ignoring him. "I'm sure we could climb over again. Maybe I could lower the drawbridge with magic."

"Is that what Mag would have wanted?" Artie asked quietly. "For you to risk yourself for her? I want to save her too, but we have to think practically."

"I am," I snapped. "I don't know the first thing about magic. I know your sister showed you a few useful tricks, but can you teach me everything I need to know? Mag could."

We stood in silence for a minute. There was shouting and an odd amount of squeaking on the village side and I could only imagine what horrible torment Mag was suffering all because of me. I should have been the one to stay behind, not her. Maybe that was my role as the Rose, to sacrifice myself so Mag could keep going.

Artie must have read my expression, because he said, "You weren't meant to stay behind, Penelope. You're supposed to do something much bigger than that. I can sense it."

"How?" I asked, bitterly. "The amulet is gone, I barely know anything about magic, and we have to get to a swamp neither one of us has even seen before."

"We'll find a way," Artie said, reaching out and touching a few strands of my hair. They were bright silver. "You are the Silver Rose, after all."

I nodded, thinking, I'll come back and save you soon, Mag. You can count on it.

* * *

We continued following the Duckweed River north, toward the swamp and the kidnapped Kaninen. The closest village was a place called Wolf Bay. Presumably, it was called that because werewolves lived in the area.

"We have to go through an open field to get to Wolf Bay," Artie said. "The full moon was a few nights ago, so we should be safe, but if werewolves are in the area, we won't have any cover. But we'll have to risk it, if we want to reach the swamp. With any luck, the Kaninen will help us rescue Mag."

If she's still alive, I thought glumly. I shivered as I remembered those guards rushing us, trying to prevent us from escaping, their faces grotesque in the torchlight. To distract myself, I asked, with a nervous laugh, "You seriously don't believe werewolves live here, do you, Artie?"

"No, but you never know. Weird things do happen. Who are we to say that there aren't any werewolves around?"

Ten minutes later, Artie and I were sitting around a campfire. We had nearly collapsed from exhaustion and had decided to stop for the night. I appreciated the warmth of the flames. Talking about werewolves had me on edge. Everything out of the range of our light was pitch black.

"Arrroooo!" a howl sounded in the distance.

"Artie!" I whispered, leaping to my feet.

"I know. I heard it too." He had drawn his knife. I fumbled for my sword.

We stood there, back to back, staring into the darkness. Nothing moved.

"Maybe, it was nothing," I said hopefully. But, no sooner had the words left my lips than a great, snarling brute leapt from the night and fell, tumbling onto Artie.

I watched in horror as what appeared to be a giant wolf-man attempted to tear at Artie's throat. Artie, for his part, was doing pretty well holding it off, keeping his knife pointed at it, so it couldn't draw nearer, not unless it wanted a knife to go through its chest.

I had to do something. Artie would tire long before the wolf and, if this really was a werewolf, he would be in serious danger of turning into a monster himself.

My sword had as good a chance of hitting Artie as the wolf-man. I searched the ground wildly. The nearest thing to me was the campfire. A burning stick was half off the blaze, providing a torch. I seized it and flung it with all my might just as the wolf-man stood. It struck the creature in its back. It yelped and leapt away from Artie.

Rushing forward, I dragged Artie to the safety of the other side of the clearing while the wolf-man attempted to bat the fire from its fur by rolling in the dirt.

Artie appeared to be dazed, but at least he was still clutching his knife. If the wolf-man attacked again, I wasn't sure if I could fight it off and protect Artie at the same time.

The sound of racing footsteps attracted my attention. My opponent snorted and looked around. I took advantage of the moment to yell, "Beredan!" The wolf-man yelped as my magic bound him. I had to lean against a nearby tree to catch myself, as silver dots danced in my eyes.

"What's going on here?" a man's voice said.

Blinking the silver away, I turned in time to see the silhouettes of two figures against the firelight. One of them was bending over Artie.

"Don't touch him," I said, distracted. My magic weakened and the wolf-man broke free, vanishing into the distance.

I started after him, but I hesitated when my eyes fell on Artie.

The woman kneeling beside him straightened. She had long, blonde hair that seemed to glow against the flames. A man with dark brown hair and an extravagant, curly mustache was standing behind her.

"What happened?" he asked.

"Artie... attacked... by a... a werewolf," I said, shuddering.

"We have to get them back to the house," the woman said. She knelt next to me and said, "Come along, dear, Zachary will look after your friend. My name is Anne Stone."

"Penelope," I muttered. "Will Artie be all right?"

"We'll do the best we can," the man, Zachary, said, "but first we have to make it past the werewolves. Wolf Bay is right past those trees."

I looked to where he was pointing and was surprised to see a thin tendril of smoke drifting over the trees.

Anne took my arm and led me forward. Zachary lifted Artie in his arms and carried him.

We didn't see any more werewolves as we made the short trek to the village, but that didn't stop me from repressing a shudder. A howl pierced the night again as the trees thinned out around us and we stepped out onto cobbled stone.

"In here," Anne said, ushering me inside a squat building near the edge of the village. Zachary and Artie came in a second later.

I stood awkwardly as Artie was lowered onto a pile of cushions on the couch. I gulped as I saw the long scratch across Artie's throat.

"Will he be all right?"

Anne entered the room with several damp cloths and knelt beside Artie. "He'll live. Lucky for your friend, its not the full moon and he was only scratched. If he was bitten, he would turn into one, regardless of the moon. But since it's only a scratch when the moon in waning, we can cure him before the sun rises."

"Why do we have to cure him before the sun rises?"

"A bite affects the victim automatically, but a scratch takes longer to work its way through the body," Zachary explained. "The boy still has time."

"How do we know if he's cured?"

"Its up to him, actually," Anne said, with a sidelong look at me. "He needs something worth living for. If you could simply make him remember anything he cares about, he will have the power to remain human."

What did Artie care about? I hadn't known him long enough to know.

He groaned and his teeth began to elongate into fangs.

"Artie!" I cried.

Somehow my words had the effect of causing the fangs to shrink back into regular teeth. I looked up at Anne in surprise.

"Keep talking to him," she said. "It seems to be working."

I repositioned myself beside Artie and began to talk. I had no idea of half the things I said; I simply wanted Artie to hear my voice.

I talked for what seemed like hours. There was no other change in Artie, appearance-wise. He breathed steadily and all the while, the scratch on his neck began to heal until it was nothing more than a tiny scar.

Anne and Zachary didn't stay with me. They had gone to bed hours before. I didn't mind. I found it easier to sit with Artie without them hovering over us.

As the sun began to creep in from behind the curtains and my voice was about to give way, the scar on his throat disappeared. It was as if he had never been attacked at all.

Artie groaned and his eyes creaked open.

"Penelope?" he said. He sounded as hoarse as I was.

"I'm here, Artie," I croaked.

"Where are we?"

"You're at our house," Anne said, walking back into the room. She knelt beside him. "Hold still."

Artie looked at me and when I nodded, he did as she said and held perfectly still. Anne inspected his throat.

"Amazing," she said.

"What?" I said, anxiously.

"There's no need to worry. Your friend is completely cured. He's as likely as you or I to turn into a werewolf now."

Artie blanched. "What did I miss?"

I fell into the explanation of what had happened since the howl, my voice cracking horribly. I looked around desperately for a glass of water, but all I could see was a fireplace with a ship-in-a-bottle on top of the mantel.

It was a pretty ship, red with light brown riggings. A tiny crow's nest could be seen near the top. I was marveling at the workmanship, when without warning, the ship fell from the mantel into the fire, though nobody had visibly pushed it.

Zachary was the first one to reach the fire. He seized a pair of fire tongs and carefully pulled the bottle from its depths.

I watched anxiously, worried it was ruined, but when Zachary turned around, I could see that the bottle was unscathed.

"How is that possible?" Artie breathed.

"This is the Ruby Ship," Zachary said solemnly. "Its been passed down through my family for generations."

Artie gaped at him. I thought about telling him to close his mouth, but before I could, he said, "Surely, that's only a model. The real Ruby Ship is much grander. It's said to be as long as a dragon."

I felt a slight pang for Mag at Artie's words.

"This isn't a model," Anne said quietly.

"What is the Ruby Ship?" I interjected.

"It's a ship of legend," Zachary said. "It is said that the chosen one will look upon its surface and discover its secret."

"What secret?"

"Nobody knows. That's why it's a secret."

I reached out a hand to take it from Zachary, wanting to examine it.

"Its so tiny," I said.

"Its still the Ruby Ship," Anne said.

A gleam of blue flashed across the bottle's surface. I almost dropped the bottle in surprise.

"Careful!" Zachary said, seizing it from me.

"What was that?" I gasped.

"It is a sign," Zachary sighed warily. "The ruins are calling you."

"Ruins?" I said, wincing at the memory of Tealeaf.

"They're in the west of Alsmora," Anne said. "It's said that is where the first castle of Alsmora stood, before trolls invaded our land and destroyed it."

I remembered hearing about the first rulers of Alsmora: King Cecil and Queen Winona. Queen Rebecca's parents. They had fought valiantly against the leader of the trolls at the time, but they were overrun and killed. The castle had been burned. Only Princess Rebecca escaped.

A knock on the front door interrupted my thoughts. Anne went to answer it. She returned a moment later with two men in tow.

"Is this the girl?" the taller of the men grunted.

"Yes," the other said. He had straggly dark hair and stood slightly hunched. His clothes looked unkempt, like he had slept in them. He was massaging his wrists, which looked raw and red.

Artie looked as confused as I was.

"Young lady," the first man said. "I am Steven. Aatto here claims that you attacked him this morning."

Aatto glared at me with amber eyes.

"What are you talking-" I began.

"You used magic," Steven said. "That's an offense in Wolf Bay."

I looked at Artie in alarm. How did they know that I used magic?

"You're going to have to come with us," Steven said.

"Why?"

"I'm sorry," and he truly looked it, "but you're going to have to come with us. You're going to be tried as a witch."

Chapter Seventeen

Trial of the Witch

THE HOUSE ERUPTED INTO OUTRAGE. Artie, though still weak from his encounter with the werewolf, stood protectively in front of me.

"You can't take Penelope," he said. "She saved my life!"

"Be that as it may, Aatto here says-"

"But, I never attacked him!" I said, reaching out to steady Artie. We were both trembling. "I will admit I used magic, but it was on a werewolf!" Then it dawned on me. "You were the werewolf, weren't you?" I slowly turned to face Aatto.

He stared at me with liquid yellow eyes, but didn't speak.

"The whole village knows that he's a werewolf," Steven said. "Even so, it is a law that nobody can harm a citizen of this town without consequences." Artie made a noise of protest. "Yes, that includes werewolves," Steven added.

"That's ridiculous!" Anne said. "I've never heard a law like that!"

"It was passed quite some time ago," Steven said stiffly.

"Last week, if I remember correctly," Zachary muttered. "Good thing too, since Aatto's father is the mayor."

"What if I refuse to cooperate?" I asked, thinking fast. I had magic, albeit with some minor complications.

Steven shook his head. "It would be better if you didn't. Come quietly and we might go easy on you."

"Meaning you'll kill me quickly?" I demanded.

"Most likely," Steven said, sheepishly.

I met Artie's eye and we came to a silent agreement: we would go down fighting.

Artie drew his knife. "You'll have to go through me if you want Penelope."

"This will not do at all," Steven sighed. "Aatto, if you'll do the honors."

Before I had time to react, Aatto had knocked Artie's legs out from under him, wrenching him away from me. Artie lay sprawled on the floor. Aatto advanced slowly on me.

"Stay away from me," I threatened, drawing my sword.

"Take heart, *witch*," Aatto hissed, knocking me against the wall. My sword went flying, landing a mere inch from Artie's head. "Your death will be quick and painless."

Steven stepped forward with a strip of black rope. "I'm sorry," he said, binding my hands together. Accompanied by Aatto, he led me from the house. A dozen heavily armed soldiers met us outside, where they formed a rank around us. They had Queen Alana's symbol on their chests. More soldiers were patrolling the village. Steven stiffened slightly beside me.

My last glimpse inside was of Artie struggling to his feet. He met my eyes and then the door closed between us.

* * *

They shoved me into a damp stone jail cell. There was a bed against the corner and a tiny barred window a good foot above my head. That was it.

Steven didn't have the decency to look at me as he opened the cell door and propelled me inside, after loosening the rope binding my hands. Aatto grinned wolfishly at me before departing with a spring in his step. Steven sat behind an oaken desk on the other side of the bars.

"Let me go," I said, eyeing the door next to Steven. It opened to the outside. I could see more soldiers in the distance. In fact, we had passed more soldiers than villagers on the way from Anne's house.

"I'm sorry, but I cannot do that. You'll have to wait for Judge Matthew to return. He'll decide what to do with you."

"When will that be?" I spat.

"Tomorrow. He's out of town at the moment."

"I'm stuck here until tomorrow?" I asked, indignantly.

"I'm afraid so. Try and make yourself comfortable, while you still can," he said and left the room.

I closed my eyes, wearily. I had spent half the night fighting Aatto and the other half talking to Artie. I was exhausted.

I sat upon the bed and leaned against the hard stone of the wall. I had to come up with a plan, but first, maybe a little nap wouldn't hurt.

* * *

I woke up suddenly without any clear idea what brought forth my abrupt return to consciousness. It was dark. I touched the stone wall and my hand came away damp. Home, sweet, home.

"Psst! Penelope!"

I nearly jumped when I saw Artie staring at me through the narrow window. How had he hoisted himself up there? We were about the same height and I would have had to stand on somebody's shoulders to even see through it.

"Artie! What are you doing here?" I said, craning my neck back.

"It was our intention to rescue you, but we didn't anticipate the bars on your window."

"What about the front door?"

"The werewolf, Aatto, is guarding it."

"What can we do?" I asked.

"I don't know."

There was a muffled sound from the other side of the wall. It almost sounded like voices.

Artie's eyes grew wide and he said, "Somebody's coming. I'm sorry, Penelope, but we have to go. We'll rescue you tomorrow at the latest, I promise!"

Before I could respond, Artie had withdrawn his head and disappeared. I continued to stare at the spot where he had been long after he was gone. A single star was visible against the night sky. I hoped it was a sign and a good one at that.

* * *

I awoke in a shaft of sunlight. I uncurled from my uncomfortable position and stretched. My throat was perched and my stomach rumbled. I hadn't had anything to eat or drink since yesterday.

Steven walked in with a flask and a plate. I sat up eagerly as he shoved it through the bars.

"Thanks," I croaked, gulping down the water and starting on the bread and cheese.

"Hurry up, Judge Matthew will be here shortly," Steven said.

"He'll decide whether I'm guilty or not?"

"That's right."

"What's there to decide?" I said, washing down a bite of cheese with water. "I fully admit I used magic to save Artie and myself from Aatto."

"Nobody's denying you're a witch." Steven sighed. "If it was up to me, I would set you free in an instant, but Aatto's father Hareton is the mayor and he passed a law last week saying it was an offense to attack werewolves."

"This is so unfair," I said.

"I agree," an unfamiliar voice said.

I looked up and saw an elderly man with a hooked nose and watery eyes staring down at me.

"Greetings, I'm Judge Matthew. You must be the witch, Penelope Bogg. If the circumstances were better, I would say it's a pleasure to meet you."

I stared at him stonily. Here was the man who was supposed to try me as a witch trying to be friendly! I didn't need that kind of bigotry. If he really wanted to greet me properly, he would set me free and forget about judging me.

Judge Matthew sighed. "Believe me, Miss Bogg, this is the last thing I want to do."

"Then don't do it," I said, flatly.

"I wish it were that simple, but I have to follow the law."

"There's a law against witch burnings," I snapped. "Queen Alana passed that law several years ago. I know. I saw it."

"Really? But, the mayor keeps the town up to date on what is going on in the outside world and he insisted that witch trials were still alive and well. We heard Queen Alana even sent soldiers to various towns to ensure the trials were carried out."

I stared at Judge Matthew in disbelief. Who in their right mind would ever believe that?

Anger wouldn't get me anywhere, though, so I said as calmly as I could, "Your mayor is lying to you. You can contact Queen Alana yourself and you'll find out the truth."

"I'm afraid you're wrong." A small, bald man with bright green eyes walked into the room. "Thank you, Steven. You may go."

Steven left the room, giving me a small, sad smile on his way out. I tried not to grit my teeth in frustration.

"I am Hareton, the mayor of Wolf Bay," the man said, silkily. "And you, young lady, are in very deep trouble."

"No," I said. "You are. The Queen does not condone witch burnings."

"Ah, but I have a letter signed by Queen Alana herself, accepting the practice once more."

"I—you're lying!" I cried.

"No, I'm not," Hareton said calmly. "Judge Matthew, here is the letter in question."

Judge Matthew perused the document for several minutes, but to me it felt like several hours. My heart was thumping wildly, terrified that what Hareton said was true.

Finally Judge Matthew lifted his head and my stomach dropped immediately. He was looking at me with a pained, sympathetic expression.

"I am deeply sorry, Miss Bogg, but Hareton does not lie."

He showed me the letter and at the bottom I could see the line of script formed in a perfect rendition of Queen Alana's handwriting.

"Penelope Bogg," Judge Matthew said, startling me with his official tone. "Under the evidence of your admitting to magic use and the fact that Queen Alana has made such use a crime, I hereby denounce you as a witch. Hareton, as the mayor, you may select the sentence."

"My pleasure, Your Honor," Hareton said, his eyes blazing. "I can think of only one suitable punishment: witch burning."

* * *

They left me alone to prepare my execution. I sat on the cold floor of my cell with my arms around my knees. How could I escape? Artie had said he would attempt to rescue me, but I couldn't just sit here and do nothing.

I checked both pockets of my torn and stained dress. Nothing. I sat back, almost ready to admit defeat, when my hand brushed against the sheath around my waist.

I sat bolt upright. Aatto had disarmed me. My sword was still at Anne's house, but *nobody had bothered to remove the sheath.*

Frantically, I fumbled for the side pocket. After a moment of scrabbling at the leather, I succeeded in opening it.

There it was: the silver rose. If ever there was an emergency, I was looking at it.

Seizing the rose, I opened my mouth to cast an invisibility spell. I would wait until they opened the cell door, slip out unseen, and search for Artie. Then, we would escape this backwards town.

But, before I could utter a single syllable, the door burst open and Judge Matthew, Hareton, and Steven entered.

I hesitated for a second too long. I didn't know whether to fight back or feign innocence.

In the end, since they had already seen me, I only turned the rose invisible and feigned innocence. I would only have one chance to escape.

"Penelope Bogg, are you ready?" Judge Matthew asked, but he had stopped in his tracks and was looking at me curiously.

I had a split second of panic. Had Judge Matthew seen the rose? There was a tense moment where we stared at each other. In the end, though, he simply turned away. I breathed a sigh of relief.

Hareton hadn't noticed anything. He addressed Judge Matthew, as if I wasn't even there, "We can do this quickly, Matthew. My wife has dinner waiting and I don't want to be late."

My heart sank. Hareton was talking as if food was more important than my life.

Judge Matthew's eyes were sympathetic as he watched me sadly. "Come along, Miss Bogg," he mumbled.

Hareton opened the door of the cell and grabbed me by the wrist, yanking me outside into the fresh air. Luckily, he didn't seem to notice the rose. For a fleeting moment, I hoped he would release me, giving me a chance to escape. Instead, there were a dozen soldiers waiting. They surrounded us and led us through the town. Judge Matthew walked several paces behind us, whispering with Steven.

I was steered to the center of town. It was paved with cobblestones, with shops and houses on either side. There was a mound of firewood with a stake at its heart. Beside it sat a wooden platform with steps leading up to it.

A crowd of people was gathered. Some of them were jeering at me; others were shaking their heads in pity. I scanned the sea of faces hopefully, but I didn't see Artie anywhere. If worst came to worst, at least I had the rose. I tightened my grip on it. I felt braver.

Hareton, Aatto, and several townspeople I didn't know secured my hands to the stake. I quickly hid the rose up my sleeve, but still within easy reach.

Judge Matthew, Hareton, and Aatto mounted the platform.

"The accused is charged with the crime of witchcraft. Does she have anything she wants to say before we commence sentencing?" Judge Matthew said.

Where were Artie and the help he had promised? There were plenty of upturned faces, but no blonde-haired, blue-eyed, smiling face.

"How are you, Judge Matthew? I was sorry you couldn't visit me yesterday," I stalled.

Judge Matthew's eyes widened in surprise as the villagers began muttering amongst themselves.

"I'm er, fine. I had a slight cold the last few days."

"I'm sorry to hear that," I said, scanning the crowd once again for Artie. The rose tingled in my hand.

"Enough of this," Aatto growled. "Let's get on with the execution."

"Yes, yes, you're quite right," Judge Matthew sighed. "I'm sorry, Miss Bogg, but this conversation must end. Executioner."

I shifted on the dry logs underneath my feet. Where was Artie? He said he would be here. If he didn't show himself soon, I would have no choice but to use magic and then I might accidently injure innocent bystanders.

The executioner stepped onto the platform, a torch in his hand. His eyes were glinting. He wore a hood over his head, so I couldn't see the rest of his face, but he appeared to be about the same height as me.

"You may proceed," Judge Matthew said.

The executioner paused for a countless second before he whipped out a knife and with one slash had cut me free.

Everyone, including me, stood frozen for a moment as the would-be executioner threw back his hood to reveal blonde hair, blue eyes, and a roguish grin: Artie!

The crowd was recovering fast, surging toward us. Artie shoved my sword into my free hand, while he wielded his knife and the torch.

"Nice of you to make it," I said, sweeping my sword at my attackers to keep them at a distance.

"Sorry, we got tied up."

"We?"

A roar pierced the square. Everyone parted, revealing a very familiar friend.

"Sorry I'm late," Mag said. "What did I miss?"

Chapter Eighteen

Stuck in a Hollow

"WHO ARE YOU?" AATTO SNARLED from atop the platform. The crowd was stirring; they wouldn't remain still through shock much longer.

Mag, in her human form, turned defiantly toward Aatto. "Mag, and you are?"

Aatto made a growling noise deep in his throat and I tensed. He was staring fixedly at Mag. Before I could call out a warning, he lunged at her.

Mag yawned and stepped to the right as Aatto sailed past, completely dodging him.

"Not very friendly, are you?" Mag mused. She glanced in our direction and made little motions with her hands, which I took to mean, "Go!"

Hareton must have seen too, because he seized my upper sword arm in a vice-like grip and yelled, "Don't let them escape!"

Aatto tried to make his way back up to the platform to join his father in guarding me, but chaos had ensued. Some people were trying to follow Hareton's order and stop Mag from escaping, while others simply got in the way, tripping over feet and slamming into each other.

Artie lunged at Hareton, his knife in hand. Hareton kept one hand on my wrist as he dodged to the side, unsheathing a sword as he went. They went, knife-on-sword. Artie had to be careful not to hit me. I was sure Hareton would push me in front of him and use me as a shield, if he got the chance.

He was bearing down on Artie with his sword. I had to do something to help. I couldn't maneuver my own sword with Hareton clinging to me this tightly, but the rose.... Summoning as much magic as I could, I cried two spells, "Enchauta!" and "Beredan!"

Hareton suddenly stopped. Faster than I could blink, he was bound with ropes that sprang from the now visible rose. He dropped me and I staggered away from him, disoriented.

Artie quickly sheathed his knife and caught me one-handed before I could tumble off the platform.

I looked at the chaos below. Mag was standing amidst a crowd of injured villagers who had tried to stop her. Now they were all frozen in place from my spell. I glanced down at the rose. It was white. I waited for a tense minute until it was silver again. Still magical, but it had stayed white and normal for too long.

Mag was still moving, as were two people standing beside her. Even from this distance I could tell they were Anne and Zachary. There was no mistaking Anne's blonde hair or Zachary's mustache.

They said something to Mag and her wings sprouted from her back. She took off into the sky toward Artie and me. Anne and Zachary melted back into the crowd.

"Penelope, are you all right?" Artie cried, shaking my arm. "Pen!"

I blinked at the unexpected nickname.

Mag landed beside us. "Artie, what happened?"

"Exhaustion, I think."

"I'm fine," I murmured, my head still swimming.

Mag and Artie held a hurried conversation in which I only heard a couple of words and something passed between their hands.

"Here, eat this," Mag said, handing me the strangest looking flower I had ever seen. It was purple, but with an orange center that seemed to be oozing.

I recoiled from the sight, but Mag forced the revolting flower into my hand and instructed me once again to eat.

I shoved it in my mouth and chewed. It was tough and tasted like rubber. I swallowed with difficulty and stood there panting. A fiery pain erupted in my stomach and I doubled over. Artie and Mag were hovering anxiously beside me as I clutched my middle. Then, just as quickly as it had started; it was gone, leaving me with a feeling of well-being.

"What was that?" I asked in wonder.

"A flower that revives your strength," Mag said, her features elongating until she was in her true form. "Stronger than the last one Artie gave you. Hop on!"

Artie and I didn't wait to be told twice. Villagers were unfreezing rapidly, Hareton shouting, "Stop them!"

The sound of ropes snapping reached my ears. I turned and saw Hareton breaking free.

The villagers surged toward us, Aatto in the lead, when Mag unfurled her wings. Artie threw the torch as hard as he could at the firewood. It caught instantly and spread to the stage. Everyone with any sense leapt back, but Aatto kept up his headlong charge.

Flapping hard, Mag rose into the air with Artie and me perched precariously on her back. Aatto lunged, extending a clawed hand, which Artie slashed with his knife. Aatto snatched at his hand and gave a low whine as he fell back to earth.

Mag put on a burst of speed. Soon the village of Wolf Bay was nothing but a speck behind us.

* * *

Mag landed on the edge of the Duckweed River several hundred miles from Wolf Bay. Night was falling fast and the stars were our only source of illumination.

I turned to climb off Mag's back, but I was so tired, I stumbled over a loose scale and wouldn't fallen face first to the ground, if Artie hadn't caught and steadied me again.

"Thanks," I mumbled as Artie helped me to the ground.

"No problem," he said, reddening slightly.

"Penelope, do you have any food?" Mag asked.

Startled, I looked at her. Mag had transformed back into a human and she was gazing steadily at the water.

"Mag, how did you escape Silent Stream?" I asked.

She grinned, her tongue darted in and out for a moment, as though she was tasting the air.

"Never underestimate a dragon," she said. "When the invisibility wore off, those guards surrounded me. I brought forth my tail and batted them aside. They were persistent, though and converged upon me again. By the time I sprouted my wings and flew over the wall, Willow and the Woodland Warriors had arrived. They shot arrows at the guards, distracting them. I'm sure they're still taking about the bat-winged girl and the archer squirrels. Once I was free of Silent Stream, I followed your scent to Wolf Bay and met with Artie to plan your escape.

"Now, do you have any food or not?"

I reached for my bag, when I realized it was gone. When Aatto and Steven detained me, I had left it behind at Anne's. "My bag…"

"I have it," Artie said, holding it up. "I grabbed it when Mag was securing my disguise."

She shrugged. "I knocked out the real executioner, stole his cloak, tied him up, and hid him behind a building. He's probably just waking up now.

"But, enough of that, what about our supplies?"

I opened my bag and looked inside. There were a couple of carrots, but nothing else.

"Unless you want to eat vegetables, I'd say you're out of luck," I said.

"We going to have to forage then," Mag said, "if we're going to sail on the ship." And she produced the Ruby Ship from beneath her red cloak.

I gaped at her. "Where did you get that?"

Mag grinned. "Anne and Zachary are old friends of Aldrich."

Artie examined the ship. "Its small, it doesn't look as if it could hold our weight."

The blue flashed against the surface of the bottle again. I blinked and looked down at the water rushing beside us. And then it clicked.

"Artie, put it in the water."

He did as I asked and placed the bottle in the river. The ship floated to the narrow neck and pushed against the cork blocking its progress.

I fished the bottle out of the water and the ship resumed its usual position. I pulled on the cork, but it seemed to be sealed shut with wax.

"Allow me," Mag said, holding out her hand.

I placed it in her left palm. A claw popped out from her right index finger and she sawed through the wax around the cork. It was easy after that and Mag soon had it open.

"Here," she said, handing the cork to Artie. "Keep that safe."

"Wow, thanks Mag, I've always wanted a cork," Artie said, winking at me.

I had to look away quickly, but I couldn't hide my giggles.

"We need that cork, otherwise we wouldn't be able to seal the ship off later."

She handed the opened bottle to me and I placed it back in the water. "I can't put it in the water," she explained to my questioning look. "The magic of the ship won't work if a being of fire attempts it. The mermaids would never allow it."

"Mermaids?" I asked.

"Trust me, you don't want to meet them," Artie said. "They can be vicious when they want to be."

"You know them?" Mag asked.

"I've, uh, heard of them," he mumbled.

I spared Artie from having to answer further by placing the bottle into the river with a small splash.

We stared at the ship as it floated back to the bottle's neck. This time, it compressed itself until it was almost flat and exited the bottle. As the ship touched the water, a miniature whirlpool swirled around it, with the ship as its center.

The ship grew, extending until it towered over us and filled the whole width of the river. There was a crow's nest in the mast and a roaring dragon figurehead on the bow of the ship. It was made entirely of wood. I glanced at Mag, worried about her flickering fire-like hair.

As the whirlpool petered out, Artie approached the hull of the ship and tapped it with a fingernail. It made a resounding *thunk!* "Impressive," he said.

A gangplank detached itself from the side of the ship and came to rest at our feet. We hesitated for the space of a heartbeat, then climbed aboard, single-file, Mag in the lead, with Artie and his knife as the rear guard.

The floor creaked as I stepped on deck. Ropes and cables laid haphazardly in our way. We had to tread carefully as we inspected our surroundings.

A door near the back stuck as I tried to force my way in, but one good push and it scraped open. I stumbled on the threshold and stopped dead when I saw the skeleton in the chair before me.

I mouthed a silent scream and backed out of the room.

"Pen, did you find anything?"

There it was again, that unexpected nickname.

"Pen?"

"In here," I croaked.

Artie appeared at the door and took in the scene with the skeleton. "Whoa," he said, taking me in his arms and turning me away. Grateful, I allowed him to lead me from the room.

"Was that a real skeleton?" I asked as Artie removed his hands from my shoulders.

"I think so, but I don't know why it would be on the ship. Do you, Pen?"

I stiffened at the use of the name again.

"You don't like the name 'Pen?'" Artie asked.

"No! No, I really do like it," I said and I realized I did, when he said it. It was a nice change from Penny, or even Penelope.

Artie smiled awkwardly as we delved deeper into the ship.

"Penelope, Artie, over here!" Mag called from the helm.

We exchanged glances before heading in the direction of Mag's voice.

"What did you find?" I asked.

"This," she said, indicating a small octagon-shaped hole in the center of the helm.

"Uh, it's a nice hole," I said, hesitatingly.

Mag rolled her eyes. "Think, Penelope. What do you have that would fit in there?"

I stared at her for a second, and then it clicked. "The ruby!" I cried, before I remembered where it was and my heart sank.

"I was afraid of this," Mag said grimly, "I'm sure we can power the ship with the ruby, but it won't work until we've completed the Kaninens' mission."

"Can't we sail it ourselves?" Artie asked.

"We could, maybe, but do either of you know the first thing about ships?"

"No."

"Exactly," Mag said. "Until the ruby is returned, we're stuck."

Chapter Nineteen

Tarboone

"CAREFUL, PEN!" ARTIE GRABBED MY wrist to stop me from plummeting down a steep hill.

"Thanks," I said, staring down the embankment towards the river below. It was daybreak. We had decided last night that we would walk, since we couldn't sail. Artie and I were walking alone, with the ship back in its bottle. Mag had volunteered to fly ahead and scout the area. She had instructed me to place the bottle back into the water after we had filed back onto dry land. The ship had floated to the bottle's mouth and, after shrinking, sailed right in. Artie recorked it.

I regained my balance and we set off again. I was careful to stay away from the wet patches least I slip again.

There was nothing around for miles, just a flat, grassy plain with trees dotting the bank here and there.

Mag announced her presence through the beating of her wings. I waited until she had retracted them before looking at her. For some reason, the sight of Mag's human body with dragon wings sprouting from it gave me goose bumps.

"Did you find anything?" I asked, as way of greeting.

"Yes!" Mag said. "About a mile from the next bend in the river is a bridge. After flying over and going right, I soon found my way to a meadow and *it* was there!"

"What?"

"Elton Castle!"

"You're kidding!" Artie cried.

"No, I'm not!"

"What's Elton Castle?" I asked.

Mag and Artie stared at me in amazement.

"You've never heard of it?" Artie said, aghast. "Its only the most famous castle in all of Alsmora!"

"What is it then?"

"Elton Castle was the first castle built in Alsmora," Mag explained. "It was built by the first ruling family of our land, the Eltons: King Cecil and Queen Winona. Elton Castle is located in almost the direct center of Alsmora, so it wouldn't give its allegiance to any one section of the land.

"Everyone was happy under their rule, except for one race: the trolls. The trolls were an unruly, barbaric group, content with only pillage and murder. They preyed on innocent villagers, until one day King Cecil ordered an attack against their leader Talleck. Talleck was slain, but the new leader Kelraz, Talleck's brutal son, vowed revenge against the King and Queen."

"Now I know," I said, slapping my forehead. "King Cecil and Queen Winona were Queen Alana's great-grandparents and Queen Rebecca's parents. I don't think anyone ever mentioned the name of the castle to me before."

"Its easily mistaken for the castle Queen Rebecca founded," Mag said. "Elton became Kelton."

"What about this troll Kelraz? I know I've heard the name before. Didn't one of the trolls mention it the day they attacked you, Artie?"

"Laborc," Mag said, thoughtfully. "Legend says that he's the grandson of Kelraz, but he never inherited his grandfather's brains. He's been a bane to the dragons for years, ever since he overthrew the last king of the trolls and took the crown for himself. He keeps openly aggravating us, attacking Dragon Valley for no reason, hoping to stir us up into a war so he can take our land in our vulnerable state.

"Kelraz, though, was sneaky. He sent several trolls through a secret passageway into Elton Castle and slaughtered the King, Queen, and everyone else inside, except for the princess, Rebecca. She escaped and founded the castle her granddaughter Alana lives in now. Elton Castle, however, fell into disrepair without human habitation."

"How do you know so much about Alsmora's royalty?" Artie asked.

"Aldrich, naturally. He knew everyone back then."

"I'd love to visit it," I said wistfully.

"And you will," Mag said. "We're going there now. We just need to figure out how to cross the bridge."

* * *

We reached the bridge by midday. The river was at its widest here. It would be impossible to jump.

"There is it," Mag said, pointing to the spire of an ornate building in the distance.

"We're only a mile away?" Artie asked. "Its huge!"

I was studying the support system of the bridge. "Will it hold us?" I touched the bridge lightly. In answer, it began to wobble. It looked as if the next person to walk across its surface would find herself and himself plummeting to the water below.

I looked at Mag in alarm. "Maybe you could fly us across?"

Mag nodded and transformed. She leapt into the sky with me on her back. We had barely gone a foot over the water, however, when she reverted back to human. We plummeted painfully onto the bridge below. It rocked violently as we scrambled back to our side of the bank.

The three of us sat on the warm, springy grass, wracking our brains for an idea that didn't involve the bridge. After a quarter of an hour, we still had nothing.

"We could wade," Artie said finally, standing up.

"Wait," I said, staring at the water. Something had moved under the surface. I tossed a rock toward the movement and a giant crocodile rose from the water and snapped its giant jaws.

She was beautiful, in an I'm-going-to-eat-you sort of way. The crocodile had sparkling, green scales; a wide, gaping mouth full of sharp, white teeth; and the air of a predator who doesn't care who or what she may eat.

"Across the bridge, then," I said in a strained whisper. I placed my foot on the first wooden board. It creaked, but held. I was halfway across when the crocodile leapt into my path and a small, hunched figure clambered off her back, blocking my progress. The crocodile slid back into the water. The figure stepped forward, hidden by its cowl.

"Who goes there?" the figure hissed in a voice that was definitely not human. By the sound of it, I suspected it to be male. He waved long clawed fingers in the direction of Mag and Artie. "Friend or foe? If ye be a foe, depart now, unless you wish to feel my wrath!"

"We have no quarrel with you," Mag said. "Leave now, if you don't want to feel *my* wrath."

The figure chuckled, stepped into the light, and removed his cowl. It was all I could do to stop myself from gasping. He was a goblin: three feet tall; pale skin, the color of sour milk; long, bare fingers and toes; a pointed nose and ears; and a wild tuft of fiery red hair.

"I like your style," the goblin grinned. "Name's Tarboone. This is Little Darling."

I wet my dry lips. Tarboone seemed nice enough, but goblins were tricky. "Who's Little Darling?"

Tarboone clapped his hands and called, "Oh, Little Darling!"

The crocodile blinked lazily at me.

I turned around and quickly rejoined Artie and Mag.

"Who are you?" Tarboone asked.

"Penelope, Mag, and Artie," I said.

"Why are you here?" he continued. "There isn't anything on that side of the river."

"We came to see Elton Castle," Artie said boldly. "Mag says its right past the bridge."

Tarboone grunted, but refused to look at me. "The only one I know on that side is Hugo."

"Hugo?" I said, my mind whirling. Was there a survivor in Elton Castle? I couldn't help but notice the strange, red glint in Tarboone's eyes.

"Mag?" Tarboone said, tapping a long finger to his lips thoughtfully. "Aren't you related to Aldrich? How is he? Is he around?"

"He's fine. He's in Dragon Valley."

"Aaroo!"

"Not again," Artie murmured, drawing his knife and looking around wildly.

"That was nothing," Tarboone said quickly.

"That was not nothing," I said heatedly. I recognized the call of a werewolf. It couldn't be Aatto, though. This call sounded deeper and almost friendlier.

"Its none of your business, as long as you stay on this side of the bridge," Tarboone said, "but I'll tell you what, give me your last names and I'll put in a good word for you."

"Penelope Bogg," I said at once.

"Magma Everett."

"Arthur..."

"Yes?"

"Look," Artie said. "I can't tell you."

"Why not, Artie?" I asked gently.

He winced, as though I had yelled. "I just can't, all right," he whispered, looking away.

"Well, then, you'll just have to come back when you're ready to tell. Don't worry, we'll know when that is. Until then, you cannot pass." And without warning, he melted back into the shadows.

Little Darling darted forward and looked at us balefully, preventing our progress.

Chapter Twenty

Flight and Fire

"SINCE WE CAN'T CROSS, WE'LL HAVE to continue on to the swamp," Artie said, with a sidelong look at Little Darling, who was sunning herself on the opposite bank.

"Come on, we'd better get started," I said, shouldering my bag.

"The swamp should be due north of here," Mag said. "I can fly us there."

"I thought you couldn't fly over the bridge," I said, surprised.

Mag rolled her eyes. "We're not going over the bridge, we're going around it." She waved her hand vaguely northeast.

I decided to take her word for it, as Mag transformed and Artie and I awkwardly climbed onto her back. Before I knew it, we were soaring upward over the trees.

"Mag!" I cried, hair whipping my face.

"What? We're not that high," Mag said.

I laughed as we skimmed through the sky, scaring a couple of crows from their perches.

"Watch it!" an angry voice yelled.

I turned and saw that a crow had landed beside Artie, its feathers ruffled by the wind.

"Milo?"

The crow rolled its eyes. "Of course its me! Who else is this amazing?"

"Hello, Milo. I'm Artie. What are you doing here?"

"*I* was out scavenging, when this giant lizard cut across my flight path, forcing me to land!" Milo snapped.

"We're very sorry," I said.

"Whatever," he said. "If you're done wasting my time, I have to go and see Mad Maude. She was very insistent that I hang around this area until *you* showed up. Took you long enough. By the way, she wanted me to tell you to beware of the bog."

And with that, Milo took off toward the east.

"Strange bird," Mag said, shaking her head.

"What did he mean, 'beware of the Bogg,'" I said, nervously. Surely he wasn't referring to me.

"How could he possibly know your last name?" Artie said, kindly.

I didn't say anything; I had no answer. We continued on in silence. Then, Mag wobbled suddenly in midair.

"Mag-" I began, slowly.

Mag ignored me as she raced toward the earth. It wasn't until we were ten feet from the ground that she changed back to human. We fell and hit the ground with a thump.

"Artie? Mag? Are you all right?" I groaned as I examined our surroundings. It appeared to be a glade surrounded by trees.

"I think so. Stupid wards, preventing me from entering as a dragon. They're up everywhere, nowadays," Mag said, flexing her arms, as if they were her wings. "I guess we know what Milo meant when he said to beware the bog. We're in the Blue Rose Swamp."

"What about you, Artie? Artie?"

Artie remained silent. I turned to where he had landed.

He was doubled over as if he was in pain. Before I could react, he straightened, eyes strangely bright.

But these weren't the blue eyes I was accustomed to. They were now amber, like Mag's, reflecting the light within the swamp.

"Artie?" I said, tentatively.

He seemingly ignored me. Instead, he faced Mag, amber eyes glowing. "You, young dragon." I shivered. The voice that came from Artie's mouth was deep, ancient, and powerful. This sounded nothing like my friend.

"You have much to answer for," the deep voice continued. Artie raised his finger and pointed out into the swamp. "There is always a way to stop dragon fire, if only you are creative enough to use it."

He turned those amber eyes on me. "Witch, you are not alone. Remember, there are others who struggle as you do. You might find the power of the storm is within you."

Artie's eyes flickered to blue, before reverting back to amber.

The deep voice grunted. "My time with this body grows short. Witch, dragon, when I leave this host, kindly inform him that only he may retrieve the sapphire beyond the flames. Only then will you be able to find me."

"Wait! What do you mean?" I said, hurriedly. "Who are you? Where are you? Why did you possess Artie?"

Whatever was controlling Artie smiled and said, "Peace, all will be answered in time. Safe travels, young ones," before Artie slumped forward.

Mag caught him easily and placed him carefully on the ground. When he awoke seconds later, he blinked his blue eyes in a bemused way.

"Penelope?" he said in his own voice, shaking his head as if to rid his ear of water. "What happened?"

"You were possessed," I said, placing my hand on his forehead. "You're feverish."

"I'm fine," Artie said too quickly.

Mag snorted. "No, you're not. You're shaking like a leaf."

"So, what do we do now?" he asked loudly, clearly trying to change the topic.

I stared suspiciously at him before answering. "You—the voice, whatever—told us to stop some dragon fire."

"There's dragon fire in this swamp?"

"Yes, and its my fault," Mag said. "Venn and I found this place during our rebellious stage."

"Dragons have a rebellious phase?" I asked.

Mag gave a short bark of laughter. "You'd be surprised. Dragons tend to go through it when we learn how to breathe fire. With the new ability, we think we can do anything. While that may be true, at that stage, it can be dangerous."

"How so?" I said, grinning. "You said it, dragons can do anything."

Mag shook her head. "Fire at that age can be... problematic for a young dragon. We don't have much control. It just happens."

She pointed across the glade. "Do you see that light in the distance?"

Artie and I leaned in to see, and I did indeed see a faint glow.

"What is it?"

"Dragon fire," Mag said. "When Venn and I came here before, our fire got out of hand. We were playing a game, trying to see how far we could breathe fire. In the process, one of the spurts of flame hit a tree and started a wildfire. In our panic, instead of stopping it, we doused the area with air from our wings, giving the fire more oxygen to consume. Its been burning ever since. I'm guessing that's how this place became known as Everburn Swamp."

"Can we stop it?" I asked.

"According to the voice, it can be done," Mag said doubtfully. "But, you see, the problem is that its been burning for seven years. I don't know how to stop it. Dragon fire is one of the most destructive forces in all of Alsmora. It might be that the fire is now part of the swamp."

"We could try," Artie said. "I'm sure, working together, we could stop it."

"I'm supposed to stop it," Mag said. "You, Artie, are supposed to retrieve some kind of sapphire past the flames, while Penelope is meant to use storm powers."

I watched curiously as Artie's face fell. Clearly, the news upset him.

"We could spend the night here," I suggested. "Get a fresh start in the morning."

"No," Artie said. "We should do it now. The sooner we do it, the better."

"How do you stop dragon fire?" I asked Mag.

Mag pierced Artie with a glistening amber eye. "Whatever controlled you, Artie, said that there is always a way to stop dragon fire, as long as I am creative enough."

"Don't look at me," he said, defensively. "The voice just spoke through me. I don't have any knowledge of breathing fire."

"Artie! That's it!" I said.

"What?" Mag asked, shifting her gaze to me.

"You have to breathe fire, Mag."

"I thought the point was to reduce the flames."

I grinned. "Oh, it is. Have you ever heard of back fire?"

"Never heard of it," Artie said. Mag had, however. Her eyes grew wide at my suggestion.

"That's impossible, Penelope. Even if I were to try, it could cause a bigger mess than the first."

"Back fire is when you purposely start a fire to burn out another," I said, because Artie was looking at me, confused. "Fire needs oxygen, and with both sets of flames competing for the needed fuel, the air will peter out, causing both to dwindle to nothing."

"It's a good plan," Mag said, grudgingly. "But, the problem is, I don't know if I can control the back fire. I didn't do too well the first time."

"You were younger, though," Artie reasoned. "You've gained more experience since then."

Mag stalked to the opposite side of the glade, her shoulders hunched. I watched as she popped out a talon and used it to scratch a series of lines upon the stump of a dead and rotting tree.

She continued in this manner for over ten minutes, brushing wood shavings out of her way when needed. I contented myself with meditating on the ground, gazing out into the swamp, while Artie paced back and forth.

Mag abandoned her dead stump. "Very well," she said. "I've studied the problem from every possible angle and I think I can control it."

"Can you start now?"

"Now is as good a time as any," she said. "This is a peat bog. It has an oily substance that can keep a fire going, especially one as long lasting as dragon fire. It was the dry season when Venn and I started the fire. The water level was low and the oil was exposed. It spread quickly and has been burning ever since.

"But, there are conditions for my doing this."

"Such as?"

"First, you two will ride on my back while I manage the fire."

"I can deal with that," Artie said.

"Second, if the fire gets out of hand, I will fly us out of here with no arguments from you two, deal?"

Artie and I were shocked into silence.

I unstuck my tongue. "Why?"

"Because," Mag said, "I won't have you in the way, where I could accidently burn either of you. You humans are so much more fragile than I am and I'm not taking any chances. Do we have a deal?"

I didn't like it, and by the look on Artie's face, he didn't either, but since we knew this was the best offer we would get, I said, "Deal."

"On my back, please."

Mag transformed and Artie and I clambered on. She slowly rose into the sky and angled upward until she was hundreds of feet above the swamp. Maneuvering past the trees, Mag turned in midair and sloped toward the burning section of the bog.

As we swooped over the fire, I spotted what I thought to be a path. But, then Mag swerved and it was lost to the inferno.

Hovering above the blaze, Mag sent a tiny fireball spitting from her mouth, splattering onto the merrily dancing flames below.

"That was just a test," she explained. "Don't want to overdo it."

She twisted slightly so she gained a new position on her target and inhaled. I could feel her vibrating beneath me as she prepared to launch a new attack. Exhaling, Mag sprayed the area with a new round of fire.

Shooting downward, Mag circled the fire, spiraling to safety as she flew too close to a column of flames.

"Mag! What are you doing?" I yelled over the sound of beating wings, as she skimmed the top of the swamp, releasing a torrent of fire over the original conflagration, as she went.

"My job!" Mag said, soaring upward. Flames erupted from her jaws, as she flooded the area with white-hot power.

As I watched, the two fires met. At first, it combined and devoured whatever it touched. But then, the flames began to work against each other, each fighting for the dominance to burn.

Artie and I began to cough violently as smoke engulfed us.

Mag shot even higher into the sky and broke free of the suffocating cloud.

"What happened?" Artie asked through coughs.

"Sorry," Mag said. "Back fires can cause smoke."

"I can't see anything. Did it work?" I asked, craning my neck to see beyond the constricting haze.

Mag, whose eyesight was sharper, said, "Yes, the fire appears smaller." She lowered herself gently, so we could see too.

"Wow!" Artie said.

"Wow," I agreed. Mag's back fire fought with the original fire, until both blazes were no more.

Mag breathed a sigh of relief. "It's done."

I gazed into the now fire-free swamp. "That's it? After so long, no more fire."

"Yes," Mag said, sounding slightly dazed. "It's completely gone."

"That's great," Artie said, glancing around furtively. "Now, how about we go get that sapphire before the mysterious voice steals my body again?"

Mag alighted upon a patch of dry ground. "Any idea where this sapphire might be?"

I indicated the path. "If I had to guess, I would say that it's that way."

Mag inspected the trail. "Its much too narrow for a dragon, but not for a human."

"Artie and I will go retrieve the sapphire, right Artie?"

Artie was off to the side, looking slightly green. His head jerked up when I said his name. "O-of course, Penelope."

"If you two are set on going," Mag said, "I'll fly above the swamp and see what I can find from the air. I'll meet you on the other side of the path. If I can't find you, I'll return here in one hour."

We separated. Artie and I down the path to search for the sapphire, while Mag returned to the sky, glittering like a ruby in the fading light.

Chapter Twenty-One

The Sapphire Beyond the Flames

W E CREPT DOWN THE TRAIL, PAST blackened trees with the lingering and foul stench of fire. Heat still sizzled off some trunks.

The darkness was oppressive, even though we hadn't gone more than ten feet. The fire-damaged trees seemed to make our little path darker than ever. Artie and I walked closer to each other than we would normally. Neither one of us complained.

"Artie?" I said, as we felt our way through the almost total darkness. "We have to talk."

He stiffened. "About what?"

"Who *are* you, Artie? We've been traveling together for so long, but I know almost nothing about you. You haven't even told me your last name."

We walked in silence for a time, before he said, "I'm scared, Penelope."

"That's nothing to be ashamed of. Everyone gets frightened at times."

"No, it's not that. I'm afraid that I'll lose you if I tell you who I am."

"*Lose* me?"

"As a friend," he said, hurriedly. "I don't want to lose you as a friend."

We walked further through the darkness, before I said gently, "Artie, you still haven't told me."

"Promise that we'll still be friends, no matter what," he said, his eyes shining.

I studied his guarded, determined expression, before saying, "I promise that no matter what you tell me, it will not change the way I think of you."

Artie took a deep breath. "All right, I'm a th-"

His words were interrupted by Mag's roar.

Abandoning the conversation, we sprinted through the underbrush as fast as we could. Before we could slow ourselves, Artie and I had dashed through an opening in the trees.

* * *

Blinking and stumbling in the dim light, it took me a moment to register its gloomy appearance. We were still in the swamp, but in a much darker section.

Off to one side was another path, but in front of us, lay nothing but a rounded clearing with a fringe of trees. The ground was firm, so there was no possibly of sinking, but I could swear that there was water flowing beneath us. At one end, there appeared to be a stretch of water, with a bunch of brown rocks covered with moss, shifting with the current. Above us, I could see Mag circling, nothing more than a flash of ruby light.

"Pen!" Artie said, jolting me to my senses. "Look!"

I had been concentrating so hard on my surroundings that I hadn't noticed the figure in the center of the glade. It appeared to be nothing more than a rabbit. The Kaninen.

"Hello?" I said, cautiously, walking up to it.

The rabbit turned and I saw that it had ice blue fur. Definitely the Kaninen.

"Hello," he said in a squeaky voice. "I'm Frost. Who are you?"

"Penelope Bogg and Artie. Our friend Mag is the circling dragon. We've come to get you out of here."

"Aneurin is guarding me. I can't leave, or else he'll instantly know and attack. Did you say there's a dragon here?" His eyes narrowed.

"We've been sent by Blizzard to save you," I said hurriedly. "Even Mag. But who is this Aneurin?" I asked, frustrated once again at my lack of knowledge of the outside world.

Artie, however, turned pale. "A-Aneurin No, he's just a legend, isn't he?"

"Oh, no, he's all too real," Frost said, his nose twitching.

I shook my head. "All right, Artie, I'll bite. Who is this Aneurin?"

"A sea serpent of legend. It is said that his hide is so thick, no ordinary weapon can scratch him."

"Aneurin is nearby," Frost said. "His hide is made of iron. He's as fast as a leopard on both land and water. His teeth are made of steel and his tail is like a whip."

I shivered. "Where is he now?"

The gentle lap of rippling water attracted my attention, causing me to spin around.

"There's your answer," Frost whimpered.

The water parted to reveal a long, snake-like, acid green and brown body that was rising slowly out of the murky depths. Thirty feet of the coils appeared, ending with a long, tapered tail, before the head began to rise. I stood frozen to the spot in fear as the green head with an orange frill and huge monstrous black eyes turned to gaze directly at me.

"Be careful," Frost warned. "Aneurin may be small, but he's still deadly."

"Small?" Artie said. "He's over thirty feet! What do you call large?"

"Some sea serpents are rumored to be at least a hundred feet long."

"Point taken."

"Shh!" I hissed. "How good is Aneurin's eyesight?"

"Dreadful," Frost said. "He goes by smell, still making escape impossible."

I didn't dare take my eyes off Aneurin, who was weaving his head to and fro, trying to catch our scent.

"Weaknesses?" I asked.

"Only one: fire."

"He's in the water."

"Dragon fire," Frost corrected himself. "Maybe fire caused by lightning. I'm sorry, but that is all I know."

The giant head swung toward the sound of Frost's voice and began to sway before us, fanning his frill to appear more menacing.

I thought of my dismal magic. No way did I want to risk the rose again, not after all the magic I had used in Wolf Bay. I can do this, I thought, clenching my fists. "Artie, we've got to hit him with everything we've got."

Artie drew his knife. "I'm with you."

At the sound of our voices, Aneurin turned hissing to face us. He jabbed his head forward to strike. Artie and I dodged, but Frost stayed put, apparently too petrified to move.

Aneurin was too fast. I would never get to Frost in time. It was Mag who created a diversion. She had been circling above us while we talked to the young ice rabbit. Now, she dived and breathed fire at Aneurin's head, pushing him to the ground and missing Frost by inches.

"Bechulen!" I cried, throwing myself in front of Frost. A barrier sprang up around us.

Aneurin picked himself up and struck again, this time his head colliding with my shield. I shook as I poured more magic into my defenses. It became a battle of wills between Aneurin and myself, his raw, physical strength versus my magical core.

My arms were shaking from the effort of holding him at bay. Aneurin's head was slowly inching its way through the barrier. I was reduced to my knees, struggling to force more energy into the spell. But, there was no more magic. I had used it all in maintaining the shield. Everything was silver.

Light-headed, I severed the connection and collapsed, but not before I forced the last of my strength into a magical blast, sending Aneurin reeling back in aftershock.

"Penelope!" Artie cried, rushing to catch me and lowering me gently to the ground.

Groaning, I focused on Artie.

"The flower," he said.

"What?"

"The flower Mag gave you in Wolf Bay, the one with the oozing orange center, I have one in my bag. It'll revive your strength."

Artie reached into his bag and retrieved the small, purple flower.

After I had consumed it and was doubled over in pain again, I looked over his shoulder and gasped, "Artie!"

He spun around, throwing his arms wide, in an attempt to screen me as a recovered Aneurin stabbed his head in our direction. I closed my eyes, expecting Aneurin's fangs to pierce my skin any moment, but nothing happened. I opened my eyes and watched in amazement as Mag pushed Aneurin back with only the strength of her fire.

"Enchauta!" I tried, but I was still weak and I knew it was nothing more than an irritation to Aneurin.

"That won't work," Frost groaned. "He's too powerful."

"Then what can we do?" I said. The flower had recovered enough of my strength for me to stand.

"His job is to protect the mystical sapphire. Legend says that if you manage to steal it, Aneurin will obey you, at least for a little while."

"Where is this sapphire?"

"Down that pathway," Frost said, nodding toward the side path I had spotted earlier. "Go! While you still can!"

"Hurry!" Mag called from above, swooping and clawing at Aneurin's tough hide. "Both of you, get the sapphire!"

"What? No!" Artie said, his eyes wild. "I can't!" he switched his knife to his left hand. "I'm not leaving you."

"Artie, come on! You're the only one who can retrieve it now!"

I seized his hand and pulled him toward the side path. The battle between Mag and Aneurin was hidden as we disappeared amongst the trees.

* * *

We hurried down the path. The sounds of battle still rang in my ears. I felt shaky after my use of magic and guilty for leaving Mag to deal with that monster, but she was right. Artie and I had to retrieve the sapphire, before it was too late.

Engrossed as I was in my subdued thoughts, I pushed aside a hanging branch and almost stepped into the swamp. Wobbling to keep my balance, Artie caught my hand as I swung my arms in a wild circle, pulling me to safety.

Panting, I was careful not to lose my footing again in this treacherous terrain. One false step and we could wind up trapped in a mire of quicksand.

As we rounded the corner, I stopped dead in my tracks. We were in a clearing, exactly like the one in which the battle raged on, except for a curious carving in the middle.

We set to work, exploring the clearing, searching under every rock and behind every tree. Nothing.

Slumping against a tree, we reviewed our options. We agreed that the sapphire wasn't there, but where else could we look?

"Arthur!"

I saw Artie wince at the use of his full name, but he dutifully turned his head at the sound of the voice.

A ghostly white dragon floated before us. I shut my eyes and told myself that I must be experiencing a hallucination.

"This is no trick," the dragon said, seemingly reading my mind. It was the same voice that had possessed Artie. I opened my eyes and saw that the dragon was inches from my face. I tried to place my hand on the dragon's cool scales, but my hand passed effortlessly through. Artie, meanwhile, stood rooted to the spot, as if he were terrified to move.

"I am not actually here," the dragon said calmly, "but else-where."

"Where?" Artie said, his voice a dull croak.

The dragon lifted his head and gazed off into the distance, through liquid gold eyes. "You must find the sapphire," he said. "Only then can you and your friends board the west wind and locate my island paradise."

"Um, right," I said. "Back up to the sapphire. Where is it?"

"It is hidden here," the dragon gave a wry smile. "You are an expert in your craft, are you not, Arthur?"

"Unfortunately."

"Well, if you were Aneurin and knew someone skilled in your art were here, where would you hide a sapphire?"

I gazed around the clearing, but could see nothing extraordinary. It was just dirt, trees, and rocks.

The dragon floated patiently beside us. "What is there is not always what is seen."

And then it clicked. The carving in the center of the clearing!

Artie and I ran to it, the ghostly dragon right behind us. It was a stone carving of a dragon holding a rose in one front claw and a sword in the other.

"Peace," the dragon said, pointing with a front claw toward the rose. "War," he indicated the sword.

"Different sides of the same coin. You cannot have peace without war, because without it, you will never know what you had lost. The choice is yours, Arthur. Will you fight for peace, or for war?"

I saw what the dragon meant. In the middle of the rose stood a blue stone the size of a fist, the same for the hilt of the sword.

"There are two?" Artie said.

"No. They are mirror images of each other. What you do to one will affect the other. Do you understand?"

"I—I think so. If I take the one of peace, then that's what I fight for, while if I take the one of war, I'll be fighting for battle and destruction."

"Yes and no. You'll always be fighting for peace. But, remember Arthur, when you have the power to change others' lives, act with dignity. Do not cause destruction merely for destruction's sake."

"I understand." Artie said quietly as he turned to face the carving. "I choose to fight for peace." And he plucked the sapphire from the rose's center. The sapphire from the sword vanished into thin air.

"Aaahh!"

"Mag! Frost!" I cried, turning to the ghostly dragon. "Thanks for all your help, but we've got to go and help our friends!"

The dragon bowed. "Very well. I will leave you with these parting words: how you were born and what you will become is not set in stone. I know of the argument you had with your father.

People can change, Arthur. Remember that the next time you set eyes on Aneurin.

"As for you, Penelope Bogg, I would suggest sailing with the blue, rather than the red."

"What do you mean?"

But Artie interrupted me, calling, "Thank you!" as he grabbed my hand and we ran back up the trail.

Back in the clearing, I could still hear the dragon's echoing voice. "So, it has started. I will see you again soon, Penelope, Magma, and Arthur, but not until the Rose, the Knife, and the Ruby all converge on the West Wind."

I looked over my shoulder. With a twinkle, the ghostly dragon vanished back from whence he came.

* * *

I decided that I didn't like battling Aneurin. My powers were only at half-strength and his hide was as tough as steel, so I couldn't even use my sword. Artie and I rushed into the clearing as Mag bathed Aneurin in fire. While she distracted him, Frost was biting at a rope tied around his leg that I hadn't noticed before.

"You're back," he said. "Quick, get me out of this. It's suppressing my powers."

One slash from Artie's knife and Frost was free. Or... not quite. The knife had flashed across the rope, but it hadn't actually cut it.

Frost grimaced and began chewing the rope again. "Go, help your dragon."

"Pen," Artie said, grabbing my arm. "There's a spell, 'Funner.' When in need, it'll help. I'll stay here and help Frost."

I nodded and rushed forward. "Enchauta!" I yelled, aiming for Aneurin, but he barely winced.

"That won't work," Frost reminded me. "You need fire."

"Working on it," I said, dodging the tail as it swept over our heads.

The problem was that I didn't know any fire spells. That left only one solution.

"Mag! Fire!"

Mag swooped forward and sent a stream of liquid heat that I could feel, even on the ground.

Her jaws snapped shut, extinguishing the flames.

Aneurin recoiled in pain, but shook it off and roared.

"Penelope! Do something!" Mag cried.

Her words were cut short when Aneurin launched himself from the water and struck her with his bulbous head.

Mag crashed inches from Artie. She struggled to her feet, sinking her front claws into a tree, to steady herself.

"Penelope, I can't do this on my own. I need help."

I released a breath I didn't even know I was holding. "Right, let's go."

I mounted Mag, who soared into the air, banking to the left to get a clear view of Aneurin.

"Do you know what you're doing?" Mag called over the rushing wind.

"No!"

"Wonderful," she muttered, flapping her wings—one seemed to be bent at an awkward angle—and gained altitude rapidly, while I held on for dear life.

Once we had attained the proper altitude, Mag snapped her wings open and glided jerkily on a thermal until she reached a suitable angle.

"Hang on!" she warned and folded her wings into a dive. I only managed to keep from falling.

Aneurin twisted his head toward the descending Mag. He opened his mouth wide as if to swallow us whole, when Mag's jaws widened and a great expanse of flames issued from her mouth. But it wasn't enough.

He was too strong to go down against just Mag. But it wasn't just Mag. I took a deep breath and cried, "Funner!"

A stream of silver fire burst forth from the rose and engulfed the sea serpent. With two jets of fire against him, Aneurin was forced to the ground. He vanished beneath the water. Thank you, Artie's sister, for teaching him those spells.

We ended our assault and Mag landed beside Artie and Frost. I slipped to the ground and stood there, panting.

As Mag transformed back to human, I watched in dismay as the rose flashed white and then back to silver. It had been necessary against Aneurin, but I had to be more careful with the rose's magic. I couldn't afford for it to become normal.

"That was incredible!" Artie said, glancing between Mag and me.

I was about to praise Mag as well, when a movement in the corner of my eye caught my attention. Quick as a flash, I turned, ready for action, as Aneurin rose unsteadily from the water with a tremendous splash, swaying his head drunkenly.

Before anyone could say or do anything, Aneurin spoke in a deep, rasping voice, "You have removed the stone from the rose, have you not?"

Mag looked questioningly at us as Artie said, "Yes, I chose to take from the rose and not the sword."

Aneurin dipped his head. "You were wise to do so, for if you had taken from the sword, I would be bound to fight you once again." He grinned, his fangs gleaming.

"But, since you defeated me and bear the stone from the rose, it is my duty to allow you from the swamp, without additional harm. But, next time, stone or no stone, we will do battle once more. Until then, farewell."

Aneurin's head slid beneath the water with hardly a ripple to distort its smooth surface.

"You defeated Aneurin. You saved my life," Frost said in awe.

"Don't mention it," I said. "Now let's see about getting you out of that rope." I bent to examine it, but gasped in surprise when I touched it. It felt as hard as stone.

"Its strong," Frost said miserably. "Whoever captured me knew what they were doing. Neither my ice powers nor normal weapons can break through."

"Here, let me try," Mag said. She eyed the rope carefully, flicked it with a claw, and then shot a tiny flame at the rope. It sizzled and snapped instantly. "There, easy," Mag said smugly.

Frost wriggled his leg and blew ice into the air. "Yes! Thank you, dragon... Mag."

"Frost," I said. "We have to find two more Kaninens. Do you know where they are?"

"I think," he said, hesitating. "I think I heard that one was taken to a waterfall."

He turned to go. "Oh, I almost forgot. I have a message for you from the Riddle Chipmunks. They showed up in the swamp right before you arrived, but couldn't help me against Aneurin.

"Here it is:

"'Amid the land of green and changing rocks,
Travel there against the clock.
Traverse the tunnels dark if you dare
To retrieve the star and the hare."

"I'm sorry, but that's all I know. Good luck," Frost said, leaping up and creating a glittering, blue circle of ice around himself. Once the circle was complete, he instantly disappeared, leaving us with yet another puzzle to solve.

Chapter Twenty-Two

Tea for Three

O NCE WE HAD CLEARED THE SWAMP, Mag, Artie, and I decided to head west.

"The closest waterfall I know is in the west," Artie said, as we walked. After Mag's extended time flying, stopping wildfires, and battling sea serpents, she was too tired to transform back into a dragon.

"It's the best lead we have," I said. "Frost's words make as much sense as the ghostly dragon's."

We told Mag all about the cravings and the ghostly white dragon.

"Sounds like something one of my kind would do," she snorted. "I wonder who he is. I don't think I know him and I know most dragons in Dragon Valley."

"According to the dragon, he wasn't here, but somewhere else. We're supposed to see him again, after the Rose, Ruby, and Knife, or something like that, meet," I said.

Artie was reciting the words quietly to himself. "'Traverse the tunnels dark if you dare to retrieve the star and the hare.' I wonder if they're talking about..."

"What?" I asked.

"The hare has to refer to the Kaninen. As for the star..." he trailed off, avoiding my eye. "Never mind. Its nothing."

"Where are these 'tunnels dark?'" Mag said, clearly not listening to Artie.

"We'll just have to keep an eye out for it, won't we?" I said.

We lapsed into thoughtful silence as the trees thinned around us and a mountain loomed in the distance. The swampland had all but vanished, to be replaced by rocks, which turned into larger rocks.

We started up the mountain path, stumbling over loose stones as we went. There was a flash of blue and to our astonishment an ice rabbit scampered by. It stopped ten feet away, nose twitching in the air. There was a rope like Frost's attached to its leg. Had it escape from its captor? This was too good to be true.

We froze, staring at the Kaninen. Mag shifted slightly and the Kaninen snapped its head up to look at us, before it took off running. As we chased it to the top, it began to snow.

It didn't take long for the snow to camouflage the Kaninen. We stumbled as the snowdrifts built higher. We couldn't see where we were going. The Kaninen had disappeared. There was a nearby alcove in the side of the mountain. We fell over each other to get inside. Mag quickly started a fire.

"Artie, next time you see you sister, thank her for the fire spell," I said. "It really helped us out against Aneurin."

"No problem," he said, but I could see his hands twisting themselves in his lap.

"Who is your sister?" Mag asked. "I don't think you ever told us about her."

"Oh! Well, she's eighteen and a witch. What more is there to tell?"

"What's her name?" I said slowly.

Artie seemed to turn rather deaf at this point.

I glanced at Mag in exasperation and my heart almost stopped. Mag was cradling her left arm and it was green.

"Mag?" I said, swallowing hard. "What happened to your arm?"

She looked down at it herself and tried to conceal it. "Nothing," she said, hurriedly.

"This is nothing?" I said shrilly, seizing her arm and pulling it into the light.

"Aneurin's tail whipped up and struck my wing. I think there was poison on it."

"Why didn't you tell us sooner?" I rummaged through my bag in the hopes that there would be something in there that would help.

"There's only one thing that can heal her," Artie said grimly. "A potion of holly, bitterbrush, and the gemser plant."

"Do you have them?" I asked wildly.

"No, but holly and bitterbrush aren't that hard to get. The gemser plant, on the other hand, only grows in the west."

"Where in the west?" I said. "We'll go there straightaway."

"In this snow?" Mag laughed. "No, this wound won't kill me. It will hurt and I won't be able to fly for a while, but I'll be all right."

"But-"

"Drop it, Penelope," Mag warned.

I closed my mouth, but I vowed to myself that I would heal Mag's wing, if it was the last thing I did.

* * *

Since we couldn't see anything past the snow, we decided to take shifts, so nobody could sneak up on us. Maybe the Kaninen would hop by.

Artie took the first watch. I curled up to sleep by the warmth of the fire. A few hours later, I awoke and joined Artie at the entrance of the cave.

"You can go to sleep," I whispered. "I'll take over from here."

Artie nodded, but he didn't move.

We sat in silence for several minutes, until he said, "Pen?"

"Hmm?"

"I've been thinking: I think I know someone who can help us search for the Kaninens."

"Who?"

"A man named Cyrus Foster. He lives in a nearby village called Purple Falls."

Who are you, Artie? I wondered yet again. Out loud, I said, "Are you sure this Cyrus Foster could help us?"

"He's had business dealings with my father. I've always known him to be honest." Artie twitched his lips into a smile. "Plus, Purple Falls is worth a visit."

"Why?"

"Pen, Purple Falls is situated near a waterfall. We're not that far away. The Kaninen…"

I groaned. "You think it fell down the waterfall, don't you?"

"It's a theory," he said sheepishly.

Artie fell asleep while I stared out at the snow. It was entirely possible that Artie's theory was correct. The Kaninen we had seen had to be disoriented, having just escaped from its captor. It could be in pain, stumbling around in the snow. We had to find it, quick. The fire was burning low by the time Mag awoke.

Stretching, she blinked in a bemused fashion as she became reacquainted with her surroundings.

"Good morning," I said, absently.

"Its morning?" Mag said, her shoulders tightening. "Why didn't you wake me for my shift?"

"Relax, Mag, there's still several hours before daybreak."

She was examining her arm again. In the failing light, it looked as if the green was spreading. I felt sick to look at it.

"How is it?" I asked.

She dropped her arm. "Its fine, Penelope."

Artie rolled over, yawning. He got up and went to the cave entrance. "I think the weather's died down a bit," he said.

I joined him at the entrance. "You're right. Perhaps we should leave now. It might be the only chance we'll get before the snow picks up again."

We put out the fire and hurried outside and up the mountain. We slipped a couple of times, but as the night wore on into morning, the snow stopped and it was easier to find our footing. The snow sparkled in the sun as it crunched under our feet.

We reached the crest of the mountain by midday. A waterfall was to our left and a village was in front of us.

"Purple Falls," Artie said, starting toward the entrance. "Come on."

This particular village was backed by trees on three sides and a cliff face on the other, making it almost impossible for the inhabitants to be disturbed. Huge logs were placed around the outside border of the village. They were vertical, sharpened to points at the top, and arranged so they were pressed together. I didn't see any gaps. Nobody would be able to break in, or out.

"Why are we here, Artie?" Mag asked, not having been awake at the time.

"There's a merchant family here that could help us. I believe they might know where the Kaninen is, and maybe even where to find the gemser plant with all the goods that pass through their hands."

As we drew up to the gate, a guard appeared. "Halt!" he said. He was clad in the simple clothes of a local villager. He gazed at us suspiciously. "What be your business here?"

"We're searching for our uncle. You see, our father is very sick and requires his brother's care," the words flowed so easily from

Artie's mouth that I almost believed it myself. I found myself nodding along.

The man hesitated. "What is his name?"

"Foster. Cyrus Foster."

The man stared at Artie as though he were from another world. He cleared his throat and said in a shaking voice, "Cyrus Foster died a year ago. He was trapped in a burning building."

Artie looked genuinely shocked. "H-he died? I had no idea. My father isn't going to be pleased. He and his brother weren't close, but my dad was hoping to patch up their differences before... before its too late."

The man wiped a tear from his eye. "I didn't know Cyrus had a brother. I'll give you directions to his widow's house. Ever since he passed, Mira and her daughter have been lonely. It will do them good to see you."

Artie thanked the man and the three of us hurried into the village without actually running.

I leaned in close. "That was impressive."

Artie gave a dry smile. "I learned from my dad. He is the master."

We walked through the town, trying to appear miserable at the fact that our supposed uncle was dead.

We passed several houses, but the people inside simply stared out with wide eyes and closed their doors with a snap.

Speeding up, we reached our destination in the farthest corner from the gate, where there was a modest two-story house. There was a birch tree standing beside the house's right side.

We knocked on the door and waited patiently. A few moments later, a short woman with long black hair pulled back in a bun and frightened, liquid-looking gray eyes timidly opened the door and gazed out at us.

"Yes?" she said in a hushed voice.

"Mrs. Mira Foster?" Artie asked.

"Yes?" she repeated. "Who are you?"

"This is Penelope Bogg, Mag Everett, and I'm Arthur..." Artie teetered for a moment and I thought he was on the verge of saying his full name. "But, call me Artie," he finished lamely. "I'm from the crossway point between here and Yellowbird, where your husband used to send supplies down the river."

Recognition dawned in Mrs. Foster's eyes. "I see," she said slowly. "If that's the case, please, come in."

Artie and I stepped over the threshold and into the entry hall of the small house. Mag hesitated and said, "You two go on. There's something I want to check." She disappeared around the house.

"Please, sit," Mrs. Foster said, shutting the door and leading us into a sitting room with a window overlooking a pleasant garden. We sat on a couple of spindly chairs facing our hostess. "Tea?" she asked.

"Yes, please," I said.

Mrs. Foster nodded and went to start a pot. While the water for the tea was simmering, she returned and sat on the edge of her seat.

"May I ask why you are here?" she said, shifting her gaze between the two of us, as if unsure of whom to address. "I'm afraid nobody in this village is accustomed to outsiders. My late husband was the only one who associated with strangers. We've become distrustful through our isolation, but I'll do what I can to help."

"We came looking for answers," Artie said. "I remembered your husband once sent supplies through my home and we were hoping he or someone else here could tell us whether you had ever seen the gemser plant or a Kaninen before."

"Also," I said, "we have this riddle. We were hoping you might have the answer." I recited the riddle Frost had given us.

Mrs. Foster seemed to consider the two requests. She rose and went to stand beside the window. There was a young girl playing on the other side of the glass.

"My daughter Julia," she said softly. She turned to Artie. "You know I have the utmost respect for your father and what he and my husband were trying to do for the families of the Turtleshell Mountains, but I just don't know." She took a shaky breath.

"It's been a full year since Cyrus died. The shipping company has suffered. Tell me, Artie, why should I get involved, after all the pain the loss of my husband and business have caused to both Julia and myself? Answer me that."

"Because," Artie said quietly, "we're trying to reunite the Kaninens. There were children kidnapped and we're trying to get them home. Isn't that worth fighting for?"

Silence filled the room as our hostess considered Artie's words. Uncomfortable, I heard the teapot whistle and rose to retrieve our tea. Filling three mugs, I handed them out and sipped my own. It was then that I noticed our hostess's face. Pity was etched there.

"I don't know where the gemser plant is, I'm sorry to say, but I do know someone who could aid you in your riddle."

"Who?" Artie asked.

Mrs. Foster sighed. "You know who it is, Artie. I believe you've known for a long time."

He contemplated his hands as he nodded mutely. "I don't like it," he muttered. "I swore to myself that I would never face him again if I could help it, but it's him, isn't it?"

Mrs. Foster inclined her head. "It is indeed."

"Isn't there anyone else who could help?" he said, desperately.

"No."

"I hate to break up the conversation," it was Mag, standing by the nearest window with the little girl, Julia, "But soldiers have just entered the village!"

"How do you know?"

"They were at the gate. They passed by, feet from where I was hiding behind some trees. They didn't see me. They're marching this way, coming to question Mrs. Foster about Malcolm."

"Malcolm!" I spluttered. "But, why?"

"They're saying he started the fire at the gala," Mag said grimly.

"Ridiculous!"

"I'm sure it's just a misunderstanding," Mag said, "but nobody's seen Malcolm since the night of the gala. They're scouring the whole kingdom for him. Julia, I want to introduce you to my friends, Penelope and Artie. Penelope, Artie, this is Julia."

After the introductions had been made, Julia gazed shyly at me. "I hope you find your brother."

My heart went out to the little girl. "Thank you, Julia."

There was a knock on the door and an official voice called out, "Mrs. Foster! Open up, we want to ask you a few questions about the fugitive, Malcolm Bogg!"

I balled my fists in anger.

"Go," Mrs. Foster said, pushing Artie and me outside. "The Brillande Bohrender are nearby. They'll protect you. Don't worry about us. We can handle a couple of soldiers."

The way she said it, I had no doubt she could.

Once outside, Mag led us around the perimeter of the wall, toward the front gate. We stopped beside the guard who let us in.

"Thanks for allowing us in to see our Aunt Mira," Artie said. "She was so happy we could stop by."

The man smiled. "I'm glad to hear it. Mira has too few visitors. You have a nice day, now."

"Thank you, we will," Artie said as we filed past the guard.

Once we were in the trees and the village was out of sight, we ran in the direction Mira had indicated, toward the Brillande Bohrender, the bellowing driller sheep.

Chapter Twenty-Three

Bah, Bah, Gray Sheep

I ALMOST HAD A HEART ATTACK THE FIRST TIME I beheld the sheep in action. At first glance, they appeared to be ordinary gray sheep, but then I saw one unfortunate deer approach a large ram beside a patch of grass. The ram snorted and his horns rose until they were touching, where they began to spin like a drill. The ram chased the deer around a corner, before he stalked off back to his flock.

Artie, Mag, and I watched from behind a rock in an adjoining clearing. We were across a small bridge, a little way out of Purple Falls in Bohrender territory.

"Did you see that?" I said.

"They're like piranhas with horns," Artie said.

"Those are the male Brillande Bohrender," Mag said, her voice shaking slightly. "The females use their voices as energy blasts."

"Come on, we'd better get this over with," I said, wishing more than ever that I had my amulet.

We stepped out cautiously. Some of the sheep looked up at us curiously, but otherwise ignored us. They acted like peaceful sheep, but we proceeded carefully, knowing that they could turn on us at any moment with their horns, or at least the rams could.

I eyed the females. I was more worried about their supersonic voices than the rams' driller horns.

We stopped and watched in fascination as a mountain goat encroached on one female's space. She opened her mouth and bellowed at the intruder. We had to press ourselves against the side of a nearby rock, to avoid the energy wave.

The goat scampered off and we treaded all the more cautiously. Eyes upon the ewes that bellowed and the rams with driller horns, we slowly, step-by-step, made it to the center of the mountain clearing.

"Who is the leader?" I asked.

"That one," Artie said, pointing to a dignified-looking female.

"How do you know?"

"It only makes sense," Mag said. "The females are more powerful than the males. Look at the male standing next to the leader. She looks prouder than the rest and can incapacitate him by bellowing, so he can't activate his drill."

"Well, let's go up and introduce ourselves," I said squaring my shoulders.

We started forward, when a lamb appeared at my feet. I stopped dead when I saw it. The lamb gazed up at me with intelligent brown eyes.

"Hello," I said, quietly so as not to startle him. "Would you move, please?"

"Back," the lamb bleated.

I froze. The lamb had said, 'Bah,' hadn't it? For a second, I could've have sworn he had said, "Back."

We attempted to sidestep the gray bundle of fluff, but the lamb kept blocking us, with another rendition of "Back!"

Mag circled around the lamb, who turned with her, allowing us to slip by.

"Sorry," I said and dashed toward the lead female. "Greetings," I said to her. She stared haughtily at me.

"She apparently can't talk," Artie murmured.

"Hurry up, would you?" Mag said. "This lamb is bugging me, nudging against my leg."

The female looked at Mag at the sound of her voice and began to bleat shrilly. Before we could attempt to calm her down, she began to bellow. I covered my ears with my hands as we took off for the adjoining clearing.

"They definitely don't like me," Mag yelled over the bellows.

"We have to keep trying," I said.

"That won't work." The lamb was back and he had spoken.

"You can talk?" Artie asked incredulously. "You're only a lamb!"

"I'll be a full-grown ram soon," he said indignantly. "My name's Sid."

"Could you help us, Sid?" I asked, placing a hand on Artie's arm to keep him quiet. "We came seeking help. Why are the Brillande Bohrender angry?"

"Its because of her," Sid said, gesturing toward Mag. "She smells like mountain lions."

Mag snorted. "I'm a dragon. I'm only friends with lions and they live in the forest, not the mountains. They don't even like the taste of sheep."

"How do I know you're telling the truth?" Sid asked suspiciously.

Mag was about to answer when a true mountain lion padded into the clearing.

Seeing the mountain lion made me think of Cadmus, except that this cat was tan compared to Cadmus's black.

"Her name's Nimbala," Sid whispered. "She's a menace to the Bohrender."

Nimbala growled at the sight of us. The mountain lion slowly inched her way toward Sid, but quick as a flash, Mag was standing between Nimbala and her intended prey, growling and snarling. For the first time, I could see Mag as the dangerous predator she was.

The mountain lion paused and studied Mag, looking for an opening. Sid squeaked in fright and, as I placed a protective hand on him, Mag glanced at us for a split second. It was enough. Nimbala pounced. She and Mag went rolling across the rock floor, each clawing at the other.

Nimbala was on top of Mag, raising her paw to strike, when Sid slipped from my grasp and struck the lion in the side, sending her sprawling. Mag rose and pounced on Nimbala, slamming her against a rock wall.

The mountain lion roared in frustration as her back touched the cool surface of the rock. She cast Mag a hate-filled glare and streaked off down a mountain path, though she was careful to avoid the clearing with the gray sheep.

"You're a brave little Bohrender," Mag said to Sid, patting him on the head.

"I'm sorry for suspecting you," Sid said, hanging his head. "I know you won't hurt me."

"Sid, can you convince the other Brillande Bohrender that we mean them no harm?" Artie asked.

"I think so. My family and I are some of the only Bohrender who can talk. My mom is the ewe in charge."

After properly introducing ourselves, we returned to the flock's territory, Sid leading the way to the ewe who had bellowed at us. She was now nursing a newborn lamb with the same ram standing protectively over her.

Sid stopped before them. "Mom. Dad. Sophie," he said.

"Sid!" the ewe cried. "What happened? We heard the most awful growling and snarling!"

"I'm all right, Mom," Sid said. "My friends here just defeated Nimbala."

The ram stared at Sid. "How? Nimbala is almost impossible to overcome, even for the Brillande Bohrender."

"Mom, Dad, this is Penelope, Artie, and Mag."

Sid's mom glared at us suspiciously. She looked ready to bellow again. "Aren't you mountain lions?"

"No, Mom, Penelope and Artie are humans. Mag's a dragon. Mag fought Nimbala for us. She wrestled with Nimbala and then slammed her against a wall. That lion ran for it with her tail between her legs!"

"Dragon," the ewe said, "I don't know why you're here, but if what Sid says is true, you are welcome... for now."

"We're actually here seeking a Kaninen," I said. "We saw it run by about a day's walk from here."

"I have not seen it, but maybe one of the other sheep have," the ewe said thoughtfully.

A passing ewe stopped and sniffed the air. She turned and saw Mag. She bellowed and instantly chaos ensued. The sheep closest to Sid's family panicked and began to bellow and drill into rocks.

As we tried to calm them down, a tiny bleat echoed throughout the clearing.

The minute lamb Sid's mother had been nursing had stood on her spindly legs and tottered over to Mag's side. Staring up at Mag with large, brown eyes, the lamb rubbed herself against her leg. Mag gazed down at her and gently rubbed her tiny head.

The lamb stumbled toward me and the same process ensued. She sat against my leg and plopped on the ground beside me.

I stroked her silky fleece. The other Bohrender began to calm down once they realized we were no threat.

"Well, that settles it," Sid said, releasing his breath. "Sophie likes you."

As Sid said it, the other, nonverbal sheep made their way slowly forward, cautiously approaching us.

I shivered, relieved that the Bohrender had accepted us. Wait... *shivered?* An icy chill was spreading over the clearing.

"The Kaninen," I whispered.

"It must have escaped from its rope," Artie breathed.

"The waterfall!" Mag cried, pointing across the bridge. I could just make out a small, blue shape. A bigger, tan shape was moving toward it.

"Nimbala," I said. "We have to stop her."

"How?" Artie said, desperately. "Nimbala's almost on top of the Kaninen and we're way over here."

"I'll fly," Mag offered. She took a step forward, but stumbled. Artie had to catch her. And it was no wonder. Mag's arm was greener than ever and she was shaking. The battle with Nimbala had taken a lot out of her.

I took a deep breath and said, "I'll save the Kaninen." It was the last thing I wanted to do, but what choice did I have? I couldn't let Nimbala attack the Kaninen and magic was the fastest way to save it.

"I'll come with you," Artie said.

"No," I said, shaking my head firmly. When he looked crestfallen, I continued. "Artie, I need you to stay here and look after Mag. Please."

Artie stared at me for a second. I could tell he didn't like it, but he nodded.

"The Bohrender could help," the ewe offered. I jumped. I had almost forgotten the Brillande Bohrender were there.

"How?" Mag gasped.

The ewe responded by bellowing in Nimbala's direction. She was a mere foot away from the Kaninen, whose back was pressed against a rock wall. Nimbala stopped moving and covered her ears with her paws.

"Why doesn't it just disappear?" Artie asked, struggling to keep Mag upright.

"I don't know," I said. Where was that blue teleportation circle Flurry and Frost had used?

"The Kaninen doesn't have room," the ewe said, pushing me onto her husband's horns. It already resembled a drill. I climbed on gingerly. "She would need to create a clear, unbroken circle around herself."

I was feeling rather uncomfortable on the ram's horns by now.

The horns started spinning and just when I didn't think I could hold on any longer, the ram said, "I'm propelling you to Nimbala. Good luck."

He threw his head back and I went sailing up and neatly over the bridge.

The bad news: Nimbala was reviving fast. She was crouched, ready to pounce. I needed a distraction. The good news: I found that distraction. It was me, landing on Nimbala's back.

She leapt twenty feet into the air in her surprise, carrying me with her. Nimbala twisted in mid-air, which sent me careening off her back.

"Enchauta!" I cried, throwing my arms over my face. I was no longer falling. In fact, I felt weightless. I peeked out and saw that I had managed to stop my fall a foot above the ground. I was horizontal, so I easily reached out a hand and touched the rock floor. The spell lost its hold and I landed gently on the ground next to the Kaninen. It looked speechless. I looked up in time to see Nimbala race off, in search of easier prey.

"Y-you saved me," the Kaninen said, finding her voice at last.

"Of course I did," I said, blinking rapidly and taking a deep breath. The Kaninen changed from silver-blue to blue-white almost instantly. My head didn't even hurt. "Blizzard sent me."

"He did?" the Kaninen asked eagerly. Then her face fell. "What about the others?"

"Don't worry," I said, as Artie hurried up, supporting Mag. "I've already saved Flurry and Frost."

"That leaves Ice. I'm Snow, by the way. I escaped from Tristan."

"Penelope, Mag, and Artie," I said.

Snow looked ready to bolt when she saw Mag, when she frowned. "That dragon doesn't look too good."

I turned and gasped out loud. Even Mag's hair looked slightly green.

"Mag, what-"

"No time," Artie panted. "The gemser plant is nearby. I... remember where they are now."

"Where is it?" I demanded.

"At the base of the mountain," Artie said. "Sid already gave me the holly and bitterbrush. With any luck, we can get the gemser plant and heal Mag before they spot us."

"Who?"

Artie acted as if he hadn't heard me and refrained from answering.

I turned to Snow. "We have to go. Will you be all right on your own?"

"I'll be fine. Good luck with your dragon. Good-bye." We gave Snow some room and she disappeared through a blue teleportation circle.

We started down the mountain, supporting Mag between us, when a raspy voice said, "No."

I looked down and saw Mag, pale and sweaty, digging her heels into the ground.

"Mag! You should be resting. You were injured," I said.

"No," she repeated, shaking our hands off of her. She took a few steps, wobbled, and Artie and I had to catch her again.

"Stay still," I said.

"No!" Mag said for a third time, growling. "Walking will take too long. I know how long my wing has before its permanently crippled. You can't walk down, collect the plant, *and* make the potion. By then, it will be too late. I might stand a chance through, if we take a shortcut."

Artie and I shared an exasperated look, but we knew we couldn't argue with Mag. Her arm was greener than ever and we didn't want to prolong her suffering.

"All right," I said, grudgingly. "How are we getting down? A spell?"

Mag shook her head. "What do you think of falling down a waterfall?"

* * *

"Are you sure about this, Mag?" I asked. We were at the edge of the waterfall, less than a mile from Purple Falls, staring at a sea of mist twenty feet below.

"Don't worry, we'll be fine," Mag said, but she didn't sound too sure.

"I almost wish we were still with the Bohrender," Artie muttered. "Their bellowing and drilling weren't that bad."

The three of us stood there for several seconds, none of us seemed willing to jump.

"Well, come on," Mag said. "My wing won't get better just standing here."

She grabbed my hand and I, in turn, seized Artie's.

Forming a human chain, Mag leapt off the cliff, dragging us with her.

Unable to stop myself, a muffled scream tore from my mouth, but nobody could hear me over the roar of the mighty falls, ready to swallow three new victims into its fearsome maw. I shuddered, as the water rushed toward me and enveloped me in its cold embrace.

Chapter Twenty-Four

Artie's Confession

THE WATER RIPPED ME AWAY FROM MAG and Artie. Spluttering to the surface, I found myself in the center of a deep lake, feet from the torrents of the writhing foam of the waterfall. I blinked, trying to recover my bearings. The surface of the water broke again as Artie bobbed upward.

Spewing water from his mouth, he glanced over at me. I nodded once and we started searching the lake for Mag. I found her floating in the shallows, her body shuddering and her left arm stretched out at an awkward angle.

Swimming to Mag's side, I floated beside her and examined her arm for further injury. What I saw made me sick. The poison had spread and threatened to disable Mag permanently. If I didn't find the gemser plant and fast, Mag could lose the power to fly, forever.

Unable to bear that morbid thought, I pushed it from my mind and set to work. First things first, I had to move Mag from the icy grip of the water and start a fire to warm her.

"Artie! Give me a hand here, will you?"

He swam over and together we managed to coax Mag from the water and onto the shore.

Panting, we collapsed side-by-side with Mag on wet, damp sand. Ten feet away, there was a line of grass and trees. I allowed myself the short break, but then pushed myself up with a groan. Falling the length of a twenty-foot tall waterfall was definitely not the way I had wanted to spend the afternoon.

"Artie?" I croaked. "I need to treat Mag. I'm too exhausted to start a fire. I don't want to lose concentration and end up setting myself on fire. In the interest of safety, could you go retrieve some firewood, please?"

Artie inclined his head and rose unsteadily to his feet and drifted off toward a small tree at the water's edge.

"Mag," I said, speaking soothingly.

She didn't respond.

"Mag," I said more firmly. "You have to listen to me. You *will* see this through. *We'll* see this through. Mag! Answer me."

"I hear you, Penelope," she said. There was a slight pause and then, "Tell me the truth, there's not much chance for my wing, is there?"

Hating myself for doing it, I shook my head, "Not unless we can find the gemser plant and fast."

Before Mag could answer and before either of us could react, Artie sprinted back, knife drawn and a frown on his face. "We have to go, *now!*"

Puzzled, I said, "We can't go now, Artie. Mag is too injured to move."

"You don't understand," Artie said, his eyes wild. "*They* are here!"

"Who is this 'they'?" Mag asked, struggling to her feet, but I gasped.

About twenty people, all hooded, all on horseback, and all wielding knives similar to Artie's had appeared out of nowhere. It was if they had sprung out of the mountain itself.

"Mag, please tell me you're well enough to travel?" Artie muttered desperately, raising his knife in defense.

"Not with this wing," she groaned.

"Who are they?" I said. "What do they want?"

"They're thieves," Artie said, gloomily. "And they're here for me."

The thieves arranged themselves in a loose semicircle around us. One of the thieves swung herself off her mount to face Artie.

With a jolt, I realized who it was: Sylvia Quick.

Sylvia flicked her eyes toward Mag, then me standing beside her, and then back to Artie who hadn't lowered his knife.

"Artie."

"Sylvia."

"You know, Q has had everyone searching for you," Sylvia said casually.

He still wouldn't lower his weapon. "Maybe I didn't want to be found."

Sylvia sighed. "That's what I told him, but will he listen? No, he still insisted that I find you. Although, I didn't try very hard. And you have to admit; I did keep my promise." She turned back to Mag. "What happened to you, ambassador of Draval, or should I say Dragon Valley?

My heart sank. "How did you know?"

"That she's a dragon?" Sylvia smiled. "Malcolm."

Malcolm? Why would he tell Sylvia?

"My wing is none of your business," Mag growled.

At her words, many of the thieves raised their knives and pointed them at us. My latest question about Malcolm died in my throat.

Artie glared pointedly at Sylvia. "Both Penelope and Mag happen to be my friends. Now, tell the others to lower their weapons and leave us be, Sylvia. We have to treat Mag's wing, or else she may lose it entirely. Stand down, Sylvia. We don't have time to bandy words with Q."

She sighed once more. "Believe me, Artie. I want to let you go as much as you do, but you know Q's rule: his word is law. My hands are tied. I'm sorry."

"Excuse me," I said.

Sylvia's eyes flicked back to me.

"What is going on? Why were you chasing Artie? I thought you two were friends."

Sylvia frowned at him. "You haven't told her?"

Artie shook his head.

She grunted and said, "I happen to be his..."

"Sylvia!" Artie interrupted. "Please, allow me to explain. I—I owe it to them."

She nodded in agreement. "Very well, Artie. But, first, we shall escort you and your... friends into headquarters. Now that we've found you at last, Q would like a little chat with you."

"But you can't do that!" I cried, taking a step toward Sylvia. The other thieves trained their knives on me. Artie stepped between us.

Sylvia raised an eyebrow at Artie's reaction, but addressed me nonetheless. "Oh, and why not?"

"I have to treat Mag's wing!" I said, exasperated. "Look, I'm sure I can heal her, but I don't have the main ingredient: the gemser plant. If you would set us free, then I could find it and-"

Sylvia raised a hand to silence me. "The gemser plant, did you say?"

"Yes," I said. "I have the holly and bitterbrush. Why?"

Sylvia shook her head in amusement. "The gemser plant makes its home in these parts. We have tons of it at our headquarters. Its bright blue with yellow stems."

I wavered. Should I trust her?

"If you are truly Artie's friends, you may enter and treat Mag. No harm will come to you," Sylvia promised.

"Very well," Mag said. "I trust you... for now. But, if you harm any of us during our visit, I won't need my wing to tear you to pieces."

"Of course," Sylvia said. Her eyes met Artie's. "Shall we?"

* * *

It looked as if Artie was living his worst nightmare. His face was a mask of panic and he kept glancing between Sylvia and me with— was that terror?

As Sylvia organized the thieves into ranks surrounding us, Artie turned to me, as if he wanted to tell me something. I saw him shudder.

"Penelope," he said, sheathing his knife.

I looked up from tending Mag. "Yes?"

"I have to tell you something."

My hair whipped around my face, as the wind played with it, so Artie was obscured from my gaze for a moment. "Can't it wait?"

"No, its urgent."

"What is it?"

He took a deep breath, as if steeling his nerves. "Penelope," he said. "I'm a-"

"Move out!" Sylvia called, interrupting the rest of Artie's sentence.

"What was that?" I said. "I didn't catch that."

"Right," Artie said. He was breathing rapidly. "Penelope, I'm a th-"

But this time, the noise from the thieves returning home drowned him out.

I shook my head as Mag, Artie, and I began to walk. "Artie, you'll need to speak up if you want me to hear you."

We marched through a valley of grass and flowers as Artie hyperventilated. A fat blue hummingbird flitted by on its way to find nectar.

I lost sight of the hummingbird among some bright blue flowers with yellow stems. Gasping, I hailed Sylvia, while Artie looked longingly back over his shoulder at the waterfall.

"Sylvia! Isn't that the gemser plant?" I asked eagerly.

"Indeed, it is. But, there's plenty where we're going."

"How much further?" I said, as I patted Mag's shoulder.

"Not far. Another five minutes, at most," Sylvia said. "Do you see that rock in the shape of a dragon's head? That's our landmark for the lake. We're heading for that mountain."

Artie's eyes grew wide. Hurriedly, he faced me. He opened his mouth, but no sound came out.

We were passing by a maple tree permanently bent to the left. The mountain was looming nearer.

"Penelope! I'm-" but Artie was cut off when Mag began to cough like a cat with a hairball. I turned to her until her fit stopped. We were so close to the mountain that it blocked out the sun partially.

Artie paled as the rock face of the wall cast us in shadow. We seemed to have arrived. The thieves were being much louder than usual. I gazed sympathetically at Artie; he almost looked as if he had given up telling me whatever it was.

But, as Sylvia pulled a hidden lever that opened the rock wall entrance of the hideout, Artie clenched his fists. His resolve appeared to have hardened once more and he took a deep, shuddering breath.

Walking down a stone passageway lined with torches, we passed between the rays of dancing light. Voices could be heard from the next chamber.

Turning full around so he was walking backwards, Artie traversed the well-worn path while facing me. "PENELOPE!" he yelled, his voice bouncing off the walls. "I'M A THIEF!"

I heard that. Shock creased my face as I looked at Mag to see if she had heard as well. Mag looked as stunned as me, confirming that I had indeed heard him correctly. And from the silence coursing through the room, we weren't the only ones.

Judging by the ragged, but splendidly dressed occupants, I knew we were now in a room full of master thieves, not petty criminals who roamed the streets of any city, but professionals who could steal from you as soon as look at you. There was obviously money here, a lot of it.

There were two thieves, a man and a woman, seated upon a raised platform in highly ornate chairs. The woman had honey-blonde hair just like Sylvia, while the man had black hair and a pointed nose.

Both the woman and the man appeared startled by our sudden arrival, even though the thieves had been causing a racket ever since the waterfall.

Recovering slightly from my shock, I turned forcefully toward Artie. "You-" I began, but realized his pained, uncertain expression and softened my tone. "You're a thief? Why didn't you tell us sooner?"

"I wanted to," Artie said miserably, "but I couldn't-" whatever else he was going to say was interrupted by the man.

"Welcome back, Artie! Its been too long, my boy."

"Yes, it has," Artie said, though clenched teeth.

The woman gasped and ran to meet him. "Oh, my little Arthur! How I missed you!" She grasped Artie into a hug, which he allowed until he saw our curious expressions and gently extracted himself.

"Hello," he said, gazing down at the floor to avoid meeting her eyes.

The woman examined Artie from head to foot, clucking with disapproval as she said, "I told him not to do it, Artie, but will he listen?" She spotted us. "Welcome to the Quick Hideout. The only safe haven for thieves nowadays. I'm Yolanda Quick and this is my husband and the leader of our organization, Leopold Quick."

When Artie was slow to react, Yolanda said to him, "Why, Artie, have you not told them?"

"Told us what?" I said slowly.

Artie took a deep breath and said in a pained voice, "I'm not just any ordinary thief. My name is Arthur Hamilton Quick, son of Leopold Quick, the Master of all Thieves."

Chapter Twenty-Five

The Race for the Flower

O F ALL THE REVELATIONS ARTIE HAD disclosed that day, his being the son of Leopold Quick was the last thing I had expected. Sure, I may have suspected that Sylvia was looking for him, but I could never have imagined Artie was a Quick. Leopold Quick was a thief crime lord and I had been traveling with his son! I gaped in pure astonishment at Artie. Why had I never realized it before? Artie had stolen supplies in Silent Stream, had lied smoothly to the guard at Purple Falls, not to mention that he was skilled in fighting with a knife, which, now I came to think of it, was typically a thief's weapon of choice.

So, why was I so shocked? The fact of the matter was that I had grown up with stories of vicious thieves stealing young children in the night and even after all this time, I hadn't bothered to consider the ludicrousness of the very idea. Now, faced with the fact that one of my best friends was a thief, my thoughts became so jumbled I didn't know what to think.

"Artie, I-" I began, without any clear idea what I was going to say. But, Mag saved me from a potentially awkward conversation by groaning out loud.

With a jolt, I remembered Mag's injured wing. I had precious little time to heal it.

"Thief Master Quick," I said, with a hurried curtsey. "It is a pleasure to meet you, but as you can see, Mag was injured and she requires immediate medical attention."

The older Quick started in surprise, but calmly addressed Sylvia. "Is this true?"

"Yes, Father," and I understood that Sylvia was Artie's older sister. I felt myself smiling slightly, despite the situation. Here was his source of magical knowledge. "The dragon Mag was injured by Aneurin. If you will give me leave, I will personally accompany Penelope to the storage room to heal her."

"I'll come too," Artie volunteered.

"No, Artie, I want you to stay here," Leopold said. "We have matters to discuss." Artie's face fell, but I was secretly relieved. I didn't know what to think about him at the moment. "You may escort our guests to the storage room, Sylvia. Return when-"

"Quick!" a harsh voice yelled and I turned in time to see a man with curly black hair and cold, gray eyes enter the room. There was a knife strapped to his belt.

"What is the meaning of this, Quick?" the man demanded. "First, you send us on a wild goose chase to hunt down your brat," he jerked his head in Artie's direction. "And now you would allow these commoners to wander the sacred halls of our order? They know nothing of the subtle art of thievery! We cannot trust them, am I right?!"

A dozen of the almost one hundred thieves in the room roared their approval.

I stared at the man in both horror and anger. Didn't he realize Mag needed help? If I didn't start soon, she could lose the ability to fly altogether!

Sylvia must have been thinking along the same lines, for she said, "Stand down, Tristan. Can't you see we have an injured dragon? We have to retrieve the gemser plant, *now!*"

Tristan? Wasn't that the name Snow had mentioned when she said she had escaped from her captors? I narrowed my eyes at the curly-haired thief.

"Exactly why we don't want that beast in the rest of the hideout," Tristan said, heatedly. "Haven't you heard the stories?

Dragons hoard treasure! If we're not careful, that monster will rob us blind!"

I couldn't take it anymore. I faced Tristan and growled, "Look! We don't want your treasure! We're just here for the healing properties of the gemser plant. Then, we will never have to see each other again and even then it would be far too soon."

Tristan bared his teeth at me. "This isn't the end, girl. You will pay for speaking to me so." He swept away, a couple of the thieves trailing behind him.

I took a deep, shaky breath, trying to calm my nerves. I felt a hand on my shoulder. When I looked up, I saw Mag smiling at me. "Thanks."

"Nobody calls my friend a beast," I said. Turning to Thief Master Quick, "Sir, may we go to your storage room for the gemser plant?"

"Yes, of course you may. Sylvia, I may not agree with everything Tristan said, but he is right about one thing: we can't have visitors wandering around the halls unescorted, so stick close to them, will you?"

"Of course, Father," she said. "Penelope, Mag, if you will come this way."

Sylvia led us toward the same exit through which Tristan and his followers had departed. I looked back only once and that was to see Artie standing in the center of the room, arms across his chest and staring off into the distance, a look of hopelessness on his face. I felt a brief pang of guilt, before Sylvia steered us around a corner and Artie was lost to sight.

We plodded down a stone hallway, Mag walking slowly. We emerged into another room like the one before, but unlike the main chamber, this one was much smaller, with five arches leading out from its depths.

"Which way?" I asked. All the arches appeared the same.

"This way," Sylvia said, heading for the door, second to the right. The thieves in this room studied us carefully, as if they were calculating the best way to steal from us.

"You will always know which way to go, thanks to these," Sylvia said, pointing to a blue orb planted at the top of the arch. "Blue means storage. Green is treasure. Diamond is for weapons. Purple stands for sleeping quarters and the mess hall. And gold is the exit."

I spotted a red orb. "What about that one?"

"Hmm? Oh, that is for the main chamber, the one we just left."

We entered the blue tunnel and were soon in a long and twisted hallway.

"How did the thieves know Mag was a dragon?" I asked. The question had been bothering me since we were in the main chamber.

Sylvia laughed. "Draval? That's the first three letters of *Dragon* and *Valley*. The thieves have always known about the dragons, even before Malcolm told me." Her eyes gleamed brightly. "Dragons are said to keep hoards. We would be fools not to protect our treasure. We've followed their movements closely for years."

"Dragons don't hoard treasure," Mag said with as much dignity as she could muster.

Sylvia grinned. "Good to know."

"Sylvia?" I said, after a few minutes.

"Yes?"

"What did you mean earlier, when you told Artie that you had kept your promise?"

"He asked me not to tell our father that he was at Kelton Castle. He's my brother, so I agreed." She refused to say anymore on the subject.

I knew we were reaching the end of the tunnel when I saw a bright orange pinpoint of light in the distance.

Sylvia paused. "This isn't right. Come on!" She started running. I followed close behind, while Mag brought up the rear at an easier pace.

Tearing through the tunnel, Sylvia and I raced toward the light. I almost slipped on a puddle of water in my haste. Grabbing Sylvia's arm, I righted myself and together we hurtled through the chamber opening.

Coughing, my eyes stung as a stream of smoke engulfed us. Mag pushed her way in, but covered her nose from the stench.

The contents of the chamber were on fire.

"Tristan!" Sylvia cried and I saw three figures hurrying through another opening across the room.

"Bavasnor!" Sylvia produced a bracelet with a small mermaid charm on it.

"Bavasnor!" I said, copying her. The jet of water issuing from her bracelet doubled in strength as my magic took hold. Steam formed as the water hit the fire.

Panting, we ended our spells, and Sylvia approached the middle of the storage room. Oddly enough, I didn't see silver. It looked as if combining my magic with another witch or wizard prevented my vision from changing.

The storage room was a large, circular area, big enough for both Mag and Aldrich in their dragon forms, with room to spare. In the center was a pile of ash.

"I don't believe this!" Sylvia cried. "Its all gone! Every last bit!"

"What's gone?" Mag asked, stepping further into the chamber.

"The gemser plants!" Sylvia said. "Tristan and his gang burned it all."

I felt like my heart had stopped. "You can't be serious!" I gasped. "What about healing Mag's wing?"

Sylvia sighed. "Unless you know of another batch of gemser plants, our stock won't regrow until next spring."

Mag slumped to the ground, her gaze unfocused.

I didn't cry; I was in shock. There had to be a way to help Mag, there just *had* to be! Hadn't I seen another batch somewhere?

And then it clicked. I *had* seen another gemser plant, outside the hideout. If only I could get to it. I didn't know my way around as well as Sylvia or Artie might, but as long as I followed the orbs...

Working fast, I recounted my discovery to Mag and Sylvia. Mag's eyes cleared and she appeared hopeful again. Sylvia, on the other hand, looked dubious.

"I don't know, Penelope. I promised my father that I wouldn't let either of you out of my sight. We would have to move fast, there's no way Mag could keep up."

"Mag's wing doesn't have much time," I said quietly. "We have what, twenty minutes? Sylvia, allow me to retrieve the gemser plant." Sylvia opened her mouth to argue, but I overrode her. "I promise I'll only go outside, grab the flower, and return. Please, stay with Mag. Tristan might return."

Sylvia was silent for a moment, then, "All right, Penelope. Follow the gold orbs. There will be a small door at the end. When you reach it, say 'Anoffen,' and it will open. It will lock after it closes, so when you return, say 'Anoffen, Sylvia Quick has granted me entrance,' and follow the blue orbs back to us."

"I'll be back soon," I promised, turning to go. "Oh, and Sylvia." She looked up. "Thank you." I sped off, entering the maw of the golden orb's dark tunnel, in a desperate attempt to save my friend.

* * *

I practically flew through the tunnel, as if I had wings. But fast as I was, it still took me one of my precious minutes to traverse the tunnel and enter the adjoining chamber.

Too slow, I thought, eyes flicking to the next set of arches. Spying the golden orb off to my right, I dashed across the intervening space and into the passageway, grateful that no other thieves were in the vicinity.

I hurtled through the stone hallway as fast as I could without tripping over the uneven ground and was met by a somewhat smaller chamber than the ones previous. This had only two choices, one red, one gold.

Choosing the gold arch, I ran through its depths, thinking all the while. *Why did Tristan and the other thieves burn the gemser plants?*

I was so distracted with the unpleasant possibilities that I almost crashed into a closed wooden door with a brass lock.

Spitting brown and silver hair out of my mouth, I reached out and seized the lock. "Anoffen!" The door swung ajar with a slight creak and, after breathing calmly to disperse the small amount of silver in my vision, I dashed outside.

Blinking in the bright light, I was blinded for a moment. Once my eyes adjusted, I searched for the route the thieves had used while escorting us to the hideout. I found a trampled piece of earth and took it. Covering the well-worn path, I remembered that it had taken roughly five minutes to walk from the lake to the hideout. It had taken five of my precious twenty minutes to get outside. If I didn't want to spend half my remaining time going from the hideout to the lake and back again, I would have to run.

I set off, jogging, so as not to attract attention. There was the bent maple tree. I sped up. Panting, I saw what appeared to be the dragon head rock Sylvia had pointed out. Slowing to a grateful walk, I searched the area for any sign of blue.

As I pushed aside a bush, I caught sight of the same blue hummingbird from before. It gazed at me with beady eyes.

"Hello," I said. "Do you know where the gemser plant is?"

The hummingbird buzzed its wings and flitted across the path to the other side of the dirt lane.

As I tracked the hummingbird's progress, I realized that the bird had seemingly disappeared at the edge of the path. Grinning, I peered closer and saw the hummingbird amidst a sea of blue flowers with yellow stems.

I observed a gleam of triumph in the tiny bird's eyes.

"Thank you," I said, hurriedly picking a handful of flowers. I would have to remember this place, if I ever needed another supply.

Turning on my heel, I full out ran back toward the Quick hideout, not caring if anyone saw me. I had used up two my remaining fifteen minutes running toward the gemser plants and another two searching. With only eleven minutes left, I wasn't about to take any chances.

As I approached the secret entrance, I called out, "Anoffen, Sylvia Quick has granted me entrance!"

The door creaked open and I sprinted into the gloom, the door slamming shut behind me. I knew I should use more caution, but only ten minutes remained, so I ran over the uneven ground, somehow keeping myself from tripping over rocks that I knew lay in my path.

Emerging into the first chamber, I saw that it was the room with only two choices, this time red and blue, instead of red and gold. Taking the blue arch, I followed the twisting hallway, until I reached the next deserted chamber. This time my choices were: red, blue, green, purple, and diamond. Choosing the blue path, I sprinted through the tunnel's depths, until I spied the gentle white light, marking the entrance of the next chamber.

Hurtling into the light, I skidded to a stop, panting, as I beheld Mag and Sylvia standing in the center of the room.

Unable to speak, I contented myself with holding up the gemser plants I had picked.

"Penelope," Mag said, seeing the miraculous bouquet of flowers. "Thank you."

"No time to celebrate," Sylvia said. "We only have seven minutes remaining. Penelope, you good for making the potion?"

"Water," I croaked.

Sylvia sprayed a jet of water from her bracelet into my mouth and I gulped gratefully.

Still tired, but unwilling to wait, I pushed up my sleeves and said, "Ready. What do we do?"

"Have you ever made this potion before?" Sylvia asked.

"No. I've heard the theory, but if you have the knowledge and experience, I am yours to command."

"Very well. Mag, you'll have to transform back into a dragon. Penelope, first you'll want to put your cauldron to a boil," Sylvia instructed, indicating a nearby cauldron.

As I sprayed water into the cauldron's depths, Mag transformed. Everything seemed normal, until I realized the green had shifted from her left arm to her left wing. The area looked acid and inflamed, but Mag simply shook her head and lit the underside of the metal.

Once it was hot, which took only seconds with dragon fire, Sylvia said, "Add the holly and bitterbrush, in that order, and stir in a slow circle. Once the potion turns light green, add exactly three petals, or one flower of a gemser plant."

I placed the holly and bitterbrush into the cauldron and stirred slowly. It didn't take long for the green holly and the yellow bitterbrush to turn light green, at which time I plucked three blue petals from one of the gemser plants and dropped them in.

"Good. The potion is almost ready," Sylvia said. "Mag, would you please heat up the cauldron again? Penelope, this is very important. While Mag is busy with the fire, you'll have to stir the potion counterclockwise, until the potion changes to a bluish-green paste. Neither of you should stop before then."

I began to stir counterclockwise, careful to stay out of the range of Mag's flames. Mag, for her part, only opened her mouth a fraction of an inch, so as to control the stream. After a minute of stirring, I could barely lift the stirring rod from the blue-green contents, and Sylvia deemed it ready.

"Now comes the tricky part," Sylvia said. "Mag, you're going to have to drink half of this, while Penelope massages the rest into your infected area."

"What will you do?" I asked.

"The potion stings, a lot. Trust me. I'll hold down Mag's wing, so she doesn't jerk it up while you are applying the potion."

The three of us moved into position. I scooped half of the potion into a cup Sylvia provided and climbed onto Mag's wing, while Mag prepared to drink the rest. Sylvia placed her weight on the wing tip and nodded once.

I began to rub the mixture into the green area of Mag's left wing, wincing as my friend's throat contracted in a gulp and she tried to jerk me off, Sylvia just barely managing to hold her down. As Mag sat panting, the cauldron empty beneath her, I continued to massage in the potion, all the while trying to speak soothingly to her. Mag somewhat relaxed and steadied her wing, which made it easier for me to work the remaining potion into the fading green of her red.

As the last residue of green was replaced by bright, new red, I applied pressure to Mag's joints, and she didn't wince. Overjoyed, I called Sylvia up and together we checked her wing for further injury. When neither of us could find any hint of damage, we slid off her back and I proclaimed her whole and sound.

Mag roared in triumph, flinging her head back in pure happiness, sweeping both wings high into the air as she tested them to their limit.

Sylvia nudged me. "Good job. I didn't think you would make it back in time. The potion itself takes five minutes to make plus a minute to work into the skin. If you were off by even a minute, all would have been lost."

My head spun, through exhaustion and through the knowledge that I had saved Mag's wing with only a minute to spare.

Mag lowered her head to look at me with her amber eyes. "Penelope, thank you."

"No big deal."

"Oh, but it's a very big deal. You gave the power of flight back to a dragon, one of our most precious gifts, so again, Penelope, thank you."

I shifted in embarrassment. I had only done what I believed was right.

"Penelope, by helping me, you have enacted the final stage of a dragon guardianship. If ever you are in trouble, any dragon, guardian or not, will be required to help. Even Amarina."

"What about Sylvia, though? She did as much as me."

"Untrue, Penelope," Sylvia said. "I may have known how to make the potion, but you were the one who actually did it."

"And," Mag said, "you didn't give up, even when I had lost hope."

"Mag, you didn't lose hope, did you?"

"I did. When I saw the gemser plants burned, I thought my wing was lost. But you, you remembered the plants outside and risked capture from the other thieves to retrieve it for me. That is no small amount of friendship you showed me. We had to trust each other to do the right thing. I had to believe you would find the gemser plant and save my wing. You had to trust me about leaping off the waterfall. The combined trust cemented our bond as witch and dragon guardian.

"There's just one thing we still have to do. Repeat after me: *I, Penelope Alice Bogg, promise to uphold the sacred trust between witch and guardian as long as I live. Beredan.*"

I took a deep breath and repeated the words. A tingling sensation started at the base of my neck.

Mag recited the words for herself and once she was finished, the tingling sensation had evolved into a feeling of peace.

"Want to go for a ride, Penelope?"

"Yes, but we're stuck down here."

"Not at all," Sylvia said. "Look up."

We obediently did as she said and saw an opening large enough for a dragon above our heads.

"That's a natural opening in the mountain," Sylvia explained. "We placed the gemser plants here so they would receive full sun all day long."

"Shall we?" Mag asked casually.

I hesitated. "What about your wing? Are you strong enough?"

Mag snorted. "Of course I'm strong enough. Now, come on."

I climbed onto my friend's back and she extended her wings to their full length. It was as if her wing had never been injured. Flapping twice, hard, Mag soared into the air and flew once around the perimeter of the storage room, before she rocketed upward. We breezed through the opening with barely an inch to spare. We were outside.

I gasped as Mag propelled us further into the sky, spiraling upward until the land below appeared to be nothing more than a patchwork quilt that some giant had created.

Once we were level with the clouds, Mag straightened into a glide.

I broke the silence. "Mag?"

"Hmm?"

"Now that we've completed the dragon guardian final stage, what does that mean for us? We're bonded, but is that it, or will anything special happen to us as a result of it?"

Mag paused. Then, "The only other time this has happened was when Cessala and the witch defeated the golden dragon.

"Before they were bonded, they were strong, but after, it seemed none could harm them. Many tried to separate them and tell them falsehoods concerning the other, but Cessala and the witch never fell for it. They could always seem to find the other, no matter where in Alsmora they might be. And they could never be persuaded to betray the other, even if forced. So, Penelope, what does this tell you about our bond?"

I considered what Mag had said. No lies could fool us, we could always find each other, and we couldn't betray the subject of our bond. I ran this past Mag.

"Correct," she said, turning her head to look at me. "Bonded humans and dragons are rumored to be stronger and faster than usual. Want to test it out?"

"Do it," I said.

Mag flattened her body and the wind rushed over the two of us as she sped through the clouds. She performed a loop-de-loop in midair, which almost caused me to slip to the ground. Hanging on for dear life, I couldn't help but help in exhilaration. Straightening out, Mag came to a stop and flapped in place. Turning her head to me, we both grinned.

We settled into peaceful silence, drifting along, but always careful to stay within sight of the Quick Hideout.

Chapter Twenty-Six

Thief versus Thief

AG LANDED ON THE GROUND and I dismounted before Sylvia.

"There you are. We have to head back to the main chamber. They'll start to wonder at our long absence."

After Mag was human again, the three of us started for the red arch. "We haven't been gone that long, have we?" I asked.

"Twenty minutes to heal Mag and about thirty minutes of your flying, we've been gone for almost a whole hour."

"Even if they sent out a search party, they couldn't catch us now. Right, Penelope?" Mag smiled.

"You could fly us out of here within minutes," I said.

"But what about Artie?" Sylvia murmured softly.

"What about him?" I said carefully. I still wasn't sure about Artie, now that I knew the truth.

"He's a good kid, Penelope, he is my brother after all."

"He didn't tell us he was a thief until after you captured us," I said, flatly.

Sylvia sighed. "Don't be too hard on him. Artie loves being a thief, but he has a problem with Dad stealing from innocents. On more than one occasion, they've argued that point. In fact, that's what they were arguing about the day Artie left."

"What do you mean by 'innocents'?" Mag said as we emerged into the next chamber.

"Good people, those that don't take advantage of others. Whether rich, poor, or in between, Artie can't stand to steal from those who have never wronged a soul. He's perfectly willing to steal from those that cheat others, as long as he sees it happening, but if a family is struggling, or if somebody puts their money to good use, Artie can't morally steal."

"Why would that cause an argument between him and your father?" I said with a frown. "That sounds reasonable to me."

"You don't know our father. He's convinced that thieves are superior to everyone else in Alsmora. If you have an opportunity to steal from anyone: innocent, guilty, rich, poor, a cheat, dear old dad doesn't care, as long as they're an easy target. Artie's soft approach angers him. The day Artie left, he missed robbing such an easy target that they argued for so long, I'm surprised their voices didn't give way. Artie's missed easy targets before, but this one put Dad over the edge, this target was rich."

"What happened?" I asked. The Artie I knew, or thought I knew, wouldn't purposefully rob anyone, but there *was* that awful merchant back in Silent Stream...

"Dad has great people skills, nearly all thieves do, but he just doesn't know how to act around Artie, a thief that more often than not refuses to steal. They had argued and yelled, nothing out of the ordinary, but Dad was fed up with him, so he assigned Artie to steal from a rich local merchant known to be traveling alone in our direction.

"Artie stationed himself by the side of the road, hidden in a thicket of bushes. A poor family was walking down the path at the same time and he saw them drop a coin. He was about to retrieve it and give it back to them, when the merchant arrived. From what Artie's told me, he retreated back into the bushes and watched the man dismount his horse and take the coin. Artie said he would have stolen from him right then and there for daring to steal from this family, when the merchant hailed them over and returned their coin, plus another bag of crestas. Apparently, the merchant had once been poor himself and knew what it was like to go hungry. The merchant went about helping the poor whenever he could.

"Artie was so touched by the man's kindness that he allowed both parties to leave without ever revealing his presence. Dad was, of course, furious. They argued again. Artie said that, as thieves, we should use our gifts of theft to help those less fortunate and punish those responsible for their misery, but only if they were caught misusing their powers, for if you can't see them abusing it, how can you rightly punish them?

"Dad's argument was that we're not judges to determine the guilt of our victims, that we should care only for ourselves and the thief nation. The one place Dad will not condone thievery is in our own halls, so you two are safe from theft, until you leave."

Finished, Sylvia looked to Mag and me for our reactions.

"I can see their reasoning," Mag said. "Your dad is a predator, and should not predators prey on the weak to survive? But Artie is the dog among wolves. His efforts to save the lambs from the wolves are noble, indeed, but when trapped in this den of wolves, he is far outnumbered."

My thoughts had strayed back to Silent Stream. I had seen that man attempting to cheat that family of the little money they had, just so they could buy bread. Artie had resorted to theft only when it became clear that the man was a crook. That was noble, right?

Our talk had led us straight to the entrance of the main chamber and there was yelling inside. We were at the end of the passageway, peering into the throne room, but none of the thieves in the chamber had spotted us yet, so I stopped to listen.

"You just had to come after me, didn't you?" I recognized Artie's voice.

"We needed this opportunity to talk!" the second voice belonged to Leopold Quick.

"Some opportunity!" Artie said bitterly. "You forced me here!"

"What did you expect? You ran away!"

"For good reason! Dad, you can't just steal from innocents!" Artie shouted.

"Not this again! I'll steal from whomever I please!"

"Did you have to send your thieves after me? Maybe I didn't want to be found!"

"I told them not to harm you!"

"You just don't get it!" Artie said. "You told your thieves to drag me back, even if I was in the midst of something important! What if I was in a fight and to capture me was to forfeit my life? I was harassed by trolls for information about the hideout, before I even made it past Yellowbird! Where were you then?"

"It never would have come to that. Besides, they would have incapacitated your opponent, troll or not!"

"Well, *Dad,* if you must know, I was in the middle of something important! Did you see my friends? We were *trying* to find young ice rabbits kidnapped from their home! It's the only way the Kaninen leader will help us! I was actually enjoying myself traveling with Penelope and Mag! Now, thanks to you, they probably hate me for what I am and I'll lose my two closest friends! I hope you're hap-"

He broke off when he saw me marching toward him. I stopped when I was a foot away. I had made my decision.

"Penelope, I-" Artie began, but stopped short when I reached out and gave him a big hug. Silence. Nobody moved or spoke as I extended the hug by an extra few seconds, before I broke contact.

"That," I said, "is for being a good friend."

I looked Artie straight in the eye. "Artie, I will never hate you and neither will Mag. You've proven to be trustworthy and seriously, why would I hold your past against you? You're my friend, Artie, and nothing will ever change that."

I turned to Thief Master Quick. "Sir," I said. "Thank you very much for allowing us access to your lair. It was an... enlightening experience to heal Mag's wing within your halls."

"Wait, you saved her?" Artie yelped.

"Indeed," Mag said. "But, if I ever find the thief Tristan, he'll wish he was never born."

"I'm sure we've all felt like that at some point," Thief Master Quick said, with a slight smile.

"This is much worse, Father," Sylvia said. "Mag has every right to feel as she does."

"This is... most distressing," Thief Master Quick said, lacing his fingers together in contemplation. "Please continue, Sylvia."

Sylvia's eyes darted around the room and I knew she was checking for Tristan or any other possible spies.

Thief Master Quick appeared to have noticed this as well, because he said, "Thieves, attend to your duties."

Every thief in the chamber, save the Quicks, all pretended to be engaged with one task or another as Sylvia held a whispered conversation with her parents.

I knew the thieves were focused entirely on the three Quicks on the platform, so Mag and I took the opportunity to tell Artie, in whispers, of the dragon bond.

His eyes grew wide as he listened. When we finished, he said, "I can't believe this! The last time something this momentous occurred was-"

"Was about a hundred years ago," I finished.

Artie hesitated, then said, "Did you mean what you said, Penelope? That we're still friends, and nothing will ever change that?"

"Artie," I said gently, "you should know me better by now. You've never stolen from us and you've been nothing but generous on this quest."

"How many humans would agree to help strangers they only just met, especially if one of them happened to be part of a race they mistrusted with treasure?" Mag said. "You are truly one of a kind, Artie Quick."

"Please, I try *not* to use my last name. Too many bad memories with him," Artie said, gesturing toward his father, who frowned as Sylvia continued her tale.

"Artie," I said. "Your name is part of you, and no matter what your father has done, that's no reason to be ashamed of who you are. Call yourself by the name 'Quick' and you may forge a new identity for yourself, away from your father's influence."

"You still want me on your quest?"

"What part of we don't care who your father is, don't you understand?" I said fiercely. "Thief or no thief, you're still our friend, and you're coming, whether you like it or not."

Artie grinned. "That's all I needed to hear."

"How can this be?" Thief Master Quick said, causing us to jump. "Thieves," he said, his voice echoing. "A breach in conduct has arisen. Terrible Tristan McGraw's actions almost crippled one of our guests!"

There was a yell of outrage from the assembled thieves.

"What happened?" one thief asked.

"You know our guests?" Thief Master Quick said. "Artie's two friends: the witch Penelope and the dragon Mag. When Sylvia escorted them to the storage room for the gemser plants, Tristan and several other rogue thieves burned every last scrap of flower and stem, so as to prove useless."

"The dragon looks fine to me," another thief said. There were murmurs of agreement.

"That's because Penelope raced the clock to retrieve the gemser plants grown outside," Sylvia said angrily. "It wouldn't had been necessary if-"

"If that beast had never entered these halls." Tristan and his cohorts had arrived.

"What do you want, Tristan?" Sylvia said, her voice dripping with venom.

"Temper, temper, Sylvia," Tristan said. "That's no way to talk to a fellow thief, especially here."

"Answer Sylvia's question," Thief Master Quick said with a frown. "What do you want?"

Tristan made a great show of sighing. "To business, I suppose. All right, Quick, you ask what I want? I only have two requests. First of all, I want you to get rid of the beast within our halls."

"Mag is *not* a beast," I growled.

"Second," Tristan said, ignoring me. "I want you to stand down, Quick. You've grown too soft over the years, becoming more and more like your brat," he gestured toward Artie. "We've lost so much treasure on campaigns to find him and what do we have to show for it? Your brat crash-landed in our lake and dragged back here! What was the point of sending us out to search, if he basically handed himself in? No, Quick, you are no longer fit to lead. Stand down and thieves will once again be feared across Alsmora, but only with me at its head."

A dozen or so thieves cheered at this pronouncement, while the others, even Artie, drew their knives and clustered around Thief Master Quick in a protective semicircle, facing Tristan.

Artie, himself, who was at the front of the pack, said, "I may not always agree with my father, Tristan, but you are unfit to lead. Look what your leadership has gotten us: our whole supply of gemser plants burned to the ground because of your fear and anger. How are you best suited to guide the thief nation if you can't even see past your own prejudices?"

Tristan narrowed his eyes at Artie. "You've gone too far, *Arthur*, you and your father. You'll see. Thieves," he said, addressing the chamber at large. "If you are tired of blindly following the rule of the Quicks, than come with me! We'll form our own league of thieves and it will be far more successful than the Quick operation will ever be."

Tristan and his two followers, the ones who had burned the gemser plants, turned on their heels and strode from the room. After a furtive glance at the other thieves, a dozen others departed to join him.

Relaxing, the remaining hundred or so thieves settled into their former positions around the room.

Returning to his place beside Mag and me, Artie said, "We haven't seen the end of this. Tristan is a coward, dictated by fear and a lust for power. He hasn't changed since I last saw him."

"Maybe we should go," I said. "The thieves have already done enough for us and I'd hate to see them to suffer on our account."

Artie snorted. "Pen, Tristan would have challenged my father with or without our presence. It was only a matter of time."

"Besides," Mag said. "We still don't know where to go. Now that my wing's healed, I can easily fly us to wherever it is we're going."

"What is this?" Thief Master Quick demanded. "Did I hear you say you were leaving again, Artie?"

"Yes, Dad. We have to finish our quest. You can't keep me here forever."

"Artie, I–" Thief Master Quick began, but Yolanda Quick placed a hand on her husband's arm.

"Leopold," she said gently. "We can't keep Artie here if he doesn't want to stay. Make up with him. Don't let him leave until you come to an understanding, but allow him to leave nonetheless."

Thief Master Quick slowly nodded. "Yes, dear." Turning to Artie, he said, "Artie, when you stood up to Tristan, I must say, I was impressed. I–I didn't know you had it in you."

"…Thanks, Dad."

"I may not have always agreed with your decisions, like when you lost all that treasure to that wealthy merchant, or the time you dropped my sword in the lake to keep me from harming that scholar, or the time–"

"Leopold," Yolanda said, quietly and dangerously.

"Oh, uh, you're quite right, my dear. The point is, though I may not agree with your past actions, seeing you today, friends with a dragon and witch as Sylvia tells me, well, Artie, I'm proud of who you've become."

Artie stood there, speechless, and then in a voice thick with emotion, said, "I'm proud of you too, Dad. You may not have always been there for me, but you're still the best father in the world, in my book."

They stood there, father and son, both staring at the ground, too embarrassed to look up.

"Is that the best we can get out of them?" Sylvia asked her mother with a sigh.

"I believe so," Yolanda said. "Leopold, isn't there something else you wanted to tell Artie?"

He stared blankly at her.

"How you *won't* be sending thieves out to search for him again?"

"Oh, yes, of course. No thief in this hall will be sent to track you down this time, Artie."

Artie and the other thieves looked relieved at the news.

"Well, this is great," I said. "We just have one problem."

"Oh, and what's that?" Mr. Quick said.

"We still don't know where to go," I said. "All we have is a riddle."

"A riddle, huh? Well, recite it, I love a good puzzle."

Mag, who had the best memory, faced Mr. Quick and said,

> "Amid the land of green and changing rocks,
> Travel there against the clock.
> Traverse the tunnels dark if you dare
> To retrieve the star and the hare."

"Hmm? And who gave you this riddle?"

"A Kaninen," Artie said.

"Really?" Mr. Quick said. "I didn't know they was still around."

"Can you solve the riddle?" I asked, anxiously.

Leopold snorted. "Do thieves like treasure? 'Amid the land of green and changing rocks.' Yolanda, my dear, doesn't that sound like the oasis we visited on our honeymoon?"

"I believe you're right, Leopold," Yolanda said, thoughtfully. "Oh, I remember the green palm trees of the desert. It was so beautiful."

"So, we go to this oasis, 'traveling there against the clock,' to the land of green palm trees and changing desert rocks?" Artie said.

"Sounds like it," I said. "What about the last two lines? 'Traverse the tunnels dark if you dare, to retrieve the star and the hare.' Could that be at the oasis?"

"If it is," Mr. Quick said. "I've never seen it."

"It may be hidden," Mag said. "We could go to the oasis and search for it."

"If we could find these tunnels, we might be able to save the Kaninen, and then I can, uh, come back and visit you, Dad," Artie said, awkwardly.

"Well, first things first," I said. "How do we get to this oasis?"

Chapter Twenty-Seven

Sand Dunes All Look the Same

I HAD TO ADMIT: THE THIEVES HAD GROWN ON me during my time with them. I still didn't trust them, except for Artie of course, but as long as we were inside the Quick Hideout, no thief bothered us. I kept glancing over my shoulder to ensure nobody was sneaking up to steal from me, though.

All in all, I was glad we were leaving. Artie's parents had given us directions to the oasis, saying we would have to fly over the Sand Dune Desert before we found it.

"Remember, it's right past the desert," Mr. Quick said.

"And don't forget," Yolanda Quick added. "If you reach the flower fields, you've gone too far."

Trying to keep all this in mind, I stood off to the side, beyond the entrance of the hideout with Mag in her human form, blinking in the new morning light, while Artie and his family said good-bye.

"Oh, my little Artie," Yolanda said. "Oh, my baby. Please, be careful."

"Mom!" Artie protested as she hugged him.

She released him and Sylvia stepped forward. "Good luck, Artie." Then, she whispered something to him, something that I couldn't make out.

Artie blushed and said, "I am not, Sylvia!"

She smiled knowingly and said, "Whatever you say, Artie." Then, she too hugged him and stepped aside.

Mr. Quick stood before Artie. "Good luck, son. Rob a couple of trolls for me, will you?"

Artie smiled faintly. "Of course, Dad." They gave each other an awkward handshake and Artie made his way to Mag and me. I thought I could detect relief on his face.

"My thieves have given you supplies," Mr. Quick said. "That should last you until you reach the oasis. If you run low, I would suggest stopping somewhere to steal some provisions."

We waved to Artie's family as we crossed the packed sand surrounding the Quick Hideout, onto a stretch of grass and trees, before we started toward the Sand Dune Desert.

* * *

Hours later, we stopped and ate lunch beside a rather scraggily tree, examining the shifting sand before us. We were at the very edge of the desert.

"Are you ready to cross?" Artie asked, checking his bag of supplies.

"I suppose," I said. "It shouldn't be that far."

Mag transformed into her dragon self again. "It will be faster to fly," she explained. "Don't look at me like that, Penelope. We need to get there quickly. Besides, I keep telling you, my wing is fine."

I finished packing the saddle bags on Mag's back and went to stand beside her ruby head.

"Do you feel it, Penelope?"

All I could feel was the wind swirling the sand around me. When I expressed this to Mag, she said, "Sand storm's coming."

I blanched. I had never seen a sand storm before, but had heard they were dangerous. "Is it... safe to go out in this storm?"

"What other choice do we have, Pen?" Artie said, joining us. "My father said the oasis is right past the Sand Dune Desert. We'll just have to fly in a straight line and hope for the best. It'll take too long to go around."

"We trust your judgment, Mag," I said. "I know you'll see us there safely." I hoisted myself onto her back, ready for takeoff. Artie swung up behind me. Mag leapt into the sky and angled toward the south.

At first, the flight was calm. We were buffeted from time to time with a gust of wind or a blast of sand, but the real trouble didn't begin until an hour after departure.

Mag's breathing became labored and she slowed, as she tested herself against the sand storm. It blew us side to side, up and down, this way and that, with us barely hanging on. Artie and I were forced to cover our mouths and noses against the swirling sand.

I willed Mag to succeed as she fought against the onslaught of the storm. Artie murmured several encouraging remarks.

Then, things went horribly wrong. Mag broke free of the wind and sand, but only for a moment, before she was pelted with faster wind and rocks, which made several dinging sounds as they bounced off her scales.

Mag threw herself against the storm, only to be pushed back, until she was virtually at a standstill. A torrent of wind pounded into her from all sides, pushing her to and fro, without any means of escape.

A jet of wind blasted Mag to the right, flipping her upside down. Artie and I each grabbed a spike and hung on doggedly. I felt my grip slipping, the blood pounding in my head, as I dangled fifty feet in the air.

I was coated with perspiration as I strove to hold on. The sweat on my hands made the task slippery. The spike slid from my grasp and I found myself falling to earth, Artie calling my name.

I was screaming. I could see Mag right herself with effort. A tiny dot broke away from Mag and within a second, Artie had joined my fall.

Tears were streaming down my face from the rush of wind. As Artie caught up with me, I reached out wildly and somehow seized his hand.

Mag swooped down, but the wind prevented her from sailing underneath to catch us. She flapped her wings, trying to stay in place, but the additional wind caused us to plummet faster with every second.

I opened my mouth to cry out a spell, but billowing sand rushed in, threatening to choke me. Somehow, I was able to gasp out, "Enchauta." Instead of crashing, we slowed to a gentle stop and landed with a soft *thump* on the ground.

I rose to my hands and knees, coughing up sand as I watched Mag tumble head over tail, her scales a bright scarlet as the wind knocked her away from us, into the heart of the storm.

I stood rigid, shocked at the forces of nature, until Artie tapped my shoulder.

"She'll be all right," he said. "Mag will make it out. But, you know, we do tend to fall off Mag a lot."

I smiled slightly, before closing my eyes. My bond with Mag told me she was due south of our current location.

Taking stock of our supplies, I was surprised to see Artie had managed to grab one of the supply bags before our fall.

Artie blushed. "I seized the strap just as Mag flipped. Should prove useful, right?"

"At least we won't starve or dehydrate," I said, shielding my eyes from the unforgiving afternoon sun. "Come on," I said, trudging south. "Mag's this way." I was grateful that Artie didn't argue, but followed me silently down my chosen path.

Time, in that barren landscape, was difficult to guess. I knew we had been walking for some time, but every sand dune and every grain of swirling sand looked the same, so I couldn't be sure whether or not we had made any progress.

I only became aware of night, when the land turned a dusky purple and cool shade swept over the land.

I blinked. Was the day really gone? We had only been walking for five minutes, or five hours, I wasn't sure which.

We finally halted beside one of the endless sand dunes and made camp. As we munched on a couple of apples and coughed on sand, I thought I could hear the sounds of nocturnal animals scurry past. A coyote howled, drowning out everything else in the otherwise flat landscape. It must have wandered down from a nearby mountain.

I closed my eyes and leaned against our sand dune, concentrating on Mag's presence, which was still to the south. I hoped she had escaped the storm.

We sat in silence, on opposite ends of our camp, surrounded by the howling wind, when Artie said, "Pen?"

I opened my eyes. "Yes?"

"What are we going to do after we save the Kaninens and your amulet is returned?"

"What do you mean? We're going to go back to the castle. I'm sure Queen Alana will accept you, after we explain the situation. You're not like other thieves, Artie."

"Thanks, but what I meant was, what are we going to do about your training? You won't get any at the castle."

"We'll decide after we save the Kaninens," I said, turning away. "Its late. Let's get some sleep and we can continue this conversation in the morning."

"No, I'll stay awake and keep watch. I don't want anyone sneaking up on us."

"Wake me around midnight and I'll keep watch until dawn. We'll both need our rest for tomorrow."

But truthfully, I felt wide awake. What was I going to do after I got my amulet back? It was true that I needed to continue my training and it would be difficult at the castle, but I desperately wanted to see Lydia and Malcolm again. What were they doing right now? Lydia was probably still looking for the person who started the fire. At least she was safe. As for Malcolm, had he really started that fire? If so, why? I sighed as I drifted off into a fitful sleep. For now, Malcolm and Lydia would simply have to look after themselves, like Artie and I would have to do in the desert tomorrow.

* * *

It felt as if I had only been sleeping for seconds, when Artie shook me awake. I shivered in the cold desert night and sat against a sand dune to keep watch, fingering the strap of the bag. Artie dropped off to sleep nearby, his gentle, steady breathing mixing with the soft noises of the night. I thought I heard the coyote howling again, but it never came close.

When dawn came, we had a scant breakfast of apples and biscuits, which did nothing to alleviate our thirst. We had one canteen of water and we each took a small sip before continuing on our way.

I walked in a slightly southeast direction, following my connection to Mag. Artie didn't complain. He just trailed behind me, carrying the bag of supplies.

Our trip through the desert morning was pleasant, a soft breeze played across our faces, but we were soon exhausted from walking in the slowly shifting sand.

Around midmorning, the gentle breeze had turned into another miniature sand storm, like the one that had thrown us off course the previous day.

Shielding our eyes, mouths, and noses from the stinging sand and the blistering sun, we plodded farther, never deviating from the course I set forth.

We took periodic sips of water, but soon, our supply reached a dangerously low level. I heard the squawks of birds and was dismayed to find vultures circling above us. I tried not to look at them.

As noon neared, Artie and I halted. We were too exhausted to continue. We stood, shaking and trying hard to remain awake and alert.

"Pen," Artie said, his voice a dull croak. "Is there a spell to make it rain?"

"Perhaps," I said. It was hard to talk. "But if there is, I don't know it. Mag hasn't taught me that one yet."

Artie handed me the canteen. "Here, take the rest of the water. There isn't much left, but there's enough."

I firmly pressed the canteen and our precious supply of water back into his hands.

"No, Artie," I said. "Either we both share what is left, or we get none at all."

Artie hesitated and then took a carefully measured sip from the canteen. I did the same. There was now only the tiniest mouthful remaining.

Slightly refreshed, I plodded forward into the hot afternoon, when I thought I heard the whimpering of a dog.

Artie and I exchanged looks and then hurried as fast as we could, slipping and sliding through the sand, until we reached the base of a creosote bush and found a coyote stretched out on its side, panting. I checked the animal's forehead and found it burning.

"Artie, I need water."

He handed over the canteen without complaint as I reached into my bag and extracted some leftover bitterbrush. Remembering what Mrs. Hexley, the castle healer, taught me one rainy day, I grabbed one of the leaves from the creosote bush. Crushing the bitterbrush and the creosote leaf, I sprinkled a few drops of water on it to make a paste. Praying that this would work, I placed the mixture on the coyote's forehead and poured the last of our precious water into its mouth.

A moment later, the coyote stirred and licked my hand. I gave a sigh of relief as it gingerly rose into a seated position and licked Artie as well.

I slumped against the creosote brush, pleased to have helped the coyote, but also painfully conscious of my own thirst.

The coyote seemed to sense my discomfort, for he cocked his head and gazed at me with curious eyes.

I smiled and said, "I'm glad you're all right, but would you happen to know where we could find some water?"

The coyote stood, nudged my hand until I rose, and trotted in the southeasterly direction I'd been following.

Artie and I shuffled behind our guide, moving so slowly we were almost at a standstill. The sand continued to billow around us. The coyote turned his head away, but didn't pause in his battle against the elements.

After what seemed like hours of fighting the storm, the sand ceased pelting and the wind died down. The sand storm was gone, leaving the desert to the south flat and finally still, while the storm raged behind us.

The coyote barked, loud and sharp, and startled, I glanced down. The friendly canine was wagging his tail, and running east, toward what looked like a palm tree, growing beside a spring of water. I could see a mountain in the distance.

Laughing, Artie and I ran after the coyote and entered what appeared to be an oasis village.

Kneeling, I glimpsed my hair in the water's reflective surface. It was almost pure silver, except for a few strands of brown near the top of my head. I filled the canteen with cool, sweet water and gulped down several mouthfuls. Handing it to Artie, I looked down at our guide. The coyote was lapping up water as well.

"Thank you," I said, gratitude swimming within me. The coyote raised his head, water dripping from his muzzle and padded away, further into town.

Artie and I stayed by the spring. My connection with Mag told me she was right on top of us, but I couldn't see any sign of red in the small oasis or the surrounding sky.

Then, I heard the soft swish of wings. Mag emerged straight from the sand storm's depths, the dust sparkling off her scales.

We waved at Mag, who dived toward us. A foot from the ground, she transformed back into human, and landed lightly beside me. "Good to see you again, Penelope, Artie. I've been searching for you everywhere. That was my third trip into the desert."

I smiled up at her. "Good to see you too, Mag."

And we stood together, three friends in a paradise among the sands, happy for the moment in each other's company.

Chapter Twenty-Eight

Information for a Price

"**W**HAT DO WE DO NOW?" I ASKED. "We're at the oasis, but where do we find the 'tunnels dark?'"

Mag sniffed the spring of water. "I smell trickery here, but this makes no sense, the scent is coming from below ground."

"Maybe there's a secret passageway," Artie said, tapping the earth.

"How would we go about finding it?" I asked.

"We could jump in and swim to the bottom," Mag suggested.

"Too simple," Artie said. "Besides, anyone could find it if that was the case. Luckily, a friend of mine lives here. He should be able to help us find the entrance to the secret passageway and sell us goods, for a price."

"Let me guess," I said. "He's a thief, right?"

"Right," Artie said. "He said that if I ever needed to find him, to look for the red house with the blue roof."

"Colorful. That shouldn't be hard to spot," I said.

"What can I say? Leon loves rubies and sapphires. Which reminds me, Pen, don't mention your amulet to Leon. He might steal it from the Kaninens himself."

We walked down the streets, searching for the red and blue house. The roads were congested with people, all pushing and shoving each other. It took all my concentration not to lose Mag or Artie in the crowd.

We passed several small houses and outdoor markets as we searched. None of them were red or blue.

I stopped to admire a model ship-in-a-bottle, feeling drawn to it because of the Ruby Ship, which was safely in my bag.

"Looking to buy, my dear?" the haggard woman behind the stall said.

"No, thanks," Artie said, steering me away from the woman.

"You know, those who admire my ship are destined for great adventure," the woman called after us.

I could feel the woman's stare on my back. I shuddered. Her talk of destiny and great adventures unnerved me.

The people before us parted as we reached a fork in the road. I studied the buildings in both directions, looking for any sign of red and blue.

"Leon should be here," Artie said. "All these trinkets and jewels are a thief's paradise."

As if on cue, someone shouted, "Stop, thief!"

A boy with dark, shaggy hair and an impish smile, roughly Artie's age, came running down the street, carrying a gold watch, and chased by a guard.

"Leon!" Artie said. "Hurry, we need a distraction!"

"Aldrich is going to kill me," Mag muttered, transforming back into a dragon, as Leon ran past. She roared, causing both prey and pursuer to jump.

I scrambled onto Mag's back as Artie grabbed Leon's arm, pulling himself and the dark-haired thief beside me. Mag tensed and sprang into the sky, the man chasing Leon shaking his fist at the departing dragon.

"Thanks," Leon said, his impish smile still in place. Focusing on Artie, his smile became wider, if that was possible, and said, "Artie! I haven't seen you for ages! How are you?"

"Fine, Leon," Artie said. He sounded exasperated. "What did you steal this time?"

"Oh, this. It's nothing. Just some fancy watch I conned off some man." It was a golden pocket watch with a blue star etched on the inside cover. I had a vague feeling that I had seen it before.

"Right. You're going to have to return that."

"You and your rules, Artie," Leon laughed. "Don't be so quick, Quick. I need to make a living too."

Artie forced a smile and said, "We've come for your help, Leon."

"My help? You're welcome to all the treasure I have, but never the rubies or sapphires."

"Not that kind of help. Leon, this is Penelope. Penelope, Leon."

Leon shook my hand and whistled. "Nice one, Artie."

Artie glared. "Penelope is a witch, Leon. We're sitting on our friend, the dragon Mag."

"Greetings," Mag said.

Leon's grin was as wide as ever. "I never thought I would ride a dragon! And a ruby one at that!"

"Leon! Focus!" Artie said, snapping his fingers in Leon's face to gain his attention. "We're searching for the underground chamber beneath the spring. Have you heard of it?"

For the first time, Leon's grin faded. "You're not seriously going back to the oasis, are you? Tristan's down there!"

"What?" I spluttered. "What is he doing here?"

Leon shrugged. "I don't know, but man, did I score! Tristan was targeting the same watch."

Artie's eyes grew wide. "Leon, give me that watch!"

"No way, you just want it for yourself," Leon said, clutching it to his chest.

"Please, Leon, you don't understand," Artie said. "If I'm right, this is the mystical Starclock."

Mag gasped and dropped a couple of feet.

"The what?" I said.

"The Starclock is a tiny chip of meteorite that has the power to slow down time," Mag explained tightly. "Its much too dangerous."

"It sounds cool," Leon said. "I think I'll keep it."

"Leon!"

"What? I'm not giving it to Tristan, am I? Relax, Artie."

"Do you know how to get into the underground chamber?" I asked sweetly, shooting Artie a look that clearly said later.

"No," Leon said. "Recently, people have been going to the spring and just disappear. It's weird. I tried to follow someone in once, you know, to get at this ruby they had. Anyway, whatever opened for him wouldn't open for me. Its like it won't reopen until whoever's inside comes out again."

"Thanks, Leon," Artie said. "Where should we drop you?"

"At my house. It's farthest from the spring, to the right."

"We'll also need some supplies," I said.

"Ah," Leon's grin returned. "Now that's going to cost you."

"How much?" Artie said through gritted teeth.

"Its barely anything, you'll hardly even notice its missing," Leon said.

"How much?"

"Just a tiny scale," Leon said. "It could be the smallest one you've got for all I care."

I glared at Leon, not liking the thief and said, quietly, so only Mag could hear me, "What do you think?"

"I don't like it, but it seems the only way to secure his help. Go ahead, Penelope. The small one, by the base of my neck is loose, anyway."

I pried the scale loose, relieved when Mag didn't wince, and turned to Leon. "Mag has agreed to your terms. Here's the scale."

I made to hand the ruby scale to Leon, but Artie beat him to it.

"Not so fast, Leon. I need you to give me the Starclock in exchange for the scale," Artie said, holding it out of his reach.

"You're no fun," Leon pouted. "Yes, I promise. Happy?" Leon said, as he and Artie traded. It was then that I got a good look at the Starclock. I had indeed seen it twice before, once in Kelton Castle and again at Dragon Valley.

In a daze, I spotted Leon's house as Mag dived for the ground. I shook my head, trying to clear it. The sooner Leon was off Mag's back, the better. The impish robber was nice enough, but I still found it difficult to trust a thief, except for, of course, Artie.

* * *

We hid behind a palm tree at the spring. After dropping Leon off at his house, Mag had become human once more and we walked back, so as to not attract even more attention. We had returned to find Tristan and his two cohorts, the ones who had burned the gemser plants, standing by the water's edge.

"I bet it was Leon," Tristan grumbled. "He never knew what was good for him."

The thief on the right, a hunchbacked man, with pointed teeth, said, "What about the master? He won't be happy when he hears the Kaninen has escaped."

"We'll worry about him later," Tristan snarled. "First, I want to use the Starclock to ruin Quick."

Next to me, Artie balled his fists.

"It won't do us any good until we find it," the man on the left said. Three gold teeth flashed as he grinned. "Let's just go take it from Leon."

"Yeah," Tristan said, cracking his knuckles. "That will teach the little upstart to steal from me."

After they had departed in the direction of Leon's house, we came out from behind the tree and stopped next to a large, flat rock.

"We have to go warn Leon," Artie said immediately.

Mag shook her head. "We'll never make it before them, unless you want to alert them with my massive presence."

"Leon will be all right, Artie," I tried to reassure him.

"You're right, Miss Bogg. Leon will be fine." I turned and saw Aldrich standing behind me. "I met Leon once, years ago. He is a troublemaker, but very resourceful."

"Grandfather! What are you doing here?" Mag said.

"I was investigating some strange occurrences in the oasis," Aldrich said. "But, someone stole my watch."

"Do you mean this?" Artie asked, taking the Starclock from his pocket.

"Yes! How did you get it?"

"Leon stole it," I explained. "We traded for it."

"I see," Aldrich said slowly. "Well, I'm sorry to cut this short, but the leader of the Fire Storm elites has requested a meeting and I don't want to be late. Mag, look after the Starclock. We'll discuss your transforming in a populated area when I return. For now, head for Cherry Grove and look for Mad Maude. I'll explain everything later."

And without another word, he tapped the flat rock. It moved to reveal a hole, through which he disappeared. Before I could take a closer look, the rock slid back into place, sealing Aldrich off from the outside world.

Chapter Twenty-Nine

The Cherry Pits of Direction

CHERRY GROVE WAS ONLY ABOUT FIFTY miles southeast from the oasis. After several fruitless attempts to shift the rock, we had to admit that Leon was right. Aldrich had simply disappeared. Mag transformed back into a dragon and we flew swiftly away. Two hours later, she glided over a mountain range, followed by a blue streak of water that glittered and sparkled when viewed from the sky above. Cherry Grove sat on its banks.

"Ah, the Golden Glimmer River," Mag sighed. "They say if you time it just right, the water will turn gold and a dip in the river will grant any wish."

I rolled my eyes. "Next you'll be telling us that the reason nobody can find the fairies is because they live in flowers."

Mag didn't answer as she began to circle the village. She touched down on the outskirts of Cherry Grove. The air smelled of the cherries, all ripe and juicy. My stomach rumbled. We hadn't eaten since breakfast that morning, which seemed like a long time ago.

After Mag was back as a human, we wandered the streets slowly, on the lookout for Mad Maude, but also painfully aware that we didn't know what she looked like. We stopped to talk to several people, but nobody could tell us a thing about her.

"I think I've heard of her," they would say, with bemused expressions on their faces, but nobody could tell us anything further.

"She has to be here somewhere," Mag said. "I can detect her scent."

"You can?" Artie said.

"Yes, it smells of magic and it's powerful, too."

"Where does your nose say we should go?" I asked.

Mag lifted her nose to the air. "That way," she said, pointing straight ahead to a small park, with cherry trees growing all around. But, before we could do more than take a few steps in that direction, a deep, grating voice growled, "Stop!"

I spun around and came face-to-face with green, muscled arms, a club clasped in one gigantic fist. I tilted my head back and saw the cruel, scowling face of Laborc.

Within seconds, my sword was out. I hadn't used it since my training session with Artie in Tealeaf, but I felt braver holding it. Out of the corner of my eye, I could see Artie gripping his knife and Mag readying her claws.

"What do you want, Laborc?" I demanded.

He was looking at Artie. "Thief, I should have known you would have allied yourself with these two."

"Laborc," Artie said, stiffly.

"What do you want?"

Laborc turned his dark, hate-filled eyes on me. "My master wishes me to make you a proposition."

"Your master?"

Laborc ignored me. "He knows the Kaninens have stolen your amulet, witch, and he would like to offer his services in helping you retrieve it."

"Meaning what?" Mag snapped.

"Meaning that he'll get your amulet back from the Kaninens and return it to you. All you have to do is stay away from Mad Maude and leave the last Kaninen where she is. What have the ice rabbits done for you, except send you on a wild goose chase?"

I looked at Artie and Mag. Neither one had lowered their weapons.

"Do we have a deal?"

I turned back to Laborc and pointed my sword straight at his heart. "No deal," I said, my voice deadly calm. "I made a promise to Flurry that I would save every Kaninen and *I will keep that promise.*"

A line of red was trickling from where the point of my sword met Laborc's skin. I recoiled, drawing my sword away in horror.

Laborc sneered at me. "So be it," he spat. "My master charged me with leaving you in peace after our little conversation. Don't expect him to be so lenient with you in the future."

He disappeared into the nearest stand of cherry trees.

I lowered my sword shakily.

I felt Artie's hand on my shoulder, "You okay, Pen?"

"Yeah. Yeah, I'm fine."

"Come on," Mag said, retracting her claws. "Mad Maude is still straight ahead."

I wiped the blood off my sword, as we made our way across the park, the grass springy under our feet. A huge crowd of people was blocking our way to the oldest and most bent tree I'd ever seen.

"She's over there," Mag said, indicating the tree.

"You've got to be kidding me," I said. "How are we going to fight through all these people?"

"Excuse me," Artie said, tapping a nearby bearded man on the shoulder. "We're looking for Mad Maude. Is she here?"

"Aye," the man said. "But, she's at the center of the throng. Folks come from miles around to see her."

"Could we slip by?" Artie said. "We're kind of in a hurry."

The man nodded and stepped aside, leaving us a clear view of a woman sitting against the trunk of a tree.

She had wild white hair, sticking up as if she had been struck by lightning; a long, pointed nose; and pale blue eyes that seemed to pierce through my innermost thoughts and feelings.

I had the strangest sense that I had seen her before.

We waited while she talked in quiet voices with a young woman sitting across from her. They seemed to be discussing a toad problem. Bored, I looked at the cherry tree. A purple lizard climbed down the side and came to rest on the older, wilder woman's shoulder.

The young woman left and Mag, Artie, and I stepped forward.

"M?" I asked, stopping dead. I hadn't seen her since I was eight in Tealeaf, but there was no mistaking her wild, white hair.

"Greetings, oh wise one," Mag said, nudging me in the ribs and bowing to the old woman. "We are weary travelers in search of directions. Can you help us?"

"I might," she said, her voice high-pitched and cracked. "But first, thou must tell me thy names. You," she said, pointing a crooked finger at Mag. "Name, species, origin. And speak honestly, dragon."

Mag looked taken aback, but she answered dutifully. "Name: Magma or Mag for short. Species: dragon. Origin: daughter of Storm the Savage and Starlight the Fierce and Beautiful." She spoke quietly, but her eyes never left M's.

"Very good," the woman purred. "You," she pointed at Artie. "Name, weapon, and astrological sign."

"Name: Arthur, but I prefer Artie. Weapon: the knife. Astrological sign: well, I was born in March."

"When in March?"

"The fifteenth."

"Ah, so you are a Pisces, sign of caring and forgiving. Symbol is the twin fish."

"You," she turned to me. "Name, place of birth, and fact about trolls."

I sighed. "Seriously, M, do I have to answer?"

M stared at me without blinking. "Yes."

"Name: Penelope. Place of birth: Tealeaf. As for trolls, they are vicious monsters who attack innocent people."

"How do you know? How many trolls have you met?

"Two," I said.

"You should meet Hugo, then. But, you answered my questions, so I am obliged to help."

"Wait, you didn't tell us your name," Artie said. "Are you Mad Maude?"

M stared balefully at him. "That's none of your business. And, speaking of business," she pulled out a handful of cherry pits.

I gaped at her. Was she mad?

M rolled the pits in her hand, which produced a slight clacking noise. "Here's how the game works: I will toss the pits onto the ground. Cissy here," she patted the lizard fondly, "will collect the pits. Your job is to retrieve as many as you can and I will use your winnings to read your direction."

Yep, I thought with certainty, definitely mad.

"You!" the woman shot at me, causing me to jump. "You will play against Cissy."

The crowd pressed in.

Oh, great, I thought, humiliated in front of everyone, and by a lizard, no less!

"Ma'am, can't Artie or I help?" Mag asked.

"No, I sense in this one much doubt and confusion in the way of seeing. She must learn how to see on her own."

The crowd snickered. Artie pulled me aside and whispered urgently, "If you get into trouble say, 'Zanalent.' Sylvia taught me this spell."

"Ready?" M said. "Begin!" And she threw the cherry pits onto the ground. Cissy hopped from her shoulder and rolled the pits back to her mistress, who placed them in the wide sleeves of her faded blue cloak.

I was shocked at how fast the lizard was. I would reach for a pit, when the little purple monstrosity would dash forward and steal it through my fingertips. Soon, Cissy had delivered almost half the pits to M. I had not collected a single one.

Frustrated, I cried, "Zanalent!" Half of the remaining cherry pits zoomed into my outstretched hand, even going so far as to take one from Cissy, who was rolling it to M.

From then on, I was the faster contestant, summoning cherry pits into my hand, until I had three-quarters before me.

"Enough," M said, and the lizard sprang onto the palm of her hand. "I have never seen a traveler collect the pits in that manner before. You have truly learned how to see."

"Thank you," I said, warily. What was the point of M pretending not to know me in front of all these people?

Now that the contest was over, I could see tiny arrows sketched onto the sides of the pits.

"May I see them?" M asked.

I relinquished my hard won cherry pits to her. She studied the inscriptions carefully.

"It is as clear as day. You will go north on a great ship. Your actions will have far greater consequences than you can possibly image. But for now, you have more pressing matters closer to home." She abruptly stood up. "You will accompany me to my house. She turned with a swish of her cloak, Cissy hopping onto her shoulder again.

Mag, Artie, and I exchanged looks and hurried after her. She led us on a winding tour of what seemed like the entire village, until we reached a small house in the center of the square.

"Welcome, young travelers," M said, gesturing us inside. "We have much to discuss. Its good to see you again, Penelope."

Chapter Thirty

Mad Maude

THE FIRST THING I NOTICED UPON ENTERING M's house was the crow. He was sitting on a perch just inside the door. He reminded me of Milo.

My suspicions were confirmed when the bird said, "Maude, about time. Where did you pick *them* up?"

"Hello, Milo," Mag said in an exasperated tone. "What brings you here?"

"I happen to live here," Milo said, haughtily.

Ignoring Milo, I turned to the woman and said, "So you *are* Mad Maude. You were watching me throughout my childhood in Tealeaf. Why didn't you tell me who you were sooner?"

"I couldn't," Mad Maude said. "If I told anyone my true identity, it would have put both me and Cissy in danger." Cissy nodded sadly on the table. "Its nice to see you again, my pet," she finished fondly.

I blushed and said, "Its good to see you too."

Mag interrupted impatiently. "This is all well and good, but we need your help."

"Oh, what kind of help?"

"We were tasked with looking for three Kaninens," I said. "We have one more left to find. Have you seen it?"

Mad Maude cackled. "Do yikties poison their prey?"

"Yes," I said, hesitatingly.

"Indeed," she said, smiling crookedly at us. "Just as it is certain a yikty will poison its prey, I know the location of the Kaninen."

"You do? That's wonderful!"

She simply smiled.

We sat there waiting for her to speak, but she continued to stare at us with unblinking eyes.

Mag cleared her throat. "So?"

Mad Maude shifted her attention to Mag. "So, what?"

"So, are you going to tell us the location of the Kaninen or not?" Mag asked, exhaling smoke from her nostrils.

"Of course I could tell you, but you never asked me."

"Will you please tell us where the ice rabbit is?" I said, giving Mag a stern look.

"She's not too far from here, or so Cissy reports. Unfortunately, the Kaninen's captor is protected by powerful enchantments. Only advanced spells can take down his defenses."

"What are these spells?" I asked.

"I can't tell you."

"Would you tell us, please?" Artie asked, speaking up for the first time since we had entered the house.

"No."

"But-"

"I would be glad to tell you," Mad Maude said, "but I don't have the faintest idea which enchantments were used."

"So, we're stuck?" I said, grimly.

"Not necessarily," Mad Maude said. "We know where the Kaninen is, the problem is getting it."

"Where is it?" Mag asked.

"In a cave. I tried to send Milo in to investigate, but he refused to enter."

"Don't blame me," Milo said. "I may be all but invincible, but even I don't dare to tackle a yikty."

"A yikty?!" I cried. Dealing with Wansetop had been bad enough.

"It's the only way if you want to find the Kaninen. The yikty is the captor," Mad Maude said gravely.

Mag, Artie, and I exchanged dark looks. None of us looked too excited by the prospect.

"You don't have to go yet," Mad Maude said. "This is summer. Come winter, the yikties will have to hibernate. If you can wait a few more months, you can slip in and out quietly."

"A few more months?" I said, sitting down heavily. I couldn't believe my ears. That poor little rabbit, lost and alone for another few weeks at least was more than I could bear.

"Well, if you're sure," Mad Maude said. "It should take you a day on dragon back to reach the cave. When you get there, you'll find a narrow hallway. Follow it until you wind up in a chamber. There will be three archways to choose from. Use your magic and say, 'Endoraken.' It will reveal which path to take. Yikties are rarely stationary, so it could be anywhere. Each archway will have a different challenge, so be ready."

"We are in your debt," Artie said. "Is there anything we can do to repay you?"

"Yes," Mad Maude said, turning to me. "When you see your mother, my dear, please be so kind as to say hello from me."

I didn't say anything. Mom. Would—would I truly get to see her again? After the game with the cherry pits, I figured Mad Maude knew what she was talking about. I hoped so.

"You should leave today," Maude said. "The sooner, the better, especially considering Blizzard and his deals. He just can't get over his grudge against the dragons."

I felt as if my mouth had gone dry. Wetting it, I said, slowly, "You know about my amulet?"

"I'm the one who crafted the setting for the amulet, wasn't I?"

"Hold on," Mag said. "Grandfather told me the ruby came from us. How could *you* have crafted it?"

"Ah, my dear young dragon, how little you know. Your kind did indeed possess the ruby first, but when it made its way down to Alice, she knew what it was. She gave it to me for safekeeping. I polished it up, created a setting for it, and gave it to Penelope when I thought she was ready."

I remained silent. I was thinking about my mom and how it had been her last wish for me to have the amulet. Without my knowing, she had been preparing me ever since I was a child. I swelled slightly with anger. Had she only ever thought of the dragons? Had she ever truly done anything for me without it leading back to my supposed destiny?

Maude gazed at me with sad eyes. "Do not be too hard on Alice," she said, as if she had read my mind. "She did the best she could at the time. Besides, you should be grateful. She gave you a normal childhood, at least until Tealeaf... until you had to leave."

I sighed. "I know, I just wish-"

"-that she had told you herself?" Artie asked quietly.

"Exactly. I don't blame you, Artie. You told us yourself in the end, but my mom never told me anything before she... disappeared."

"Not true," Mad Maude said. "I distinctly remember Alice telling you that the pendant was powerful. Truthfully, it was really the ruby. The setting is all decoration. Right, Cissy?"

The purple lizard inclined her tiny head and stared unblinkingly at me.

Perturbed, I shifted my attention back to Mad Maude. "So, about this cave? You said the yikty guarded it with spells and enchantments?"

"Hmm? Not his own. Yikties can't use magic. Any magic you encounter will have been created by a witch or wizard. And the only enchantment I know of is the one on the individual hallways, the ones that will challenge you. Not that you will have much problem with that. No, the real danger will be the yikty himself."

There was a thump outside that shook the windows. Cissy scampered up Maude's shoulder. Milo flapped his wings in indignation. But, Mad Maude just sat there calmly. "He's found you," she said in a whisper, tossing me a pack of supplies. "Get going. We'll hold him off."

"Who?" I asked, as Artie and Mag shepherded me to the back door.

Mad Maude selected a staff from the wall. "Why, the wizard who injured your mother and kidnapped the Kaninens. He's figured out a way to transform himself into a golden dragon at will."

Chapter Thirty-One

The Compressed Tunnel

"THE DRAGON WHO BETRAYED US A hundred years ago is nothing more than a human!" Mag cried, stopping dead, her hair flaring up. Artie pulled me away before I was burned.

"It would appear so," Mad Maude said calmly.

"The dragons have known you for years. Why didn't you tell us sooner?" Mag snapped, starting to pace around the room.

"What good would it have done?" Mad Maude asked. "You dragons would have gone crazy trying to find the golden dragon."

Mag opened her mouth to respond, but there was another thump from outside. This time, dust fell from the ceiling.

"We can talk about this later," Mad Maude said. "Save the Kaninen. Go, now!"

On the threshold, I looked back at Maude. She was rolling cherry pits on the table. She waved to me to leave and mouthed what looked like "Ohen." I closed the back door behind me as the front door burst open.

I was in a garden. Mag and Artie were feet away, scrambling over a fence. At least Artie was. Mag sprouted her wings and flew over.

Praying that the intruders wouldn't notice, I joined Artie at the foot of the fence. "Ohen," I whispered.

I was suddenly floating a foot off the ground. I waved my arms to regain my balance and saw that the magic had affected Artie as well.

"Penelope, what-" he began.

"I don't know," I said, honestly.

"Control it," Mag said. "Think of the direction you want to go and concentrate."

Up, I thought and shot upward. Artie jerked to the right. I grabbed his hand to steady him. He seemed to have less control than me.

Mag waved frantically for us to follow as Mad Maude's back door inched open. Straight, I thought and dragged Artie along with me.

We tumbled over the fence as the magic dissipated.

"Hurry!" Mag landed beside us and contracted her wings.

"No!" a roar sounded on the other side of the fence. There was something familiar about that voice.

"Penelope, Artie, move!" Mag said, tugging us to our feet. There was a stand of trees nearby. We ran and hid ourselves just as the wizard-dragon burst into the air, fanning his wings.

I shrank back against a tree, shielding my eyes against his golden hue. His brown eyes glittered dangerously. After eight years, he had found me at last.

Mag growled beside me and took a step forward as the dragon circled the trees. Artie and I seized her arms to hold her back.

"Now isn't the time, Mag," Artie said.

"Let me go," she hissed, ceasing her struggle, but glaring at us.

"Mag, you'll get your revenge," I promised, "but he caught us by surprise. Wait until we can do the same to him."

Artie and I released her. She didn't move.

"What do we do now?" I asked. There were only a few trees covering us and the golden dragon was continuing to circle.

"I could fight him," Mag suggested hopefully.

"No. Artie, what do you think? Artie?" I turned around and found him kneeling on the ground, examining an ordinary boulder. "What are you doing?" I asked shrilly. Now was not the time to play with rocks.

"Thieves have been here," he said.

"How do you know?" I asked, instantly joining him.

"The symbol," he said, pointing to the rock. Etched into the rock's gray surface was a "Q" with three lines to its right.

"What is that?" I said, squinting at it.

"The sign of the Quicks. It's supposed to symbolize our speed with thievery."

"How do we use it?" Mag asked, staring intently at the golden dragon.

"It's a tunnel," Artie explained. "Sylvia designed the spell. If I etch a standard, everyday Q next to it, the tunnel will open. It's a little like the passageway in the castle where we met, Pen. This is what the riddle meant. *These* are the changing rocks. For security reasons, only thieves can use them. They can choose where the tunnels will send them. That makes it harder for anyone to accidently stumble upon the Quick Hideout."

I frowned. "Wouldn't that make it easier? You could just ask for it."

"The dragon's head rock is the closest to headquarters. Sylvia enchanted each thief's knife to open most of the passageways. That's why I gave you my knife, Pen, so you could get back in your room. Only four knives were enchanted to open the path to the dragon's head rock."

"The Quicks," I breathed.

"Right. Besides you two, my parents, Sylvia, and I are the only ones who even know about that passageway," Artie said. "I can't see enemies marching on it from the outside and winning, can you?"

"No," I said. Then an idea struck me. "Can we use it to find the Kaninen?"

Artie's eyes widened in surprise. "As long as we can name it, we can find it."

He drew his knife and began to carve into the rock when the smell of smoke reached my nostrils. I turned around and saw the golden dragon bathing the trees in fire.

"Artie, hurry!" I said.

Mag was halfway through transforming. "Its no good," she said, reverting back to her human form. "The trees are too close together."

My eyes watering, I coughed, "How are you doing, Artie?"

"Almost done. Pen, you have to get rid of the smoke."

"Penelope, come with me," Mag said, grabbing my arm and pulling me out from the cover of the trees.

"What are we doing?" I demanded as Mag released me.

Without answering, she transformed into her true form. "Get on," she said.

I climbed awkwardly onto her back and she sprang into the air, banking to the left toward the golden dragon.

"Bavasnor!" I cried, sending water toward the fire. It couldn't quite reach.

"Cover me!" Mag called as she spiraled above the trees and with a quick flap of her wings she propelled the water to its destination and put out the fire.

Steadying myself with the help of a spike, I turned full around until I was facing the oncoming dragon. He opened his jaws; flames building behind his fangs in his halfway open mouth.

"Beredan!" I cried the first spell that came into my head. Ropes sprang from nowhere and wrapped themselves around the dragon, binding his wings together. The flames died in his mouth as he plummeted to the ground. I slumped against the spike and, grinning, faced Mag. "We did it," I said.

Our victory was short-lived, however. A snapping noise could be heard below. Mag and I exchanged looks and then peered down. The golden dragon had spread his wings, breaking the ropes instantly. He was pelting back toward us, aiming for Mag's underbelly.

"Pen! Mag!" It was Artie, waving to us from the tree line. I looked down at him at the exact same moment as the golden dragon, who changed course for Artie.

"NO!" I cried as Mag dived as fast as she could for the ground, but the golden dragon was miles ahead.

"Beredan!" I yelled desperately. Ropes exploded forth once more, but the golden dragon was ready. He dodged and the ropes continued downward, wrapping around Artie instead.

Cursing my aim, I did the only natural thing: as Mag drew level with his tail, I leapt off her back onto the golden dragon. The wind whistled through my hair as I stood precariously on his back. Step by careful step, I made my way to the dragon's head, dodging protruding spikes.

The dragon began to try and buck me off. He was twisting and turning, but I held on doggedly, determined to remain airborne and give Mag the chance to gain the upper claw.

A flash of red darted past my eye and I looked just in time to see Mag gaining. The golden dragon was so preoccupied with me; he hadn't seen her. To ensure that it stayed that way, I reached for my scabbard and the hilt of my sword.

The golden dragon's green eyes sparkled maliciously. He had noticed Mag and had chosen that moment to twist away from her. As Mag soared back around, I gained control of my weapon and plunged it awkwardly in between some loose scales on his back.

The dragon roared and began to shudder violently. I would have been thrown off, if I hadn't been clutching a spike. As it was, I stumbled to my knees and struggled to rise. Tears streamed from my eyes as the wind rushed past.

The dragon fell into a dive, with me just barely clinging to his back. One hand seemed glued to the spike, while the other couldn't seem to release the sword. The dragon landed hard on the ground, jolting me. He was breathing heavily.

I pulled the sword free and saw it was stained red with blood. Trying to swallow my revulsion, I sheathed it and leapt off his back, rolling upright.

The dragon ignored me. He was glaring at something to my right. I followed his line of sight and caught my breath. The golden dragon was looking at Artie.

Artie was struggling to free himself from the ropes. He was lying in an awkward position and I saw his knife out. He was trying to cut himself free.

"Artie! Watch out!" I cried, as the golden dragon lumbered toward him. I ran forward, seizing my sword in the process.

He looked at me upside down. His eyes widened and he redoubled his efforts to escape.

I could never make it in time. The dragon was almost on top of him.

There was the soft swish of wings and next second, Mag had dropped from the sky onto the rogue dragon. The two of them fell away, snapping at each other's throats.

"Artie!" I rushed to his side just as he managed to break the ropes with his knife.

"Pen, you were fantastic," he said, sitting up and rubbing his wrists. "I've never seen anyone jump off an airborne dragon before."

"Thanks. Did you open the passageway?" I said, replacing the sword once again in its sheath.

"Yes, its ready when you are, but we have to hurry. After an hour, the 'Q' I drew into the rock's surface will disappear and the tunnel will be completely cut off from us. We'll be trapped underground forever if we don't make it out in time." He pointed to the rock, which had moved to reveal a hole large enough for a fairly thin person to slip through.

"We'd better grab Mag, then. Mag, come on!"

I helped Artie to his feet and waved to her. She was still wrestling with the golden dragon. She must have heard me, though, for she immediately changed back into her human form. She was able to slip to the ground and run toward us. The dragon was bigger and bulker and couldn't change direction as fast as Mag the human could.

Once she reached us, Mag immediately leapt into the hole. Artie slipped in next. After one more fleeting look at the golden dragon that was trying to kill us, I slid into the hole and followed my two friends.

The rock slid back into place above my head, hiding the enraged dragon, and plunging me into complete darkness as I landed painfully on a hard, dirt floor. I shivered as the overuse of magic caught up with me. I blinked several times.

"Penelope," someone said in my ear and a hand slid into mine. I jumped before I recognized the voice.

"Artie?"

"Yes, Mag's here too."

"Is this the secret passageway?" Mag's voice said.

"Yes. The cave with the kidnapped Kaninen." Artie requested, then paused. "We have to go to the right."

I did so, but collided with something hard and from the sound of it, I wasn't the only one.

"Stop!" Artie said. "We need some light."

A second later, Mag's hair caught fire. I spotted a burnt out torch nearby and set it close to Mag's hair. It lit instantly. Artie took the torch from me as her hair went out.

From the light of the torch, I could see that there were two dark paths before us: one left and one right. Mag and I had run into a wall.

"Everyone to the center of the room and grab hands," Artie instructed. "And go to the right."

With Artie and Mag on either side of me, we did as Artie said. The torch threw our shadows across the wall, elongating them and causing me to squeeze Artie's hand tighter than usual.

We were walking, but we didn't seem to be moving. There was a light at the end of the tunnel, but it wasn't getting any closer.

"Its not working," Artie muttered.

"What?"

"We're walking in place. The tunnel won't allow us to continue."

"Why not?" I said nervously.

"I don't know. Sylvia's led me this way in the past and its always worked for her."

"Maybe we have to go through a test," Mag suggested.

"No, that's not it," Artie said, slowly turning to face me. "You have to lead us, Penelope. I'm such an idiot. Its just like the tunnel at Kelton Castle."

"What? Me? But, I don't know my way around this tunnel."

"Sylvia said that if I always followed her and those like her, I would never get lost. I think she meant magic users. You're the only magic user we have at the moment. You were able to do it last time," Artie insisted.

"She could have meant following a thief," I pointed out.

"No, Penelope. I'm sure of it, we have to follow you if we want to get out of here."

I looked between Mag and Artie. Artie looked deadly serious and Mag nodded in encouragement.

"All right. The cave with the kidnapped Kaninen," I requested.

Artie smiled and handed me the torch. He took Mag's other hand.

"Why do we have to hold hands?" I asked, as I started forward.

"Only the wielder of the torch can find their way. Your magic is passing through to us, so Mag and I can see where we're going as well. Look, the tunnel's already a lot brighter with you in charge."

It was. When Artie was holding the torch, I could barely see past three feet. Now, the whole passageway was lit.

After what seemed like no time at all, we were at a dead end with a low ceiling. I couldn't stand upright, but had to duck my head.

"Now what?" Mag said.

"We can let go now," Artie said. "We're here."

"But-"

"Look up," he said. "Do you see that darker circle on the ceiling? That's our ticket out of here. All I have to do is draw the sign of the Quicks on that surface."

There was a rumbling down the hall. Artie blanched and fumbled for his knife.

"Our hour is up," he said. "I have only seconds to get us out of here."

The rumbling was getting closer. The ceiling was pouring dust on us. Artie was hastily drawing into the rock.

"Done!" he said and touched the stone with his hand. Sunlight streamed in as the rock covering our exit slid away. Mag sprouted her wings, seized my hand and Artie's shirt and launched herself into the air, just as the tunnel closed.

We hung there, suspended in midair.

"That was close," Mag said, setting us gently on the ground.

"Too close," Artie agreed. "Does anyone see the cave?"

"Turn around," I said. In front of me was the gaping mouth of a circular cave. Few trees dotted the flat, barren land, making me feel exposed. If the yikty guardian showed, there would be no place to hide. We would be completely at his mercy. Still, if this was the only way to save the Kaninen and get my amulet back, I was willing to do it.

"Come on," I said, drawing my sword. "We have a yikty to defeat."

Chapter Thirty-Two

Separation in the Cave

THE MOUTH OF THE CAVE SMELLED LIKE mildew. I turned my head away in disgust and saw that Mag and Artie had wrinkled their noses as well.

"We'd better go in," I said, straightening my shoulders. "We won't find the ice rabbit by standing here."

Mag and Artie nodded and together, we crept slowly to the cave's maw.

"I'll go first," Mag whispered. "If there's a yikty in here, it'll have a hard time facing off against a dragon."

I could think of no argument for that, so trailing behind Mag, we entered. The cave was slightly damp. I tripped over a rock and caught the wall to steady myself. My hand came away with a layer of moisture.

Artie, who was behind me, reached out a hand to steady me. "This place is freezing," he said.

"Yikties like the dark and the cold," Mag said, from the front. "That's why fire is so effective. They can't stand the heat."

Artie and I followed Mag deeper into the cave. The sunlight outside was growing fainter behind us, until it was only a pinprick of light. I had kept the torch from Artie's shortcut and passed it up to Mag.

We tried to be quiet, so we could sneak up on the yikty, but unfortunately, our feet slapping against the wet rocks were loud. They echoed around the passageway.

Mag paused. "There's a chamber right in front of us," she said. "I can hear the yikty, be careful."

We emerged into the next chamber and saw that the cause of the noise was no more than an echo, but from which of the three archways in front of us, I had no idea.

"Endoraken," I said, just as Mad Maude had taught me. The middle arch flared up at once with a soft blue light, but then so did the left path, and a second later the right path dazzled me with its brilliance.

"What happened?" I said. "Wasn't the spell supposed to reveal the yikty's presence?"

Artie was studying the ground in front of the center path. He picked up something to show it to us. "Its part of the yikty's armor. It molted right off."

"Then, the yikty's that way," Mag said.

I wandered over to the left path. "There's some more over here," I called, holding up a piece of shell.

"Here too," Mag said, now kneeling before the right arch.

"Now what?" I asked miserably. "How was the yikty able to fool my spell?"

"It's an old thieves' trick," Artie said. "Leave a sign of your presence in multiple locations, so your pursuer won't know which way to turn."

Mag banged her fist against the rock wall. "So what are we supposed to do? It'll take too long to test every path and it might move at any time."

"I think," Artie said quietly, "that we're going to have to split up."

I stared at him incredulously. "What?! No, Artie, its much safer if we go together."

"I agree," he said, "but what would happen if the yikty discovers us and decides to escape. We'd be too busy checking every path, it would be long gone before we noticed."

"This leaves us vulnerable," Mag said. "When one of us finds the yikty, how will the others help?"

"If the yikty isn't down our path, come back to this chamber and wait for the second person to appear. Then both will take the third and correct path."

"I don't like it," I said.

"It's the only plan we have," Artie said grimly.

I gazed at the three arches. Was it my imagination or was the left arch glowing slightly brighter than the other two?

"I'll take the left path," I said.

"I'll go right," Mag said. Her eyes sparkled with fierce excitement.

"That leaves the center for me," Artie said.

We clasped hands and I knew Mag and Artie were thinking the same thing as me. Would we ever see each other again?

* * *

I had a bad feeling about my chosen path when the archway sealed itself behind me. I looked back and saw nothing but a solid rock wall.

"Mag! Artie! Can you hear me?" I whispered as loud as I dared, in case the yikty was nearby. They didn't answer, but a roar from deeper inside the passageway did.

I slowly turned and examined my surroundings. I was in another stone chamber. The walls were completely smooth, which struck me as odd. Who would spend all this time smoothing stone in a random cave?

I started forward, my right hand clasped on the hilt of my sword, while my left trailed along the moisture-covered walls. I hadn't gone more then ten feet when a creaking noise from above attracted my attention.

I rolled away just in time to keep myself from being squashed flat by the rock that had dropped from the ceiling. I lay shaking an inch away.

"So weak," a soft and dangerous voice said, echoing around the room. "To think the mighty Silver Rose was almost crushed by a meaningless rock."

I gritted my teeth and stood up, backing away from the rock until my foot hit a curious sort of puddle. I glanced down and hopped away with half my shoe burnt off. I had stepped in a puddle of water that was strangely hot. It was the only hot area in the room. Fire seemed to dance across its surface.

"And so the little heroine is defeated by the very substance her friend hates," the voice laughed. "I set the traps for her. Boiling water from the mermaids. So hot, even dragons would feel the pain of the heat."

"Who are you?" I demanded. "Why are you doing this?"

"Who am I?" the voice purred. "Why, Penelope, I'm hurt you don't recognize me. After all," a figure stepped from the shadows and I gasped, tripping away from the woman.

She was tall with long, brown hair and green eyes that gazed thoughtfully at me. Her smile was pleasant, just as I remembered it.

"I am your mother," she finished.

"You can't," I said, my voice trembling. "You can't be my mother. She died two years ago."

"No, Penelope, I'm very much alive. Watch." She held out her hand and a ball of flames appeared.

Unbidden, memories of my mother conjuring a ball of flames flashed through my mind. She used to do that for me when I was small and afraid of the dark.

"You've done wonderfully, sweetie," she said, holding out her hand. "Come with me, we'll find your friends and escape together."

I longed to take her hand, to rush to her side and bury my head in her shoulder and cry, but I looked again at her smile and saw it had changed. A moment before, it had been lightness and sweetness, now, however, she was leering at me with malice. I searched her eyes and saw they had turned hungry and black.

I unsheathed my sword and slowly placed the tip against her throat. "You aren't my mother," I said quietly. My voice only shook slightly. "'A rock, watery flames, and the shade.' The Riddle Chipmunks were right. You're one of the challenges sent to stop me."

The woman began to dissolve into dust. Her legs disappeared, followed by her torso, until only her head remained and still I didn't remove my sword.

"We could have been happy together, Penelope," the head of the apparition said. "You, me, Lydia, and Malcolm. Now, watch as your mother dies before your eyes again."

I stumbled forward as the dark version of my mother vanished. I was left with an empty room, a lingering feeling of dread, and tears in my eyes. I shivered as I continued through the chamber to the very back.

Questions rose in my mind. What if that had been my mother? Had she been trying to contact me? Did I kill her a second time? A moan escaped me as I wiped fresh tears away.

"Now, now, now," a deeper and deadlier voice cooed. "There's no need for tears. You'll see your mother again soon."

The speaker stepped forward and I forgot my misery as I looked upon the face of a giant scorpion. A yikty.

"I'm so glad you made it," Wansetop said. "It wouldn't have been any fun without you. Your friends aren't here to save you now. Prepare yourself. You won't escape me this time."

Chapter Thirty-Three

The Scorpion in the Dark

"WANSETOP? *YOU'RE* THE GUARDIAN of the Kaninen?" I said, taking a step back and raising my sword.

"Certainly, you didn't expect me to trust this task to one of the morons of my nest, did you? I am the leader of the yikties and wanted to kill you personally."

"How did you know I would be here?" I asked, stalling for time while my mind worked furiously, trying to come up with an appropriate spell. A giant scorpion bearing down on me: definitely an emergency.

Wansetop waved an imperious claw. "My master alerted me to your presence. He said he knew that old fool of a witch Maude would tell you of the rabbit's location, so he placed me here. You have fallen into our trap, Penelope Bogg."

He lunged at me and I ducked, but my knees were shaking. I couldn't fight him again, even with the rose and my sword, not after how he paralyzed me last time.

"You cannot escape me, Bogg," Wansetop whispered. "My master has given me permission to do what I will with you. You are only delaying the inevitable."

"How did you manage to create a copy of my mom?" I asked, backtracking down the chamber. I spotted the Kaninen, tied to a protruding rock in the shadows. Its ears drooped miserably.

"A mere trick by my master," Wansetop said, carelessly waving a pincer. "It was meant to show you your worst fear and it worked."

My worst fear? What did my mom have to do with my worst fear? I shook the thought from my head. Wansetop was just trying to distract me and it was working.

"My friends will be here soon and then we'll defeat you," I said, trying to sound braver than I felt.

"They'll have to get past the traps first. They reset after every challenger. They will never reach you in time."

"Penelope!" Artie's voice called, echoing around the chamber.

"Ah, they're here," Wansetop said. "I'm almost tempted to let them through, just so they can witness your failure."

Wansetop turned away and as he did so, his tail scraped a stalactite. It wobbled precariously. This gave me an idea, an impossibly stupid idea, but it was the only chance I had.

There were shouts from Artie and Mag as they dealt with the three challenges: the rock, the boiling water, and the apparition. Meanwhile, I used the distraction to circle around Wansetop until I was directly behind him. I only had seconds before he turned around.

Mag and Artie's shouting died and there was complete silence in the hall once more.

"Ah, a pity, but I think your little friends are dead," Wansetop said, turning. It was then that I acted.

Before he knew what had hit him, I had leapt as high as I could, right onto his tail, which I used as a springboard to launch myself into the air toward the stalactite. I struck it with my sword.

For one terrifying moment, I thought it hadn't worked, but as I fell back toward earth, the stalactite screeched against itself as it broke loose and aimed right for Wansetop.

I was racing the rock, I willed it to win, to surpass me and crush the giant, *disgusting* scorpion, but I had had a head start. I closed my eyes, ready for his pincers, when *oof!*

Something had stopped me mid-fall. I opened my eyes and found myself hanging from Artie's hand. Mag, in human form, but with her wings extended, was clutching Artie underneath his arms, keeping us all aloft.

"Don't let go," Artie said through clenched teeth.

"Don't worry," I said, weakly.

Below us, there was a crash and I looked down to see Wansetop with a stalactite on his head.

"He's not dead," Mag said. "It takes a lot to kill a yikty. If I had to guess, I'd say you just stunned him, Penelope."

I shuddered at the thought of fighting Wansetop again. "Come on, let's rescue the Kaninen and get out of here."

"I'll get the Kaninen," Artie volunteered.

"Penelope, we should check on Wansetop," Mag said.

I nodded grimly.

Mag landed. Artie took off for the ice rabbit, who was still tied to the rock, while Mag and I continued toward the stunned yikty.

"You... cannot escape... me, Penelope Bogg," Wansetop said slowly, as he tottered about.

"Its over, Wansetop," I said. "You're defeated."

Wansetop shook his head almost imperceptibly and seemed to gain control of himself. "You... shall... never... win,... Penelope... Bogg,... not... as... long... as... my... master... is... one... step... ahead... of... you."

"What's wrong with him?" I asked Mag.

"Artie used the Starclock. It slowed down Wansetop."

"Why didn't it affect me?"

"Oh, it did. We saw you destroy that stalactite in slow motion. It wore off when Artie grabbed your hand."

Mag and I took a step closer to Wansetop, when the sound of breaking rock reached our ears. I looked up just in time to see the cave's ceiling collapsing upon us.

"Run!" I yelled. We weaved our way toward Artie. He was still twenty feet away, cutting the Kaninen free. My only thought was to make it to him before the cave fell, trapping us. I caught a glimpse of gold from where Wansetop remained, but I didn't stop to dwell on it.

"Artie!"

And he was there. Artie appeared at my side, clutching the quivering Kaninen. I released a breath I didn't know I was holding, grateful that Artie was still alive and not crushed by a rock, when a red, velvety canvas extended over us.

I squeezed my eyes shut and waited for the sound of falling rocks to abate. After what seemed like an eternity, there was silence and the red canvas withdrew from over our heads. Artie released the Kaninen, while I looked around for Mag.

She was standing beside me in her true form, panting. "Are you all right?" she asked.

"Fine," I said. "Was that you protecting us?"

"Yes, but Wansetop escaped. That golden dragon came and snatched him. There's no chance of catching him now. We'll have to wait and try again another day."

"We'll be ready for him," Artie said. "Just remind me never to get on your bad side, Penelope. I don't fancy getting in between you and a stalactite."

We laughed as afternoon sunlight streamed in through the destroyed ceiling of the cave. Our mirth and relief was contagious as we fell over ourselves, unable to stop, until the light faded from the land and plunged us into the darkness of a starless night.

Chapter Thirty-Four

Transparent Parent

"EXCUSE ME," THE KANINEN SAID, stepping forward. "Thank you for saving me from the yikty. I'm Ice."

"Nice to meet you, Ice," I said. "I'm Penelope. This is Mag and Artie."

Ice jumped at the sight of Mag.

"Relax," Mag said. "Blizzard sent us."

"Oh," Ice murmured softly. "Well, good. Where are the others, Snow, Frost, and Flurry?"

"They're fine," Artie said. "We already saved them."

Ice's face broke into a smile. "That's wonderful! Are you going back to Kaninen territory, now?"

"Yes, just as soon as we see you off, we're on our way," Mag said.

"By flying?"

"Naturally."

"No need," Ice said. "I can transport all of us there instantly."

Before any of us could respond, Ice leapt above the rubble and created a blue circle around the four of us. I watched, fascinated, as everything around me blurred ice blue for a moment. When it cleared, Mag, Artie, and I were standing in the middle of a bridge over a small stream. Ice was nowhere to be seen.

"Where are we?" Artie asked.

"Why, you're back outside Elton Castle," a familiar voice said.

I spun around and saw the goblin and the crocodile. Tarboone was leaning against the bridge's rail. Little Darling, meanwhile, was floating lazily in the stream.

"Greetings, Tarboone," I said cautiously. "Where did you come from?"

"Oh, here and there," he said, shrugging. "Little Darling and I had some business to take care of. I was alerted that he," Tarboone gestured toward Artie, "finally told you his full name. Arthur Hamilton Quick, huh?"

Artie nodded slowly.

"Great. I'll introduce you. Just go inside the castle after I leave."

"Wait, Tarboone! Why are we here?" I called.

"You were summoned," Tarboone said. "Ask the witch inside. She's the one who wants to talk to you."

He waved his hand and leapt back aboard Little Darling. They sped off around the corner, to introduce us, I guess.

I squared my shoulders. "Come on. We're here. We might as well explore Elton Castle."

We crossed over the bridge and found ourselves on the opposite bank, which was a grassy field dotted with trees. Elton Castle loomed in the distance, past several hills and an expansive and colorful flower field.

"There it is," Artie said in wonder. "I never thought I'd live to see Elton Castle."

"You sound excited," I said.

"Are you kidding? It's a thief's paradise."

Artie must have seen my expression, for he said, "Not that I'm planning to steal anything, of course."

"Of course," Mag said. "Now, let's get inside, before that crazy goblin returns."

Mag led us through the flower field, up the cobbled walkway, ending at the old oak door. The big handle was so heavy, Artie and I had to work together to even lift it.

The knock was a resounding boom. A moment later, the door opened and I was enraged to see who was on the other side: Laborc.

"You!" I cried, drawing my sword.

"Hello," the troll said, politely. "May I help you?"

"Why are you in Elton Castle, Laborc?" Mag demanded.

"Laborc? I think you're mistaken," the troll said. "My name's Hugo. I'm the custodian of Elton Castle."

With a glance at Mag and Artie, I lowered my weapon. I had to admit that he was very different from Laborc. Laborc would have tried to beat us to a pulp immediately, but Hugo was actually wearing reading glasses and holding a book under his arm.

"Will this take long?" Hugo asked. "I'm at the most exciting part of this book. The hero is just about to confess his love for the fair princess."

"Um, right," I said. "I'm Penelope. These are my friends, Mag and Artie. We're looking for someone, Hugo. A Kaninen named Ice. She was transporting us to Kaninen territory. Have you seen her?"

Hugo froze and I could see him studying us with a shrewd expression, as if he were sizing us up.

"She's not here," he said slowly. "There's someone else who wants to talk to you, though."

"Who?" I said.

Hugo opened his mouth to respond, but before he could, a familiar and excited voice said, "Penelope? It really is you! Your hair's silver!"

I turned around and saw... my mom?! She looked just as I remembered her with her long brown hair pulled into a bun, her green eyes that were sparkling with amusement, and her smile that was nowhere near the sneer the imposter had worn.

"M-Mom," I spluttered. "What are you doing here?"

Mom smiled sadly and that's when I realized I could see through her. "Mom? Are you a ghost?"

"No, Penelope, not a ghost." She glanced at Hugo. "Do you think we could continue this inside?"

"Of course," Hugo said. "Right this way."

We followed them inside and Hugo closed the heavy door, throwing us into darkness.

"I don't like this," Artie whispered to me. "How did we get here? They were expecting us."

"Hugo seems all right," Mag said grudgingly.

"And its my mom, we can trust her," I said.

I tried to keep the excitement out of my voice, but it was no good. Calm down, I told myself. Remember the cave. But, this transparent version of Mom didn't act threatening in the least. She was floating—*floating*—along, grinning from ear to ear.

Mom and Hugo led us through a damaged entryway that must have been grand in its time, but now was crumbling and falling to pieces. A dusty chandelier was lying on its side in the center of the room, broken beyond all repair.

"We can talk in the library," Mom said. "Hugo says he won't mind."

"No, and I might be able to help shed some light on any questions you may have," Hugo said.

The library was to the right of the entryway and it was magnificent. It was at least three stories tall, but time had not been kind to it. Half of it lay in ruins, with books spilling to the ground, missing half their pages. Fallen shelves were blocking access to the ruined sections and it looked as if the room would collapse if they were moved.

But the books still on their shelves looked proud and stately, if a little sad. It was as if they could remember all the important people who used to read them and wondered at their absence.

"I've done a lot of work already," Hugo said proudly. "When I first came here, the whole library was unusable, but I've been able to clear out a space to work and read."

"Its very nice, Hugo," I said smiling. I was itching to check out a few of those books.

"Thank you," he rumbled, pleased.

"You're not like other trolls, are you, Hugo?" Mag said.

"No, I've never agreed with Laborc's bloodthirsty ways. I prefer to spend my time as a scholar."

"I take it the silver rose has reactivated your powers," Mom said as we all took seats on the floor.

"Yes, it—What do you mean *reactivated?*"

Mom's smile turned, if possible, sadder. "That night in Tealeaf, your magic protected you from the golden dragon. It was so much magic all at once. Your father and I were trying to get you children to safety, but the rogue dragon was following us. We moved as quietly as possible, but magic itself is unpredictable... You were unconscious, Penelope, and magic kept bursting out of you at odd moments. You somehow caused a tree to sprout yarn balls all over its branches.

"The dragon was getting closer all the time, following your magic. Your father sacrificed himself to slow him down. In order to protect you, Malcolm, and Lydia and escape from the golden dragon, I cast a spell on you so your magic wouldn't return until Lydia's own magic surfaced. It has laid dormant these last eight years."

I gaped at my mom. We stared at each other for a full minute before I looked down at my hands.

"So that's why it never surfaced when I was thirteen," I murmured. I looked my mom full in the face. "I understand why you blocked my magic, but why did I have to wait for Lydia to turn thirteen? Why not when I turned thirteen?"

Mom sighed. "I didn't know when, if ever, I would finally escape from the golden dragon. And you had such little control back then. I figured it wouldn't overwhelm you now at sixteen, like it would have done at eight."

I sat in silence, digesting the information. Next to me, Mag cleared her throat. "Mrs. Bogg, what are these powers the silver rose supposedly reactivated?"

Mom gazed at me steadily. "Penelope, did you meet Cadmus?"

I started. What did he have to do with anything? "Yes. I met him right after I got my magic."

"You were always good at listening to plants," Mom said fondly. "But, you were born with the ability to talk to animals."

It was like a storm cloud battering at my brain with all the new information my mom was throwing at me. "No," I said hoarsely. "I couldn't talk to animals until I met Cadmus. There's no way..." I paused as a new idea struck me. "It... it was one of the powers you blocked, wasn't it?"

"Indeed," Mom nodded. "It was the strongest aspect of your magic. I was afraid any glimmer of magic would draw the golden dragon to you, like a moth to a flame. I was taking no chances, so... I blocked everything."

"Well, that's just great," I said, unable to keep the sarcasm out of my voice. "Really wonderful that I was safe all these years, but now I have no control over it. Every time I use a spell, I see silver, and-"

"If I may interrupt," Hugo said, placidly. "But, that goes away with practice."

I sighed, exasperated.

"We don't have time," Artie said. "We have to defeat the golden dragon before he causes even more chaos."

Hugo shrugged. "I'm sorry, but time and practice are the only way."

"Train with Mad Maude," Mom said. "She can teach you more magic and how to control-" She began to flicker in and out of focus.

"Mom?!" I shrieked in terror. She was disappearing before our very eyes.

"I thought you said you weren't a ghost," Mag said.

"I'm not. This is a projection of myself from a different location. Even I don't know where I am. Tarboone alerted me to your presence in Elton Castle."

"Then where did he go? He's not here now," Artie said.

"Tarboone's an old friend. He contacted me through a scrying mirror. No, he doesn't know where I am either."

"Tarboone insisted on having your names," Hugo said, "because the spell anchoring Alice here only works..."

"...when I know exactly who I'm talking to," Mom finished. "Penelope, I have to warn you..." Her voice was getting fainter. "I love you, darling. You, Malcolm, and Lydia. I'm ending the connection. You'll be in Kaninen territory in a minute. Good luck, Mag, Artie, and Penelope."

At my name, everyone and everything around me vanished in a blue blur.

* * *

When my vision cleared, I was standing next to Mag and Artie in a forest. I heard a squeak of surprise and looked down at the ground to see Ice jumping away from me.

"There you are!" she said. "I arrived and you three were gone for nearly twenty minutes! Where were you?"

I glanced at Blizzard, Flurry, Frost, Snow, and even Cadmus, who were standing beside Ice.

"There was a slight detour. Anyway, Blizzard, I held up my end of the bargain."

"Yes, yes," he said. "Your amulet. Here it is." Blizzard held out the amulet to me, the ruby shining in the early morning sunlight.

My fingers had barely closed around it, when Blizzard said, "We must be going. You have done us a great service, Penelope Bogg. We won't forget it." He and the young Kaninens disappeared back into their cave.

I shivered. Blizzard's words were kind, but as cold as ice.

"Well, now that they're gone, I have a message for you," Cadmus said. There was a piece of paper lying at his feet. He picked it up in his mouth and handed it to me. It was covered in cat spit and badly torn, but I could still make it out:

Penny, help! I found who started the fire at the gala. No! Please hurry! I can't handle him on my own. He's... too strong. Bavasnor! Helppppp!

"Lydia," I whispered. The writing was in a barely legible scrawl, but I still recognized my baby sister's handwriting.

"I have to save her," I said, hastily fastening my amulet around my neck. I didn't even smile at its familiar weight.

I made as if to bolt, I would have to run if I wanted to get there in time, when Artie grabbed my hand, stopping me.

"Let me go, Artie!" I frantically tried to pull my hand free, but he simply tightened his grip.

"Penelope! Pen, calm down!"

I was so surprised, I ceased my struggles, but I continued to breathe rapidly.

Artie squeezed my hand gently, but didn't let go. "Now, Cadmus," he said. "Why is it written like this? I seriously doubt Lydia would write 'no' or 'Bavasnor' if she was truly under attack."

"She was using a special type of magical paper that wrote her words in her handwriting as she dictated them. We were attacked." His eyes looked haunted. "The golden dragon. It was all Lydia could do to stop him from setting Charlotte and me on fire. Lydia escaped with Charlotte, while I came to find you. I only just got away. I don't know where they went. I'm sorry."

I had gone cold during Cadmus's explanation. I roused myself. "We have to go find her."

"Penelope, listen," Mag said. "To save her, we very likely will have to face the golden dragon again. We barely escaped ourselves last time." Her expression turned sour. "We need more training and the only person who can help is Mad Maude."

I looked to Artie, who nodded, sadly. "It's the only way, Pen."

I sighed, but recognized their logic. "Fine, but we *will* save Lydia," I said fiercely, before allowing Artie to steer me toward Mag, who was back in dragon form. I didn't let go of Artie's hand as we started our return flight to Cherry Grove. Neither did he.

Character List

1. Penelope Bogg- witch-in-training, chosen by the dragons, friend of Mag and Artie

2. Mag Everett- red dragon, friend of Penelope and Artie

3. Artie- skilled with a knife, secretive, friend of Penelope and Mag

4. Aldrich- white dragon, grandfather to Mag, member of the dragon council

5. Lydia Bogg- younger sister of Penelope and Malcolm

6. Malcolm Bogg- captain of Queen Alana's guards, older brother of Penelope and Lydia

7. Alice Bogg- witch, mother of Penelope, Lydia, and Malcolm, presumed dead

8. Sylvia Quick- thief, daughter

9. Yolanda Quick- thief, mother

10. Leopold Quick- thief crime lord, father

11. Venn- green dragon, friend of Mag

12. Amarina- pink dragon, jealous of Mag

13. Cadmus- lion cub, offers advice to Penelope

14. Grrwrath- leader of Cadmus's pride, father of Cadmus

15. Willow- squirrel, leader of the Woodland Warriors

16. Tarboone- goblin, friend of Little Darling

17. Little Darling- crocodile, friend of Tarboone

18. Cissy- purple lizard who hangs out with Mad Maude

19. Mad Maude- healer, found in Cherry Grove

20. Queen Alana- Queen of Alsmora

21. Casimir- court wizard

22. Wansetop- giant scorpion, also known as a yikty

23. Milo- annoying crow
24. Shell- female Riddle Chipmunk
25. Mel- male Riddle Chipmunk
26. Sid- Brillande Bohrender
27. Nimbala- mountain lion
28. Anne- wife to Zachary, helps Penelope and Artie, from Wolf Bay
29. Zachary- husband to Anne, helps Penelope and Artie, from Wolf Bay
30. Aatto- werewolf
31. Hareton- Aatto's father, mayor of Silent Stream
32. Leon- thief
33. Mira Newton- mother, found in Purple Falls
34. Julia Newton- daughter, found in Purple Falls
35. Blizzard- Kaninen leader
36. Flurry- young Kaninen, daughter of Blizzard
37. Frost- young Kaninen, found in the Blue Rose Swamp
38. Snow- young Kaninen, found near Purple Falls
39. Ice- young Kaninen, found in the yikty's cave
40. Hugo- nice troll, booklover
41. Laborc- evil troll
42. Aneurin- sea serpent
43. Tristan- leader of the rogue thieves
44. Golden Dragon- evil, started a war between humans and dragons a hundred years ago

Glossary

Anoffen- Open

Aun evas comren- Invisibility

Bavasnor- Water

Bechulen- Protect

Beredan- Bind

Brillande Bohrender- Bellowing driller sheep

Enchauta- Stop

Endoraken- Reveal

Funner- Fire

Henatin- Warm

Kaninen- Ice rabbit

Lanasan- Slow

Ohen- Up

Sacakan- Search

Sten henaus- Wand out

Yikty- Giant scorpion

Zanalent- Collect